It's safe to say, and most would agree, Mr. Joe Stampfli writes what he feels and he feels what he writes. It is no surprise to those around him, his success at writing fiction fits him like a well-made glove. Mr. Stampfli's stance of doing so revolves around two simple but extremely well-thought-out plans, always write something better than what he wrote last but never as good as what he writes next.

First and foremost, I dedicate these pages to my friend and brother Ty Ritter and with him come the heroes that follow. To them I say, "I whisper no sad song of sorrow, for that is a meal you have all had far too often. Instead I painfully write this story as I see it through the eyes of my brother."

This story has life, a spirit and a soul. I gave it that. To my lovely wife, Linda, thank you for giving me the chance. Forever and always. And of course, last but not of the least, a shout-out to my homies, Evelyn and Ryan, thanks for the touch-up.

Joe Stampfli

PROJECT MOTHER'S DAY

AUSTIN MACAULEY PUBLISHERS™

LONDON * CAMBRIDGE * NEW YORK * SHARJAH

Ordering Information
Quantity sales: Special discounts are available on quantity purchases by corporations, associations, and others. For details, contact the publisher at the address below.

Publisher's Cataloging-in-Publication data
Stampfli, Joe
Project Mother's Day

ISBN 9781647501167 (Paperback)
ISBN 9781647501150 (Hardback)
ISBN 9781647501174 (ePub e-book)

Library of Congress Control Number: 2021913073

www.austinmacauley.com/us

First Published (2021)
Austin Macauley Publishers LLC
40 Wall Street, 33rd Floor, Suite 3302
New York, NY 10005
USA

mail-usa@austinmacauley.com
+1 (646) 5125767

The definition of bravery can only be defined by those who commit the act, the same is to be said for an act of valor. I would like to thank all of the wonderful people involved with Project Child Save. Not only for their continuous and heroic acts of bravery but also for the inspiration to write this story. God bless you all, and may your journeys bring a safe recovery for those whom you collect.

Tigers' Day

Saturday, May 10th, the day before Mother's Day; from the doorway of a moderately sized home in a quiet city in Orange County, Ryson steps from the threshold with the twins, Molly and Madison. They are their own reflection, at four years of age, there are no differences between them, the same green eyes, same light complexion, and both already with shoulder length, light chestnut hair.

Ryson checks his watch before the three of them step off the porch, it's 11:20 a.m. and although the knowledge is useless, it does, somehow, make him feel in charge, but knowing the decision to leave the double wide stroller at home was not his, has already weakened his authority. They can both walk and insisted on doing so.

Like lukewarm lava, they mosey down the walkway, and once to the minivan, sadly waiting in front of the garage, there is already an argument as to who gets which car seat. This Ryson blames on both sets of in-laws, it's an under-breath mumble along the lines of, "Yeah, thanks for not collaborating when it came time to buy safety restraints for your grandchildren."

Truth of the matter is, he has been looking forward towards today, of course minus the mall and the minivan, but any full-on dad time with the girls is always a plus. As for the mall and the minivan, well, the mall can't be helped, having already put it off too long considering tomorrow is Mother's Day. The minivan because his truck is in the shop.

There's a predictable wave of quiet that ripples through the back seat as Ryson cautiously backs down the driveway and into the street. The girls from day one always found movement to be quite pacifying, especially reverse.

As much as Ryson would love listening to the updates and search status for the still missing Nixon helicopter, he turns off the radio in hopes of finishing their mall plan of attack.

"All right, my ladies, so what's it going to be? We still all on board with the bracelet and if so, which one?"

The twenty-minute drive and discussion only furthers the debate as to do we go bracelet or perfume.

With the debate once again narrowed down towards bracelet, the option where they should park now simplified.

"Well, girls, how about we start with moms favorite store and see where that gets us," Ryson says this more as a compromise than any real discussion and so now makes a right turn leading into the mall's parking lot.

The second large department store they come to is where they'd like to start, Ryson begins up close in his search for a place to park, then back and forth, till maybe mid-lot before he finds an open slot and here, they park.

Within eyesight of the doors they plan to use, Ryson turns off the engine and waits the few seconds it takes for silence to surrender and the girls to chatter once again like infant circus monkeys, words just strewn together without that help of any dots or dashes.

"Okay, okay, okay, now listen girls, you know the drill right? Holding hands at all times, stay close, and most important, stay focused soldiers."

They both giggle and agree.

Ryson has brought them to this place in hopes their search and shopping end's here, there's a brief pause at the front doors and it's just long enough to inject a last thought in hopes of shortening their visit, "Mom has lots and lots of perfume, but a charm bracelet, now that's something special."

It's an eager 180 foursome and not so much for another with their backs now to the parking lot Ryson slowly opens the door and the three of their own choice step through, neither knowing life has already crashed forward and collapsed. The evilness of mankind is just waiting for Ryson to get caught up.

Parked near the entrance to the lot Ryson and the girls pulled into sat quietly in a sort of dormant state a small, white, utility van, and in it are four men, who only, when Ryson and kid drive by, are they then rattled alert.

The Spanish being spoken in the small, white van has about it a sense of chaos and destruction, the words…and no stroller. Lay thick with accent and contempt from one of the men in the back.

The driver sees Ryson and the girls pause for just a moment at the front doors and knows, in that one single heartbeat, those two are for whom they've come, and for whom they've waited.

The movement sets forward and the machine quick to engage, the driver, his passenger, and the two in the back pre-wired with enough experience to safely say what happens next has already been written, just needs to be played out.

The white van rolls up and somewhat past the doors were Ryson and the girls were last seen, from the sliding door of the van, two men exit on their feet and already in motion simply because the van never comes to a complete stop.

From the same sadistic casting, surely all four were poured, though I doubt any are related, but the similarities between them could not go an-noticed, all in their twenties, brown complexion, brown hair, five feet inches, one hundred and seventy pounds and all four with thick South American accents. The two that did not get out our just wearing jeans and T-shirts, the other two are indeed dressed for their parts.

The man that leaps out first is wearing gray overalls, gray cap, and rubber boots. His outfit complete with a security tag hanging around his neck. Even on a good day, all the true mall security will see is Mr. Maintenance Guy and think nothing more of it.

Maintenance man's movement does not slow, he quickly disappears down a trash and recycle alley commonly shared by two large department stores. At the end of this alley is a thick steel door and a cinderblock wall, this only slows his progress for less than 90 seconds.

The second man that leaps from the slow moving van does so just as quickly, only this one lingers, but only long enough to adjust his disguise before he reaches the doors, and now, he pauses in the same space Ryson and the girls did as if he can still taste the lingering essence of all three and not just the two he's come to consume.

To blend here and slip in unnoticed is objective one. The jeans, T-shirt, tennis shoes, backpack, ball cap, and cell phone all carefully chosen to look as though he belongs as he steps through the doors he is a predator; pure and simple and almost invisible.

The predator strolls through the store as if he two might be shopping for Mother's Day, coming to a self-standing column of cheap watches and moving in pretending to take a closer look, he idles with his phone in hand and focused on Ryson and the kids.

The three have made it to about mid-store and are now standing in front of and over a display case; it's busy so they have to wait for someone to help them. In the meantime, the discussion continues as to which one.

Glancing down at the phone in his left hand and seeing the still empty screen, he now removes one of the watches from the column as if he's made some kind of decision as to what moms getting for Mother's Day. When in fact, he has no mother, and the rest of us can only believe he most likely consumed the dead carcass of his own mother shortly after gnawing his escape from her womb.

Now the phone vibrates like an itch in the palm of his hand. The message reads 'Set.'

Replacing the watch in a calmly manner, as if still contemplating the purchase, he now keys in his response but does not hit send. Turning and moving towards the prey his thumb hovers over the send key, the other hand already tightly gripped on a two foot steel pipe slid down the front of his pants.

It's his attention to detail, that, for one, makes him extremely efficient and for another extremely successful. In the few steps, it takes to reach Ryson and the girls he has already retained visual image of the area and has visually map his escape out the side doors.

Just before he reaches the space directly behind Ryson, he pushes the send key, texting the word 'Go.' And now exchanging the phone for a small can of mace in his left rear pocket, and with the right hand, withdrawing the steel pipe.

Ryson is leaned slightly over the display case when the store goes dark, he does not have time to react or more tightly gather the kids before an explosion goes off in his head.

Ryson, of course, collapsing, first hitting the display case then to the floor. His grip weakens leaving his children to fend for themselves. And so shall the tiger feed.

After replacing the pipe down the front of his pants, he sprays both girls with the mace and now tucks one under each arm. The movement to the side doors, even in the dark, quick and precise, the kids coughing and choking as they struggle to breathe.

From the ceiling above, Ryson had hung some cardboard displays of various kinds of jewelry; it's one of these that slightly deflect the deathblow meant to shatter the spine at the base of Ryson's neck. The pipe lands equally across his head and neck, thus sparing his life but leaving a five inch gash in the back of his skull.

Ryson is quickly to his knees but the numbing buzz in his head in the darkness has him questioning where we might be. He hears the girls crying and choking from somewhere buried in the darkness in front of him, although why this is he's not quite certain.

Like only a father would, he gets to his feet and without hesitation, staggers and stumbles towards their cries, even though they have now fallen silent.

When Ryson does find the side doors, he finds the exit empty and the sunlight on the other side painfully blinding, and yet, through the doors, he knows the cries ended. He stumbles more into the doors and through than spending any time attempting finesse in his exit.

Ryson wobbles to a stop just outside the doors, hoping for orientation of any kind and now finds himself in some sort of alley between department stores with half a dozen large trash bins.

The quick head movement right reveals a steel door and a cinderblock wall, it also sends blood from his head on the glass doors behind him like, it was flicked from a large paintbrush. The quick look left has the same effect.

The look left also reveals the rest of the alley and then the large parking lot out front were most likely you would find their minivan, although in his current condition he does question this. Panic and fear seize control with such penetrating force; every fiber of his being is locked like soaked with superglue. The panic so thick and saturating he is unable to force his own movement in any direction.

Shattered silence seems to fill all the space around him at the same time, the noise loud enough to startle Ryson from the dark place to which he was falling. The steel door to his right explodes open with enough force it sounds like a gunshot and backs Ryson up a couple of feet; until his back is now flat against the doors were his own blood has already been splattered.

What emerges from the doorway that not only surprises him but baffles his ability to think clearly and therefore, he is slow to react.

The young man in a gray jumpsuit is obviously in a hurry and judging by how hard we kicked the door open is not going to let much get in his way, but the young child he drags along with him, she clearly does not want to be there and is putting up a struggle as they pass by.

13

Because of this his own focus towards the other end of the alley and parking lot the man in gray does not see Ryson, or just does not care, either way, he just keeps moving and dragging the young child behind, he has both her wrist in his right hand and when she can keep up she, runs, when she cannot, he drags her.

As strange as all this is, stranger still is the fact that not until; Ryson and the little girl make eye contact, does he realize he needs to do something. In the eyes of this small child are many horrors all rolled into one and a look so frightened it pulls Ryson in their direction as if they share a rare earth magnet moment.

Ryson catches up as gray jumpsuit boy nears the end of the alley and he reaches for the little girl, she, in one last act of defiance, pulls hard enough to free one of her hands and reaches back towards Ryson. Their hands lock and their souls united, Ryson already knows, he saves this one.

He slows their pace long enough so maintenance boy finally looks back and their eyes meet. Ryson sees surprise, then fear, and then anger and now gray boy reaches into his overalls and withdraws a small frame revolver, probably a 38.

What gray boy does not see is the small, white van pull up and stop at the top of the alley, his focus is on Ryson and the bullets he wants to put through his head.

Before gray boy can get the gun high enough to fire and because he still has momentum, he plows into the side view mirror and door of the van without firing the weapon. The impact carries with it enough force that when he rebounds, it staggers him forward and he drops the gun, also loosening his grip on the little girl.

The gun bounces, stopping only when it hits Ryson's left foot. In one quick motion, Ryson pulls and with a whipping action, sends the little girl behind him and away, slow enough to keep her on her feet but fast enough to move her back and out of the way. Now, he picks up the gun.

The gun discharges twice and nobody more surprised than Ryson. Both rounds tear through the gray overalls sending the man in them dead to the ground.

When the small van starts to move, it does so slowly because now it has to steer around the dead guy. For no reason other than pure spontaneous instinct, Ryson reaches for the van and catches the handle on the sliding door. It's the

14

vans own movement that pulls the door open a couple of feet, Ryson stumbles but stays upright and gets a look inside.

On the floor and covered with a brown tarp are two small lumps and one small leg protruding from underneath, the shoe is gone but on the small foot is the Scooby Doo sock he put on the twins no more than two hours ago. Ryson does not see the barrel of the gun, he feels it pressed against the side of his face, then…click, then nothing but darkness.

Terrence knows it was a gunshot and then something speeds away, he backtracks only out of curiosity and sees to bloody bodies in the street, he finds one for sure D.O.A. The other with a head and face wound. Quickly, he removes his own shirt applying it to Ryson's face and head slowing the flow of death as now another bystander dials 911.

The sound of sirens approaching sends Terrence back the way he came. He can't stay, and for sure, he's got nothing to say. What he does not need at this point is any kind of interrogation.

The lights did flicker on but only for an instant when Ryson first gets to the hospital, it was the sudden and abrupt end to the sirens that seem to tug on his upper eyelids. And now, through the thinnest of slivers, Ryson can just make out the words "emergency" high over his head and knows this is a hospital, but with absolutely no understanding as to why they would bring him here.

And then the warm embrace of an opiate long kiss good night.

The surgery goes well, the repairs fairly straightforward, they remove what's left of Ryson's top front teeth, there was no damage to the gums but when the teeth shattered, they caused nerve damage to his upper lip right side, leaving his face permanently scarred. It took twenty-seven stitches to close the gash in the back of his head and as for the ring finger on his left hand… Well, there's not much they could do about that, although the pinky finger on the same hand after it heals should be good as new. And the bullet they took out of his neck, it is now evidence.

During the surgery, memories and visions bouncing around the inside of Ryson's head were nothing more than abstract whispers and illusions that he could not comprehend due to the drug-induced coma where he currently resides. But as the medications begin to wear off, there comes this darkness slowly at first and somewhat translucent but soon to a place so dark everything here hides in a darkness so thick you can almost lean into it for support.

The second flickers of light seem to come just shortly after the first but only this time along with the trickles of light seeping into his awareness, so, too, are the sounds and smells of the inside of a hospital, and the pain.

There are times in life, especially as a parent, when panic can squeeze you with such lung collapsing force that you will gasp in absolute horror for that next breath, for Ryson this was one of those moments.

Ryson lay motionless for almost three days in that hospital bed but on the third day just before dinner rounds, with his wife, Pat, at his side and a nurse cleaning some of the hoses leading to and from the bed, Ryson takes a series of short breaths followed by several seconds of no breathing at all.

One alarm sounds, than two, still Ryson's not breathing. Before that third alarm could sound and the call for the crash cart made, Ryson begins to inhale with such force it causes him to sit straight up in bed, eyes wide open and with a look of fear so disturbing Pat, who was standing now, collapses to her knees.

When normal breathing finally returns to him, he is facing Pat, who is now in the bed next to him, thanks to the orderlies and also semi-sedated, thanks to a quick thinking nurse and says, "Where are the girls?" Even though he already knows, but it's one of those questions we ask while doing our best to subdue and ignore the reality. Pat's reply even though now slightly slurred is, "Sweetheart, that's what we would all like to know."

"Yes, Mr. Willows, we would like to know that as well," this voice soft and feminine but with authority comes from out in the hallway and now stepping through the already open door, then closing the door behind her, is a light-skinned, light haired, five foot nine, pretty sort-of woman in a two-piece business suit, light gray, dark line pleats, and even with the jacket being somewhat bulky, it was obvious somebody needs to eat more or exercise less.

"Hello, Mr. Willows, my name is Margo Hops, my partner, Mr. Marks, and I are with the child and youth protective services, we are a federal task force and as of yet have not been assigned to this case so just as soon as Mr. Marks gets in here with a tape recorder, we will take your statement and proceed as necessary."

"Well, if you're the feds, then this must be pretty serious or maybe even something on the lines of international right? Let me ask you... Feds   or no feds, do you have any idea where my children are?" the tears streaming down their face were indeed the answer to his own question.

"No, Mr. Willows, at this point, we do not know where the children are, and yes, I am very sorry to say, we do suspect this case does fall under international child endangerment laws."

Now. in through the closed-door, steps a somewhat balding man and too young to be doing so, six foot, medium build, light brown skin, dark hair, at least what's left of it, and carrying a tape recorder in one hand and an unopened bottle of water in the other, handing the water to Margo, he now clicks on the tape recorder and shifts his full attention to Ryson.

"Will, good evening, Mr. Willows," he turns but only the upper part of his body, "and to you as well, Mrs. Willows," who was still resting quietly not saying much but paying very close attention in a blurred world sort of way.

"So, tell me, Mr. Willows, what the hell happened? Exactly how much do you remember?"

Ryson's clarity for an instant gets the better of him and he barks without thinking, "What the fuck did she mean by international laws?"

"Listen, Mr. Willows, I'm not going to pretend to know what you're going through, I can only sympathize and it's not because I am not a father but this job does not allow it. Now I really need you to focus more on the answers than your own questions. We both want the obvious, Mr. Willows."

"Now, again, Ryson, exactly how much do you remember especially in regards to the inside of the store and out along that trash alley? And also, do you have any idea who the man was who saved your life?"

Ryson does his best to recount the events starting with leaving the house with the girls, to seeing the emergency sign over his head when they wheeled him in here. He does not remember the moments after being shot in the face or the three days he spent lying in this bed.

"Nicely done, Mr. Willows, and this," Tom Marks says with absolute admiration and respect, he can clearly tell Ryson is in a great deal of pain and judging by the fresh blood now seeping through the bandages around his neck and face, this conversation is over.

"All right, Mr. Willows, now listen to me, with the pictures and descriptions of your kids your wife has provided us, we are already into this at full speed and you have to trust that we are doing all we can, now here's my card, you call me if you remember anything new. As far all your questions, there will be somebody of local authority to come by very soon and they will have access to all of the facts as we know them, and they will answer your questions. Thank you, Mr. Willows, get better, we will be back in touch."

The two detectives politely walk out of the room. Tom Marks leaving the tape recorder on no doubt, so the two of them could make their own private remarks.

Sometime around midnight, Pat's parents by request of the hospital showed up and convinced her to go home with them for the night.

That very next morning at 6:45 sharp, Ryson, who was already awake, could hear the breakfast service commencing out in the hallway, and now feeling just a little stupid for not ordering any, but, then again, it is just hospital food. Then through the doors comes what appears to be an orderly carrying two trays of breakfast. Reluctantly, for sure, Ryson says, "Sorry, man, I did not order any breakfast, although now I wish I had."

"That's all right, neither did I, good morning, Mr. Willows, I just figured what better way to get acquainted this morning than over a meal that was clearly meant for somebody else, all in a day, right?"

Setting both trays down on the wheeled bed tray and now making direct eye contact, this new food bringing friend says, "Will Thorne, that's me, I already know who you are and I am what two detectives probably referred to as the local authority." They shake hands,   Will now grabs one of the trays, plops down in the chair on the right side of the bed with the tray now balanced in his lap, fork in his left hand as he begins to eat and talk at the same time.

"So yeah, how fucked up is this shit? Although I got to say for a guy who three days ago was clubbed, cut, shot in the face, lost a finger, then damn near bled to death, you don't look half bad. You, my friend, are a survivor."

"Now, so far I believe I know what you know, and I believe I know what the two detectives know, so instead of you asking a whole bunch of painful questions, both mental and physical," this was obvious to Will, given the way Ryson winced at even the smallest bits of breakfast, "why don't you just let me do all the talking for now?"

"First off, let's start with the obvious, where are your kids? On the transcripts I got last night you asked, were they in that light blue minivan? And yes, Mr. Willows, we believe they were. We have video of that part of the parking lot but not much overview of the trash alley, but what we can see is a Hispanic male with what looks to be something under each arm dives headfirst

18

into the minivan, to me and the others, what it seemed he was carrying were small children. The description your wife gave us was a pretty good match. The video is not all that great, pretty cheap and grainy, but I got a copy whenever you're ready to look at it."

"The minivan now pulls away, you show up, they come back, shoot you, you shoot one of them, and then they leave their dead buddy behind and drive away, where to at this point, we do not know. Nice shot by the way." Ryson says nothing, just nods. Will then adds, "They were quite crude in the assault but the overall plan and the fact they targeted twins was somewhat sophisticated. That's why the visit and involvement by the feds."

"At this point, there are a dozen different agencies, including local P.D., in five counties looking for your children twenty-four hours a day. And the guy you shot, he comes back a Colombian national with a history of drug smuggling for the Bolivian cartel. So what that means is, the feds have already involved foreign relations just on the off chance there successful in smuggling your children out of the country."

"Well... What I miss Mr. Willows?" Will again makes eye contact with Ryson, hoping to get a feel for how he is digesting all of this.

Ryson surprisingly solid, now asks, "Who was that little girl? And how in the hell did these guys walk into a major department store and shut down all the power?"

Now Will pulls out a small paper tablet, opens it about halfway, then places it down on the upper part of his right leg above the tray and reads from it, "Okay, so the little girl's life you saved, her name is Trina Match and she is six years old. And as near as we can tell, the poor little thing had just stepped out of the dressing room, she was alone in when the lights went out. Her and her father, Arthur, were at the store, so Trina could pick out a new dress to wear on Mother's Day."

"Now, as Trina stepped out of the dressing room to model one of her choices, the whole store goes dark. Now dad is some distance away, looking for more dresses in her size, and being that they both were at about mid-store when the lights go out, it was really dark and, in the commotion, loud enough that when Trina calls out for her dad, he does not hear her. And when Arthur calls out for his daughter, Trina, and now basically, he's just standing there yelling in the dark, he does not hear her reply if, in fact, there even was one."

"Understand? The rest of this I got from a six-year-old. Trina says as she came out of the dressing room it got really dark and scary so she stood there in the dark and calls for Dad, she does actually hear him calling her by name from somewhere in the darkness. But before she can call out the second time, something from behind impacts the right side of her face and head, then a hand held tightly over her mouth, dizzy and can't breathe, she is now lifted and carried somewhere into the darkness."

"When they find light again, they are going through a door and into some sort of alley with big trash cans, as they come through the door, bad guy loses his grip on the little girl, having to now grab both of her wrists in just his right hand. The two now, he dragging her basically by her wrists, head up the alleyway where they meet you, you know the rest."

"What was your other question?" Ryson, in that instant, could not remember, he was still trying to process the first answer, then, Will answers it for him, "Oh yeah, how do these guys just walk into a major department store and completely shut off all the power, I mean, isn't that difficult?"

"Yes, that's not easy, Mr. Willows. And that's one of the reasons why the feds are already involved."

Will now folds and puts back the paper pad from where it came, finishes the last few moist oats in the bottom of the bowl and says, "Absolutely not, Mr. Willows, it's just not that simple."

"You see, all the major department stores because of their large electrical demands, they are not part of the mall electrical grid, they take their power right from the street. Each department store has a small electrical substation in their basement, the power comes into here, then up to what is called the charge room and into large circuit panels. Now, from these panels, the current is sent through the electrical wiring, which feeds electricity throughout the entire store. So yeah, first you have to get past all the employees, find your way back to the maintenance section, locate the charge room which was indeed locked, get past that, and into the charge room in order to shut down the main power panel."

"And now because the backup system is what's known as a static control system, which means the backup power is actually dormant until main power loss. During main power loss, the voltage bleed causes a coil/condenser to collapse, sending a main charge to the backup panel and if you are not standing right there at the ready to disengage the circuit, the batteries kick in and then by its own design you cannot cut power to the system until the batteries have completely drained and that takes about four hours."

. "So this guy, whoever he was not only did he get into the charge room, he knew to wait for the static control system to attempt powering the backup and then he shuts down all power. And of course as you are quite aware of, immediately after this, it gets very dark. Also, I believe, before the guy goes into the charge room but after he picks the lock, he shoves a thin slice of aluminum into the key slot which renders the lock useless.

"The door itself is designed to not lock from the inside, so after he leaves, you could no longer unlock the door. Yeah, that damn door had to actually be removed by the hinges so they could reset the system and restore power."

All Ryson can say at this point is, "Wow," and then he starts to cry, it's not a sob but clearly tears trickle down both sides of his face.

Will now stands, both hands still holding his food tray and places it atop the wheeled bed tray then gently nudges it out of the way, now standing over Ryson, he places both of his open hands onto Ryson's chest and applies some pressure. He, too, has tears in his eyes as he says, "Mr. Willows, I am not going to hide the truth from you, what I know, I want you to know, I also want you to know, I am here for this, all of this, no matter what."

"On that note, Mr. Willows. Here's what you need to do, first, get out of this sickness infested shit hole and go home, do your best to put yourself back in working order, I will come by the house, maybe a day or two. Here is my cell and home phone, call me if need be." As will turns and heads for the door, he quick glances back at Ryson and says with half a smile. "I pity the fool when they find out not only did you steal one breakfast you did not order, you stole two."

Laughing slightly, Will heads through the doors and disappears.

Ryson's tears are still drying on his cheeks and painful as it is he bends the tiniest of smiles. The next morning, Ryson goes home after being fitted for temporary dental implants.

Ryson's brother, Lee, and Ryson's wife, Patricia, were at the hospital bright and early on the morning of checkout. Lee had managed to put on a happier man's clothes today and Ryson did for sure appreciate it. Patricia on the other hand, well, let's just say… Good thing she is not driving, yes, still fairly well medicated, and who could blame her.

Pulling up to the house, then slowly into the driveway, Lee's truck barely fits without blocking the sidewalk path past the house. As the truck goes quiet and Lee retrieves the key from the ignition, the three of them now realize what a quiet ride it was on the way over.

When they reached the front door, it was obvious to Lee neither of the two wanted to enter the house, Pat, with all the apprehension in the world laying across her shoulders like a cement shawl, painfully does manage to unlock the door. Lee steps in first like he was happy to be there, yeah, still wearing the happy man's clothes.

Dark and stuffy the inside of the house, badly needed the air exchanged, stale and uncomfortable with the temperature at a level that has wilted all the plants, Lee says, "Seems from the smell of things you two have some windows to open, or not, either way, I shall leave you to it." Hugs them both and says, "Love you both like cheap sex, you got my number," and heads for the door. Ryson sort of mumbles Lee's name to turn him around, now bringing them face to face from across the room and says, "Thanks, Lee."

Lee winks, nods, and through the door, he shuffles.

As Lee backs out of the driveway, it's finally the site of their minivan that shatters what little remains of his emotional shield he had left, and the tears that flowed he let do so…because…sad is sad.

The following day, some family, some friends and a phone call from Will Thorne saying he was coming by in the morning around nine, after breakfast. The day sadly sombers forward like this until dark.

At 9 a.m. sharp, there is a quiet tapping at the front door, assuming it is Will, Ryson yells from the kitchen, "It's open, Will, come on in, coffee's almost ready and I hope you don't mind the site of a few bazillion dead ants."

The sound of a woman's voice startles Ryson but only because it's not what he expected, but then again, with Francine, it never is. The tiny frail voice chirps good morning as Ryson lifts his head from the daunting task of a bazillion ant kill cleanup, and of course, as always, the voice does not match the body.

"Ryson…I don't know if you know this, but there is a man sleeping in a car in front of your house. Been there since about 6:30, when I took Jake to school, there was no car but when I got back maybe 6:40 car was there, guy covered up with a coat sleeping. Still there now."

22

Turning on her toes in an attempt to appear graceful all 300 pounds of her heads back towards the front door moving through the house with the speed better left to those who have the ability to stop quickly.

Ryson follows Francine through the living room until they are both now sharing space on the front porch, both looking out towards the street when Ryson says, "Yes, Francine, I know who that is."

Francine steps off the porch, cuts right into the yard towards her house in silence and in just a few steps, already sucking wind. "Thanks, Francine," Ryson doing his best to be polite, and Francine a partial wave with the back of her hand means she heard him but makes no vocal reply.

As Ryson gets close to the car parked in front of the house, he can hear a phone alarm attempting to wake the sleeping driver. It's only when the phone alarm go's silent does Will begin to stir, Ryson sees this as he approaches the back of the car, decides to let him come around on his own terms, makes a U-turn back to the house, back to the ants.

At 9:17 a.m., again light tapping at the door, "Come on in, Will, it's open. I'm in the kitchen." This time the voice from half way to the kitchen did not come as a surprise, "I hope there's some fresh coffee Mr. Willows," and now through the door-less entryway into the kitchen steps, Will Thorne holding an empty coffee mug, and as he does so, he says, "technically, I am not late, been here since 6:30, now where's that coffee?"

"Grab a mug, or... I guess you can use the one you brought, put it right there, hit brew, I think it's hazelnut. And yeah, I have already been informed as to your sleeping arrangements. Nothing happens around here without Francine knowing about it."

"God damn, these fucking ants been killing and cleaning these nomad mother fuckers for an hour now." Ryson pauses and it seems like he's almost in tears, he takes a breath and without turning around to face will he says, "Wow, I'm sorry Mr. Thorne, it's just been that kind of morning."

"So why so early, Mr. Thorne? You know you could have just knocked on the door when you got here."

Will, who is waiting patiently for his mug to fill, first says, "Yep, hazelnut," then, "yeah, I figured as much, but just thought maybe you were still sleeping, did not want to be freaking anybody out."

"But, now, listen, Mr. Willows, why I was so early, I was supposed to meet with Tom Marks, you remember him, right? And Margo Hops, detectives from the hospital, well, Tom and I were supposed to meet at LAX this morning. He calls a couple of days ago telling me that he has a case file he thinks I should see, he proceeds to tell me some of what is in it and says I should meet him at L.A.X. in the morning at which time he would give it to me. But while I am sitting in traffic to get on the 105 Tom calls and says he is going to miss that flight, tells me he will send the file to me, then again touches base on some of the details it contains."

"First off, how are you and Patricia holding up?" along with a couple of sips of hazelnut coffee comes a little slower pace. Will ask this question out of true concern and not curiosity.

Ryson gives him a so, so and that Pat went to stay with her sister and brother-in-law in Gorman for a couple of days. It's probably better this way, maybe it will help clear her head. Ryson says this but knows it's not true.

Ryson now asks, "Hey, Will, if you are local authority, then why are the feds sharing info with you?"

"It's probably my charming disposition or just simply that I am a hell of a lot of fun to hang out with," Will responds first with this but then gets serious. "Very good question, Mr. Willows. You see, is what happened, the federal government, three years ago, decided to implement a separate branch within the child welfare department, calling it Child Safe Care Services, this is now because of the funding an entire network within in the U.S. dedicated to tracking collecting and maintaining data files and information regarding any and all non-domestic kidnappings."

"So, the feds appointed one police department substation within each county to appoint one officer to maintain local records regarding these types of kidnappings and they would also be the contact liaison to the feds, that's me, that's why I'm the one they called the day you landed in the hospital and that's why I'm here now."

Done with the ants, Ryson refills the coffee pot with a hazelnut pod and hits brew. Now the both of them sit down across from one another at a small round kitchen table.

"So why you, Will?"

"Volunteered, I have been a beat cop in Orange County for eight years and in that eight years never once did I put in for a promotion or ever rank above beat cop, anything above that just meant more rules and regulations. At least, as a beat cop, I know I am making a difference in my own county, so when this came along and of course it was for the kids, I was all in, sorry to say not much to really do till you came crashing in, and so now here we are."

Will stands and heads to the coffee machine with empty mug in hand, Will withdraws Ryson's mug from the machine and says, "Do you need something to happen to this?"

"No," was Ryson's response, "works for me just the way it is." Will sets the mug on the table in front of Ryson and turns back towards the coffee machine, does his thing, hits brew, and stays standing next to it in hopes for a quicker brewed second cup.

Will waits patiently admiring the hissing, spits, and sputters of the machine that now brews his cup of vanilla cream. So far happy with his selection mostly because of the aroma.

Ryson cups both hands around the mug in front of him and without looking up, speaks in a voice and manner that reminds Will as to just what this man has been through, "So, in this report Mr. Marks has for you does anybody, anywhere, have any idea, where my girls are?"

"Ryson... You remember what I told you when we first met in the hospital, it doesn't matter, I'll say it again. I want you to know what I know. That file Tom has I have every intention of sharing its entirety with you. But for now, here's all I know."

"Tom tells me the people that took your children refer to the day they did it as Tiger's day or even as the day the Tiger feeds. These groups are referred to as a Tiger team. And evidently, the day before Mother's Day is Tigers day."

"Federal intel gathered within the last four years indicates an understanding of our own predictable local behaviors on their part, the bad guys. So much so that these Tiger teams are assembled with specific targets predetermined and, in your case, twins. These teams also know that the day before Mother's Day is the best chance they have at achieving this."

"Like I told you in the hospital, these guys, in their own trial and error sort of way, knew you or somebody like you would show up the day before Mother's Day, and with their prize."

"So at this point in time, Mr. Willows, we do not know where the kids are, but we do have a pretty good idea who took them. For sure, this team came in from South America, the feds tell me they know this because of a tattoo the guy you shot had on the back of his neck. It's the word 'death' followed by

25

two $ signs. Death and $$. What this signifies they're not quite sure but at least we do have some continuity between us, them, and your kids."

"So, basically, because of the guy you killed we now have a better understanding of who we are dealing with."

"Hey, listen, Mr. Thorne, about that guy I shot. I'll be honest, I don't really know what happened or how I killed him, I remember bringing the gun up and pointing it at his chest, but really only to scare him and stop his advance. But when the sliding door of the minivan opened and I saw my little girl's foot, the gun just went off, it was at that point I remember removing my finger from the trigger and out from the trigger guard, that's when the gun went off the second time, I no way pulled the trigger of that gun twice."

Will with a thin smile and shaking his head in wonder says, "Good thing that gun went off twice because the first round was not going to stop him from using that seven-inch folded blade we found under his body from probably cutting you in half. It was that second bullet tearing through his heart that saved your life, Mr. Willows."

"I guess it's true what they say, we are all just ordinary men until we are forced to do extraordinary things," Ryson says this, but for the first time, he realizes what this means.

"So what can I do to help? You know what, Mr. Willows, the best thing you can do right now is simply keep it together. I have read your file and checked into some of your background, your tour in Vietnam and the work you did body guarding some of the dignitaries over there, and then now the body guarding business you and your brothers have built appears to be quite successful. So you seem to me a pretty solid guy, just be that. I am only just one small component in this large machine doing everything possible while using all available resources to find and return your kids to you."

The buzzing coming from Will's front pocket forces him to stand and remove a cell phone, replying quickly with dancing thumbs, Will speaks out loud what he is typing, "Thanks, Tom, for sure, see you at four."

Will picks up his empty mug from the table and checks his watch, then says, "thanks for the coffee Mr. Willows, I will be back in touch just as soon as there is anything new, and when that file shows up, I'll go over it and let you know what I find."

Slowly standing, as if trying to lift a man three times his own weight, Ryson stands and says, "Thanks Mr. Thorne."

They shake hands, Will heads for the front door, Ryson right behind him.

At halfway, Will stops and at the same time saying, "Arthur Match, yes, Arthur Match. That's the guy who's little girl you saved." Turning now to face Ryson, Will continues, "I think he would like to say thank you. Okay I gave him your number? Too late, already did." Will turns back to the front door while saying, "I'll let myself out." He does and closes the door behind him. The house fades to silence, Ryson still standing where Will left him, and now all that can be heard is just the sound of a slow beating heart.

Petting Zoo

That same evening somewhere between toy-fully playing with a suicide solution and dinner, Ryson's cell phone comes to life with the song *Love Me Tender* but not Elvis, it's the version from Gary Hoey. When the number shows, it's not listed or in the contacts Ryson answers it anyway, he thinks it's Will Thorne.

The voice that replies to Ryson's hello, Ryson can tell right away that it has a sense of pretend calm to it.

"Hello, Mr. Willows my, name is Arthur Match, I think maybe Will Thorne told you I would be calling."

"Yes, he mentioned that."

Not sure where this conversation is going Ryson is still trying to remain neutral.

"I realize, Mr. Willows, that for you there is no really great time for us to do this. But right now, I am in sort of an emergency, I do not at this point think it is life-threatening but believe it or not, you are absolutely the only one I thought to call."

"It seems I have just recently acquired a petting zoo and because I fired the staff of four that took care of the goats and sheep, believe me, no other choice. Anyway, you still with me, Mr. Willows?"

"I guess so," Ryson says, still neutral.

"Anyway, for the past two nights, I have been coming down here to feed these animals and tonight was supposed to be the last night I had to do so, that's what I was doing when I got the message from Will Thorne saying that it was okay to call you."

"As I finished keying in your number and hit send, the cord I am pulling to release the feed through a tube that travels up into the ceiling somehow tears out and part of the tube and the valve controlling the flow of feed then falls, almost killing me and causing the door of the feed room to slam shut and by some magical force of nature, the door is now locked."

"But wait, it gets better. The valve I yanked from the ceiling and is now lying on the floor is what stopped and started the feed flow, without it I have no way to stop or stem the flow of feed coming from a hole in the ceiling, so basically, the feed is flowing into the room through a hole I have no way to plug. At the rate it seems the feed is falling, best I figure, perhaps an hour or so, and I should be standing chest deep in it."

Ryson's neutral buoyancy begins to take on water, "Mr.? Ryson struggles for the last name then just says, Arthur, are you sure you shouldn't be calling 911?"

"No can do, here's where you need to trust me, Mr. Willows. You have to believe me when I say this is about our future and the future of your kids as well. So no more questions. I need you to get in your car right now, drive over here, it's just in Santa Ana, twenty minutes from you tops. I am texting you the address right now, worst comes to worst, there is a window I can easily break and crawl out, call me when you get here, I am sliding the key under the door right now so don't break any laws getting here," Art now pauses and waits quietly for a response.

"Jesus, Arthur, really, hey... If I get down there and find you dead and buried in a room full of goat chow, I'm going to be pissed."

"That's not funny, just hurry, thanks."

In the twenty-six minutes it took Ryson to reach the warehouse and call from out front the animal feed had become ankle-deep and now has slowed to just a trickle.

"Hey, Mr. Willows, no rush, buddy, I am pretty sure the feed danger has passed. That little door next to the big door is not locked, come on in, hey, my car still out there?"

"Well, if your car is a gray Dodge truck then, yeah, it's out here."

This reply from Ryson weighs heavy with suspicion.

"Oh that's right, the truck, forgot about that, those three large bags of cans in the back I'm supposed to drop off at the recycle place on the way home."

Ryson steps closer to Art' truck to inspect its cargo and says, "What no beer cans?" and heads for the smaller of the two doors in a protruding section of the large warehouse.

"Nope, no beer cans, and that's because they were collected by that little girl you saved, my little girl. Yeah, she collected most of them at school and at our local park, it seems her gymnastics school is doing a recycling fundraiser, oh boy."

"Now how's about you unlock this door and we talk face-to-face. Now come through the smaller door, go straight just past three or four stacks of tires, quick right, and now that door you are looking at with key on the floor in front of it is the feed room, open that, would you?"

Even before Art could finish the sentence, he could hear the key dancing around the inside of the lock and then freedom.

Handshakes and smiles, one in joy' the other in sorrow and in each other's eyes, one hides the sadness the other shares his pain. And even though Art told himself that he would be strong for Ryson, when they embraced, Art could feel the weight of the world on this man's shoulders, Art wept, and Ryson for a moment lets him do so. It's a simple hug and no longer than normal but the moment is forever cast in stone.

Art finally stepping back and attempting to regain his strength and composure but clearly in his voice, it's no doubt a work in progress.

"It's nice to finally meet you, Mr. Willows, I am just so very sorry it had to be like this." Ryson responds first with a tiny smile then says respectfully, "You and me both, Mr."

Ryson who is now done with pleasantries says, "Geez, I don't know what is worse, Mr. Match, the smell or the noise in this place."

"Shit, this is nothing Mr. Willows, hell, I have already fed the goats," Art says this as he heads back into the feed room. "As for the smell, why don't you get those two large rolling doors on either side of the warehouse open and let's get some fresh air in here, I shall finish feeding the sheep."

As a hunger hush finishes making its way through the rest of the animal pens, that line half of the warehouse on one whole side with a feeding lane right down the middle splitting the rows of pins into too long single rows, goats on one side sheep on the other, things begin to quiet down.

"So, tell me, Mr. Match, how does all of this affect my kids and change our futures?" Ryson's question follows him as he walks over to the pins where Art is just finishing dumping the last two buckets of food into a wooden trough in the last pin of unfed sheep, and now says, "How about we stop this whole proper name thing and just go with first names only. You can call me Art."

"Yes, that's fine, you can call me Ryson."

Art steps back through the small gate of the pin he was just in, now Art and Ryson stand with-in arms-length of each other, Art with an empty pail in both hands raises both arms, what he says starts with sort of a whisper.

"All of this and including another larger facility out in Riverside County, that houses and maintains the llamas, camels, and as I understand it, a couple of elephants. As of 9 a.m. tomorrow morning, I become owner and general manager. Now come on, let's go sit down, we have a lot to talk about."

When Art returns from the feed room with two bottles of water and minus the two empty pails, Ryson has already taken a position at a round card table in a metal folding chair just outside the feed room.

After placing both bottles of water on the table, Art sits down in the chair directly to Ryson's left, leaving only a couple of feet between them.

Now from Arts pocket, he retrieves a small kid's diary, the kind you would buy at just about any kind of card shop and give to a small child, he then places it on the table in front of himself.

Without opening the diary, Art begins to speak as if reciting what's inside it, "Tiger team, it's what they call themselves. They can come from just about any small city or town in South America, they come into the United States, usually looking for a very specific item or items. And in this case, your twins. And then, it seems in a single heartbeat, they can disappear."

Ryson does not hide his confusion when asking how do you know about all this Tiger shit, "Art?"

"Let's just say I am extremely resourceful and the less you know as to how I obtained this information the better," Art says this, no doubt, as a matter of fact.

"Well then, Art, I guess it's your turn for the one-billion-dollar question. Do you have any idea where my kids are?"

This statement and the tears that are forever paired with it, further fuels what Art feels for this and he knows he has made the right decision.

"Ryson, the only ones that know where your children are, are the ones that have them. Not even the ones that took them know where they are now," Art drops this statement like a sandbag only to test the level of Ryson's strength and composure.

It's a simple head nod from Ryson but it speaks volumes, it's the lack of a vocal response that makes the most noise. Again, Art knows he has made the right decision.

"I truly believe that your kids are no longer in this country, I am quite sure they were taken out of the country within hours of them being taken from you, and the only reason the two detectives assigned to the case are not telling you this is because they themselves cannot verify this information. But in all past dealings with these types of kidnapping teams, it's hard to think otherwise." (That is a quote directly from the detective Tom Marks.)

"You know, he and his partner, Margo Hops, they really do mean well and I think they will be useful to us in the future, notice, I said future. As for local help, this guy, William Thorne, will definitely be of some help, his heart absolutely is in the right place."

Ryson rings in, but doing his best not to sidetrack the conversation, "Yes, I have dealt with will a couple of times now, he seems pretty genuine."

"So what I'm saying is this, at this point the U.S. government does not have a system in place, local or otherwise, to chase these guys down on foreign soil, thus, retrieving your children. If that is going to happen, it can only come from the private sector and by private sector, I mean us."

"First of all, how do you know for sure my kids are no longer in this country, and what are you saying, we form our own Tiger team and steal back my own children, do you know how ridiculous that sounds?"

Art was already in a subconscious level on board with this concept, he just did not realize how much until Ryson actually speaks it out loud.

"You know, Ryson, that's not as farfetched as you might think. I did find two cases where that's exactly what happened. There was a Canadian couple in 1999 that somehow retrieved their twins, and then in 2001, a couple from Arkansas come home from Columbia with their triplets. How this was done is not public record and I could not find anybody that would care to discuss it. So, before you start saying how ridiculous this all sounds, I think maybe what's ridiculous is that were still sitting here talking about it."

"And, yes, Ryson, without any doubt, those kids are no longer in this country, I drove to Sacramento to gather this information myself because in the state's capital, there is a library that houses all of the FBI's declassified criminal investigations, and a whole section on kidnapping, foreign and domestic."

"These Tiger teams do not even rent hotel rooms, they live in their chosen vehicle until the job is done, at which time, the vehicle is abandoned and the whole party is moved out of the country, and then… well, that's what we need to find out, now don't we?"

Art leaving the last part of this statement a question in hopes of furthering Ryson's path from denial.

"Well, geez, Art, it sounds like you don't think I am being all the dad I should be right now, well, that's horse shit! Because from the very moment I could speak clearly again, never mind the fucking pain, I have spent every waking moment and I am quite sure most of the sleeping ones as well with my head, heart, and soul engaged in this nightmare, every phone call, every conversation, every place, person or reason I could confront I did, hell, that's why I'm here now. And so far, all I have learned from you is some shit I already knew and some other shit nobody has any real proof, as of yet."

"What I do know is this," Ryson's voice almost seems to hide in the form of a whisper, "they're just gone. Saying this out loud fractures what's left of a hollow man," then when Ryson repeats this a second time, "they're just gone," his head falls forward onto his crossed arms at the table at which time, he finally emotionally collapses and is no longer making any attempt to not do so.

For every tear that now falls from Ryson's eyes, the world just becomes that much heavier.

Art knowingly makes no attempt to comfort nor console, not because of his own wisdom but simply for the fact that here before him sits a man in such a darkened place he knows from experience many do not return, and also a man who saved himself from this very same horror. There are no words. You just leave the moment be. You save your own tears for later.

Within just a couple of minutes, Art could tell Ryson was attempting to regain some self-control. Art pushes a stack of paper napkins in front of Ryson, leaving his hand to come to rest on Ryson's right shoulder. Ryson embraces the compassion and somewhat folds beneath it and then grabs half the stack of napkins.

Art applies some pressure and a gentle push to Ryson's shoulder and says, "So, then we find a way, and we hunt and we chase these Tiger fucks to the ends of the earth if need be."

Reaching for the rest of the paper napkins and leaving the used ones to form a pile on the floor, Ryson finishes mopping up before lifting his head to a full upright position.

"Art, why are you doing this? Why are we here? Art, this is not your fight, you do not have to be a part of this. You talk as though I have a choice in all this or even the means to truly make a difference, you have to understand, Art, that even if Pat and I liquidated everything we have, it would probably be worth about as much as a couple of round-trip first-class tickets to Phoenix, and that includes money from the body guarding service. From the outside, it seems quite profitable but, in all reality, due to the expenses and overhead, there is not much cash flow at this point, and even that belongs mostly to my brother, he, being the primary investor/owner."

"So, all I can do is continue to do the best I can with the resources I have available to me, and I am real sorry, Art, that you don't think this is enough, but it's all I have."

"You could not be further from understanding my position or place in all of this, Ryson. Let's start with this place," Art remaining seated, follows this statement with stretched out arms and small movement at the waist left and right. Returning his arms to a closed position in front of his chest, Art falls silent, staring forward and avoiding eye contact with Ryson, Art starts with this, "What you did for me, as a father, I can only say thank you, because any other attempt to find balance short of returning your own children to you would simply be the gift you gave to me."

"But what you did for my little girl," Art can no longer hold back his emotions and lets slip just a few tears before he rechecks his strength and continues, "what you did for her, is a debt that must be paid and as long as your kids are not with you, this debt is a broken soul and cannot, and will not, be abandoned."

"So it starts right here," Art stands and continues to speak, "I had every intention of closing the books on this place when the A-hole that owns it runs down and kills an eleven-year-old in a crosswalk on a Sunday morning after an all-night celebration of some sorts. It was his third D.U.I. offense in two years, yah, he got twenty-five years with no possible way for early release. I've been this A-hole's accountant for six years now and as I see it, he got what he deserved, should have been more."

"I actually did begin processing the paperwork to liquefy his petting zoo, but when it came right down to it and of course, when you came along, I realized I simply needed to acquire some insurance and refile for a business license and this whole operation goes back into production, and so, I remain ethical through all of this, one third of the profits will go to the victim's family, the other two thirds will go directly into a non-profit organization, that's you."

Ryson, of course, with surprise and confusion, "What?"

"So, you see, Mr. Willows, you do in deed have the means, in fact, you had the means the moment you grabbed my little girl's hand and intervened, so now you and I are one and the same, what I have is yours," Art now steps closer to the table, a sense of sadness and strength in his voice.

"Sometimes, life just has to hold still, at least long enough for some of the lost pieces to be gathered, it's obvious neither one of us want nor chose to be here, but we are, and now those lost pieces are your children. So here, my life stops and becomes something else, it's a debt that must be paid and cannot be considered as such until your children are safe and in your arms. So, take this as my surrender to you, whether the journey takes a few days or an eternity, all I have and all I can gather, I give this to you."

Art now moves right to the edge of the table and in his voice, now, rings a sense of strength and anger, "So what say we work together, I will be finance and intel, you be search and recovery... I mean unless none of this appeals to you."

If Ryson thought his knees would support his own weight, he would have attempted to stand, he could only nod his head and repeat the slow words, "Yes, yes, yes."

Giving Ryson a moment to collect his reply Art, now sits down in the chair directly across the table.

"Of course, Art. Art, there is no life for me without them and no fucking land far enough for them to hide my children, you point me in the right direction, I will hunt in hell if need be."

This time when the two of them make eye contact, who they see now is different from when they first met.

"I really am very sorry, Art, that I cannot contribute more financially but obviously what I do have belongs to this cause as well, I also have two brothers who I'm sure will give all they can afford. It's learning to manage without me, they will find most disturbing, but believe me, they will understand."

"Oh, I think they will do better than just manage," Art approaches this topic somewhat hesitant at first and Ryson can tell.

"This is what I bring to the table, Mr. Willows, it's not just the money, there is a whole bunch of shit we've got to know. That's what I do, so like it or not, hear is what I have already done."

"Are you familiar with the Marietta and Temecula area?"

Not waiting for a reply and just assuming, so Art continues and now, without any hesitation.

"Well, it just so happens I am one of the accountants hired to do the financial growth and profit assessments for new development in both Marietta and Temecula, so a couple of days ago, the financial allocation for manned patrol and security for the two malls that are being built, one in each location comes through my desk."

"I simply put in a bid on behalf of you and your brothers, me knowing the bottom dollar my bid or I should say, the bid submitted by level 1 security was five thousand dollars under allocation. They called the next day. All that's left now is the three of you sign the contracts, hire a handful of retired cops and military personnel for each location, and now you are in the mall security business."

"It just does not get much easier than that, so whether our business here takes a few days or longer, when it's over and your kids are safely in your arms, you simply go back to what you were doing only better."

"I also need you to sign and fill out all the paperwork in your new employee package."

Ryson question, "I have an employee package?"

He has to squeeze in because Art never really slows down.

"Yeah, we don't want the feds fucking with the money." The disgust in Art's voice is obvious and Ryson can tell Arts been down this road before.

"We cannot risk money flow issues, so what I did was hire you whole time as my personal bodyguard, I think it's absolutely reasonable in thinking that my family and I need full-time protection, in case they come after my kid a second time."

"And, yes, it's a sweet package because, it's not every day I get to hire somebody who was the bodyguard for Pat Buchanan when he was running for president."

The simplest of grins and a confession from Ryson ensures Art that indeed the two of them will no doubt make a difference.

Ryson's grin is labored and full of guilt and this is obvious even to an untrained eye, well, don't be too impressed Art.

"I just happen to be in the office the day the Buchanan campaign wagon stopped in town, couple of their security guys have some sort of stomach problems, so we leave them behind in the office and I go with the other two and help bodyguard Pat Buchanan."

Art, who is obviously still impressed, asks, "So, how was that?"

"It was cool, I watched him eat lunch."

Art, doing his best to subdue the obvious amusement, lets a small chuckle escape his chest.

Ryson always tells that story the way he does for just that response.

"So, Art, what's next?"

"I think we need a recon mission, not quite sure where you're going just yet, or who you are going with, but we need eyes on intel. This limp I have will stop me from going with you," Art says this as if it was one of the hardest things he's ever had to say and does not elaborate.

"But somebody does have to go with you, preferably a woman. I think our best bet at obtaining information as to where your kids are is to perhaps explore the purchase angle of these children and or children like them."

"So, Ryson, you let me get to work on this, you need to go home and get your affairs in order and of course, get your brothers up to speed, and no, at this point, we are not asking for money from anybody, you or otherwise."

"Let's get out of here, I will see you in a couple of days." Art now slides a business card across the table in front of Ryson and says, "My office and all my phone numbers."

When Art stands from the table, he has a small look of concern on his face, then says, "How about I close and roll up the back doors and you put the feed pails back in the feed room, I am not in a hurry to get back in there."

Ryson, of course, understanding, gets up, gathers the pails, and heads to the feed room.

When Ryson reaches the closed door of the feed room, the small sign hanging from a nail in the door makes less sense now then the first time he read it, it says "knock before entering." He flips the sign over and now it reads "leave key in lock when in feed room, door will lock if shut."

With Art within shouting distance. Ryson shouts, "Hey, Art, did you knock before you entered the feed room?"

Arts reply is hesitant, "Yes, just the first time, after that, it did not seem necessary."

Ryson leaving the pails, shutting the door and placing the sign in its proper orientation, heads away from the room saying to himself, "You have got to always check both sides of the coin." He makes sure Art can't hear this.

As the two of them stood in the warm summer darkness between their two vehicles, both knowing less of one another but at the same time, sharing the same understanding of hope and trust, Art reaches out his hand and says, "Yes, we fight."

Ryson quick to the shake and says, "We fight. See you in a couple of days."

Handshakes and smiles, one in joy the other still in sorrow, but now with some hope.

The quick arithmetic tapping came in short burst, then silence. Knowing this to be the front door, Ryson attempts to hide in the warmth of post slumber, thinking back to a day when not answering the front door was an option. Now the sound of wind chimes resonating through the house means they found the doorbell and it's time to get up.

From the top of the stairs, Ryson can see through a window over the front door and already tell his early visitor is Will Thorne, now at mid-stairs, he pauses and in a slight mumble he says to himself, "Only what's in front of me."

Twisting the knob on the front door and leaving it to open on its own, Ryson shuffles through and towards the kitchen, trying to sound somewhat awake Ryson semi-trumpets, "Good morning, Mr. Thorne. You are just in time for coffee."

Before Ryson can reach the kitchen, Will's reply and the tone in which it was delivered sends a freezing bolt of panic and fear through Ryson, stopping him cold in his tracks.

"Listen, Mr. Willows, there is no need for pleasantries this morning, I just rather we do this right here on the porch," Will says this as if tomorrow the sun does not rise.

A slow half turn towards the front door, Ryson finds Will still standing on the porch in a sort of lean and holding a brown collapsible folder in his left hand and on his face and in his eyes, the world and all that's wrong with it.

Before Ryson's knees buckle, sending him to the floor in a blubbering mass of crybaby jelly, Will speaks up and avoids the disaster.

"No, no, no! Stop thinking the worst, Mr. Willows. We still do not know where the children are, good, bad, or otherwise. But at the same time, I have no good news neither."

Ryson finishes the turn and now heads back towards the front door, with this short journey complete and Ryson now at the threshold, Will steps back and away from the door, so Ryson can step out onto the small porch.

There are two round columns holding up the porch overhang on either side of the steps leading up to the house, on one of these, Will now leans against, not so much for comfort but for support, the brown collapsible folder still in his left hand.

There is a moment of silence but not long enough to be uncomfortable, Ryson's attempt to voice his curiosity is quickly washed away by the strange melancholy sounds of Will's voice.

"I was thirteen when I decided to become a cop," Will brings this statement forward as if Ryson had asked the question.

Ryson, at this point, chooses to just listen.

"So from thirteen on, my life revolved around the anticipation of that future, I did everything I was supposed to do, good grades, no drugs, stayed out of trouble, did my four years of college, and then right from college to the police academy. And yes, I believed it was time for me to make a realistic difference. I know how textbook *cliché* this sounds but it's true, all I wanted was to go out into the big scary world and make it better, you see, I assumed the authority of being a police officer was a platform from which I would spring. Yeah, right. Second day on the job, we pull over a speeder, simple ticket, except this fucker comes out shootin', luckily, my training officer knew what to do because I was frozen in the passenger seat."

"So, right there, I realize my authority means dick, and the only ones playing by the rules are the innocent. I spend the next four years entrenched in day to day street battles with drug dealers and users, sex offenders, the unruly homeless, and domestic violence, as if, in most of the population, it was hereditary."

There is a pause here, it's duration is not based in time but thought gathered.

Ryson sticking to his choice for silence, takes a breath that simply signals, I'm listening.

"And, now, here I go with the textbook *clichés* again, but hell to a higher court, I swear there were times you could bust some crackhead for beating up his kids at the end of your shift and that same fuck could be back on the street before you."

"At some point, right around the four-year mark, it was obvious at street cop level the only difference I could make was to simply slow things down and temporarily halt the progress of all things wicked mean and nasty."

"And now, the obvious choice at this point to me was to move up, higher classification, better pay, and more authority. So I start taking criminal law classes and begin to study for the sergeant's exam, and also the detective requirements. Still wanting to make a difference."

"But what I found on this several month journey was bucketful after bucketful of rules and regulations, regulations, and more regulations."

"Had it not been for the in-department memo I had received saying Orange County needed seasoned cops for a couple of positions opening up along with the new substation. I would have checked out of the cop bizz right then and there."

"So I moved to Orange County, it still had all the same rules but the things you had to fight at street level were far less than in L.A., and at least it gave me a chance to get more involved in the local communities."

"Bored to tears and in no way making a difference in the evil doings of mankind. I decide to check out of the cop bizz one more time. And yeah, you guessed it, wham! Another in-department memo, except, this time, it's the feds and they would like a volunteer to be liaison in a new task force being headed up by the F.B.I."

"It would be one substation per county and that liaison would be in direct contact with the F.B.I. regarding any and all matters relating to the abduction and kidnapping, foreign and domestic, of children under the age of 16."

"I could not sign up fast enough. Getting a chance to work with the F.B.I. and help kids, hell yes."

Ryson, shifting his weight and now deciding to lean against the house, then folding his arms into his chest, and in doing so, letting will know he still has the helm.

"With the little amount of training involved, at first, I just assumed it would be a sort of training as you go thing. The only thing training really offered was, I did get to meet and spend some time with F.B.I. personnel. Including Tom Marks and his hottie partner, Margo. My one and only true mistake through this, and right up till this point was to believe if any kidnapping happened in Orange County I would be there go to guy."

"So, before you ask, yes, there was two. Both local and each time. it was a pissed off father not happy about his visitation rights. I filled out the incident forms and submitted them to my F.B.I. contacts, end of story."

"And then, you. For the first time since the two of them stood together on the porch, they finally make eye contact."

What Ryson sees is a man in chaos and turmoil as to the question, "What am I if not for my own convictions and decisions?"

"I was not prepared for the emotional aspects of something like this and for that, I so dearly apologize for. I was led to believe that if a situation just as this was to happen, protocol would be put in place and we would all work together, fuck... I believed that right up and until I read this report."

Will now leans forward and away from the pillar, just one half step with his right leg. Ryson thinking Will is going to hand him the brown folder makes a short reach with his right hand but staying in his lean against the house, Will instead reaches and withdraws a legal size, white envelope from his back right pocket and gently places it in Ryson's already outstretched hand, after doing so, Will retreats back to the pillar and again looking for support more than comfort.

The envelope is not sealed, so the contents are easily withdrawn. With obvious wonder, Ryson's voice cracks just a little. Inside the envelope was a round-trip ticket, first class to Bogotá, Colombia. It has William Thorne's name on.

"Okay, Mr. William Thorne. So you're taking a trip, going by yourself and you ponied up the big bucks, seems your flying first class. What does this mean? And why come tell me?"

The connections between these new turns of events are somewhat obvious but Ryson chooses to let Will elaborate.

"While I was standing in line two days ago to buy that ticket, I realized I was doing so for three reasons. The first was to ensure my life has purpose and meaning before I quit the force. The second reason was so I myself understand the commitment I am making. The third reason was that you understand that this shit ain't over and I have no intentions of backing off."

After I read this so-called report, that by the way, was finally delivered by messenger and it looks like it was assembled by somebody in their sleep. With a look as if Will had just been made fun of on the school playground, he holds up the brown folder and tells Ryson, "I promised Tom I would not share this with anybody, and me being a man of my word, I shall just leave this right here and forget where I put it."

Will let's go of the folder waist high and does not watch it hit the ground... Ryson does.

I called Tom even before I finished reading what the F.B.I. refers to as local intel assessment because what's inside this report is everything we already know. And really just barely that. So when I finally reached Tom, I asked him, "How in the hell is this report in any way supposed to help me on this case?"

His reply was, "It's not supposed to and we no longer require local authority interaction, the F.B.I. thanks you and keep up the good work."

I tried to ask him if there was any new events regarding this case, he says, "And I should not be telling you this, but our contacts in South America say they have seen nor heard anything regarding this case. And now he tells me in some sort of F.B.I. voice of authority, your services regarding this case have run their course, let the F.B.I. handled this."

"At this point, I haven't a clue as to what the F.B.I. is doing in regards to the safe return of your children, I think we can all horribly and safely assume that your kids are no longer in this country, and I personally believe there is nobody to follow their trail in hopes of a recovery if these children are to be brought back, Mr. Willows, I believe it can only happen within the private sector. Now...to be sure, I will not be interfering in any secret or underground F.B.I. ops, I will be posing as a gem investor looking to purchase some emeralds."

"I do actually have somebody in South America I can use as a contact. I have some leads on two separate locations where it's possible they are using some of the illegal emerald trade routes for human trafficking across different borders and these same people deal in kids. So, as a gem buyer, yeah, I am going to go take a look around."

Will lets the moment fall silent, he realizes he so needs Ryson's approval because if the F.B.I. tells him to back off and the father of the kidnaped children tells him to back off, back off he must.

He would hate to walk away, thus leaving himself without purpose and he being quite sure the damage would be permanent to himself and his future. But truly and most of all, where would that leave the children?

Humbled, confused, and by destiny's design, a liaison. If ever there was writing on the wall. Ryson, again, sees hope.

"Are you sure you won't come in for a cup of coffee, Mr. Thorne? I am quite sure we are all thinking the same thing. And also, you can call me Ryson."

"Thanks, that would be nice, and of course, you can call me Will."

Ryson steps forward leaving his position of lean against the house, he hands Will back the ticket, turns, and steps through the open door, pausing just long enough to ensure movement on Will's part.

Ryson stops mid living room halfway between the kitchen and the front door, he waits for Will to clear the doorway and is in the house before asking, "So tell me, Will, what the hell did your training officer do to that speeder who came out shootin your second day on the job?"

Wills reply was quick and precise as if he had been waiting this whole time to finally answer this question.

"Ah, gezz, that crazy fucker, Pete Shorts, yeah man, the department called him quick draw. That son of a bitch, I kid you not, rolled out of the squad car to a one knee prone position and fired three times hitting Oscar Wickets once in the neck and two through the chest, poor kid was dead before he hit the ground. And I never even unbuckled my seatbelt."

Laughing, but understanding how that just is not funny, Ryson turns towards the kitchen and says, "Yeah, all in a day."

Now they share a real chuckle and head into the kitchen. Will closes the front door and as he leaves the entryway, he returns the plane ticket to his back pocket.

They talked for some time like old friends just trying to catch up. Eventually and before the first cup of coffee completely consumed, the conversation rolls back around to matters at hand.

Ryson understands the fact that he is in no position to keep any secrets and has no intention of doing so.

Somewhere around halfway through cup number two, Ryson comes up for air after a full explanation regarding his and Art's meeting and conversation, Ryson's voice now slips humbly into a warm place of hope and trust.

"Will, I can only tell you the very same thing I told Art. I have no boundaries to what I will do or endure to have my children safely back with me. I also now have some understanding why each of you would choose to help."

"At this point, all I can do is say thank you because I am at a complete loss emotionally for any other words, how can a man in my shoes feel anything less."

Ryson fights back the tears, because it's not time for tears anymore.

Will, not knowing his place at this point in the big picture, says, "So what now?"

Ryson's voice still in a place of humble but absolutely certain what has to happen next, "I say we all work together and fight the same fight."

Again, Will is quick and precise with his reply like he is always two steps ahead, "Yes, sign me up, I would much rather this be a team thing."

"Also, I think it would be best if Art and I had some one on one time, so why don't you call him later, set up a meeting, he and I can do lunch today, talk about you and perhaps learn something about each other?"

"I think that's an excellent idea, Will." Ryson says this as he drops a coffee pod into the machine for cup number three, hits brew, then thinks to himself, *Going to need a bigger machine*, as it's Will's turn at the coffee pod carousel.

The two of them stand in the kitchen and to each; the other seems like an old friend who they should never have let life put so much distance between them, the conversation simple in words but not so in life.

The quick two thumbs that come from the kitchen door that leads out to a patio into the backyard catch them both off guard, Will more than Ryson is slightly startled just because he is closer to the five foot high, five foot wide female individual on the other side of the door, he can tell this because of the full-length window with no curtain and only a small baby gate covering just the bottom portion.

The first couple of words that come out of her small puffy mouth are slurred with excitement but the ones that follow are quite clear.

Mistaking Will for Ryson, even though they are making eye contact, she holds up a large orange tabby, her voice loud enough to wake any neighbors

44

still sleeping, and at a pitch only equal to its own level of rising excitement, "This your cat, Ryson?"

Will stays frozen in surprise and left speechless as the woman's questions just keep coming.

"Is this your cat, Ryson? Did you get a new cat? I found it in my yard, do you know how it got there? Did you put it there so I could keep it? Do you know who's cat it is? Should I just keep it? Somebody probably did not want it. Have you seen this cat before? Does it look hungry to you? Should I just keep this cat so I can take care of it?"

Without glancing away from the window, Will ask Ryson, "Is that your neighbor Francine?"

"Yes," comes Ryson's reply.

With a smile as big as all life itself, Will nods his head and says, "Yes, Francine, you can keep the cat."

In the book of happy, page one. There is a photo of what true happiness should look like, that's the look Will got just before Francine pranced from the backyard as if now keeper of the baby Jesus.

Will turns towards Ryson with a good portion of smile still intact and says, "See there, you just made a new best friend, and I finally got rid of that damn cat, things are looking better already. I've been leaving my car windows down for two days now, hoping that furry, little ball and chain would finally crawl out and disappear. Yes, things are already looking better."

Will puts a quick rinse to his empty cup and leaves it open side up on the counter and now heads out of the kitchen towards the front door, before leaving the kitchen, Will states, "All right then, I got stuff to do, you got stuff to do, I will wait to hear from you."

Will moves out of the kitchen with a slow pace and without turning around, asks Ryson, "Has Francine ever told you how tall she is?"

"Yes, many times, how do you know Francine? And what do you mean you finally got rid of that damn cat?"

When Will makes a quick glance back towards the kitchen as he moves slowly through the living room, Ryson is now standing in the doorway with half a smile.

Wills answer is, "That's a whole another story for a whole different day."

Will finishes moving to the front door but stops short and now turns completely around to face Ryson, who was one step into the living room but not moving.

"Hey, Ryson, I'm not going to ask this right now, but next time we meet, the question how's Patricia is going to come up. I hope she is okay."

"Thanks, and yes, next time."

Will believes this to be so and nods in agreement, turns back to the front door, opens it but does not look back and says, "Be strong," and now closes the door behind him. As Will steps onto the porch, he glances down at the brown folder still where he dropped it, he smiles not because a chapter is ending but because life is a new.

"Be strong," the words come easy enough. It's the strength or the lack thereof that comes at the highest price. Ryson retreats back into the kitchen, pulls up a chair at the table with cell phone in hand, "It's time to make some calls."

Ryson retracts the half-eaten pop tart from his lips when Patricia's older sister, Chelsea, answers the house phone on the first ring. Her hello is pleasant and Sparky like she is not with a care in the world.

"Good morning, this is Chelsea."

"How's things, sweetheart? It's Ryson."

"Well, I guess it depends on which side the bed you rolled out of this morning," Chelsea still somewhat sparky but it's just an act. "There's good days, there's bad days, today, I am not quite sure. Mom was here early to take Pat and Rose to some fancy shoe store downtown, I am not even sure what time they left."

Ryson is noticeably relieved, "Ah that's all right, I don't care all that much for that phone conversations anyway, over the phone, she just seems so unattached and anyway, I will be up there tomorrow afternoon, I'll bring something to barbecue, any chance she will come home with me?"

Yesterday, at this same time, this question comes from the heart, today this very same question, though still from the heart, Chelsea can tell something is different.

"What's going on, Ryson? Have you learned anything new? You sound different."

"No, Chelsea, there is nothing new but we are working on it. I will catch you and Dan up to speed tomorrow."

"Hey, Chelsea."

"Yes, Ryson?"

"Thanks, you're the best. See you tomorrow."

Chelsea goes back to being sparky, "Yeah, yeah, yeah, see you tomorrow."

Ryson sets the phone down and pushes it several inches away before leaning back in the chair with his arms crossed in front of his chest. His gaze falls on all the many souvenir magnets placed in sporadic fashion on the refrigerator, you could trace their lives together, before, during, and after having kids in these colorful magnetic depictions. He wonders now what magnet depicting this true life experience would look like, to which he would gladly place within their families' magnetic journey but only if there were others to follow.

His heart and soul believes there's more magnetic adventures to come. So, for the time being, Pat will have to rely on her own family, this thought saddens him true enough, but it also fuels.

10:20 a.m. The commuter train clanking across the market street bridge signifies so. It's only two blocks away, and the noise snaps Ryson from the fridge.

Towards the end of pop tart number two, Ryson finds Art's number in contacts and calls his cell phone.

The lack of any sort of surprise in Art's voice when he answers the phone makes the call seam predetermined, "Good morning, I was hoping to hear from you this morning, I need your social security number and I have some paperwork you need to sign."

As a sign of trust, Ryson recites his social security number over the phone and does not ask its purpose, instead he jumps right into catching Art up to speed with the Will thing.

With the details of the early visit from Will explained, the best Ryson could do over the phone and of course they share a laugh over the cat thing. But when all is said and done they both agree it would be far better if William Thorne was with them then not. Without hesitation, Art agrees to call Will and meet for lunch.

Before they hang up, the conversation rolls back around to where it began.

"Now, listen, Ryson. I really do need you to sign some paperwork for me, so after my lunch date, I'll call, and you can come by the office, and hey! don't forget that brown folder on your porch, I really want to see what's inside."

Ryson has already embraced this chain of command, it's for the greater purpose. The two of them understand this. Ryson's only reply can be and was, "Got it, I'll be there."

"Sounds great, Ryson, I will see you this afternoon."

They both hang up, Ryson shuffles out to the porch and brings in the brown folder, then delivers it to the kitchen table.

Ryson stands empty in heart and empty in soul, that's the feeling he gets while staring down at the folder, he also knows inside that folder exist only torment and chaos, and so chooses to forgo the agony of investigation.

A shower before he calls his brothers, a much better idea.

Art rarely had butterflies in his stomach, he has always been one of those guys were most times the world in general would roll off his back like water off well-oiled boots. But this phone call is different, Art takes a moment to really gather his thoughts before he keys in William Thorne's number.

Two very important things have to happen before the two of them can move on to launch, the first being that Will does indeed choose to join their team as a team player, the second, he and Will must be able to get along, they have to right away, like one-another. Will's number keyed in Art hits send while keeping his fingers crossed, literally, it's a thing with Art.

Will's one and only true regret as being a police officer and investing eight years of his life to protect and to serve is that he never became a cop at all. It's not to say that the last eight years were without any reward, it's just time he feels could have been better spent.

There is a door at the end of a small hallway to which Will now strolls, with all the goodbyes said and his locker cleared out, that door is all that's left of this chapter in his life. Without hesitation, Will steps through the door and into the parking lot, he pauses, just on the other side, allowing the door to slowly close on its own, with his back to it, eyes forward, he waits and he listens.

The lock Will hears engage after the door comes to a complete stop he no longer has a key for, this pleases him and a smile indicates so. It's a short walk from the door to his car and with each step, the sun got just a little brighter.

From the open trunk of his car, Will can hear his cell phone ringing from the front seat where we left it, along with the driver door ajar. The number calling is unknown but Will knows just on instinct it's time to move and cannot answer it fast enough.

In his head, he tries not to sound like an eager schoolboy.

"Hello, Will Thorne."

Forgetting he no longer is on duty this comes across far too professional. The voice on the other side, pleasant and respectful, "Hello, Mr. Thorne. My name is Arthur Match, Ryson tells me we should talk and that perhaps, we are already fighting the same battle."

"Indeed, Mr. Match, and you can call me Will. I was hoping you would call, and soon. I think we both realized time is of the essence here. And I would really like to hear what you have to say. I have absolutely no desire or authority to interfere with your plans, I am only interested in if somehow we can either work together or maybe at least share information."

"Ditto on this end, Will, let's have lunch. And please, call me Art."

"I am getting in my car as we speak, where do you want me to go, Art?"

Art could not be more pleased by Will's eagerness and attitude and already was looking forward to meeting him. Hoping with what sounds more like confidence then giddy schoolboy chatter, Art says, "Can you do the food park there in the Brea-mall, say twenty minutes?"

"Sure thing, Art, not a problem, see you in twenty."

"I'll be the one camped in front of Mrs. Fields cookies. On my table will be a shoebox with a hole at one end. Please, when you sit down, do not block this hole. I need to do a favor for some new friends."

Will, too, was pleased with Arts eagerness and attitude, the wee bit of mystery and intrigue welcomed, "Can do, Art, know the place well."

Wills only thoughts while leaving the police parking lot on that final time were only about the future, to this very day, he cannot remember driving away from the substation, he only remembers again chasing tomorrow.

Back in the kitchen and probably smelling a little better, but as of late, that's all he can ask.

The things we derive pleasure from no matter how simple or intense it's our emotional state that allows us to experience these things and as of late, Ryson no longer has a grip on this reality.

Sadness, anger, fear, these are now his emotional center and from these, he finds no pleasure, he's hoping lunch with his brothers might somehow blow some sunshine up his ass on a smoky day like today.

Calling Jesse's cell phone, Ryson considers to be one of the last guarantees left in this world. Because anything other than death and he sometimes

49

questions this, Jesse is going to answer that phone. He has always been a drone to the phone, and I mean all phones. If a phone ringing and he is close enough to answer it, he will. Ryson believes if Jesse was plummeting to his death and his phone was to ring, *yes*, he no doubt answers it.

On the second ring, Jesse answers as if he has just decoded a secret message, "Hello, my brother, how's things?"

"Hey, Jesse, strange to say the least, but for sure moving forward. Ryson now asking the question, and so how's my favorite brother?"

"Hey, about the same, but enough about me, how's the case going? Any breaks? Anything new?"

Jesse's insistence on being kept up to speed was only equal to that of the oldest brother, Lee, as brothers go, the three of them have always been extremely compatible, Ryson, being the youngest, so the older two always looking after him. Jesse, being the gay one, providing the other two with real-world wisdom and sometimes fashion, leaving Lee, the oldest and the younger, too, always looking to him for advice, guidance, and structure. So when the three of them decided to go into the bodyguarding business together after Ryson came home from Vietnam made perfect sense and has ever since. So between the three of them there really is no favorite.

"No, Jesse, and believe me, I wish there was, but hey, that's not why I am calling."

"Well, spill, it little bro, what can I do for you, you just name it."

"Well, believe it or not, Jess, this is about what I'm going to do for you. How's about I come by the office, say noon and I'll bring the meatball subs and a gallon of Hawaiian Punch."

Jesse speaks from a true level of excitement, "Oh, baby, you had me at meatball sub. Lee and I will see you, noon-ish. Love you, bro."

Ryson's reply, "Right back at cha."

They both hang up at the same time and do indeed share the same little smile.

Food Park

Will finds Art eighteen minutes later right where he said he would be. And of course, there on the table, a shoebox and in one end a three-inch hole pointing away from Art and the table, along with several cookies and two bottles of water.

Will enters the food park through a set of doors on the right side and somewhat forward of Art's position. Art is already looking that direction and sees Will come through the doors, the description close enough that he can assume this to be who he's waiting for.

Will turns a few degrees left moving towards the table because he, too, has found his lunch date. Staying away from the front of the shoebox, Will comes around the table to Art's right. When Will is close enough for a handshake Art stands and they do so. They talk for a couple of minutes while standing, mostly about Ryson and the kids.

Art can clearly see that Will is more interested in the cookies than the shoebox, this brings a large smile to Art's face, Art motions but without pointing to the chair directly across from his and tells Will to have a seat, "But please, don't move the chair or shoebox."

Doing as requested, Will does his best to quietly and without contact take a seat at the table but clearly his primary concerns are the cookies. Because his first question is, "So, what's up with the cookies?"

Teasing Will now, Art slides in Wills direction the cookie sitting in front of himself that he has already eaten half of and says, "Here, you can finish this one." Will's face gets a little puffy but before he can throw some sort of cookie conniption fit, Art smiles, withdrawing the half-eaten cookie followed by, "I'm just kidding, Will, I really bought the cookies for you. I'm just not that big on the whole pastry thing, candies, that's my sweet tooth weakness. So help yourself, enjoy."

A couple of chumps into his first cookie, Will finally comes up for air, assuming one of the bottles of water is his, Will unscrews the lid, takes a small sip, puts the lid back on, then raises the bottle slightly, and now making eye contact with Art and says with a thankful nod, "Thanks, Art."

Without glancing down so as to maintain Art's attention, Will now ask, "So, ah, we gonna talk about the shoebox, Art?"

Art makes a quick glance at the watch on his left wrist, then speaking softly but it a tone loud enough for Will to hear him, "Yeah, we got a few minutes here, let me tell you a story." Will can tell Art is almost giddy at the chance to do so, so he sets his sights on another cookie and let's Art continue.

This story starts back a couple of years ago when Pauline Staples pulls into a gas station somewhere in Azusa, at eleven p.m., alone. She has to go inside the small minimart to prepay for gas because all she had with her was cash. When she gets back to the car, she finds these two guys stealing her gas and putting it in their own car directly on the other side of the pump. As she gets closer and tries to say something, one of the guys grabs her. So now, as this is happening, some other dude pulls into the gas station right behind the woman's car, and it's obvious to him something is not right, he gets out and asked the woman if everything is okay. Now she starts to really struggle and yells for help.

As luck would have it, the dude that just got there is an ex-marine and Vietnam vet, and he jumps into action, he separates the woman from her captor and this happens easy enough but then this guy pulls out a large knife and the two start fighting. The bad guy does manage to cut Mr. Hero but it doesn't help. Hero boy gets the upper hand and really starts to beat the shit out of bad guy.

The other brother, who is still stealing the woman's gas, sees that his younger sibling is taking a real beating, so now he pulls out a gun and fires twice at hero boy, missing both times, but one of the bullets hits the woman in the elbow of her right arm, shattering the bone and destroying most of the elbow, leaving only skin and muscle holding the arm in place. She goes down and before the shooter gets a third shot, Mr. Hero abandons his attack and retreats.

The two brothers as if nothing had happened get back in their car and simply drive away, except, of course, one of them severely beaten and bleeding quite badly.

Cop's show up, they take a report, haul the woman off to the hospital, hero dude declines medical attention.

Couple of days later, hero boy is down at the local precinct going through mugshots, trying to identify the two bad guys, and he does. But as the investigation moves on, it turns out the two brothers are sons of a Bolivian relations ambassador, so, of course, the father has diplomatic immunity.

When the F.B.I. contact the father regarding the matter, he simply says the sons were not in the country. And because the video of the incident taken by the gas station surveillance system was of such poor quality, the F.B.I. were unable to identify the two brothers in the video, and, therefore, had to drop the case. Hell, the F.B.I. never even went looking for these guys.

"So, how do I know this? Well before you ask, let me explain. I was hired by the city of Temecula to oversee and confirm overseas investors cash and accounts for the new malls they are opening up out in that area."

"It was the father's name, the ambassador, that caught my attention because I actually remember the name from the gas station incident from the articles I had read in the U.S.A. Today. So, now, I go through the ambassadors investment proposal with a fine-tooth comb because he is not calling himself an ambassador, and this becomes shady, to say the least, come to find out, what he wants is a piece of real estate in the food court."

"The proposal is for a Mediterranean *café*. He lists it as a profitable franchise, to which there are already two other locations. One of those locations just happens to be right here."

Art intends to tell Will to not look around, "We don't want to be noticed," but instead, halts the moment to test Will's control over his own curiosity.

It had been some time since Wills last visit to this mall, knowing this and on instinct alone, when he entered the food court from the parking lot, he automatically re-mapped most of the food court in his head, even before he found Art.

Without any change in body position whatsoever, Will says, "Is that the same Mediterranean *café* behind me forty feet and off my left shoulder?"

"That's the one," Art makes no hesitation with his answer, trying not to seem overly impressed but it was difficult, because he was.

"So, anyway, a couple of weeks ago, I come down here to see what's up, I sit right here doing some serious damage to a steak sub and fries while watching the Mediterranean *café* people set up and get ready for the lunch rush.

At about 11:45, two new guys show up and it's obvious they are in charge and to me yeah, they looked like brothers."

"I sit and watch them taking turns tending the cash register and until I'm done with my own lunch, I watch them proceed with regular lunch operations. Of course, I have a suspicion as to who these two guys are, so later when I get back to the office I," Art pauses here, remembering that he and Will don't really know each other and backpedals, "well, let's just say, I looked them up. And what I found was, no, they are not wanted and there are no charges pending in the U.S., but as I read on, I find there is a fugitive warning on both of them along with a contact number, so I call."

"I tell the woman who answers the phone who I think these two are, the phone clicks a couple of times and then a man's voice comes on. He tells me is Colombian Secret Service and would I please elaborate as to how I come to know this, and I do."

"When I'm done, he thanks me, he then tells me his name and gives me his personal number, he also informs me there could be a reward, so if in fact these two are who he hopes they are he will be in contact, although he does not say how, the phone just goes dead."

"The very next afternoon, he calls back and informs me that, 'Yes, the brothers have been positively identified and that there is a reward,' and how I go about collecting on an international reward for fugitives."

"I informed secret service guy I am not interested in the reward, and if there is a way to be compensated for pain and suffering, it should go to the woman those two ass holes permanently disfigured and damaged. Then I ask what now happens to the brothers, I really wasn't thinking I would get an answer but all of a sudden, me and secret service guy, our best buds and he can't wait to talk about these two and the horrors that await. I actually hear him take a breath like he is just too excited, then he starts in."

Seems these two brothers were on a fishing trip and meeting friends in some remote high mountain fishing camp in Venezuela, on their last day, there an unexpected storm rolls in early and the two brothers and their pilot leave anyway.

About thirty minutes into this flight, the storm catches them and they make an emergency landing in another high mountain village, but now they are in Columbia, and when they land, there is damage to the plane, enough so it can't take off.

Well, somehow, these two brothers end up in a four-wheel-drive van as passengers; this van belongs to a private school and is the only way down off the mountain that time of year. One Saturday, a month some of the students and a driver go down this mountain and to the village at the bottom. They collect mail, food, goods and such, and there is also a train stop.

In the van with the two brothers are, of course, the driver, who is also part of the security for the school, brothers don't know this.

A brother and sister, eleven fourteen, and eleven-year-old girl. The brother and sister were going home via the train, the other girl was going for a tetanus shot and antibiotics for a cut on her foot. At some point on their three-hour journey down the mountain, a rockslide lets go and a couple of large boulders slam into the back section of the van, spinning it, so the rear of the van is now hanging off the road. The next couple of boulders hits the front of the van, pushing it off the road, sending it backwards, rolling on its wheels down, and through a narrow drain channel carved in the side of the mountain.

When the van finally comes to a stop, there perched atop some of the debris from other landslides, following the same trench they just did and the van is almost level and completely intact. And nobody seriously injured. It snows for the next two days and there is no rescue attempts, they don't hear anything from anybody. Without question, there is no way down without help.

They start to argue over the few supplies they have and somehow, the brothers end up killing the driver, hoarding all the supplies and for two days, following the scuffle the brothers, take turns raping the 11-year-old little girl.

Finally five days into this whole thing, a couple of guys on snowmobiles reach the van, but when they do the brothers take the snowmobiles at gunpoint, leaving the two rescuers with the van and the rest of the survivors.

All the brothers have to do is simply follow the snowmobile tracks that led the rescuers to them write down the mountain and into the village at the bottom.

When the brothers get to the village, as you would expect, they were quite anxious to get the hell out of dodge and they do so that very afternoon.

Luckily, one of the rescue guys hikes for a day and a half to the village and all were eventually rescued.

Both, Art and Will, take a deep breath, Will says nothing, Art checks his watch, then removes a small remote from his front pocket, and sets it on the table in front of him, Art then continues his story.

After secret service guy finishes telling me this story, he quickly and abruptly says, "Thanks for all your help," the phone then clicks a couple of times and then dial tone. As I'm still sitin' there, the phone, not quite cooled down from the last call, it rings again, this time, the number is unknown, "Well, fuck, you know, I've got to answer it."

Will smiles, nods his head *yes* and says, "Yeah, I would have to answer it as well."

The voice on the other end has a thick Colombian accent and sounds extremely important. He introduces himself and then ends with, "This conversation is not being recorded and this line is secure." Now this voice becomes somber and even emotional. "Thank you, Mr. Match, on behalf of myself and the country of Columbia, we cannot thank you enough. And as a father perhaps, now the healing can begin, and for that there's just no words."

"The country of Columbia owes you a favor, do not be afraid if ever in this country to ask for it. Now, on a more personal note, Mr. Match, if you could see your way towards videotaping the arrest of the two men that attacked my little girl, we can just forget about the reward and why don't you just tell me what you want?"

"At this point, I am so absolutely touched by this man's pain and gesture all I want to say is, you owe me nothing. I hope the brother's burn in hell and you're welcome. But I realize the moment these brothers are hauled away, that woman from the gas station never gets justice. And believe me, I know how that feels."

"So, what I end up saying to the man is, I hope to never understand your pain and I am truly sorry for you and your little girl, and so, no, sir, I can take nothing from you, you have already had to part with far too much. But once these brothers are taken away, if there is any financial compensation left behind, perhaps, it could land in the lap of the woman who lost her arm because of these two vicious animals."

"The favor you say your country owes me, well, yeah, someday that could come in handy. You tell me when and where these two are to be arrested and where I send the tape, because, sir, we are both fathers and I believe we feel the same. To cause pain and suffering to a child, this is the last evil act anyone should be allowed to inflict."

As a father, to a father, the saddened voice replies, "I would consider it a privilege to someday meet you, Mr. Thorne." A couple of clicks, then dial tone.

"And so, here we are. What happens to the woman who lost her arm? I don't know, I did what I could do."

At11:51a.m., Art sees the two brothers come into the food court through the same doors he and Will did, he pushes the start button on the remote, two beeps from inside the shoebox indicates the scene is now being recorded. The brothers enter the Mediterranean cafe through a single door by the back wall, then appear at the cash register through doors leading from the kitchen as they are putting money into the cash register from a small zippered pouch, two women approach the cash register and are now standing directly in front of the brothers, both women lean forward in unison over the counter, and you can tell they say something to the brothers and by the time spent leaning forward it was obvious, it was not just a couple of words.

The brothers say nothing, but the big eyes and both their heads say they are listening. The two women are clearly from the same mold and even though they shared similarities, it is also obvious that they are not related. When the two women return to a normal standing position, there is a look on both the brothers faces... Just fear.

The two women turn to their right seemingly engaged in light conversation and moving to the same door the brothers used to enter the Mediterranean *café*, they stop just at the door in front of it, there is no longer conversation between them. When the door opens, the brothers exit. The four of them without conversation or even eye contact remain as a foursome and calmly head towards and then through the doors from the food court into the parking lot. From there and in broad daylight, it seems they move into darkness and disappear.

Getting lightheaded, Art finally takes a breath, Will kind of snickers and says, "What the hell did you think was going to happen, Art?" Art snickers as well and adds a shrug to his shoulders, and they both laugh just a little.

Art pushes stop on the remote, two beeps from the shoebox says the video camera agrees. The two finally introduce themselves to one another, after introductions Art says, "so Mr. Thorne what's for lunch?"

Will's reply is just as playful, well hell Mr. Match, "Baby, you had me at steak sub and fries."

After the visit to the steak hut, they belly up to a fresh table. Conversation is light and mostly about pricing but it does lead to their common goals and the two of them begin to trust one another. When the last of the crumbs were picked clean from the plastic basket, the stake sub once called home, they both agreed it was time the three of them got together and start working on a plan, sooner than later.

They part ways from the food court with the understanding, stay close to your phone. Art heads towards the mall, Will out the doors, he came in, but both heading, no doubt, in the same direction.

Brothers

There are several food and drink combinations the three brothers without haste could agree on, the meatball sub from Anthony's and a liter of Hawaiian Punch was just one of those combinations, so when the news regarding the current meatball shortage finally reaches the front counter, Ryson was very disappointed, to say the least. Leaving with two meatball subs and a chicken Parmesan sub was no doubt going to be an issue.

When Ryson reaches the back-parking lot of level 1 security, he can tell the other two are already here. The keypad on the back-door forces him to place the plastic bag containing two bottles of Hawaiian punch on the ground. Once the code is entered, the door, because it's under spring tension, opens on its own about four inches, using his foot now as a wedge, Ryson simultaneously finishes opening the door, grabs up the Hawaiian Punch, and disappears inside, allowing the door to slam and lock on its own.

Ryson finds his two brothers, Lee and Jesse, in the back office/lunch room, and after some discussion, the three of them decide to cut the two meatball subs in thirds, leaving the chicken Parmesan sub in the bag for Ryson to take home.

Ryson holds nothing back, attempting to purge every last detail as he does his best to bring his two brothers up to speed, they talk, they eat, and of course, they are ecstatic regarding the chance to get into retail security and do not have any hesitation in signing the contracts to do so. They both, of course, want to help in any way he and Art seem fit. It's obvious they're close and the conversation's genuine.

The two brothers would like to go with Ryson to Art' after lunch but Ryson convinces them, not today. The three of them finish watching a rerun of Gilligan's Island and are glad they did, even though the ending was common knowledge. The last thought they share together before hugs and see you later was they agreed and shared Ryson's unwillingness to investigate the contents of the brown collapsible folder.

It's a thirty-minute drive from level security to Art's office and in that thirty minutes, Ryson's thoughts drifted between yesterday's and tomorrow's, and he can only hope that soon again, one will lead to the other.

As the second quarter falls through the purchase of time, it chatters down a meter a block or so from Redline Financial. Ryson just now remembers Art was going to call when he got back to work after lunch with Will, so he may not be there yet.

Ryson feels his phone come to life within the short journey from his pocket to eye level when he checks see if he has missed a call. He sees Arts name and answers, "Good afternoon, Art, how was lunch?"

"Excellent, like a match made in heaven, yeah, he's with us Ryson, now, where are you?"

"A block away on foot, you didn't tell me there was no parking around here, so I'm heading your way."

Art quickly replies in hopes of slowing Ryson's advance, "Slow down, I'll meet you halfway, we'll get coffee."

Ryson's reply is one of patience and for some reason, understanding, already there. Before they hang up, Art hears him mumble, "Sticky bun."

With coffee and sticky buns in hand, the two of them had back up the street to Art's accounting business, Redline Financial.

Sealed moving boxes and a half dozen folding chairs scattered about is not what Ryson was expecting when he followed Art through the door. "Geez, Art, going somewhere?" Ryson's question is one of curiosity not concern.

"Yes, indeed, bigger, better, more parking. And as fate would have it, within walking distance of your house, purely coincidental, I assure you. That H and R building on Adams finally came back on the market after the fire. I waited seven months for that damn place to dry out, shit, the fire damage was minimal; it was all the water they used to put it out that caused most of the destruction. Luckily, the management company split the building into two separate units and I got the lesser damaged of the two." Art pushes together a couple of boxes and gathers two folding chairs for a makeshift table during the new rental property soliloquy and now tells Ryson to sit, they both do, but only for the sake of the sticky bun.

Art picks up the brown folder Ryson placed on the boxes between them, along with the sticky buns once the box table was complete. Thankfully, before Ryson has to ask Art may be looking through that later, Art tosses it atop a stack of smaller boxes, saying to himself more than anything, "I will go through that later, maybe I'll find something interesting."

Ryson's obvious relief does not go unnoticed when he says, "Yeah, that sounds good."

"Okay, so, let's talk employment, sign these," Art hands Ryson three sheets of paper he withdraws from a briefcase he had not noticed. Now Art gets somewhat businesslike. "As of right now, you are employed full time with full benefits as my families and my personal bodyguard. What you made last year plus fifteen percent.

"I have already looked at your last two tax returns, you three have done pretty well," Art's way of saying "there's room for improvement."

Those numbers will go up as level I security gets into the retail security bizz, but for that to happen, I need you and your brother's signatures on some contracts.

"Believe me, that's not going to be a problem, Art. You call, they will come down. They would like to thank you in person anyway, they would also like to help, so don't be afraid to ask for it if need be,"

Ryson would like to see that happen, but is in no position to ask.

When it seems quiet all of a sudden Ryson calmly ask, "So, Art, what's next?"

Art makes eye contact with Ryson and says, "You ready?"

"Absolutely is now and always the answer when we're talking about my kids."

Art picks up his phone and starts pushing buttons, "Well, let's just see how on-board Mr. Thorne really is." Moving the phone to his ear Art does so with apprehension and wonder.

Will answers halfway through the first ring, and like they have been friends since childhood Will says, "Yo, bro, what's up? Hey! If you're calling to ask for the rest of those cookies back, that just is not going to happen."

"Yeah, we might have to talk about some cookie issues. But that's for another time. Hey, can you be at the new shop tomorrow night say seven-ish, I think I'll have some furniture by then, you Ryson and I will decide together what we do next."

Will's reply is, "Be there by seven, got it, I'll bring the cookies."

"Hey, Will, if you bring cookies, you may have to share them."

"Maybe, we'll see, see you at seven. Later, Art," Art hears dial tone before he can say bye.

Art puts the phone back where it was and says nothing, the moment lingers like a straw in a thick shake. Art seems to be weighing the probable odds as to which direction the straw will travel, when the words, "I still think we need a female," quietly falls from his lips.

Without waiting for an explanation, Ryson chimes in, "Seven-ish, new place, tomorrow night. What else I need to know?"

Art nods his head and says, "Yeah, two to three days, something like that, you be prepared to take a trip. Now get out of here, see you tomorrow night."

Before Ryson can stand up to go, Art looks him in the eyes and cautiously asked him, "how are you doing, Ryson?"

Ryson's face contorts slightly towards anguish and despair, his voice humbled with hope. He checks his emotions and chooses to now truly thank Art.

"Art, I know you have your reasons for being here, and I have listened to your definition of gratitude and personal debt. But the fact of the matter is, you are here by choice. I can only at this point thank you for seeing that if we do nothing, nothing gets done and my kids don't come home, thank you, Art, for the chance to at least try."

Art is touched and responds with, "Ryson, my own child was a single heartbeat away from the same moment that stole your children, but it was you that saved her, I am just trying to return the favor." Art cries just a few tears, Ryson does not. Instead, Ryson says, "We can only try to make it right." And now Ryson stands and begins to leave, with his back to Art, Ryson says, "I love you, man."

"What, are we dating now?" Art begins to laugh before he can finish that sentence and so does Ryson. Almost to the front door, Art calls out and Ryson stops, he turns to face Art.

Art does not stand but says, "Hey, I still need a name for our charity." Ryson smiles and with purpose and forethought loudly announces, "Project Mother's Day." Art nods and smiles. Ryson leaves. Art writes it down.

Hemet

That next morning, Ryson stood quietly, sipping a mug of fresh brewed glazed donut. And from the moment he stepped into the kitchen, something seemed different. Everything looks right but it's not. Head still fuzzy from sleep and now sitting at the table with a half mug of coffee slowly losing its aroma as it cools, it's the smell of warm sugar, as if somebody had just baked a batch of homemade sugar cookies that replaces the aroma of glazed donut. The smell is faint, causing Ryson to gently sniff, check the air around him by slightly moving his head side to side. The smell is warm and pleasant and for an instant, steals Ryson from the chaotic world around him, but only for an instant. Puzzled by the smell and it's fleeting moment, Ryson sits silently, pondering things to come.

At 10:26 a.m., the house phone rings just as Ryson clears the threshold of the front door. Now, standing on the front porch, he mumbles as he pulls the door halfway, "Just somebody trying to sell me something," timing the other half just long enough to confirm his suspicions, he mumbles again as he heads down the walkway to his car, "Like I fuckin' need something from those people."

First stop is the store. As much as this aspect of life displeases Ryson, the ride out to Hemet and the afternoon to follow, made this particular trip painless. The only confusion was whether or not to bring beer. With the few items purchased now stowed in the back, Ryson finds himself reluctant to start the car. First because it's a long drive out and second, for sure, it will be an even longer drive back. Ryson's apprehension to start the car is replaced by surprise and being somewhat startled when the car seems to start itself. It's only the grinding of the starter that tells Ryson to first let go of the key. and indeed, he did start the car but certainly not on a conscious level.

Ryson refers to the drive out to Hemet as the drive with many faces. This time for reasons of sadness and sorrow, and the fact that he has never taken this ride alone, Ryson puts those thoughts away and just drives. A few faces of life do catch his eye along the way, but just a few.

One hour and twenty-seven minutes later, Ryson merges onto the Hemet off-ramp and exits the freeway. The road to the house winds back on itself a couple of times then up the mountain. The small market was there in an instant and Ryson almost missed the driveway. Braking hard enough to almost skid, he slows enough to make the entrance. More mad at himself for not buying the beer when he had the chance than what it's going to cost now at what he refers to as "Little Joe's Stick-Up Market." It's a small market surrounded by a dirt and gravel parking lot with a raised wooden walkway spanning the front of the building. There's a few wooden steps leading up to the front door at mid-building. He's only been here a couple of times and from here, the house is just six minutes away.

Halfway between his car and the front door of Joe's market, there is a sound emanating from inside the store. The sound is reaching Ryson's ears in bits and pieces but it's obvious it's an argument. Within just a couple of paces, he is now at the bottom of the five steps, leading up to the front door. The heated argument going on inside the store stops his progress, he pauses and listens. The female side of the conversation Ryson hears quite clearly because she must be close to screaming at the top of her voice, saying, "Well! I am just too fucking sorry my tits are just not big enough for you!"

It's a screechy voice like one that would belong to a diving pterodactyl. She screams again, "And just who the fuck is supposed to pay for these tits anyway?"

The male side of this argument speaking loudly but not screaming is just as heated. Ryson now hears his reply to the diving pterodactyl, "Now listen, Josephine, I will pay for every penny of it and they really don't have to be all that much bigger anyway. Now just calm down."

Josephine's reply is, "Well, you filthy fucker, and even after I pierced my tongue and let you have an…"

The voice from behind Ryson comes at such a surprise that he quickly pulls his right hand out of his front pocket to maybe have to defend himself, causing his watchband to catch on the way out loosening its safety clasp and causing it to fly off his wrist, then land not far in the soft dirt. The voice belongs to a young man that bounds past him and halfway up the steps. He's twenty something, thin, and really tall, close to seven feet. Tall boy lands mid-steps

64

with both feet and freezes, without looking back at Ryson, he leans slightly right with just as much bent knees trying to get a look through the window just right of the door and says, "I said, they still fighting about her tits? or should I say, the lack there of?"

Ryson fumbles with a response while he is trying to get all the dirt off his watch. "I guess so," is all the response, he dares in fear of letting out the burst of laughter he's having trouble containing.

Evidently, the two arguing inside hear tall boy land on the steps because the silence from inside the store follows the echo of his landing.

Tall boy, with one long stretch step, moves to the front of and just left of the screen door, leading into the market. Now turning just his upper body towards Ryson, tall boy says, "You coming in or what, city slicker?" and smiles. Ryson can only chuckle and does, but before he can answer, tall boy pulls the screen door open towards himself with his left hand while still looking at Ryson, tall boy now says, "After you, sir," and holds the screen door open, revealing the inside of the store.

The figure that appears at the doorway from inside, surprises both of them, just as Ryson commits to step three up the stairs. The portly fellow with way too much hair on his head as well as his face, grunts a couple of times as he quickly moves past tall boy, then Ryson and heads around back. Ryson finishes his assent ascent, then steps through the doorway into the market. He has been here only twice before and only as far as the parking lot so what awaits inside is a mystery.

The diving pterodactyl greets him with, "Morning, special on eggs, raised local, just got a damn too many." It's the same voice from outside, just several clicks down on volume.

Ryson quickly locates the source of this horrid audio infraction by quickly moving his head to the right letting, his eyes fall and settle on a strange creature perched atop a padded barstool behind a small counter. She is partially leaning on an antique cash register to her left. It's a tiny woman of a thing, not circus tiny, just small and probably not legally considered a midget. Her hair and body thin, straggly and the color of dried figs. There is ugly and then there is "what the fuck is that?"

Ryson goes with the latter.

"No thanks, just beer."

He pays the twenty-one fifty and lets slip a glance while she retrieves change from thirty dollars, not because he can't turn away from the train wreck, but wow, how desperate do you have to be to even fathom the repair. He exits the store dumbfounded and laughingly so.

The short drive to the house from the small market seems to find Ryson in a much better place, perhaps the day and in it, he may find some sunshine.

The entrance to the driveway is really all that can be seen of the house from the street. if it were not for the large standing mailbox and the reflectors next to it, finding this place would be very difficult. The narrow, dirt driveway descends somewhat to a level plateau, which leaves most of this property at a lower level than the road leading to it. The driveway ends in a teardrop configuration along the right side of the house. This is where Ryson finds Danny already fussing with the B.B.Q. on the patio adjacent to the driveway and garage.

Danny is already at the walkway along-side the driveway before Ryson gets turned around and parked, standing there with both hands in his front pockets looking like the last kid picked for the team.

With the key off and the car quiet, he hears Danny walking around the back of the car, then catches his approach to his door in the side view mirror. When he first married into this family, Danny was already part of it. Their relationship early on, because of their differences, was just that of generalized acceptance but lacked any real sort of friendship. As a tree doctor, Danny was as "tree hugger" as they come. Here's a guy that is not only hugging the tree but shoving a thermometer under its bark and checking its pulse, but after a couple of Christmas's, an Easter or two, and some Thanksgiving dinners, the two of them became friends and even consider each other real family, so the long hug after Ryson exits his car was to be expected.

The words, "How's Pat?" he whispers in Danny's ear. This ends the embrace and Danny pulls away saying, "A lot of medication, it seems like way too much, but when it starts to wear off…"

Ryson can hear the despair in Danny's voice and this brings tears to both of them, not crying, just tears.

It's clear for now she will not be okay without it.

Together, they remove the items from his backseat. There is a fridge in the garage and the short journey, there, is in silence. The patio area is covered but not enclosed, its openness allows the area to spill into the front yard. It's where

Danny and Chelsea do most of their outdoor entertaining. Because the back of the property falls away at such an incline, there's just not much you could do with it. Although it does lend itself to a nice wooded view out the back windows.

On the patio is a built-in brick barbecue, a picnic bench, and a couple of lounge chairs. After putting away what Ryson brought in the fridge they keep in the garage, they head back out to the patio.

It's Danny's voice that breaks the silence only a few feet from the garage, "So, what's going on Ryson? What do we know? I realize you would rather not talk about this, but Chelsea and I only want to help in any way we can."

Ryson stops short of the picnic bench that clearly they both were intending to occupy and says, "Listen, Danny, you and Chelsea are already doing more than enough. There is no place better for Pat than right here right now. This is her best chance to survive, I know that and you know that Danny. She needs to be right here."

They both have their backs to the door that leads from the house into the patio area when Chelsea appears in the open doorway.

"Did not hear you pull up," these words from Chelsea in the doorway quiet the two of them and they turn to face her.

"Hi, sweetheart," is Ryson's response as they move towards one another. The hug idles then leads to a supportive embrace. When Ryson feels Chelsea's knees getting weak, he suggests they all sit down. The three share the same side of the bench with Chelsea between them.

"So, how you holding up, Chelsea?"

Before she responds to his question, Chelsea takes his hand and applies a soft, steady pressure, "We're alright, all things considered. But I have to say, for what you've been through, you don't look half bad for a guy that was shot in the face and had a finger almost ripped right from his hand just a few days ago. I don't know how you are out and about already."

"There're times the pain does slow me down, that's for sure, but there's just no time for that."

Danny and Chelsea can hear the conviction in his voice and for reasons of love and compassion, sit quietly.

"It's bad," Ryson's voice cracks. Chelsea exhales with a soft groan. Danny clears his throat trying to hold back the tears.

"So, where is Pat? And hey, where's Rose today?" being cautious as to who might be listening, he lowers his voice.

Chelsea lets go of his hand, she turns and scoots to better face him but does not get up.

"Ryson, I wish to fuck I had something positive to bring to the table here because you look like a man that could really use it, but I'm afraid I can't."

Ryson has always admired Chelsea's candor and honesty. She did not tend to sugarcoat stuff. She is the older of the two sisters slightly by age but far more in maturity.

"Like I said, when you called yesterday morning, Mom talked Rose and Pat into going to some shoe store downtown. I tried to tell her it was a bad idea and in fact, before they could even get out of the car in the parking lot, Pat starts looking around the inside of the car for the twins. She begins to panic when she can't find them. Mom and Rose had to convince her that I had them to get her to calm down enough to take more medication, so they could get her home. Dr. Marks has had her pretty doped up since then, so she is in her room sleeping. As for Rose, she went home with grandma for a couple of days, my mom and Rose bonded from day one as if that eleven-year-old little girl was blood to this family."

"So, Ryson, talk to us," Chelsea scoots back and now closer to Dan.

"At this point, the general consensus is that the twins are no longer in this country, not because they have been seen, but because of who took them. He starts here and ends with so now you know what I know. You asked me to share this burden, which is good, considering this all lands right in your laps. So you tell me, because only you two can, how do I save any of this? Do I stay where clearly my wife needs me and should be able to depend on me to be here for her, or do I try to play superhero and attempt to rescue my kids? Is one or the other even possible? Or do I lose them all simply because I made the wrong decision?"

"Well, Ryson, you're right, this is bad," Chelsea says this with a layer of sentiment like she has an ace up her sleeve. "Though I fail to see the complexity in your decision, I understand what brings us here but I also understand where you go next. You follow what's honest in your heart, you breathe only those breaths that sustain life. That's where you find your answer. Ryson, what's here, Dan and I got this. She's my sister and all of us, as a family, will be here for her. You have my word, I shall see to it she survives."

"Now, Mr. Willows, I need you to know what I feel. Those two, little girls are worth far more than any of us, you can only sacrifice all we have for their safety. It's what parents do, and from you, sir, I have never seen anything less than that. I love you, Ryson, but for every second we sit here, it sounds as though them girls are moving farther away, in distance and in hope."

Ryson is speechless and stumbles for even the thinnest reply, so Danny steals the moment.

"So, how come nobody's asking what Danny brings to this party, slash nightmare?"

Before anybody can ask, Danny starts right in, "I think when Chelsea says follow the honesty in your heart, part of that honesty you can measure as courage, and as far as you being a superhero, well, if ever there were a time to fill them shoes, I think it would be now. And I would like to add, not because I think all the decisions have been made, but at one end of the spectrum, this information could be useful in the right hands. Part of what my division does is not only track local forest stability and regrowth but we also monitor those same patterns globally using satellite imagery. So, for instance, if somebody wanted high resolution intelligence on certain places other than military and government installations, I could probably work that out. Like they say in the forest business, if you can see it from space, the U.S. forest service can tell you what color it is. It's complicated after that but I think you get the gist of it. And as far as family goes, I reserve the right to make my own promises, and rest assured, there is nothing more important to me than this family. So when things are happy, we all sing and when things are sad, we all cry. She's in good hands, Ryson."

Ryson uses the bottom edge of his shirt to wipe away a few tears but declines a tissue from Chelsea who has retrieved some from her back pocket and is willing to share.

Ryson stands and faces the two of them, his emotional state rattled by Chelsea and Dan's allegiance and their convictions, "And what if I don't come back?"

He not only says this, so he himself can hear it spoken out loud but also to clarify the dangers of this reality.

Chelsea and Danny stand and there is a group hug. Chelsea whispers, "We can't tell you what to do, Ryson, we can only tell you we love you and we are family either way."

He finally accepts a couple of tissues from Chelsea and luckily there is just enough to go around.

"I think I'll go sit with Pat awhile, maybe she has something to say about all this, he knows she will not, but it feels good to at least include her."

One step into his exit, Ryson stops, he is still facing Chelsea and Danny, eyes drier now, he says, "I love you guys, Pat and I are lucky to have you"

Before he can step through the door between the patio and the house he's just opened, Chelsea stops him by saying, "Hey, Ryson, Danny and I are trying to pick out paint or wallpaper not sure, but anyway, we are going to take a run to Home Depot, so take your time, when we get back, maybe we think about food," there's now a short pause, "or we don't."

Ryson takes a semi-deep breath not saying anything, the exhale is without any sort of cleansing properties as he sadness on his face says it all. He does not let the door close completely behind him because that is not how he found it.

The room is well lit. There are two large windows in the back wall with the curtains drawn fully open, and from the halfway open window on the right, he can feel the warm afternoon air working its way in, and yet, the room feels so very dark.

Pat is sleeping quietly but becomes somewhat restless after Ryson comes into the room. He carries a small, under-stuffed, short back chair across the room and places it is as close to the bed as he can without making contact. For the first few minutes he sits in the chair, he thinks only of Chelsea and Danny and how they were so quick with their evaluation and input. It will not make driving away from here any easier but perhaps, there will be something to come home to. The sound of Chelsea and Danny's truck rolling up the gravel driveway towards the street shifts his thoughts from them to Pat and the kids.

He so desperately wants to tell Pat of his plans, but each time he tries, the sadness wells up inside him to the point of emotional collapse. With every thought of the kids, a sense of panic squeezes his guts and chest crippling him to the chair. It's only the sound of Chelsea's voice still echoing in his head, "Farther away, farther away, farther away," that pulls him from the grips of an oncoming panic attack. The strength he finds in her echo brings Ryson to his feet, Pat is sleeping quietly with her back to him, her knees drawn up slightly to her chest, a thin sheet wrinkled and balled at her feet. He places both hands on her shoulder, and still he cannot find the words.

Danny and Chelsea knew he would be gone when they got back. Ryson also knew this as he stood in the kitchen writing the note.

"It's your strength I now pair with my own, I'll keep you up to speed. You have my number. Love you both, lots and lots."

It was exactly one year to the day, Ryson had returned home from Vietnam when he found Pat, ex-high school girlfriend of two years working at her parents' bakery. He did not know this before he walked in the door, about the bakery or the fact that she worked there. He was there to get cookies for the grand opening of Level 1 Security. He was sitting when he heard her voice call out number seventeen. He knew the voice right away, he stood and looked towards the counter, the angel that captured his view made him weak in the knees. He knew from that very moment, he and Pat would share a life together. As this replays out in Ryson's head, it moves towards the twins and how much the two of them wanted kids. He has both hands on the steering wheel, when in unison, they begin to tremble. A moment ticks by and it gets worse. Now because of the tremble in his hands, the front of the car starts to quiver. The small market he was at just a couple of hours ago comes up on the left side of the road. Without thinking, when the driveway appears, he turns in. When he brings the car to a stop, he is safely in the parking lot.

Confused and somewhat disorientated, he turns off the car and rolls down the window. Still trembling but it is subsiding with every breath of air he can suck in from the open window. The sadness consumes the sorrow, the sorrow only shadowed by the fear that he does not come back and Pat is left to suffer yet another loss. The trembling gives way to tears, and the tears he allows because he is out of options, but this gives way to crying, then sobbing. It feels right, so Ryson let's go.

A couple of minutes into this tearful cleansing, Ryson finally notices movement out of his left side peripheral. When he glances left, towards the front of the market, there on the walkway in front of the door are two young boys maybe eleven or twelve but definitely not teenagers. In each of their right hands is an ice cream cone and some flavor of ice-cream. The two boys are locked in a stare at him and on their faces are looks of puzzlement and concern. The young boy, who was standing in front of the propped open door, takes a couple of steps backwards to where he is consumed by the shadows inside the small market. Boy two, who is slightly right of the door, remains motionless and stares, except for the small movements between his tongue and the ice cream.

Ryson shifts his attention to the inside of the car, searching the glove box, then center console. It's here he finds a fistful of folded fast food napkins and proceeds to mop up the snot and tears. Avoiding the re-glance in fear they have called the crybaby police, his focus stays in the car.

It's not until he is using the last napkin to finalize the cleanup he notices movement towards his car. When he turns his head left looking out the open window, he sees the young boy that had previously backed into the market now walking towards him. He is at best only a few feet away, the young boy heading towards him is of average kid height, brown hair, T-shirt, shorts, tennies, and now he has an ice cream cone in each hand. The cone in his right hand he appears to be licking quite feverishly as he covers the rest of the distance within a foot or two of the window.

Somewhat cautiously when the young boy is arm's length from Ryson's open window, he lifts the ice cream cone in his left hand to the window toward Ryson. He, of course, can only take the cone from the boy and does so without question, his right-hand crossing over his chest, but he does not fully withdraw it to the inside of the car, he just sort of suspends himself. They are looking at each other as the young boy lowers his ice-cream a few inches down from his mouth, and with three or four nods of his head the young boy simply states, "Life," then turns and slowly walks away.

He watches the two boys as they walk across the parking lot and disappear somewhere along the road. The three of them making sure none of this ice-cream goes to waste.

In those cold, sweet moments of frozen dairy bliss, right up until there was nothing left but finger lickin's, he checked out.

With the last finger cleaned, he knows that somehow that kid saved him. He did not even get to say thank you for the hope or the ice cream, but he cannot escape the thought that someday he just might get that chance. Ryson reaches for the key, and when the car comes to life, he knows it's time to go, the kids come first.

Art and Lila were spending the day bossing around the movers, Art more so than Lila. They still have no furniture but it is supposed to be on its way. Lila has always hated telling people what to do, so whenever it came time to move in the twenty four years they have been married, Lila would simply make a list of things she wanted to see happen, along with clearly marking all boxes as if later they would have to be reassembled taking on shape and structure.

Per instructions, before they could leave, the movers stacked boxes that were to be stored on site in front of the two storage areas Art and Lila had created at each end of the L-shaped building. Because it is a corner unit the front half is somewhat rounded whereas the back half is more squared.

Art's attention slipping from the task at hand to the fact that now, because the movers have left, Lila has removed the outer button up shirt she was wearing leaving just a thin yellow, deep V cut, short sleeve T-shirt with white lace sewn at the arms and neck. The neck opening loose and roomy, causing it to fall forward exposing braless cleavage but not quite full boobs.

Every time Lila would lean over the boxes as she deciphered her code as to which one she would scoot into the storage area next, Art would steal a peek. Beginning to grow tight in the groin, Art checks his watch.

The beauty to which Lila possesses, not even forty years of age nor twenty-four years of marriage could wrinkle the very fabric of her sexuality, her pale skin, and delicate Asian features lend well to her five-foot four-inch frame and slightly larger than average breast. And the fact that Trina is at Grandma's, Art makes his approach. Lila does not feel Art right on her heels as she pushes one of the boxes into its position in the storage area, the sound of Art pulling the curtain closed behind them startles her, but only long enough for her to get turned around.

When Ryson pulls into his own driveway it's four p.m. sharp. He turns the car off, withdraws the key, and starts to exit the car but decides to stay put, reclaiming a molded image of himself still pressed into the driver seat. The thoughts of this day and the many faces that have been in it are still swirling around the inside of his head like mystic Indian smoke. The thought of going into the house and all its silent shadows unnerves him, so he decides to walk the five blocks to Arts, even though he is two hours early, it's better than the house option and the walk will do him some good.

From there love den and the pleasures of passion Art and Lila could not hear the furniture delivery guys banging on the back door, after a couple of minutes with no response, the two delivery guys decide to leave the truck and walk around to the front.

Ryson covers the distance of five blocks far too quickly and is disappointed it was not much farther.

At one end of the short block is a three-story dental complex with a courtyard and some sort of fountain that sits next to it, Ryson comes to this first, there are two smaller units past this and then Redline Financial sits on the far corner.

In the front corner of the dental building closest to Ryson is a coffee house, from here, he can see the front door and some windows of Redline Financial to which he sees no movement or activity.

Ryson does not see the movers approach the front door of Redline Financial because he is busy ordering coffee and a couple of croissants.

Art sees the two men approach the front door as he exits the love den, he is quite certain because of the matching jumpsuits the furniture is here., Moving towards the door, Art now looking through the window, can read the logo on one of the jumpsuits, he opens the door and in a post love den response, he is probably far too chipper, "Hey, what's up, fellas, I sure hope you brought something that looks like furniture, come on in."

As mover one comes through the door, he says, "In a truck out back, looks like furniture to me."

"We knocked on the back door guess you did not hear us," mover two now comes through the door and closes it.

Art still somewhat chipper replies, "Yeah, sorry about that, that backdoor definitely needs a doorbell. Come on, we can walk through."

In single file, they head to the back door.

As Ryson exits the coffee house, he glances left, checking for any activity at Redline, seeing none, he takes up a seat on the edge of some sort of fountain in the courtyard that is adjacent to the dental complex.

After the snack, he stands in an attempt to brush all the croissant flakes off his shirt and pants with the back of his hand and ends up accidentally smacking the half-full cup of coffee right from his grip. The lid free cup hits the ground with the open end straight up, it does so with enough force to send up a coffee curtain chest high. There is no time to react and he thoroughly expects to be drenched.

It seemed gravity had rescinded its offer of escape because once the coffee curtain drops, all that remains is only a couple of small splatters left behind on his tennies. The rest of the coffee is quickly consumed by a gentle slope and a two-inch floor drain in the cement at his feet.

Ryson picks up the cup like it belonged to somebody else. Calmly, he deposits the trash in a can, just as he reaches the sidewalk, he turns left really fighting the urge to look back, and wins.

A couple of minutes later, Ryson is at the door of Redline Financial and now he can see movement inside. When he spots Art through the window, he and somebody in a gray jumpsuit are just setting down a large box and then disappearing through a curtain towards the back building. Ryson checks the door to see if it is locked, it is not, he steps in, and closes the door behind him.

Before he can announce himself, there is a voice coming from his left and behind a stack of boxes, as he turns that direction, Lila steps into view, her voice as pretty to listen to as she is to look at, "Can I help you?"

"Hello, there," he says this with a smile on his face, "my name's Ryson and I'm early."

"It's nice to finally meet you Ryson Early," she is just kidding and they both snicker. "Well, come on in, Mr. Willows, I'm Lila, Art's wife." They move towards each other, when they are within arm's length from one another, Lila stops and puts out her right hand, Ryson follows this lead and does the same, they shake hands.

Lila moves and a little closer, she does not let go of Ryson's hand, she looks into his eyes and says, "I have something for you."

She now lets go of his hand but does not back away.

Lila, with both hands, now removes a chain and some sort of medallion from around her own neck and slowly lifts it high enough to slip it over Ryson's head, then around his neck. Now, she hugs him.

She whispers thank you and leans her weight into Ryson embrace, he can feel her tremble, she says it again, "Thank you."

When they separate, Lila's strength comes back to her and she again looks into his eyes and with the strength of her own woven courage says, "No tears, Ryson, no tears. But evidently that belongs to you."

"I don't understand, Lila, how does this belong to me?" his question is one of suspicion and concern.

Arts reappearance through the curtain startles all three of them, considering he almost runs into the two of them. Art's genuine pleasure in seeing Ryson is quite obvious and the fact that he is early, even better still.

"Hey, Ryson, didn't expect to see you already, but nice of you to drop in. I see you two have already met," Lila smiles and takes Art's hand and she

75

replies, "Yes, we have, now how about the three of us go sit down and I will tell the two of you a story."

Lila leads them back through the curtain, Art just appeared from and into the back part of the building, at the same time, asking if all the furniture is off the truck.

"Yes…and the two young men responsible well tipped and sent on their way."

In the back room, there are two tables already set up, the smaller square table and four chairs sits in the kitchen area, and then a much larger oval table with eight chairs sits more center in the room, Lila pulls up a seat at the smaller of the two, as she does so, she asked Ryson to join her, then asking Art if he would grab some bottled water from the fridge.

Before Art can take his place at the table, Lila starts with, "Art already knows some of the story but until today, I have never told anybody the entire story My mom and I are the only ones that know, and that's only because she was there with me."

Zippered with intrigue, the two now stay fastened to their silence, letting Lila have what is obvious a much-needed moment.

"I was nineteen when my father died and shortly after, that my mom comes to me asking if I would like to go to China with her to trace and meet some of our family's history and still living members, I said, 'of course,' and two and a half weeks later we were on our way. At the end of our stay in the village, where my father was actually born and raised, we go to this really old Buddhist temple a couple of hours away, my mom finds out that some parts of this temple are now open to the public and just can't wait to go see it, so we go."

"At first, the temple looks deserted, and if it was open to the public then where is the public? We were the only car in the small, dirt parking lot. Most people would just turn and go home, my mother is definitely not most people, so we go bravely inside. It's dimly lit with small windows surrounding the upper part of the large building, allowing only enough light to softly illuminate the entryway."

"Past this, the windows get larger and along with well-placed, candelabras we can now see what the inside looks like. To our left is a series of small animal statues embedded in a wall, in front of that a large bank of small candles, some lit some not, on the floor in front of the candles are two straw woven flat baskets, both with money on them both paper and coins."

"Mom now strolls over while fishing through her purse like she's been here a dozen times and places all the money she could find in her purse in equal portions into each woven flat basket, and now is going to light some candles using a small stick and stealing a small part of a flame from an already lit candle. Before she can get the flame close enough to an empty wick to call her own, there is a hand that gently touches my shoulder, gentle or not, it scares a small scream right out of me."

"The hand that was on my shoulder drops and is now hanging at the side of an older, maybe fifty-year-old Chinese monk and next to him is his double, only a few years younger, both wearing a brown robe cut and stitched from the same pattern and material. The older monk begins to speak to me in a Chinese dialect my mother and I cannot fully understand, and we both speak fluent Chinese. It's obvious the older monk wants to shake my hand, so we shake hands."

"His handshake was firm, yet pleasant, but nothing special. It's when the monk releases my hand that something extraordinary happens, there was an emptiness that followed the release and the sense that I was only a single breath away from being nothing, to the point where I was truly afraid to breathe. When I did finally take that breath, it was the single most cleansing moment of my life, and that is the only way I can describe that."

"The two monks quietly share a few words, don't have any idea what they were saying, but now the younger of the two monks reaches for my hand. I'm hesitant and even back up a wee bit, the monk is persistent and I somewhat reluctantly obliged, but it's not a handshake he wants, he tugs on my hand and arm, just enough for me to understand we are going for a walk."

"The two monks lead, my mom and I follow, the younger monk, holding my hand the whole way. We make a couple of turns down a couple of hallways and end up in a large open room."

"In this room are several life-size statues of children, I would say age wise probably ranging from two to early teens, boys and girls. The four of us stop at the entrance to this room and the monk holding my hand lets go, I hold my breath, expecting the same strangeness as last time with the older monk, but nothing."

"Now the older monk starts speaking to me again in that same old dialect, and it's obvious I do not understand him, but it doesn't stop him from doing so."

"The monk, who is speaking, now motions for us to follow him, the younger monk holds his ground and does not move but motions with both hands for my mom and I to do what the older monk has asked."

"The older monk does not wait for our decision to follow; instead, he turns and starts walking away. Of course, my mother does not hesitate, she eagerly obliges and follows, I do as well, I am just not as eager. And indeed, the younger monk stays behind."

"In the center of this room is a small group of statues and it looks to be the monks intended destination, my mom and I are a few steps behind the monk as he reaches the group of statues and stops, he turns our direction and waits for us to join him."

"The statues we are now standing in front of our quite remarkable, I am not really sure what they were made of, it looked like some sort of light colored metal, the tallest of the statues was a woman in a full-length gown and at her sides are children, two on one side and one on the other. The woman's arms are at her sides, making it possible for them all to be holding hands, they are all life-size and, on their faces, it's obvious the four of them are in a very happy place."

"Puzzled as to why he brought us here but glad that he did, the monk now withdraws what resembles a medium-sized flat spoon from somewhere I don't know. He lays this spoon looking thing at my feet and he kind of goes down on one knee to do so and does not stand up afterwards, instead, he makes a couple of grunting sounds and looks up. When he is sure I am looking down at him, he picks up the flat spoon, the very same one he just sat down, and proceeds to pretend, as though he is going to use it to remove a gold looking medallion, which is one of several that have been set into the bottom part of the dress the woman statue is wearing, he goes so far as to wedge this spoon tool under one of these medallions but does not attempt to force it out."

"He, again, lays this spoon thing at my feet and slowly stands up. The monk, when he stands, is not saying anything but he begins to gesture and in quite the assertive manner, and as strange as I think all of this is, I know what he wants me to do."

"So I, now, go down to one knee just as he did, I pick up the spoon and slowly move it to the same medallion, when the monk does not try to stop me, I proceed to wedge the flat part of the spoon behind the medallion because there seems to be just enough space to do so."

"Without any real effort, the medallion pops out and bounces loudly causing echoes throughout the room until it comes to a rest on the floor just in front of me, in a moment of guilt, I look up not really knowing what to expect."

"The smile on the monk's face is not just one of happiness, this is a facial expression of extreme jubilation, I glanced towards the young monk who is still standing where we left him in the doorway and on his face, the same look."

"I, of course, pick up the medallion and stand up, facing the monk with the medallion in one hand and the tool in the other. I can only assume the look on my face was one of confusion and wonder."

"The monk is still smiling as he points to the spoon tool in my left hand and then points to the floor at my feet. I gently bend down and place the spoon on the floor. As for the medallion, I leave it resting in the open palm of my right hand. The monk who is still smiling raises his open right hand and slowly closes it, making a fist, and with his left hand, he points to the medallion, I, close my hand around the medallion and the monk acceptably nods, still smiling."

"Okay, so now it gets weird," Lila says this just to make sure Art and Ryson are paying attention.

They both in tandem say, "Oh, yeah, now, it's going to get weird."

"The smile slithers slightly to less than jubilant and Mr. Monk now gets all serious, not in an angry way but there is a sense of importance to what he wants to tell me."

"Pointing to my stomach, and I mean within just a couple of inches so there is no mistakes as to his reference when he says, 'And I know this now but I did not know it then.' But what he says is, 'Early in life, and as his reward you give him this when he saves her.' He now actually does touch my stomach."

"This message was written on a small piece of rice paper in a common Chinese language the younger monk gave us as we were escorted from the temple to the parking lot. The rice paper message lasted a couple of years as did my curiosity, after that, I, kind of, probably out of the fear of the unknown, put it out of my head and there that medallion sat in my jewelry box. Until Mother's Day of this year, when I took it down to my jeweler and had him set it in a backing and put it on a chain, so you could wear it around your neck. So you see, Mr. Willows, it truly does belong to you."

Ryson is speechless, he cradles the medallion in the palm of his hand relieving tension on the chain around his neck.

It's an unimpressive medallion, on the front is an engraved depiction of the very same statute from which it came, it's seems slightly larger than a silver dollar and on the back is something written in Chinese. It looks to be solid gold and very old, there are no dates on the medallion, and along the edging of the medallion looks like some kind of large feathers front and back.

Ryson is studying the Chinese writing on the back when Lila says, "From what I could learn, the language dates back to the Ming dynasty era and it reads 'The angel to children.'"

Ryson gently allows the medallion to again take up the slack on the chain as it now hangs freely around his neck, he looks at Lila and remembering her wishes of no tears and seeing she was doing her part, simply smiles and says, "Thank you, Lila, I will do my best."

Lila, who is of course choking down her emotions, says, "Well, you have a pretty good start."

Art and Lila are looking at each other when she says this.

Art loves what she has done and it's his lack of words that tell her so, he only smiles, he then picks up her hand, and gently kisses the back of it.

Lila remarks, "Well, there you have it, now let's all get back to work."

They all three smile.

Art and Ryson commence to moving furniture, Lila goes back to her storage plans.

2 More

Will's hesitation and the lingering moment his finger hovers over the send key, May interprets as a weakness in their understanding, she questions his delay. William, this name she only uses when it's just them, "If this is about me, maybe we should talk about that some more before you call him."

"It's not like that Masha, (May's full name) you and I are solid here, we just need them to be as well, what you bring here I believe is not only necessary, but will absolutely better our chances of success and survival."

Will hits send, May agrees but says nothing.

Art and Ryson are having a water break when Art's phone is awakened on the counter right behind them, before Art picks it up, he glances at Ryson, saying, "Everybody's going to be early today, I love it, it's Will."

"Hello, Mr. Thorne, how's things?"

"Listen, Art, I realize this is going to sound a little strange but I did not come alone, but hear me out. I realize we don't have any history together, and you have no reason to do so but you have to trust me when I say, this could be very important and you should really hear what this person has to say."

"Of course, Will, if this is important to you and what we're doing, then it's important to Ryson and I, who is already here, by the way, now where are you?" Art's decision and voice are clear indicators he is having no problem filling the shoes of a leader.

Will fumbles with the location, "I think we are parked just outside your back door."

Arts pleased they are already here, and is not afraid to show it.

"O, great, I will open the door and have a looksee."

The word looksee trails off as Will hangs up.

As he and May get out of the car, the door closest to them opens cautiously, Art steps out just far enough to get a good look, seeing them both approach the

81

door Art smiles and says, "Nice to see you, come on in." He waits till there through the door, he, being the last, then pulling the door closed and locked.

Act 1

Handshakes and hugs while Will introduces May to Art and Ryson, and now because of the commotion, Lila has joined the party as well.

With informal introductions done, Lila can clearly see that May is extremely uncomfortable, but first turns her attention to Will.

"I, Will, I'm Lila, Art's wife, it's nice to meet you."

"Right back at you, Lila, Art talks a lot about you."

The hug lingers and for both of them it's for different reasons. For Lila, the strength she feels in Will's embrace is a sense of courage and determination, and for Will, it was like he was sharing a moment with a sister he's never had, and being an only child, this was a sensation completely unexpected, but well received.

Now, Lila turns to May, they stand face to face, Lila slightly raises her arms from her sides and turns her hands palms up, and without hesitation May responds by placing her hands palm down on to Lila's.

Lila's voice gently resonates with the sounds of mother bird in charge of the nest, "Come sit down, sweetheart, and tell us how you fit into all this." May smiles and already is starting to relax. Lila with one hand leads May to the larger of the two tables in the room, Lila taking a seat at the far end of the table while scooting the chair to her left, out and away for May.

The other three, Ryson, Art, and Will, come to the table but before they can sit down, Lila instructs them to get water and whatever they want from the kitchen, and tells Will to get a large plate from over the sink for the cookies he brought.

The three men take seats at the table, Will alongside May and across the table from him, sits Art, and to his left, Ryson, he is now sitting between Lila and Art and across the table from May.

Before Art and Ryson can get completely settled, May's eagerness gets the best of her and she starts right in.

"First off, my name is Masha Blume, but you can call me, and I prefer to go by, May The first thing I want you all to know is I have no intentions of causing even the slightest ripple in what you all are trying to do here. I can't have that and will not, so at any time, once you've heard what I have to say and do not want me, here you just look me in the eyes and ask me to leave. I will do so without hesitation or question."

May does not pause long enough for rebuttal, instead she now stands with her back to the kitchen area, hands at her side, she takes a small breath, and kinda gently bites the right corner of her bottom lip, nods her head up, and down slightly and says, "What you see is absolutely what you get."

It's here Art and Ryson share the same brain because what they're looking at is a five foot six, hundred and eighteen pounds very pretty, semi-dark skin, nice body, but a little chunky in all the right places. So at this point, Art and Ryson will just wait and see what she has to say. Lila does not share the brain of the other two, but it would be nice to not be the only woman in this man's club. So, in silence, they all decide to give May her moment.

"I only want to help and without question, I believe I can, I'm already pretty much up to speed, given the relationship between Will and I. So, let's start there," May smiles and sits down.

"Will and I have been in a relationship just as far back as probably both of us can remember, our lives have crisscrossed, I believe, since middle school, and there's just not much we don't know about one another. So, yeah, we confide in each other and have for many years."

"I remember reading the story in the paper on Mother's Day and being absolutely staggered with anger and sadness like I just did not know which way to fall. And this happening the day before Mother's Day, and in my own neighborhood."

"At first, it was the sadness of having your children taken from you," May pauses here and her eyes water, she meets Ryson's stare from across the table and softly says, "I am so very sorry, Ryson." A couple of tears do fall but May's strength and anger stem the rest.

Like pepper on the tip of your tongue, Mays voice now stings a little, "I remember being furious at Will for letting this happen, so much so I called him pissed off and looking for a fight," she quick glances at Will, he confirms with a nod. "Over the phone, he does a quick breakdown for me of what's going on and a couple of days later, we meet for dinner."

"It's then Will informs me as to what has transpired and he is going to quit the force and if he got half a chance to go rescue those children himself, he would without hesitation."

"I believed him, and envied his passion and purpose."

"When Will tells me he's coming here tonight to attempt to formulate a plan of intel and observation regarding the whereabouts of the twins, we both knew I was coming with him. And so it's about purpose and making a stand for something you believe in. It really is just that simple for me."

"What I bring to the effort is this, let me start with my parents, in particular, my father. As strange as this might sound, my father was an Iranian rocket scientist. He is no longer a rocket scientist but is a great father and also still Iranian. At the end of the seventies because of missile embargoes and pressure from the U.N., his division is closed and dismantled."

The Ayatollah decides some of the scientists will be retrained in agriculture and ships my dad and some others to Australia. '

"Well, the first chance he gets he stows away on a cargo ship headed to the U.S."

"Long story, short version, he meets my mom because her father, my grandfather owned the apartment building he was living /hiding in at the time near Chinatown in San Francisco. My dad convinces her and even pays her to marry him so he can become a U.S. citizen. She does, they end up falling in love for life and are happily still married to this very day."

The other four smile, May continues, "For a long time after I was born and really even into my teens, my father still believed the Iranian Secret Service was looking for us, though he chose not to hide, what he did do is prepare us in case that day ever happened. With me, it was all education and self-defense, it seemed to me whatever we were doing as dad and daughter somehow related to one or both of those things. With my mom and himself, it was always about finance."

"My grandfather on my mother's side passed away before I was born and when he did, he left the apartment building to my mother. Within weeks, they sell it, they use that money to buy what is now the third largest hobby rocket manufacturer in the U.S. The point I'm trying to make here is that I have never allowed life to tell me where I belong in it, I have seen far too much in regards to the uglier sides of those that feed on the rest of us."

"It's the children and how in so many countries they're treated as a commodity, this I find most disturbing and our neighbors to the south being some of the worst. What they did to Ryson," May does not make eye contact in fear of losing emotional control, "they do on a regular basis, and so yeah, I'd like the chance to say, not on my watch, and maybe dish out a little payback."

May falls silent, Art jumps in. "Well, hell, sweetheart, you had me at hobby rockets."

They all laugh, including Art.

"Now, seriously, is there anybody here that would like to ask me to leave?" Art leaves this question to idle on the table as if it is up for discussion. It is not. Just as well, nobody speaks up.

"Agreed, stay as long as you like," Art winks and adds, "but you may very well leave on your own before this night is over."

Act 2

On the table in front of Art is a black leather medium-sized organizer. Art clears his throat and partially opens the organizer, but before its contents are revealed, he gently re-closes it and returns it to its previously dormant state, he leans back in his chair and it seems is almost in tears, clearing his voice, it's obvious he stumbles around these words, "Let's talk about trust and honesty. I only bring this up because I myself have a confession and this is something that could certainly interfere and cause trouble down the line, so my suggestion is this."

"Everybody in this room right now should be thinking the same thing, I am not saying it's time to hear everybody's life stories and confessions, but I think, as a collective, if any of us here like say, have a warrant for their arrest, or maybe you got a dead guy in your basement, that kind of stuff there. We should probably talk about that now as opposed to later."

Art g silent and nervously shifts around in his seat like there could be a comfortable position in it that he's not yet found.

"I'd like to hold off on my turn in the box if you don't mind, Art, at least until I hear what you have to say, not as an ex-cop mind you, only out of curiosity."

All others at the table silently agree with Will.

Art cannot entirely conceal his smugness nor his anxiety, "I am sure you are all aware of the fact that the Nixon presidential helicopter on display next to the Nixon Library not more than six miles from here three months ago disappeared from the face of the earth and has not been seen since. Well, I stole it, and still have it, and now, I don't know what to do with it."

It's Arts delivery and factual honesty from which these words are carried that makes this statement not only believable but without any doubt, the truth.

There is now of course, a bewildered silence at the table, as if May, Will, and Ryson had just been handed a euphoric stone. The looks on their faces in some strange way were all the same.

Almost in perfect timing, the three bewildered reply, "Why would you do that?"

Will then adds, "How did you do that?" Will continues to voice his concerns, and the fact that he is impressed did not go unnoticed.

"Art, geez, you gotta give it back, every government and local authority in the U.S. is looking for that damn helicopter. You do not want to be the guy found with the keys to that heli in his pocket. If you know what I mean."

"Art, how in God's name did you steal (Marine one) from right out in front of the Nixon Library? The only video they have of the night it was stolen is from a single camera on the roof of the south east corner overlooking E. Yorba Linda Blvd. and all they got is four point three seconds of a large amount of water leaving the parking lot and draining away down the street."

"How, Art, how did you do that, and for God sakes, don't tell us where it is. Just give it back. Hell, I believe you could just send them a note telling them where they can find it."

Ryson's only comment when Will takes a breath is, "Why!"

Art looks at Lila who still has not said a single word regarding this topic, it's a look that continues to say "I know, I know." Art now turns towards Ryson but is addressing the whole table, "Absolutely, Ryson, why is what's most important here, I will make this quick, so we can get on with what's important."

"I only take time to explain this because I can't have you guys thinking that this is somehow normal behavior for me, well, it's not. But sometimes what we do for the sake of our children is not always rational. First of all, you need to know that I was already extremely pissed off at this city regarding legal actions they took for unpaid utility bills about a year ago, to which those unpaid bills were not even mine. But we aren't talking about that."

"Trina, my seven-year-old daughter, for her first ever book report, she chooses to do it on Nixon and the library, we drive by it all the time and she just loves getting a look at the helicopter in the parking lot as we drive down the street. So when it came time to start the report, the first thing she wants to do, of course, is go see the helicopter up close and personal."

"So, we go, just her and I. I park in a handicapped spot as close to the helicopter as possible, I put my handicap plaque on the mirror, the last thing I do before I shut the door is grabbed my cane, Trina and I make our way to the copter as we stroll through the gate, we finally see the security guy sitting in a folding chair near the stairs leading up and into the helicopter."

"Now evidently, ass-wipe with a tin security badge and a solid fourth grade education sees me get out of my car with the cane and studies my ability to stay upright as I walk with a slight limp, using my cane not so much for balance or support, it just hurts less when I use it. But in the couple of minutes, it takes to walk to where he is, he determines I am far too handicapped to ascend or descend the few steps, it would take to get in and out of the helicopter."

"I try to tell piss-head I am absolutely able to go up and down a few steps without a cane or any other handicap device for that matter."

"I kid you not, it's at this point Mr. Security Man assumes a defensive posture and says in his best security voice, 'Sir, I need you to step away from the helicopter,' and now he radios for backup."

"This scares Trina and she starts to cry. I can't believe this is happening, so rather than make a scene and risk being arrested, because I know if I'm still standing there when piss-head number two shows up, I was going to let it get ugly."

"Forgoing the traumatic experience of seeing daddy go ballistic, I take her hand and lead her back to the car, but before we get in and drive away, I make a promise to her that day."

"Two weeks later, I told her that she and I have special permission to go to the place where they clean and repair the Nixon helicopter, and there, we will have the helicopter all to ourselves. I made sure to even drive by the library just so she indeed would see the empty space."

"And before you ask, yes, what an amazing day it was. We spent all day playing, eating, and doing a book report all about Nixon, and the Marine One helicopter, sorry to say there was no photography allowed."

"As for how I stole it, well, that's a story that will just have to wait, the point I was trying to make is first of all, I did it because I knew I could, and I am if anything, just a dad. Second, if this is to be even slightly cohesive," Art makes a circular motion with the index finger of his left hand in regards to all sitting at the table, "some basic foundations will have to be established, but for right now, let's just stick with honesty among the five of us here, especially if it concerns the five of us here."

"Okay, so we good?"

Everyone at the table agrees, "Yes," and there are no further confessions

Now 5

Art laughs out loud while making eye contact with May from across the table with outstretched arms and pointing his index fingers one each at Ryson and Will, he says, "With you being a part of this, May, you just saved these two from having to show up in Paraguay as a gay couple from San Francisco."

Ignoring the puzzled looks and not waiting for a confused reply, Art turns the table over to Lila after some introductions.

"Okay, first business, let me officially introduce Lila here," Art with his left hand, palm up with half extended arm gestures towards Lila, "she is a very important member of this tribe."

Lila quietly smiles, somewhat.

"She is in charge of the finance and also president of our charity, to which Ryson here," Art same gesture towards Ryson, "is the creator and sole benefactor of Project Mother's Day. I will let her finish."

Art sits back with a bottle of water.

"Well, I think you will find me far less wordsy than Mr. Chatty Cathy over there," Lila says this with half sugar, half salt.

"Project Mother's Day is a non-profit organization devoted and dedicated to the safe recovery of children thought lost forever, and of course, any and all kidnapped children, foreign or domestic. In its financial account as of present is thirty-four thousand dollars. This money coming from a very generous benefactor and owner of a large petting zoo who is donating out of the goodness of his own heart one third of its annual income to Project Mother's Day."

"What this means is there has to be a receipt for everything. We are absolutely legitimate and I intend to keep it that way."

There are tears in Lila's eyes, then a few tumble down her cheek, she obviously struggles emotionally with what she wants to say next.

The words that poetically dance from the lips of Lila's soft whispers are in Chinese and directed towards May and Will when the short poem is finished Lila translates it to English, but this time above a whisper.

It means, "To choose your own destiny for the sake of a child, there is an angel that shall watch over you in hopes that someday you can save them all."

Lila dabs the last couple of tears as she catches them mid-cheek with a tissue that appears from nowhere, "I believe you three are about to make a difference, and anybody trying to interfere, at least on this end will have to come through Art and I. We will do whatever it takes to get the three of you in and then however many out of whatever country you're in when it's time to go."

These words from Lila are quickly digested and its Ryson who speaks first, "When is it, time to go?"

Art clearly is done fucking around when he reengages the group, speaking clearly and with the voice of authority asks, "Does anybody here have a problem taking a business flight at 8:15 tomorrow morning, destination, Paraguay International?"

"And, yes, Ryson, it's time to go. I will have the new tickets before sunup, I need May's passport and social security number, and nobody show up here tomorrow morning without I.D."

"Lila and I…" Arts voice now becomes quite serene and melancholy. "If there's a better way to go at this, there's just no time to explore, you have to go now, the plan easily adapts to three and also because of May gives us two separate objectives, and that's going to be helpful."

"The plan, as it stands now, is based on things we need to know. Along with what intel Lila and I have already acquired, it's enough to move forward, but just barely. So, here's what we should do, that is if we all agree."

"The three of you will be landing in Paraguay tomorrow at 3:51 p.m., Will and May as a married couple, looking to purchase or adopt twins, Ryson as a closet pedophile. You do not know one another, so there should be no conversation or contact."

Art again unzips the leather organizer, and this time to its fully open position laid out in front of him, the first thing he removes is a map, it's the same size as the organizer, it's hand-drawn and all of the words are in Spanish. Art slides this to his left and towards center table.

"When your plane lands, there should be a minivan in slot six, blue zone, I don't know what that means, you two will have to figure that out on your own." Art lifting his head from the organizer and glancing at May and Will, "If you can't find this, move on, as long as you leave the airport in a minivan, who you rent it from is no matter. Get a map, now drive to the Marx Hotel in the city of Kings Throne. Should be about fifty minutes south of the airport."

Art pushes the hand-drawn map to Will as he is retrieving a small piece of paper from an inside pocket of the organizer, and on it is two strange sets of numbers, this, he pushes to May.

"The first number you will use to contact a local adoption agency, the second number is for a far less legal agency than the first, point is, you two would like to beg, borrow, adopt, or steal, or purchase twins, and preferably, girls under the age of six."

Art reaches across the table and gently removes the map from May's feathered fingertip grip and now slowly places it in front of Ryson.

The tone and sadness in Art's voice now brings to the table a reality of just where the three of them are about to go, it's very quiet, except for Art's voice. Art turns left in his chair and now facing Ryson eye to eye.

"Ryson, I'll be honest with you, I originally believed it would be Will who was to head first into this area, because it's there this all becomes very real and I have no doubt it's going to shock and horrify you. Just as it would anybody in this room. But, Ryson, I think it's safe to say, you probably more than the rest, but go you must, and you must go as something you're not."

"The closet pedophile act should keep you from getting in any real trouble but still give you a chance to look around. You will just have to work that any way you can."

The third item Art now withdraws from the organizer is a train schedule, it, too, is in Spanish and clearly printed from somewhere off the internet. This, Art also places in front of Ryson.

"Ryson, when you get off the plane, you need to go to International Terminal B. There is a train boarding platform there, first buy a ticket to Red Valley, East Station. I wrote all that on the back of that train schedule. Check into a hotel, there's two, I'll leave that your choice, you will then be in the area known as Neighbors Cradle.

"Neighbors Cradle resides in the lower part of Paraguay and almost makes up a third of the country, it's run by a newly self-installed paramilitary and dictator, they call themselves 'The Dark and the Light.'"

Art shakes his head and in an exhale of dirty air, he says, "Yeah, whatever, but it's in this area I believe your kids have been moved through or will be soon, if they were indeed taken by a Tiger Team, and I believe they were, then it's in parts of the Neighbors Cradle they call home."

"In and around the hotel areas, there are several gentlemen's clubs, my contact in Brazil says you will find kids, boys and girls, dancing in some of these places as young as nine and ten years old. Ryson, I would start there."

These words hang in the air like the stink of a wet dog, then, silence.

it's Ryson's moment to take, the others know it, so they wait for his response.

Ryson leans forward, placing his elbows on the table, then allowing his chin to come to rest atop the back of his overlapped hands. He is visibly shaken with a slight tremor in both his hands and arms.

"It's their laughter I hear in my head and sometimes it can become so loud I can't hear anything else, I take this hunt to the grave and beyond if need be, but I will follow their laughter. I only hope it can help guide me."

Ryson lifts his head, eyes dry and says, "How do we communicate with each other after we leave the airport? Also… I have a brother-in-law that works for the U.S. forest service, and he has access to high resolution satellite imagery. Anything he can do to help he will."

Art has a grin that carries with it a sense of surprise like Santa brought you what you didn't ask for, but was thinking.

"You tell this brother-in-law, I will very soon be calling. As for how we are going to communicate, Lila has already taken care of that, I'll let her explain."

Lila jumps eagerly right into the conversation, "We will be using what is known as an e-box. Paraguay only has two cellular carriers, and these two are defined by what we would call an area code, but because they are both single band, you will have to buy phones at the airport with proper chips. It's how the Paraguay government controls all cellular communications in and out of the country."

"Basically, the e-box allows us to communicate globally but it is not a secure system, and it can only be used for text messages. In order to make an

94

international call, you would have to find an unlocked landline to which there is only a dozen or so in the whole country. The hotel where May and Will are going in Kings Throne is one of them."

The conversations for the next hour or so goes from personal experiences to hopes and dreams, then coming full circle back to here and now.

When there is just a couple of the strange raisin cookies left on the large plate from which they have all been nibbling it's Will who finally says what the other two have also been thinking.

"So, Art, you gunna tell us how you liberated Marine one from its enclosed and anchored position and then somehow put it someplace where nobody on the planet can find it?"

"You tell us how you did it and I will tell you how to give it back, with no one the wiser as to who took it," when Will says this, for some reason, it seems genuine.

"Well, hell, that's an offer I can't seem to refuse."

Art was hoping somebody would ask but never thinking it might include resolution.

"It's late, so how's about we play a little game of one question," when Art says this, he gets up but tells the others to just sit still.

From the kitchen area, Art retrieves a medium-sized, duel-wick, jar candle. Before he takes the few steps back to his chair, Art, from the kitchen, dims the hanging lamp over the table they all share, the room takes on a cozy, gray shadow that starts to dance as he puts fire to the wicks. With the candle now in the center of the table and next to it the lighter that lit it, he sits down.

"The candle is to remind you of the one question you each may ask when I'm done because it would take far too long to fully explain how I am now in possession of a national treasure, but what I can do is read to you the launch procedure I used that night to acquire said treasure. But afterwards, just one question each. It's late, we all have a big day ahead of us tomorrow."

"The whole plan hinged on two things; the flatbed trailer and the national deficit. All of the work on the trailer was done to such a degree that once I backed this modified heli hauler into the fenced area and alongside my prize, that heli was already mine. And the fact that all exterior surveillance systems were shut off because the library was actually closed due to the lack of funding, well, that was just a gift."

"So, with the budget crisis in full swing and my trailer ready to go, one more run through the numbers, because it's always about the numbers, Art winks at Lila, obviously and without question, always about the numbers."

Art now withdraws several index cards from the organizer that have been stapled together and starts to read, "We will just start at the top."

Cut large gate padlock (bolt cutters)

Unbolt from ground anchors (5/8–two-inch ratchet)

Loosen main blades (5/8–1/2 wrench) fold towards tail then strap.

Fully open large gate.

Back in flatbed/remove tarp, put in truck cab.

Close large gate/hide truck cab.

Check perimeter on back wall.

Remove plastic sheeting from flatbed, install on fence, 360 degrees, secure to asphalt with two-sided sticky tape, two inches wide.

Attach airbags and wire all eight to remote control relay system, do not plug in battery circuit! Strap relay system to door handholds.

Check trailer for debris. Plug in magnets (confirm low power).

Connect airbag system battery/turn on remote relay.

Secure all tools and miscellaneous in gear bag (leave by exit fence).

Set timer, open bladder valves to full.

Place gear bag over fence, climb over.

Retrieve remote sending unit from gear bag (not truck cab) turn on.

Check power output.

Check time (two minutes thirty-seven seconds), inflate airbags.

Check time (five minutes thirty-seven seconds), check height with fence indicator, turn magnet power to full.

Check drift, deflate airbags.

Slit plastic through fence, wait, and listen. Open gate, check payload (remove all plastic).

Close gate, check perimeter on walk to truck cab.

Hookup, pull out.

Cover with tarp/confirm gear bag in truck cab.

Drive careful.

Will barely waits for Art to finish, "So, basically, you created a swimming pool using plastic sheeting and the fence that surrounds and supposedly protects one of the city's most treasured possessions to make it your own?"

"Yes, next!" Will smiles, giggles, and shakes his head.

May and Ryson give a look to one another, it is somewhat of a blank stare as each of them finish the thoughts in their own heads, then its Ryson who says, "Ladies first."

May looks at Art through eyes of wonder and respect and then smiles, "You brought your own water, because, well, first, you needed a lot of it and second, buoyancy and the time allocated was critical. Holy cow, Batman, that must have been one very complicated set of numbers." They all laugh, including Lila. Then almost at the same time Art and Lila quietly mumbled, "To say the least." They all laugh a little more.

When it's Ryson's turn, he has two questions and cannot decide which one to ask. He chooses what intrigues him the most.

"How did you know the helicopter would be magnetic? 99% of all modern aircraft is intentionally without magnetic properties, because it seems to me you had a lot riding on the fact that once you turned on those electromagnets they were going to align the helicopter over the trailer all by themselves." Art smiles and is clearly impressed.

"On one of the late-night recon missions, I brought a small magnet and checked it for myself. Evidently, there is a metal plate maybe twelve to fourteen inches wide in the belly of that helicopter from nose to tail, probably some kind of armament to protect the prez."

Ryson stands, he's sitting directly to Art's left so Art does the same, as they stand Ryson says, "Sir, I am in awe of all that you did, but what humbles me the most still, is why you did it."

They shake hands and man hug.

"That's my exit," Ryson moves from one person to the next, handshakes, hugs and kisses and to each one he whispers, "thank you."

"I will show myself out the front, I'm walking home, what time you want us here in the morning, Art?"

"Let's go with seven, your ride to the airport will be here at eight, get some sleep, see you then."

Ryson does not reply, only a handshake over his head indicates he heard Art correctly. The night air warm even for mid-May, it felt thin and easy to breathe and Ryson was glad he chose this mode of transport.

"I guess it's true what they say, to live life to the fullest, you must learn to do the impossible. And I'm quite sure, Art, that giving it back will be far less complicated, in fact, I think you already know how, and yes, Art, you lose the trailer, but as long as you travel at least a couple of miles from where it's been, unhook it, leave it covered, and simply drive away, and for sure of all that is holy, don't look back, ever. I don't think there will be any questions asked, and that is my professional opinion."

Art does not reply to Will, instead he turns to Lila and in the hug they share he says, and not in a whisper, "I think we will all be okay."

May answers back, "Indeed. Good night, Art," now May moves towards Lila, Lila meeting her halfway and now Will moving in to make it three, the group hug lingers, but only because there is already some love.

Art walks them to the back door, Lila stays behind. May disappears first out the door but before Will can do the same he and Art shake hands, it seems they both have something to say but do not, it's a respectful nod and handshake man-hug that says "good night, Art, see you in the a.m."

Art lets the door close gently by itself.

It was a restless night and for obvious reasons, although there was one reason far less obvious than the rest. The fountain where Ryson spilled coffee danced in and out of his head all night long.

At 6:32 a.m., Ryson orders a hopscotch double whammy no whip cream, venti, and can already see the fountain for which he came.

Ryson's approach to the fountain is in more of a head down position, although he has come to see what sleep could not chase from his head it was the coffee stain that seemed to steal his focus, and also how bleach white the concrete is that surrounds this fountain, it looks as if it was poured this morning, except, of course, for this horrid coffee graffiti now at his feet.

It's the sound a sprinkler makes burping out the air that has filled its pipes that draws Ryson's head and focus up at the fountain just in time to see water jettisoned from the very top of such a magnificent creation. He now stands silently and slack-jawed in awe and a little weak in the knees.

The site before him towers another ten or twelve feet even beyond his own reach. It's an impressive fountain to say the least, its depiction and grandeur is clearly with intent and purpose, as to what that may be is not quite sure.

The fountain itself from base to highest point is surely close to thirty feet, the base maybe sixty feet in circumference, the other two tiers share the same thickness just slightly less in diameter, on top of and kind of to one side of this three tiered, circular, slightly staggered tower stands three large Thor-type hammer's, hammer side up, and they are placed in a triangle using a little over half of the space on the very top tier.

Standing on these hammers are several children with their arms stretched high over their heads slightly wider than their shoulders, the palms of their hands are turned up but their heads and faces are not.

There is a large globe of the planet resting in their palms evenly spaced so they all share and support the weight. And from the top of the globe several streams of water arc out and down into the lower tier, which is surrounded by the collecting pool.

There are two other children on the top tier of the fountain, they are set off to the farther edge and are holding hands, they seem to be in an animated position as if they are running towards the other children and the globe. All the children with obvious joy and happiness on their tiny little faces.

The whole fountain is covered in small handprints and on the base, there is a plaque that reads "freedom to be, if not for them, then who?"

The depiction and reasoning for this fountain no longer eludes Ryson, it's an obvious statement and one he can no doubt connect with, this moves him and he lowers his head, eyes still open and again, he is greeted by his own caffeine graffiti, the only stain on a pearl white carpet of cement.

When Ryson tries to leave a one-hundred-dollar bill with the manager of the coffee house in hopes the stain can be removed, she informs him there is already a fifty-dollar bill in the cash register for this very same reason. The woman who owns the property and also maintains the fountain refused to take the money and said, "My father would want it this way."

"It's a kind gesture, sir, but your stain is not the first and I suspect it will not be the last."

Ryson smiles and is speechless, not because he was unable to speak, there just did not seem to be anything else to say.

He walks the couple of minutes it takes to get to Redline Financial quite slowly as his head is in a very strange place, knowing quite well he and that fountain share a destiny.

Ryson taps lightly on the front door of Redline, it's early, and in some strange way, he still has hopes he will wake from this nightmare soon. Lila comes through a curtain and to the front door, he watches her do so and stifles the screams in his head.

"Good morning, Ryson," they hug. "Morning, Lila. Come have a bagel to go with that coffee, Ryson."

Lila turns and heads back from where she came, he follows.

From the other side of the curtain, the voices of Art, May, and Will signify he is the last one here. Lila takes his hand and the two walk in together.

Morning to all and to all hugs and kisses, with the greetings complete Lila continues to set out some dishes.

Art and Lila seem to be more nervous and on edge than the three that are actually leaving, Art tells everybody to sit down and eat something, including Lila.

Ryson, May, and Will dig right in, Art and Lila do use the plate in front of themselves but only pick at what they've deposited.

Art from his seated position places a legal-size envelope in front of Ryson, May and Will and as he does so he tells them what's in it.

"In there, you will find the name of the city and the hotel you should end up at, the text message number for our e-box and two thousand dollars in traveler's checks. I wish we were sending you with more support than this but for right now, it is what it is. Get a working local cell phone, establish communication, we will move forward from there."

When the airport shuttle driver knocks on the back door while loudly announcing who he is and also his intentions, there's a sense of relief in the room, saving the five of them from any further need for uncomfortable nervous chatter.

With the luggage loaded and the cars locked up, the three say goodbye to Art and Lila, promising to make it a quick trip.

As Art watches the shuttle leave the parking lot he has no doubt the three will comeback intact, what it is they can accomplish before doing so is now mostly up to them.

Lila is waiting for Art as he comes back inside, first, because she hates goodbyes, but mostly to inform Art that May and Will left the travelers checks behind, to which, Art replies, "Figured they would, just did not want Ryson to feel bad."

Lila smiles and hugs him, then lovingly whispers, "You've done the right thing, you've given him a chance."

The three sit quietly in the shuttle van for the first couple of miles, it is Will who finally breaks the silence.

"He stole Nixon's helicopter, Ryson, I think it's safe to say we are dealing with an extremely resourceful individual and I myself feel pretty confident in the fact that he can make things happen. And then there's Lila."

"I can speak from experience when I say, when it comes to brilliant mathematicians they see the world differently than the rest of us and I am damn glad she is on our side. But the point I am trying to make is that when we land in Paraguay, the three of us only have the three of us and if May and I get in any trouble, you, my friend, I call first. I would hope you would do the same. We go in together, we come out together."

May and Ryson spend the next few minutes playfully and even sometimes, laughingly, teasing Will about how they promise not to leave him behind, and if need be would be willing to take a small caliber bullet to the leg if that's what it comes down to, but really, nothing bigger than a .22.

They all three laugh, and indeed it does chase away some of the butterflies, but after it's funny, they do agree, we all leave together.

As they approach the international terminals, all agree, as we step from the shuttle van you don't know us and we don't know you, they quietly say goodbye, but never lose eye contact until actually seated on the plane.

Each in the same place, each going in the same direction, and yet neither of the three have any idea where this takes them.

Everything Poison

The smell brought with it a level of depression. The moment the outside air was no longer being filtered, it squeezed its way into the cabin unobstructed and well before they could reach the gate after landing. The odor itself truly was not all that unpleasant but it seemed to have an emotional component the three of them could not have prepared for.

They keep eye contact as long as possible through security and luggage pickup. When Ryson moves towards the stairs leading up and out of the terminal to the train platform, he glances back and winks then disappears.

Eleven minutes later, they purchase cell phones from different vendors almost at the exact same time.

One by one, they log into the e-box and almost instantly the three have messages waiting for a response, May responds first because her texting abilities, as Will always puts it, "Are a force to be reckoned with." Her fingers zip across the keys like she's owned that phone for months, Will is always kind of impressed, and again reminded of her gift of handheld electronics, Will shakes his head and proceeds to thumb his way through his own response.

Almost directly over Will and May's head on the third floor, Ryson is doing the same thing.

They all three respond with their messages of moving forward with a single digit number Art assigned to them and hit send. Ryson is on the train and seated, May and Will are now just exiting the parking garage in the minivan when the e-box and the local cell system processes and resends the messages to one and all. May's voice is pleasant even when truly annoyed, well... She glances at Will, it isn't going to be fast, but it will work. Will does not take his eyes off the road, instead, he takes one hand off the steering wheel placing it over May's hand she has resting on the seat and with a light squeeze, says, "We will just have to wait and see what you can do about that later, but right now, how far before my first turn?"

The train ticket was generic seating so the empty of the three boxcars Ryson chose and takes a seat. Half a second before movement an older woman and a young boy who is maybe thirteen perhaps, her grandson step through the still open door into Ryson's boxcar and quickly take seats behind him in the last row. The two of them barely getting settled before they begin to roll away.

It is 3:41 p.m. as May and Will get within a couple of blocks of the Marx Hotel in the city of King's Throne. They are met by what looks to be armed military personnel, the few cars that are on the road along with them are funneled into one lane and are told one at a time to turn around and leave the area, when it's Wills turn, it's obvious this is no time for questions and he just does as he's told.

It's less than a mile from the man with a gun and already May has the manager of the Marx Hotel on the phone, she's doing her best to understand the managers broken English, Will can tell this by the wrinkles in her forehead and squinty eyes. "Yes! We would like to make reservations," there is a short pause than a dumbfounded response from May, "no, no, no, today." Another short pause, then in a much quieter tone, but still confused, "We already have a car," now May's face goes stupid, it's a look Will has never seen before. For a minute or so, May just listens, eyes wide open and losing the forehead wrinkles. When May hits the end key and folds the phone closed, she tells Will to pull over.

There are several small villages along the way that Ryson could see from the train and each time the train would happen upon one, he found himself intently scanning the immediate area for any signs of life that does not belong.

The loud whistle that rattles the thin glass Ryson is staring through snaps his attention away from a mud shanty village in the distance to something closer to the train tracks, there's another whistle, it is just as loud as the first but shorter in duration.

The large sign in the distance and alongside the tracks appears to grow right from the earth, the obviously intentional effect is caused by a large dirt mound placed several yards in front of the sign. The sign is large maybe the face of a two-car garage, the large lettering is in blue, the background, a simple whitewash, what the words spell out is unclear because of the language, but the large emblems painted black in each corner are quite clear to Ryson, he knows the emblem from one Art had shown them.

103

When the train passes the sign, Ryson gets a glimpse at its twin on the other side of the train as it disappears along with the other somewhere behind them as they roll by, same sign, same dirt mound, same black logos in each corner. It's the logo of the new leader of the Neighbors Cradle territory and the paramilitary he has at his disposal to maintain his power and control. When Art first mentioned these things in the comfort of Redline Financial while chomping down cookies, it did not sound all that scary, but now Ryson finds himself gripped by sheer terror, he has every intention of barfing on the floor in front of himself and is already leaning forward to do so when there is a tapping on his right shoulder, the shoulder closest to the aisle. This not only of course startles him but also to his relief chases away the need to barf, for now.

Will pulls off the road into what he believes to be a gas station, putting the car in park but nervously leaves it running.

May is not saying anything, her focus is intently consumed by the small folding map they purchased before leaving the airport, May flips the map over and then just as fast flips it back again. Before Will can finish the same question the second time around, May quite calmly says, "Drive, drive now, be careful but be quick, we are going another couple of miles on this road, when it splits go right, now just start moving. I will fill you in on the way." Will fires another question even before they're back on the road, "Well, who was that on the phone?"

"That was the manager of the Marx Hotel, it seems one of the higher-ranking military officials is having a surprise birthday party for his wife. Evidently those that do not support the same political beliefs have in the past caused as he put it, damage, and even loss of life. He tells us to rent a car and sleep in it. When I told him we already have a car, he says stay off the main road and get out of the city, find a place to park some distance from the road, stay hidden, keep quiet, and no lights after dark. The last thing he says is, 'Do this. Maybe I see you tomorrow, check-in is at noon, be safe.'"

"Okay, so I guess we're getting the fuck out of dodge and I assume you already know the way," May smiles, Will knows this but does not have to look.

"Yes, dear, when the road splits go right and I guess we find a place to hide for the night," there is no more smiles, and again, Will does not have to look.

Ryson settles back into his seat more curious than concerned, the boxcars have no walk-through access from one to the other, it can only be the old woman or the young boy.

Ryson is confronted by both, they are standing right next to him, the young boy closer than the old woman. The old woman begins speaking so she and Ryson make eye contact, the Spanish dialect she is using seems old and broken but for the most part, he believes they are simply asking for money. He "*nada, denerros*" a couple of times but the old woman keeps talking.

Ryson finally decides to give her whatever change he has in his pocket, but before he can retrieve it, the old woman takes a small step towards him, now putting herself at equal distance between the three of them, then in one motion, she takes his hand with her right and the young boys with her left, then quite calmly joins the two before she lets go of both.

It's only a second or two before Ryson withdraws his hand moving it away from the aisle, the boys hand falls limp at his side, Ryson can obviously tell there is a message here of some sort but he's just not getting it, so when the old woman now takes the young boys other hand, turning him slightly towards Ryson and placing the boy's palm on Ryson's chest, he lets her.

The woman does not let go of the young boy's wrist, instead, she forces the boys hand to make a small rubbing motion, the young boy is lethargic and will not make eye contact. Clearly, if the woman let's go, the boy's hand and arm fall back to his side.

The old woman's voice now gets a little sharp, she quietly barks a few words at the boy as she leans in to him lifting her left knee and placing it squarely with obvious force into the boy's hip. There is a thump and the child cringes with a slight wither in both legs, the woman now let's go of the boy's wrist and his hand stays on Ryson's chest.

There is a part of Ryson and even still at this point that is clinging desperately to ignorance and denial but when the boy rubs across Ryson's breasts and nipples, then begins to move further down his chest, he goes cold.

The message slams home with the kick of a mule, Ryson, now weak, kneed comes to his feet and into the aisle, he nudges the boy harmlessly out of the way while doing so.

Before the old woman can step away from Ryson, he grabs her by the wrist and forearm holding her in place, he is now standing over her, the woman's head is down and she is refusing to look up.

He can feel the old woman trembling, he knows she has already surrendered to the justifiable wrath she so completely deserves. And when he first stood up, this was no doubt his intention.

Its Art's voice and the laughter of his own children bouncing around the inside of his head that stops him from delivering a fatal blow to the back of the woman's neck.

Eye on the prize, Ryson, eye on the prize. Art could no way have predicted this scenario but the statement still holds true.

So, yeah, Ryson would rather leave this woman beaten, bloodied and dead, but for the sake of his own children, he does not, instead, he tells her when I get off this boy is coming with me.

It's clear the old woman hears this because she agrees with the nodding of her head, Ryson then allows her to slither back to the seat from which she came; the young boy, he sits across the aisle from him.

"How far from the city should we get?"

These were the first words spoken in several minutes from either one of them.

Before May can answer this question the two of them see something in the road on their left side, it's not far and it is not moving, Will slows down as they get close, when they are close enough to see color, now they can tell it is a small two-door car that has been burned almost beyond recognition.

Will has to use the other side of the road to get by this heavily charred auto as they slowly roll past now they can see that the driver is still in the car slumped in the driver seat and being the same color and consistency as the rest of the burned out car.

Will decides they have gone far enough and makes a U-turn, he glances at May and says, "Maybe, we should find something closer to the city," as they roll past the charred wreckage and remains the second time, May agrees, "We should head back a wee bit."

It's only a few miles into the retreat when May at first utters to herself, "That looks promising," then in the next moment her suspicions are correct. "You see that, Will, right there, that looks good. What do you suppose the odds are we can back this little van into one of those cement sewer sections over there?"

Will is already thinking the same thing when he pulls off the road and then alongside the four large sections of cement sewer line. From the looks of things, and by the way a small river is already flowing and rusting away, these large cement sections are surely replacements for the drainage system currently in place under this part of the road, but for now, a nice place to hide from whatever evil happens to stroll by.

It's going to be a tight squeeze and they may have to sacrifice a side view mirror, once they get the van inside, they will not be able to open the doors but they decide that's okay, it will be dark soon and just before that, they will back in and call it a night.

Ryson is sitting somewhat sideways as to keep peripheral contact with the old woman, there has been no further conversations or even eye contact for the last few uphill miles of the ride, Ryson did try to communicate with the young boy a couple of times but in both instances, the boy was unresponsive and he seemed unwilling to even attempt communication.

The train lurches forward, speeds up, slows down, and now is pulling into the station, this all happens in a minute or two and is quite a nauseating approach.

The train comes up into the platform, leaving the exit and door level with the ground outside as the train continues to slow but has not yet come to a stop, the young boy leaps to his feet, a couple of strides and he's now at the door, without looking back, he is through the door and away. Ryson comes to his feet startled and surprise and is not sure if he should give chase, but before he can step into the center aisle, the old woman with the speed and agility of a gazelle, body checks him, sending Ryson first against the window and wall than onto the floor, dizzy and confused.

The old woman does not wait to see if her check was completely successful, her stride never changes, she is through the door and in the same direction as the young boy, Ryson sees her disappear just as he gets to his feet.

When the whole thing comes to a stop, he bravely exits the train, although he does so with paranoid caution, looking both ways.

The first stop the train makes is here, "Valley East station," the second stop is West station. Ryson decides the hotel that is within walking distance of where he is now sounds like a much better choice than getting back on that train, providing he can make the short walk un-accosted. On the short walk to the hotel, he realized he would actually feel better had they clubbed him over the head, took his money, and all his luggage.

May and Will spend the hour or so before dusk rearranging the van, doing their best to turn it into a very small hotel room, knowing well enough once they go back into the cement sewer section, they're not coming out until daybreak.

At dusk, they climb in and as May playfully put it, "You dance this wagon into the smokehouse, cowboy." Will does just that, scraping both mirrors along the inside of the pipe but leaving them intact and still attached.

There's a chair and table just inside the door, Ryson drops his bags on the floor next to it and then his bruised body and withered soul in the chair. He watches the door close and lock on its own then glancing around the room, the one and only question the girl at the front counter asked him when he checked in is now even more confusing. She asked him if he wanted access to the live feed in his room, he said yes because he could hear Art saying, "There will be a lot to learn, try not to miss anything," but he never asked her just what that meant. And now looking around the room, he realizes there's no T.V.

When Ryson's new phone comes to life in his pocket, the hypnotic state he is in is not shattered until the second round of chirps and vibrations. The messages come in one at a time in the order in which they were sent, and each message ending in a number between one and five, the number signifying who of the five sent it. The first message reads "Spending the night in the minivan, not by choice, but we are okay, checking in tomorrow at noon, we hope, good night, be safe all. Love, 4-5."

Message two reads "That was one of the reasons for the minivan, shelter was a consideration, be careful, be smart, love, 1-2. P.S., no word on three, yet."

Following suit and keeping it simple, Ryson's message reads, "Wow! was quite the day but no worse for wear. Checked in at first stop, room eight. Love you all,3."

The lobby is quiet and the check-in counter empty when Ryson comes through at 9:30 a.m. the next morning. There is a sign as he approaches the front door, it's in half a dozen different languages, fourth one down from the top, he can read "Café a.m." and an arrow indicating out the door than left.

The smell of hot coffee lures him down the street and idle chatter guides him the rest of the way. The small café lends itself to that of a country cottage and for a moment, sparks a sense of normalcy like Ryson's just a few blocks from home, but one quick glance through the menu as he pulls up a seat at one of the outside tables reminds him he's a long way from where he was just a few days ago, and just as far from home. He orders what he can pronounce, it's all very good, he leaves nothing behind, except the tip.

Ryson sticks to the main road in and out of town to start his hunt for these so-called gentlemen's clubs. As he passes the occasional side-street or alley, it is all he can do to just slow down long enough to get a quick peek. The anxiety and intrepid intimidation is something he is just not used to.

Maybe a mile or so, he plays this peek-a-boo game with the alleys and side-streets, then crosses to the other side, heading back towards the hotel.

On a post in an alley just a few feet from the walkway, there is a hand-bill, its depiction catches his attention, he cannot read the caption until he is standing right in front of it, but the image is of young kids, boys and girls, dressed in evening wear, tuxedos, and beaded gowns. The ages looking to be maybe nine or ten and up to perhaps twelve or thirteen they appear to be standing on a fashion runway as if in a fashion show. Ryson moves in closer to read the print "Preteen burlesque show." And at the very bottom of the bill in smaller print, it reads, "Brought to you by the Zirana Family Troop."

In a strange sort of way, visually, it does not seem all that corrupt but the word preteen is obviously a draw to the young, the longer Ryson stands here, the more comfortable he becomes with being here, so now he starts to really look around. There is no address or location on the hand bill or an indicator as to how long it's been here so he steps back out to the walkway continuing in his direction and search.

Ryson is standing across the street from his hotel fighting the last lingering bits of anxiety when his phone chirps like a car alarm, it was the only ring tone available. The message is simple and expected but the strength it provides him is a much needed breath of fresh air, and could not have come at a better time.

"We finally got checked in, all is okay, moving forward, 4-5."

Ryson smiles, he feels the two of them being a part of this, and that makes him instantly feel not so alone.

Ryson turns to his left and now begins to walk the main road that travels towards the other end of town. On the last intersecting side-street, he pauses, not seeing any reason to continue because there is no other structures past this point, he again crosses the street putting himself on the same side as the hotel but only a couple of miles further up the road.

The building that sits on the corner where Ryson is now standing appears to be just a large wall with three small side-by-side windows along the top edge, strange though, is the circus like paint job also along the top edge, it's clearly a weak attempt at a mock circus tent but you get the message. There is no door on this side, so he walks around the corner and down several feet before he comes to what looks like an entrance.

The two, small steel doors are recessed into the wall leaving them flush with the building, and on each side of the doors are movie like posters inside, permanent frames attached to the wall, one near each door. The arched circus like print over the doors, reads. Fashion Circus. Young Fashion on Parade and a hand-painted picture right below the lettering. The scene is strange, to say the least, all of the circus background stuff looks quite normal, except everything else in the picture are kids, where there should be animals, lions, and announcers there's just kids dressed in small sequined and beaded attire, and for sure all of the outfits are extremely skimpy. At the very bottom of the picture it reads "Troop Lazzar."

There are two paper clocks one on each door and on both the time being displayed is 4:00 p.m. Clearly, Ryson is early to the party.

When Ryson is within just a couple of storefronts before his hotel, there in a window of what might be a small movie theater hangs a large poster. The first words are. Coming soon. And under that it reads "Troop Six, living Dolls." There are no pictures or images just the lettering, then at the very bottom it reads "one third the sign of the devil." The printing sort of arcs over a small triangle with a fist in the center, there is something very disturbing about this poster and what it might represent. Ryson walks away nauseous and not in a real big hurry to find out why.

When he gets back to the hotel and in his room it's dark, oddly though, because he left the curtain open. And now on the table, just inside the door, sits a small portable radio.

Ryson knows he owes the group a text, it's not his favorite thing, so he chooses to sit in the dark and just say what he feels.

"Here is where it seems as though the world has sent everything poison. I'm okay and out and about. Also moving forward. Be safe all. 3."

There is no response from either of the other four. It's best to just leave that one alone.

The first number May dials rings twice then goes to voicemail, not prepared for leaving a message she hangs up. The second number, still not prepared for leaving a message, she is for just a second relieved somebody picks up, but even that second is gone quickly when the woman on the other end answers with, "Your child or mine, child placement and relocation services, how can I help you?"

Mays mind stumbles and draws a disgusted blank, she shakes her head in contempt and manages a reply.

"Yes, good afternoon. I believe my husband and I would like to make an appointment, we are in town for a couple of days and hoping somehow that could work out before we have to go."

There is genuine dislike already with this woman over the phone and her quickness to accommodate makes her that much more unlikable, but one word unsettles May more than the rest. At some point, during their short conversation, May believes she hears this woman refer to the children as product, it's in Spanish, so May is not quite sure of its content, so she lets it go. But now sitting in the same room and just across a small table from the same woman, she spoke to on the phone, she says it again, but this time her reference to the children under her care and protection as product, May hears quite clearly.

Will, who is sitting to May's left, remains dimwitted and trying to stick to the program, but when May leans to him with her mouth almost in his ear, he's thinking this might be a problem.

May does her best to whisper, but her attempt to conceal her displeasure is difficult as she says to Will, "If this filthy bitch refers to these children one more time as product, sure to Christ, I'm going to take off one of these high heels and stab her right through the fucking heart."

Will turns to May big eyed and stiff jawed, then back to this horror of a woman on the other side of the table, "I'm sorry but we are going to have to cut this appointment short," Will is not lying when he says. "It seems my significant other is still not feeling well, it was a rough flight and then a long night as well, we'll see ourselves out."

There is a rare uncomfortable silence between the two as they make the short walk back to the minivan, the minivan chirps and the locks pop as Will grabs the handle of the sliding door, pulling at first, then allowing it to fully open on its own, he already has the thin over-shirt he was wearing off and is now fanning it in and out of the minivan door, attempting to exchange the dense urine vapor cloud that accumulates when they lock it up in hopes of circulating some fresher air before they get in.

111

May is still at a distance and stopped when will turns to her and says, "We're even now. You get one, I get one." They share a look of self-contempt and May responds with, "Fair enough."

Will smiles first and says, "All right, so what's next?"

There is a short brick wall separating the gravel walkway May and Will use to get to and from the minivan and the building they just came out of, so May takes a seat. She does not answer Will, instead she leaves a message, "Good afternoon, my name is Misha Bloom, my husband and I are in town for a couple of days and would love to meet with you, we are looking to adopt young twins and came across your number. Sorry for the late request hope you can help. My cell number is 881-5665. We are staying at the Marx Hotel. Thank you."

Both May and the machine finish at the same time.

May smug and like she already has a plan says, "We go there when she calls back, should have left a message the first time. But tell them it's about local intel, don't you think?"

Will on board and already pulling the sliding door closed, "Yeah, let's start with every newspaper and magazine rack in this city."

May climbs in holding her breath, not exhaling until she gets the door closed and the window down, "Absolutely, let's start with the hotel then head back towards the airport."

"On your directions my love, I shall pilot, and you as my compass."

"Yeah, whatever, just drive." A few seconds later, May complains, "It still stinks in here."

Then Will, "Yeah, well, you were going to stab somebody through the heart with your shoe."

They laugh, May more so than Will.

It's 5:30 p.m. when Ryson turns off the small portable radio and the room surrenders to silence. Two hours of that madness is all he has time for, he understood some and even took some notes, one thing for sure; this guy in charge down here, absolutely a madman. Goes by the name Vinzaya and pretty sure it means, I'm a fucking madman. Listening to him over the radio or even in person, no doubt the conclusion is always going to be the same. A fucking madman.

Ryson exits the hotel full of dread and bowel churning anticipation. The dread he is quite sure he can deal with, as for the other, only time will tell.

112

When Ryson turns the corner, he is quite startled and for a second, his legs and feet attempt to move in reverse on their own, but he is not surprised. The large man perched on a stool outside the door holding a Mac 10 machine pistol in his lap is what he sort of expected.

It was quiet here this morning, and now he wishes he had taken a better look around. Only half the double steal door is open as the man with a gun is in front of the closed half, as for the open half, it is wedged with a small piece of wood at the bottom, holding it open against the wall, leaving the entrance a dark void where only sound seems able to escape.

The music spilling from the dark entrance Ryson can hear as he gets close, this approach to the door and man with a gun is done so with caution, fear, and a churning in his bowel, like he's trying to make soup.

The music seems to be a slow Latin rumba but with some strange circus overtones dubbed in, it's a bizarre mix of sounds and rhythms like that which you would hear ooze from Satan's own jukebox.

When they are within speaking distance, man with a gun mumbles something in Spanish, making sure he has Ryson's attention, then says, "Troop Lazzar."

Ryson remembers the name from the posters on either side of the door he now stands in front of. He answers, "*si*." Man with the gun now flicks his head, giving him permission to enter the darkened doorway. He does so without haste, pretending as though he's done this before.

Six feet inside the doorway Ryson is met with a black wall, a dead end to his right and then a short hallway ending with a closed curtain to his left. From the curtain at the end of the hallway, there is some small beams of light sneaking past the obvious obstruction but it's the sound coming from the devils phonograph that tells him, "Go that way."

The curtain feels like thick burlap and is actually in three pieces, Ryson pauses before pushing through the nearest slit. Here, again, he is faced with another life changing moment, and he knows it.

He bravely steps through, letting the thick burlap curtain close behind him. And where he once stood, he now leaves a small part of himself, and he knows it.

It's a large room with a mixture of L.E.D., incandescent, and black light, casting shadows and causing concealment to different parts of the room. The few areas the light does find is enough to give him a sense of size and layout of the room. The only thing well-lit and fully exposed is a raised walkway at the other end of the room. The room is more long than wide and the walkways layout is that of a wishbone, allowing the V section to spread and stretch to mid room, leaving only a few feet before the wall and the ends of the walkways.

The whole thing is approximately four feet high and the back straight section ends at a curtain just before the far back wall. There is a spotlighted sign hanging from the ceiling in front of the curtain that reads "Troop Lazzar."

As much as Ryson would like to sit at one of the several tables scattered about with his back towards the raised walkway he does not. He chooses one of the empty tables closest to him where he sits with his eyes on both, the raised walkway and the burlap curtain he just came through.

There are others about, some at tables, a couple occupying stools alongside the raised walkway, and two or three just standing around, mostly men but for sure, some women as well.

The raised walkway is empty but he can tell he just missed something, and when a short older man comes out from the curtain at the back of the room onto the raised walkway with a mop and a small bucket, he is quite sure he is okay with his own late arrival.

Mop man locates whatever he was looking for towards the center of the V section and quickly gets to work, Ryson trying not to imagine what he is cleaning up attempts to avert his attention, and that's when the smell comes. The two odors he has never found unpleasant in their own right but now to smell them purposely joined together clogs his throat, leaving him to only take short quick breaths.

The voice behind him and at his left ear is close enough to feel the warm breath of the man quietly speaking into it. There is a disturbing politeness to the voice and it forces Ryson to stop breathing all together.

"Sir, you are sitting at one-hundred-dollar table, move if you would like, if not, it comes with a free drink, what would you like me to have sent over?"

Ryson struggles with enough breath to reply, so instead, slides a $100 traveler's check towards the voice and waits.

That next voice he hears behind him is a woman's. She is standing more to his left then behind so when she says, "Can I get you something to drink?"

He turns slightly left to not only answer her but see her as well.

After ordering a ginger-ale extra ice and a cigar, the next breath he takes, again, allows the combined smells of fertilizer and baby powder to once more permeate his throat and lungs, there's a slightly visible reaction he just can't avoid.

Without warning or announcement, all the lights are dimmed, except those outlining the raised walkway, when the music gets louder, he can hear somebody clapping up closer to the walkway, but cannot see who.

When the two young girls push a large, circus theme, decorated chest through the curtain and onto the straight section of the raised walkway, they hesitate, but only long enough for somebody to turn the music down to about half of what it was, now they continue to push until they reach the intersection of all three wishbone pieces.

When the two girls stop pushing and the chest comes to a rest, the three of them are only a few feet from the edge. The music levels down a little more. Now the two girls step around to the front of the chest and are facing one another, leaving themselves sideways to the audience, there are no words being exchanged, they just stand there quietly.

The spotlight on the sign over the walkway now moves down and along the same path the girls and the chest, stopping only when it has fully illuminated all three.

Even without the spotlight, Ryson could see quite clearly. The two, young girls are very young, probably nine or ten. One blonde and the other brown hair. They are dressed in pullover T-shirts and short skirts, no shoes or socks.

The music now levels up a wee bit and the girls turn to face the chest, putting their backs now to the audience. The music slowly fades and with its exit, a silence in its place.

The tiny voices aloft on such frail sounding nuance reaches Ryson's ears not as words but instead, just as simple giggles, whispers, and moans. These sounds are coming from the two young girls as they reach together and open the lid of the chest, allowing the lid to hold open on its own as they let go and together they make sounds of wonder and delight.

From the chest, they both retrieve small articles of clothing that have been covered in beads and multi-colored sequence, the outfits are just smaller versions of circus costumes, they take turns holding up a piece or two, and now it seems they plan on trying some of it on, because the two, while still making silly little girl sounds, begin to undress.

Both young girls still have their backs to the audience and are completely nude before they start trying on the small circus costumes, and for the next 30 minutes, they proceed to mix and match these articles of clothing while the whole time appearing to be in playful bliss, complete with giggles and laughter. The two girls are not shy in their behavior, exposing their body is their intention.

Most of that thirty minutes Ryson spent staring at the wrinkles in the stained cloth covering his table as the show went on. What's in his head as this happens is only anger, disgust, and contempt.

The lights and music again take life and fill the room, causing him to cautiously reengage his surroundings, the two and their chest are just now disappearing through the curtain as the spotlight moves up and again illuminating the large sign hanging over the walkway. And on the table, in front of him, sits, to his surprise, the ginger-ale and cigar he ordered.

From behind and towards his right, there is a loud voice, it cracks slightly louder than the music that's playing, not completely sure what he says the first time, but when he says it again Ryson turns to see who it is.

"Youth on the floor!" is what Ryson hears from the same man that was outside on the stool say as he now stands just inside the same curtain Ryson used to get in here. He seems pretty serious and is still clutching the Mac 10 in both hands.

Ryson was already planning a stealthy exit but when gun boy shows up, he realizes it's best to just sit quietly at the table.

Towards the back of the room he can see movement but because of their size he can't quite make out what it is when the two girls are at about mid-room he can tell it's the same two that were just playing dress-up, and now they are moving from table to table with a small decorative basket and as they do, the basket begins to fill with money.

When it's his turn, he'd rather take a bullet, he does not know how much he gives them but when one of the girls says, "Thank you," in a voice, so young and adapted he shivers in sadness and despair. He does not have the willpower to say you're welcome.

Ryson attempts to use small non-suspicious head movement as he goes back to planning his escape, man with a gun is still standing at the exit curtain even after the two girls have finished their collecting and disappeared from where they came. But now, it seems, as though, he's waiting for something.

When the lights dim, Ryson's heart skips a beat, he sneaks a peek at the exit and yeah, gun man is still there. The music comes up slowly; it's different now than what it's been since he got here. It still sounds like something from El Diablos boombox, just no more Latin rhythm, but much more sinister circus sounds with the occasional muffled lion roar thrown in.

Movement from the spotlight draws Rison's attention back to the raised walkway, the spotlight drops straight down from the large sign stopping to illuminate the curtain at the back of the walkway. Somebody slides a colored filter in front of the spotlight, causing the light to slightly diminish in its intensity while adding a bluish haze to the beam.

A small boy steps through the curtain, holding something in both hands at chest height, he and the blue haze together continue moving forward, when they reach the same space where the two girls and their chest played, the boy and the beam stop. The child looks seven, maybe eight, but could be a little older, he's dressed in a lion tamer's outfit, minus the whip. In his hand is a large plate and, on the plate, looks to be a raw piece of red meat, the boy stands statue.

The music does not change in volume but somehow, the lion roars become louder and more frequent. The little boy looks nervous and afraid. He does not look up when movement begins several feet over his head.

On a thin rope, there is a phone booth size structure covered in some sort of almost transparent material being lowered from the ceiling directly over the little boy, there is no bottom to the structure, so, as it is lowered, it appears to consume the child.

When this structure comes to a stop, a large bright light from somewhere behind it explodes into a white beam of intense shadow, casting affect illuminating the inside of the structure so completely, and even though the young figure inside is dark his shadow and outline on the thin material covering the structure is so clear you can see his eyelashes flutter when he blinks.

The young boy is still statue when a dark shadow begins to grow at his feet, the darkness grows in width and height quickly, stretching to a couple of feet over the boy's head and a couple of feet from the top of the structure.

When this darkness finally takes motion inside the structure and begins to circle the little boy, now you can tell that it's a naked man dressed in lion accents, large furry collar, lion ears, paws, and even a tale.

The first full circle lion man makes around the boy, he drops the plate of raw meat, now the lion man continues his slow cat like circles around the young boy and each time removing a piece of the child's clothing, and this, in turn, is clearly arousing lion man.

Ryson, in a glance, panic checks the exit and is ready to just bolt, but what he sees freezes him to this place in further disgust and hatred.

Gun man, who is still standing at the exit curtain, has this bizarre look on his face as if he is in some sort of sadistic trance with what's happening with the little boy and lion man so much so he now has the gun in one hand while allowing the other hand to plunge deep into a front pocket, and it's obvious by the space required, he is not counting his change.

Ryson turns back to the table, the stains, the wrinkles, the pain. He drifts deep enough in his own house of torment that when the music stops and the lights come back on he is genuinely startled, he looks up and towards the raised walkway just in time to see the cloth frame structure reach its highest point and then fold itself tightly against the ceiling. The raised walkway is empty and the spotlight now back where it belongs.

A quick glance at his exit, he slides out his chair, and is glad gun man is gone.

There is no call for youth on the floor, so he leaves another hundred on the table, hoping to not offend anyone, and hopefully, this aids in a clean getaway.

Two steps into his escape Ryson is slowed and then stopped by a voice behind him, the disturbing politeness is the same voice that informed him as to the price of his table when he first sat down.

Ryson quietly turns and confronts the voice because the question seems harmless enough, and he would like to put a face to this person.

"If it's the restrooms you're looking for, there the other way."

"Nope, I just have somewhere else I need to be," as he says this, the two of them are face to face with only a couple of feet of separation. The dark skinned, slinky piece of shit that now stands in front of Ryson smiles and says, "I hope you found the show to your liking, and the table is yours for the night if you would like to return later."

Ryson does his best to seem almost embarrassed as he leans in somewhat to this piece of shit and quietly states, I was looking for something younger.

Without hesitation, P.O.S. reaches into his back pocket and withdraws a yellow poker chip, and as he hands this to Ryson, he says, "Tomorrow night, six o'clock out front, you give this chip to one of the cabs and fifty bucks, he will take you someplace where you might find something perhaps, more to your liking."

Ryson takes the chip with a slight nod but without questions, turns, and walks towards the exit curtain.

He can already see gun man on his stool, even before he steps through the opening and onto the sidewalk, and apparently, gun man can see him as well because gun man starts talking to him before Ryson can reach the sunlight.

"Hey, man! Don't tell me you're leaving already friend, you're going to miss the best stuff you leave now."

Ryson mumbles as he steps out and onto the sidewalk, "Yeah, maybe next time." He is a few feet past gun man when he ears him say more to himself, then Ryson, "Next act, she really does pee."

Before Ryson turns the corner, he looks back at gun man and knows when he comes back for that Mac 10, he leaves a dead man as payment.

Ryson forgoes dinner and instead finds a dark corner where he and a cigar spend the next two hours trying to be any other place but here. At 9:20 p.m., the sites sounds and smells of this filthy city finally chase him back to the hotel.

In a slap to the face and a kick to the groin sort of way, they both wished it had not been this easy. But it seems that child abuse is quite the lucrative industry in parts of this country.

There were three easily spotted newsstands on the way to the airport and one less than a block away from the terminal they came out of. All four shared similar material, but the one nearest the airport actually had material regarding adoption agencies.

May first, then Will agrees, "Let's find some food and a place we can sit and go through some of this stuff before we head back."

The park they found was just a couple of blocks away from a sandwich shop and in hindsight, had they known this, they would have eaten there and not in the van, Will throws what's left of the chicken carcass in a fire pit several feet from the bench where May is just now taking up residence.

Halfway back to the bench, May gets a call and answers. It's good news Will can tell by her reaction and the fact she is already taking notes, Will hears the last of the conversation before he sits next to her and begins to read the notes she has taken. Before May hangs up, she jots down a name and address she has circled in one of the ads in the paper she has opened in front of her,

119

tapping this circled ad, she then, in her most polite tone, says, "Thank you very much, we will see you tomorrow at two. Again, thank you so much."

That was the call back from the message I left using the other number Art gave us. And when she introduced herself, she did so as simply siblings and it's the same place as this ad right here, May again taps the circled ad, saying, "They specialize in finding homes for twins."

The two sit, sifting through the rest of the papers, sometimes silently, sometimes not, "This is the second time I've seen this same ad," Will circles it and slides the paper towards May, she now glances down and reads the ad out loud, "Infant adoption and rescue," and in small print, it also reads "twins and triplets." May dials the number and waits to leave a message. The man's voice that picks up barks a welcome like a hungry Pitbull, it startles May and she almost drops phone.

"Sorry about that, the girls are out of the office and I really hate answering these damn phones." Pitbull tames down some and then, a little softer, he says, "Infant adoption and rescue, how can I help you?"

"That's all right, I am no great lover of the phone myself," May sort of fake giggles and even though it is fake, there is an attractive quality to it, meaning there is a male on the other end of the phone, Will knows this and sits quietly.

"Hello, my name is Misha Bloom, my husband and I are in town for a couple of days and would like to talk to somebody about adopting."

May here's only silence. The better part of a minute ticks by before May finally and quietly says, "Hello?"

"Okay, it looks like they have an opening tomorrow at 11 a.m., that work for you?"

That's the second time she almost drops her phone during this conversation, Will can't help but chuckle at least a little bit.

"That's fine, tomorrow, 11 a.m. Thank you so much."

May pats Will on the knee and they both nod with acceptance.

May closes her phone and sets it in her lap, she unfolds the new map and spreads it across the table, using a pen she circles an area on the map called East Ridge.

"Tomorrow morning, right there." May taps at the spot she just circled, "The second appointment is in the same place, maybe 15 minutes away. This West Ridge area is on this road but it looks like it's going to take quite a while to get there, don't you think?"

May now slides the bulk of the map closer to Will.

"Well, best guess would be," Will looks at his watch then mumbles as he uses his thumb to count across the map, "every inch is an hour and 10 minutes. From here probably with a few minutes to spare, it's three hours, making it four hours from our hotel. I would say average speed maybe 60 mph, which puts us leaving the hotel tomorrow morning at 6 a.m. That gives us an hour for any delays."

"So with that said, my dear, we should probably be heading back."

Will starts to fold the map, May interrupts, "Wait! Look at this one." On the back page of what looks like a propaganda periodical similar to a National Enquirer is the only ad in it with any color. The lettering and border is in blue. Before Will reads it, he comments, "Why pay extra for color only to have it placed on the back page?"

Now he reads it, "Peas And Pods Adoption," and in quotation, "share your happiness."

"It's on the way back, let's stop and check it out," May says this but Will does not answer back. "What, Will?"

"Well, first off, there's no phone number, just an address, second, there is just something real fucking wrong about this place and now we are going to show up unannounced, I'm not saying we are not going, I'm just saying, something fucked up about it."

May completely trusts Will's instincts and they agree, they will both be on high alert.

They do not even have to pull off the road, Will simply moves to the dirt shoulder and comes to a stop. They are both speechless for several seconds. May cracks first, "How the hell did we miss that?"

"There's no way we missed that, May, that had to have happened in the time since we drove past, maybe a couple of hours ago."

The single-story structure sits on a side street with three other structures that look just like it, they are all clearly numbered, so it's obvious the structure that looks like hell rose from its bowels and chewed free from the inside out is the place they were looking for, the structures on either side did not share the same fate, there is some minor damage but it appears to be collateral.

"Well, one thing for sure, that was not an accident, that's a message. Nobody causes that much damage and sees to it, it remains standing without maliciously making a statement, and whatever was inside is most likely still there," when Will says this, he is already starting the van.

As they drive away, they are both thinking the same thing and neither one chooses to say it out loud.

It's almost dark when they get back to their hotel in King's Throne and they, too, forgo dinner, May takes a two-hour bath, Will just sits quietly.

It's 9:35 when Will hits send, his text reads, "I can only hope that tomorrow brings with it better than what it delivered today. Good night all. 5."

May responds first, "He is such a girl. Good night all. 4."

Ryson next, and it's the one they have all been waiting for, "I believe in balance, therefore, at some point, it has to get better, good night. 3."

Art and Lila text as one, "Be safe, sleep tight. Tomorrow the sun will rise. 1.2."

Culture shock comes in many forms, the one Ryson is currently dealing with, I believe goes by the name, Montezuma's revenge, even before the sun came up, the race was already on to see which orifice could produce the most foul substance. By six a.m., he was already referring to the toilet as an old friend.

Will could not shovel the frijoles in fast enough. "One thing for sure, no one's going hungry in this hotel," he says this in-between bites. May would agree if she wasn't busy working her way through a stack of fresh tortillas.

They gather what they didn't eat and along with some bottled water, pack what they can for the ride.

At 11 a.m., Ryson, out of desperation, turns on the live feed radio in hopes the sheer volume of stupidity will somehow interrupt the 20-minute intervals of projectile secretions. Oddly enough, it does seem to help.

They both sit sharing the same face of confused disbelief, twice they both attempt to speak at the same time and each time instead they fall silent.

Will finally put's the key in the ignition but has no intentions of starting the van. He's the first to gather enough composure to say what he thinks just happened, "So, let me get this straight, for $35,000 dollars we can purchase twins, boys or girls, as young as four years old from the photos we just saw, and who are all locals to somewhere in South America. Or we can leave a $10,000 dollar deposit and when something younger comes by and not from around here, they call us, and for fifty or sixty thousand dollars, they become ours, but with no way or help in getting them out of the country. Oh, and let's not forget that the fair skinned infants will cost the most."

This is only the second time in all the years he's known her that Will has seen May cry.

"Give me your shoe, May, I will go stab that filthy beast of a woman through the heart myself."

At first there is no response from May, but once she thinks about it for a moment, she believes he would. The thought makes her smile and begins to dry up the tears.

"Oh sure, still my thunder. Listen pee boy, it's my shoe, I get to do all the stabbin' with it. Now, how about you just drive, handsome."

They share what was left of breakfast in between appointments and do attempt to strategize before the next meeting.

At 12:50 p.m., Ryson has now surrendered and is simply staying put over the toilet. By two, his legs are numb and he's forced to get up and move around to replenish blood supply to the lower extremities.

When twenty minutes slip uneventfully by without a scurry to the commode, he, in many hours, is finally sitting comfortably in a chair and not fearing the next wave of evil discharge.

"Simply siblings, my ass, there was nothing fuckin simple about that," May says this to herself out loud and even before Will is back to the van, but after she has already closed her door and has the A.C. running.

When Will gets back to the van, he cannot, no matter his effort, seem not out of breath, sucking wind like an out of shape mall cop, he plops in the driver seat only focused on the accuracy of the A.C. vents, "Fuck me, May," like a damn rabbit you are.

"Hey, the bet was, I said the stairs would be faster."

"Well, yeah, but you never said you would be calling upon your inner gazelle."

May, even though she too is completely out of breath finds the spirit for some genuine laughter.

For several minutes, they sit tight just cooling down and replaying the hour and a half, they just spent with Mrs. Gullariz.

4:31 p.m. ticks by silently on Ryson's watch as he is attempting conversation with a granola bar and some bottled water, he figured he'd treat the two like his friends, bettering his odds at a happy encounter.

It's agreed, both adoption facilities seem to be following the same playbook. Will loves being able to cross reference any given situation to that of an N.F.L. quote, so when he does, not only is May not surprised but she cannot agree more.

"Somehow, we need to call an audible, we both know we're not going to be leaving $10,000 dollar deposits all over town just in hopes they call. And even though, Ms. Gullariz, there, seemed like somebody important, I wouldn't trust her for shit."

"So now what, May? Any suggestions?"

"Well, first of all, we stop walking in the front door, don't you think?"

Things get quiet in the van for the first couple of miles as May and Will head back towards their hotel. It's a long drive, so neither rush their own process of cognitive thought.

"So, then, we find a way that these people lead us to whatever children they have access to."

"Yes, like, maybe we follow Miss Gullariz home after work or wherever she might go, it was obvious the place we just came from was far too small to be housing any of the kids she showed us in her photo album."

With most of the granola bar eaten and already on his second bottle of water, Ryson checks his watch calculating the amount of time left for recovery, it's only a five-minute walk and he's not planning on being early.

They crossfire their ideas, until within just a mile or two from their hotel, "Let's get gas now and plenty of bottled water, we'll pack enough food and water for a couple of days, and first thing in the morning, we go see where this stakeout and follow thing goes, It could mean sleeping in the van again."

"Then you, my friend, best be learning how to properly screw the lid back on a pee filled water bottle."

They would laugh if that was funny.

"Yeah, yeah, yeah, just because you, my dear, have the bladder capacity of a five-gallon bucket."

May giggles like she is being bashful, but only because it's true, "Either way, handsome, let's just keep it in the bottle."

At 5:40 pm, May pulls the door closed behind them, the last words you can hear squeezing through the shrinking gap in the door are hers as she says, "How about we eat dinner in the room tonight, then we can be dessert?"

"I'll be your cherry pie, my dear,"

We do not hear Will say this, we can only assume he does, and with a smile on his face.

At 5:50 p.m., Ryson steps out into the hallway, letting his door close and lock on its own. It is not dark when he steps out onto the sidewalk but there is a lack of direct sunlight because of the surrounding mountains, which causes large parts of the city to be concealed in gray shadow.

To his absolute relief, all he finds is three cabs sitting out front of the fashion circus and no sick pervert on a stool with a gun. He approaches the cab in front of the other two with the yellow chip in his hand, hoping to keep any conversations minimal.

"Fifty bucks and you keep the chip," those were the only words spoken by either of them in the fifteen-minute drive out of town. Clearly, the cab driver is also not interested in conversation.

It's a drive out of town with a couple of turns leading to a warehouse and industrial area sort of on the outskirts. Through the gate up the stairs, the cab driver has a way of making this sound more like an order then directions as he pulls over and stops.

Ryson does a visual through the window of the cab before he commits to his exit, what he sees is what looks as if at one time was a two story, six-unit apartment building that has now undergone personal renovations, and a large fenced lot adjacent to it on the left.

"Through the gate up the stairs!" this time the cab driver sounds more annoyed than informative.

Ryson steps out onto a dirt and gravel walkway that partially runs along this side of the street, and of course, forgoing any sort of emotional goodbyes, the cab driver pulls away.

Through the gate, up the stairs. There needn't be a question to this remark, one only needs to open their eyes.

Ryson is now standing in front of a large wooden fence that surrounds a gravel parking lot, the fence is approximately seven feet tall and constructed of vertical slats, there are gaps in some of the slats, allowing a slivered view between them. To his left twenty feet, there is a large gate on rollers allowing access to the lot for vehicles. Directly to his right, a few feet is a smaller gate and on the other side of this, is a set of stairs leading up towards the second floor of the apartment building and a small alcove.

"Through the gate and up the stairs," this time the words are muffled, and for a second or two Ryson thinks maybe they came from his own head, either way, through the gate and up the stairs he goes.

Not quite at mid-step because of his hesitant ascent, he can now see over the tall wooden fence to his left and into the lot from which this fence surrounds. At the back of this fence, there is what looks to be a covered area with a tarp and four freestanding polls held in place with four buckets of dried cement, also at the very back of this fence is what looks to be another gate, just much smaller than the rolling one out front.

Tucked into the shadows within the small alcove on the second floor comes again the muffled voice he heard from the street, it is still just as muffled, except for now, it's only louder, "Chip!" As Ryson climbs the last two stairs, then steps onto the landing at the top, he now sees the man the voice belongs to sitting on a stool with a large caliber revolver lying in his lap.

He shows the man on the stool his chip just as he asked, and sticking with the mumble voice, gun man tells him, "First curtain on your left."

The sounds of a tropical rainstorm sneak into Ryson's head slowly at first and then because it seems so out of place, he has trouble understanding what the noise is.

It's about ten feet before the first curtain along the upstairs walkway, there are two other curtains along the walkway further down, all three curtains are of the same material and clearly hang in place of the doors.

The rainstorm gets louder as Ryson turns and faces the thick burlap curtain, it is one solid piece of material, so he pulls from one side and quietly squeezes through. So far, the similarities between last night and tonight have not gone on noticed, and the minute he touches the burlap curtain, he can already tell there is a connection.

Well before the disturbing politeness of a man's voice reaches Ryson's ears, he can already tell it's the same man from last night, and also why he now possesses a yellow chip, it is this yellow chip that has now granted him access to this foul and infected environment.

There is no time to gather the room in just a glance, so the attempt is futile. There is just so much to take in, it nearly pushes him back through the curtain he came from.

Slightly forward and left against the wall is a semi-circular bar, while behind and tending to it is Mr. Chips, he has already made eye contact with

Ryson and is trying to say something, but the audio level to which they have the sounds of the rain forest playing makes hearing what he says impossible from this distance, but the come and sit hand-gesture with a point to a stool he has no problem understanding.

When the distance is narrowed to just a few inches, Mr. Chips chirps in and again with that disturbing politeness, "Sit, relax, nobody here gives a simple fuck why it is you showed up, nobody here will judge you, believe me. So tell me, what are you in the mood for?"

Panic not only for the loss of an answer but also to consider the options, this sickens Ryson and draws him speechless, he just can't show it.

Mr. Chips, sensing he might be losing a customer, begins to run down a list of options, "All right, yellow chip, here's what you got. Because of the twenty-dollar cover charge, you already owe me at least that."

"All we serve here is bottled water and soft drinks, no smoking and no drugs, your twenty-dollar cover charge includes the movie and access to the visiting rooms. The three tables behind you are not actually tables, they are action platforms that's why there's no chairs, past that as you can clearly see is the movie projection system and screen with plenty of seating in front of it. The title of tonight's first move that will start in about twenty minutes is titled Play Date. As for the second, I don't rightly know."

"To my left their, yellow chip," Mr. Chips nods that direction, "are the visiting rooms and yes, the curtains are transparent for a reason."

Ryson does finally manage some movement and slightly turns his upper body to the right. What he sees requires no explanation, and he would rather tear the throat out of Mr. Chips than allow him to give one.

"Tonight, in those rooms, you will find girls in the first three, boys in the next two, the last two are empty, ages vary, so have a look for yourself. When you find something you would like to play with, pull that darker curtain closed and now you owe me fifty bucks. Clean up after yourself, there will be no marks, bruises, blood, or injuries left behind. You will be charged for anything you damage."

The slight change in ambient lighting comes from the older couple as they peal back the thick burlap curtain and step through. The light alone draws Ryson's attention, only because the music is so loud he cannot tell there in some sort of argument.

They take empty stools to his left and continue the argument at just slightly above a whisper. The female, because she is closest to him, he can hear some of what she is saying, "Mr. Chips is not interfering," instead, places a bottle of water in front of each of them as if he's seen this squabble before.

Mr. Chips turns back to Ryson and pushes a water bottle in front of him, saying, "On the house, now go spend some money," there's a stop in thought for Mr. Chips as he turns back towards the arguing couple, loud enough for the arguing to hear him, he says, "Except for room five, right, Pauline?"

Pauline breaks from her side of the argument; she stands and tugs attempting to un-wrinkle her short skirt, doing her best at seeming feminine. Her voice belongs to a man and that he does not try to hide as he says, "As long as I get first piece." Turning quickly, his skirt flares slightly as he prances away, his partner follows. The two disappear into room five as the curtain is pulled dark.

Ryson slides from the stool hoping his legs and knees will support the weight, finding himself, still standing, he moves towards the visiting rooms, he does not have to pull away the thin transparent curtain to know who is on the other side, he moves slowly not because of his interest but only to look as though he is shopping.

The small child in room three is sitting in one of two large chairs and in her lap, she is petting a small stuffed dog, the dog is dirty, tattered and torn, but clearly, one of those spotted firehouse dogs. It's the same dog as the living version he surprised the family with a couple of years ago for Christmas. This freezes him in a blank stare, for how long he is not quite sure, but it's the sound of children laughing that finally pulls him back.

He knows where the laughter is coming from, the lights in half of the room have gone dim and the strange glowing flickers means the movie has started.

"Not today, not ever," Ryson turns his back to that part of the room and now only wants out.

By the path of lesser evils, he must walk past Mr. Chips at the bar to get out of the room and is hoping to do so without further communication.

Ryson has a fifty in his hand and would like nothing more than to leave it with Mr. Chips and not look back. Mr. Chips, although clearly gracious for the thirty-dollar tip, does seem somewhat annoyed and slows Ryson's escape with a barky question of, "Still not young enough?"

Ryson fake smiles and nods his head.

Trapped once again in Mr. Chips filthy web of description, he is lured closer with the promise of something younger.

"Well, yellow chip, I think there might be hope for you yet."

Ryson is now back on the same stool he first occupied, Mr. Chips is leaned in slightly, so he only has to say this once.

"Listen, yellow chip, it just so happens that for the next couple of nights troop six will be stopping by during intermission, they will bring five for auction, most likely just girls, and I believe a couple of those will be quite young. Winning bids include thirty minutes in a private room, the ones over there on the right."

Ryson shuffles slightly on the stool and nods his head in acceptance and consideration while doing his best to seem sincere. Leaving the fifty, he heads to the curtain and out like he and Mr. Chips have a thing.

Ryson gets past Ricky revolver in the alcove without words simply because he is preoccupied with several packs of football cards, he sees him walked by but says nothing.

There are two cabs parked out front just outside the small gate at the bottom of the stairs, both facing the wrong way and neither of them know how he got here.

Cabbie closest to the gate has his passenger window down and is leaning towards it to speak, it's a strange accent and clearly not from around here that asks Ryson, "Where you need to be, my friend?"

Without getting any closer, he bends slightly forward at the waist and politely says, "No thanks, it's close, all walk."

Stands, turns away and begins to do so.

Half a block up, he crosses the street and begins to move a little faster, faster still as he gets closer to the first place where he can turn right. His adrenaline gets the best of him, so much so he is already in full stride even before he can completely turn the corner.

It's a metered pace, considering Ryson has no idea how far or how long he may have to run. A block up and another right turn, already well winded and slowing down begins to look for the two alleyways he spotted from the stairs on his way down from the second floor of the rain forest room.

Near collapse, he finally spots the first of two alleyways, it's the further one he wants but will have to walk the seventy or eighty feet until that appears.

The second alleyway is far darker than the first, and so, when he turns and confronts it head on, the darkness pushes back, stopping him wide eyed; and wobbly.

The alleyway passes between some two-story warehouses all the way to the other end, but from here all there is only dark, darker, and darkest. Even knowing what's at the other end does not seem to shed any light on the journey.

The sound of a car's horn ricochets off the tall walls of the alleyway, it starts at the farthest end and creeps quickly from wall to wall until it finally reaches Ryson's ears one at a time. This means movement on the street in front of the rain forest encounter, this finally pulls him with some urgency into the alleyway and towards the other end.

The same horn sounds for the second time, just as he reaches the far end of the alleyway, he has to weave around some miscellaneous items to get a look at the street while still maintaining cover in the alleyway.

It's a slight lean out and look right from the alleyway but only long enough to clear the corner of the large warehouse. He is directly across the street from the far end of the fenced parking area and right of this and adjacent two stands, the two story six unit converted apartment building, he was just in a few minutes ago. Out front now are parked four cabs, not just two.

From his spot in the alleyway and from across the street, Ryson cannot see the alcove at the top of the stairs, but can only assume the man on the stool with a gun and football cards is still there.

The loud clang of the smaller gate slamming shut, for just an instant startles him and he goes to turtle, before he can de-shell, he hears a car door slam and an engine start, as the cab goes zipping by, Ryson watches it disappear up the street. Couple of blocks up, the brake lights illuminate the back of the cab and then quickly fade left, but in their place, a set of headlights.

The headlights belong to a dark blue minivan that slows quickly as it approaches his position, it slowly rolls to a stop with a slight angle towards the large rolling gait in the fence across the street.

Without warning, the gate roles to an open position, and once the minivan is inside, the gate quickly makes the return journey.

The small figures that appear on the stairs leading up to the alcove and the second floor at first seem to be alone. As they reach the top of the stairs, there is some light allowing him to get a better look.

The five small figures are dressed in yellow rain slickers, including hats and boots, they are quietly moving in single file until one at a time they disappear through the curtain and into the room he is all too familiar with. As the children cover the few feet from top of the stairs to the curtain, Ryson gets his best look.

Boys or girls, it's hard to say, the large, yellow, floppy hat and slicker made it impossible to tell who the child might be, but even from this distance, he could place their ages at about six or seven. There might have been one or two younger than that, it's hard to say. They moved with discipline and without hesitation, no doubt the last and much larger figure to move up the stairs and disappear through the curtain is there to make sure of that.

In all reality, Ryson truly does not know exactly what sadistic evils await those young children, but with absolute certainty it consumes and destroys. He does not attempt to control the tears because he knows for each one that falls, many will be held accountable.

Ryson leaves the alleyway in reverse, only stopping briefly halfway to go through a small bin of steel pipe and leaving with a hollow piece, four feet long and about one inch in diameter, knowing it's going to be a dark and scary walk back to the hotel, he could use the security as friendship.

The vibration in his front pocket for good or bad was for sure welcome contact.

The first message reads "4.5. All in. New plan tomorrow. Making a difference. Good night all."

Message two reads, lost the trailer but with it goes the problem.

"End of book report. One team one goal. Sleep tight. 1.2."

Ryson responds with, "Almost back at the hotel, long night, long walk, new plan. Will text first thing in a.m. to 4.5. Good night all. 3."

The last response comes from Art.

"Be strong my friend, keep your eyes on the prize. 2."

131

5 More

It was the same for all three, the long night brought with it more questions than answers, there was some sleep had by all, but it came in short durations filled with tossing and turning.

Ryson's first text could not show up soon enough. May and Will were up at sunrise already planning for what if's and then what's, so when the phone's chirp in tandem, it's a race to see who can read it first.

"You guys up yet? 3."

May of course hits send before Will, but their messages are the same. "Just waiting for you".

"How about you two come see me, I think I might have something for us to do. 3."

They both read this but only one responds.

"5 is already gathering food and water for the drive, we will not check out, we will text when we get close, maybe 3 ½ hours. 4."

"Drive careful, text when close, be safe. 3."

The last text reply comes from Art and Lila.

"Yes! You all be safe. 1.2."

Ryson is almost giddy with anticipation, the thought of no longer being alone here has caused him to have butterflies all morning, but just that, and no more orifice explosions, he has already decided to exclude that knowledge when the three of them get caught up.

11:10 ticks by, 11:11 idols in suspension for what seems far too long, Ryson finally puts the phone down and walks away. At 11:12, the text from May chirping in, saying they were just outside the city and what next? "Sounds like angels trumpeting from somewhere high in the heavens."

His response is simple and direct, Ryson has already thought this through.

"Follow the signs to the train station, Big Blue sign, park there, I will come find you. 3."

At the back of the lot, there is what's left of a pay, booth, after checking it for snakes, spiders, or scorpions Ryson steps cautiously out of the sun and into the shade from here he can easily see the rest of the lot.

Ryson watches a half dozen or so cars come and go in the short time it takes May and Will to get there, knowing now what's here he ponders the odds as to how many of those half dozen have come to inflict and/or to damage. He realizes the moment he sees the mini-van pull into the lot, May and Will are as he was just a couple of days ago, they do not know what unspeakable horrors await, and for that reason and this reason alone, he feels bad they're here.

But for all other reasons, he has to stop himself from joyfully skipping over to them and instead covers the distance calmly and as quickly as possible.

There are smiles, hugs, and kisses. They chatter for a moment about the ride here and also a little bit about how here is.

Ryson brings to light the first part of today's plan.

"For right now, we'll just leave the van right here, let's go into the station and have lunch, it's pretty good, not real private but they got pizza. After that, we'll go back to my hotel and I will sneak you into my room. Then we can talk."

Gunfire spontaneously erupts outside the train terminal, it's some distance off and therefore just doesn't seem all that threatening, but when the occupants of the two tables closest to them duck and cover under their table, there is a glance before they each put a partially eaten slice of pizza back on the large plate with the other half and proceed to duck and cover.

May is the last to show up, but when she does, she brings with her the large plate of pizza handing it to Ryson as she crouches so she, too, can scoot under the table. As soon as she gets settled, she grabs a partially eaten slice off the plate and says, "Well, geez, cowgirls, you can't just leave all the visuals every time something spooks your ponies."

"It's so honest, it's so pure and so exactly who May is," this pushes Ryson's funny button and he starts to laugh, Will now caught in the moment follows Ryson's lead. When May herself starts to laugh some pizza falls out of her mouth, this sends the three of them under the table into hysterics.

Another round of gunfire and this time, a little closer seems to knock some of the funny out of the moment, Ryson and Will go "rock, paper, scissors" to see who goes topside to grab the water bottles.

The three sit Indian style under the table, they finish their pizza and as they do, May and Will finish telling of their adventures, bringing Ryson up to speed on their endeavors. When they get to the part where their next effort was to follow somebody after work they could tell, somehow, Ryson has also come to the let's follow somebody conclusion.

On that note, Ryson uncrosses his legs and says, "Let's get the hell out of here," as they scurry out from under their table and stand they realize they were the last to do so.

It's a short walk to Ryson's hotel, and they see no signs of why there might have been gunfire. They check on the mini-van, but only from a distance. May sends this message to Art and Lila "We are three. 3.4.5."

Art's reply "Nice. Be safe, eyes open."

Lila's reply "Always as one."

They agree, it's better if Ryson remains to look the loner, and so, they shall not walk in the front door with him. There is a service entrance and fire escape around back to which May and Will scurry with the utmost precaution. When Ryson opens it, May and Will are there to step right in. Quietly and without words, they follow him to his room.

Ryson starts with the train ride after they parted ways from baggage pickup, he does his best at describing the journey and the events leading up till now. As sorry as he was to share all and even the most foul details to share the burden was of some relief.

There's a dance life does when things are right, it's a different movement when things are wrong, and here the movement scratches and tears at your skin, it seems the poison only wants in.

Silence follows the last few words that fall from Ryson's tongue, he's waiting for May and Will to catch up, and when they do they both agree, what's next?

Will already knows the plan, and absolutely agrees with it, May, at first, struggles in silence but it does not take her long.

Ryson is impressed how quickly not only did Will catch up, but he is already moving forward.

"Geez, Will, you would make a great detective. And yes, that's exactly what I'm thinking. As sad as it is, we wait, and when those kids in the rain slickers and who ever there keepers are leave at the end of the night we do our best to find out where they go."

May now eagerly jumps in, "We simply and hopefully follow them right back to the nest."

The three of them like some sort of musketeers nod at each other and agree, that's the plan and it's time to make a difference.

Will's focus visibly changes and before he even says it, the other two already know what plan they need first.

"All right, Ryson, so what are we supposed to do about the fact that some perverted waste of life is sitting on a stool in front of some place called fashion circus and he has our gun, or guns. He's for sure to have a backup."

"Well, we have to convince him to return them."

Both the guys look at May because for the last few minutes, she's been very quiet. Will asks, "So, what you think, May?"

"We have to lure pig man off the stool and around the corner or at least down the street, because if we want both guns, he pretty much needs to be unconscious, that's going to get far too messy for just out front."

"My first suggestion is to recon both locations, I say we do some daylight drive-bys and check out the neighborhoods. You two boys hide out in the back of the van, that way it looks like I'm alone and just out for a drive".

Ryson and will look at each other, and then back to May, "All right, let's go."

"Somebody grab little 'wap o.'"

That's the name they gave the piece of pipe Ryson found last night, "I think it was in honor of somebody's brother."

Ryson yelps out, "Got it."

They decide to leave the same way they came in and then meet at the minivan.

"You two boys comfy back there?"

"As good as it gets," they both agree. May starts the van, she has her foot on the brake and hand on the shifter, but then things go quiet up front. When the silence becomes curious, Will finally ask, "What's going on, May?"

"I can't seem to get that lunatics voice out of my head. That live feed in your room and this psycho 'Vinzaya,' you are absolutely correct, Ryson, this guy is not only, I'm quite sure clinically insane, but it's the consistency in some of his phrases, it's clear that he is hell-bent on destruction of some sorts. I think that's what he means by replacing the darkness with the light. I'm just thinking, we better be real fuckin' careful."

There is no reply from the back of the van.

It's quiet in the minivan for the first block or two away from the station, then finally some chatter from the back.

They first decide to cruise by fashion circus in hopes of finding a solution to their gun problem. The front of the building is quiet, no open doors and no man on a stool, it's too early. Just as they had expected.

I'll cruise around back, let's see what the alley looks like. May slowly drifts into the alley and is maybe a car's length in when they get a good look all the way down. At about midway, there's a small parking area maybe enough room for three or four cars but there is only one and leaning against it is some guy on a cell phone.

Another car lengths further in Ryson finally realizes the guy on the phone is the same guy from the stool and the keeper of their Mac 10.

"Oh, crap, slowdown, May, that's him. That's the guy we hope has our guns."

"Should I stop?"

"Yeah, May, inch over to the right side first, as close to the wall as you can get."

When May gets stopped they all three take a deep breath, and Ryson takes the lead, "I think we finish rolling down this alley and as soon as stool boy is next to the sliding door all May has to do is stop. We slide the door open and we let little wap-o here do the rest."

Will smiles and nods his head, "Works for me, you okay with that, May?"

"Like the smell of a new car," is her answer as she begins to move forward.

"Okay, he's almost there, when I stop, he'll be right where you want him."

Ryson tells Will, "You go out first, that way he doesn't see little wap-o tell it's too late."

Will unlatches the sliding door letting it open just enough to see some daylight through the crack.

When May stops, the door slides open, stool boy's eyes get real big, the sight of Will and Ryson coming at him scares him so much he drops the phone and sort of raises both hands to face level in a surrendering posture.

Little wap-o comes quick and stool boy drops even quicker.

They find the Mac 10 fully loaded inside the car and a loaded 38 revolver in a belt holster stool boy had on him, they do a quick search a second time and still find no spare ammo.

As Will pulls the sliding door closed, May is already on the move, they take one last look at stool boy and decide it was sure nice of him to not argue.

Ryson looks back through the rear window, but only in hopes the payment has been dealt, and stool boy no longer has the need to breathe.

T are much less interesting when they get to the rain forest building where Ryson was last night, they can see no movement in or around the two-story converted apartment, although they cannot see the inside parking area because of the fence.

May loops around the blocks a couple of times just to make sure they get a good feel for the back roads, giving themselves the best possible chance for this plan to work. It's 3:20 p.m. and they realize that they will have to wait for it to get dark before they can safely park the van and get in position in the alleyway across the street from what they now refer to as the Rain Forest Apartments.

"Fall back, regroup back to the hotel."

They return using the same method as before. After leaving the mini-van in the lot at the station they split up. This time Ryson is slightly ahead of the rendezvous and is forced to stand idle for a couple of seconds, holding the heavy steel door open with his body.

This time, when May and Will come through the door they do not wait, and Ryson follows them to his room.

May first eats the contents, then proceeds to go all artsy crafty and makes the three missing playing cards out of the small box the cereal was in. The deck left in Ryson's room incomplete and somewhat damaged, but now because of the repairs, they can use it to pass the time.

Ryson packs a bag with the stuff he does not want to leave behind if they don't come back. It's dusk when Will wins the last hand of gin rummy. You can tell the three are bonding well when after the cards are put away, Ryson comments, "Yeah, like you two aren't working me for my cigarette money." They laugh, and leave the deck where they found it, only now, somewhat intact.

Together, they leave from the rear exit and make the short walk to the van as a team, it's dark when May leaves the lot, Will as passenger, Ryson in the back, and the guns stowed safely, but close enough to be quick to use.

They park the van one street over from the Rain-Forest Apartments and at the end of a long alleyway, this gives them access to the street out front and also a quick retreat back to the van if need be.

They walk the distance through the alley retracing Ryson's steps from the night before in silence, just listening.

For the most part, the debris in the alley is the same, so as they reach the far end and now have the Rain Forest Apartments in sight, they gather a couple of boxes and a small wooden crate and better conceal their position in the end of the alley. The larger of the two crates they now use as a place to sit.

Ryson whispers the layout as he knows it from the night before, including the man hiding at the top of the stairs with a large caliber revolver and football cards. But that's only speculative, they can't see him.

The bottom half of this Rain Forest building is dark and seems to be unaffected by the upper half. There is a large double door in the center and over that and wall to wall are three large windows with equal space between them, and unlike upstairs, there is no activity. The men and sometimes couples that have shown up have all gone through the small gate and up the stairs. One man they could hear say something at the top of the stairs to somebody, probably armed stool security.

When the minivan shows up, it does so from the other direction, instead of from left to right this time from right to left. Ryson whispers, "I'm sure it's the same one." The large gate roles open just far enough to only allow the space needed for entry. Already things seem more cautious than last night. It rolls closed as quickly as it was open, swallowing the minivan like a hungry beast.

It's a sight that punishes the heart, it tears at something inside you, the three sit in shameful silence for all of mankind as the single file of tiny rain slickers makes their way up the stairs, then disappearing one at a time through the first curtain on the second floor.

They hear Ryson quietly say, "For every one of them, many will be held accountable."

Neither May or Will answer him, they are still at a loss for words.

Time can always be measured but its movement is what makes life un predictable, and even though, in one place, the minutes idle by like the drift in a small dinghy. Those same minutes can also come at you like a fire breathing dragon from hell.

Outside crouched in a dark alleyway, time passes one way, but a few feet away and up the stairs time passes another. The hell for some of us is the ability to be in both places at the same time. Because of this the three of them sit quietly in their own house of pain.

The orange glow of a vapor lamp suddenly consumes some of the darkness inside the fenced area across the street, and now some noise from the same place. There is no movement on the stairs or out front, leaving the street empty and giving Ryson a chance to go take a better look.

"I've got to see what's going on. Listen, you two, if you spot those kids on or near the stairs, whistle. I will follow you back to the Van and the chase is on, I'm going to cross the street right here and follow that fence all the way down and around the back of the parking area, maybe through the fence slats I can get a look inside."

"Stay low when you cross the street and if our friend at the top of the stairs sees you, well, hell, from that distance you're most likely just a short shadow anyway," Will says this like it's a promise. May agrees, she then adds, "And be real quiet," then smiles.

Ryson moves quickly across the street with the 38 tucked tightly in his waistband. When he gets to the corner of the fence on the other side, he pauses and listens, he then looks back across the street for any warning signs from May or Will.

All is quiet on both sides of the street, Ryson begins to move along the fence towards the far back corner, when he reaches the back corner, he again pauses and listens, and because of the darkness and distance, he can no longer see the other two.

All of the fence boards up to this point are fairly tight together and without cracks, and the fence is another foot over Ryson's head, so there is also no looking over.

Ryson cautiously peaks around the back corner getting a good look all the way down the back of the fence, almost halfway down, there is some light spilling through the fence in a couple of places, which means there must be a way to get a look inside.

Almost on tiptoes, Ryson works his way down the fence, stopping just short of the first breach in the fortress, the spacing between the boards right here is an inch or so because there has been some damage to the fence, he exhales and is preparing to take a peek when noise from just on the other side of the fence causes him to freeze.

The noise does not seem to be any sort of alarm because of his presence, even so, he stalls a few more seconds just to be sure.

The opening between the slats causes Ryson to lean his head to one side in order to get a look through with both eyes. What he sees causes him to step backwards in dumbfounded disbelief where he now stands in absolute shock.

Courage and curiosity brings him back to the fence and now with just one eye, so it's a more comfortable position he again pears through the fence and allows his thoughts to run shallow trying to understand.

Five yards inside the fence under an old-fashioned, three headed streetlight sits the minivan; they watched pull in here, it's sitting sideways to Ryson with the sliding door fully open. In front of this and closer to him is a flat sort of cart with four small wheels and a piece of rope for a handle. And on this cart, lying motionless are two medium sized dogs, these dogs had been shaved absolutely smooth, the tails ears and snouts have either been modified or removed in such a way they barely resemble dogs at all.

Standing over these dogs is a man that looks very much like the guy upstairs with the gun and football cards, next to him is a box with the same kind of yellow rain slickers the children were wearing, and what this guy is doing is dressing these dogs in the rain slickers, including hats and boots.

As he finishes dressing one, he then places this dog in the seat behind the driver's, using the shoulder strap and seatbelt to secure the animal firmly in place and in an upright seated position.

When dog man turns and comes back for the last dog on the cart, Ryson gets a look in the back of the minivan and on the bench seat in the back are three more figures that look just like the one now strapped behind the driver seat.

After dog man dresses and straps the last dog in the seat behind the passenger seat, he slides the door closed and heads towards the large gate that leads out to the street. In one quick motion, he rolls the gate fully open, he turns and now checks his watch while walking back to the dog-cargo minivan. There is no hesitation when he's close enough to open the driver door and get in, the door slams shut and the engine grinds to life, the transmission clunks loudly into gear and the minivan slowly exits the lot, and following a right turn, disappears into the night.

It's one of those times in life where you really do take two steps back, and with that done, Ryson stands silent, letting the night hide his confusion.

Ryson's knees do not have to be told to buckle when what sounds like all-out war starts on the street out front, the burst of automatic gunfire squeezes him as close to the ground as possible in a tight squat with his hands over his head.

After a couple hundred rounds have been spent and what sounded like a large burst of air, the night slips to almost quiet again.

There is less than ten minutes from the time Ryson disappears around the far back corner of the fence until what seemed like explosive forces the large gate across the street roles quickly to fully open, May and Will get a quick look at somebody walking away and checking their watch, and in the next few seconds, the minivan appears, it rolls slowly out of the fenced area and makes a right turn.

As the minivan rolls down the street and past May and Will, they both strain against the night and fear of being spotted to get a distorted view of what's inside. It's obvious there are others in the van but it's impossible to tell who or what.

May and Will expect to watch the Van disappear into the night but as it approaches the first cross street, it semi-screeches to an abrupt halt, and at the same time, there's a loud rumble now coming from the other end of the street and getting louder.

Before the two of them get a look down the other end of the street, the loud rumble is right on top of them, what drives past them is a large, O.D., green, military, troop transport vehicle. Just as they get a look at the back of this vehicle it also now comes to an abrupt halt.

May and Will lean out of the alleyway just far enough to get a look pass the minivan and there, in front of it, blocking its progress, is the same kind of vehicle now also blocking its escape.

The vehicle in front of the minivan is positioned sideways to it, the one in back is nose first with a thirty or forty-foot space between it and the rear bumper of the minivan.

For a few seconds, things seem at a strange stalemate, it's a calm before the storm sort of thing, because when the two men dressed in battle fatigues and carrying some kind of assault rifles step from behind the vehicle in front and begin to walk slowly towards the minivan; it's obvious things are going to get a little heated.

The driver of the minivan does not seem interested in negotiations, this is obvious by the way he flings his door open and bolts, heading towards town at full stride like his life depends on it.

The fire and noise that erupts next is deafening and bright enough to illuminate slightly the outside and inside of the minivan, both gunmen are standing slightly off center in front of the minivan while unleashing a steady barrage of bullets.

What's in the minivan is still unclear, all May and Will can see is the damage being done to the outside of the minivan, what's inside is sure to be suffering the same fate.

When the gun fire stops, gun man on the right approaches the minivan, he gets as far as the driver door, allowing himself a look inside. He now steps back to his firing position and waits.

A third man appears from the same place as the first two and joins them. Man three has something strapped to his back and what looks like a lit flamethrower in his hands, he approaches the minivan from the same side, the first two gunmen retreat from where they came.

Flame on, and it is extremely intense. For several seconds, liquid fire spews from the nozzle, not only consuming all of what was inside the minivan but the heat was so intense it actually makes the minivan smaller.

Just as flame boy shuts it down and his liquid fire retreats, May and Will's phones vibrate to life sending a nervous chill through both of them. The text is from Ryson, "Are you two okay?"

May quickly responds, "Yes, tucked away, you stay put, wait for next text."

Ryson stands slowly, allowing the muscles to re-stretch as he types his reply, "Okay." He moves closer to the fence and is going to take another look when the sound of a cell phone goes off some distance from him further down the fence and on the other side.

Ryson is already moving cautiously along the fence in the direction of the phone noise when he hears somebody quietly answer it. There is a small gate at the end of this fence when he reaches this point he stops. There is a gap between the gate and fence allowing him to get a look inside.

Flame boy calmly saunters back, then disappears behind the large truck he and the other two came from. A few seconds tick by before both trucks move at the same time, the one in front simply continuing on in the same direction before it blocked; forward progress of the minivan, the one behind quickly moves up, passing the minivan on the left side, then promptly making the right turn to follow the first one. Leaving behind a charred and still smoldering shell of something that once was.

Ryson is apprehensive to say the least as he begins to focus through the opening between the gate and the fence, the muffled phone conversation is close and the guy doing his best to be quiet is only a few feet away, and is also the first thing to come into focus.

Man on the cell phone is leaning against the front end of a minivan, the minivan is parked right up against the wall of the Rain Forest apartment building and under a small overhang. It's pointing almost straight at him, giving Ryson a look through the front windshield and into the minivan.

Ryson's heart flutters and squeezes a thick amount of adrenaline through his veins, he instinctively knows it's go time when he sees five small figures dressed in yellow rain slickers quietly sitting inside the minivan. There is little doubt in his head as to who these children in the van are, for sure, they're the same five he watched move single file up the stairs and into curtain number one two nights in a row.

Ryson takes a few steps backwards looking up and towards the alcove at the top of the stairs, when he has backed up far enough, he can now see over the top of the fence and directly into the alcove to where there is no body sitting on a stool waiting to put a bullet through his head when he comes through the gate.

The gate is not locked but it is latched and the noise he makes with the latch and the movement of the gate swinging open causes cell phone boy to go for the gun he has in a shoulder holster on the outside of his shirt. Ryson comes through the gate with his new .38 pointed at cell phone boy's chest, hoping it would deter him from forcing a shoot-out.

Ryson is moving quickly and fires twice, both slugs land center chest, putting a well scramble to cell phone boy's innards.

Ryson picks up cell phone boys' gun and would rather first check the ignition then rifle through the dead guys pockets. He reaches through the open driver's window and checks the ignition, the joy and the text buzz hits him at the same time, "All clear out here, you okay?"

"Yes, I'm coming out."

Before Ryson starts the van, he turns and checks his passengers. The tiny little faces that stare back, four little girls, one little boy all about six are frightened, but dry eyed.

He smiles big and winks, turns back to the front, and calmly puts the minivan in gear, and because evidently, the two shots he fired has caused no attention rolls out of the lot through the open gate like this is all just part of the plan.

The second minivan, May and Will see, pulls out of the lot looks very much like the one that was just riddled and blazed, but when it heads straight to them and pulls up along the curb right in front of their position, there is no time to run so all they can do is squeeze closer to the ground and stay quiet.

"Psssssst," May whispers, "what the hell was that?"

Will brings the Mac 10 to chest height. Then again, "Psssssst." And then the words, "May, Will, you two still there?" ring clear as Ryson's voice.

Two heads pop up over a large crate. Ryson does not give them time to ask questions, he simply blurts out and only loud enough for them to hear him, "Listen, you two, I am going up this road a mile or two and when I make a right turn, I will stop and wait, now giddy up, little doggies."

There are no questions or hesitations. May and Will make a cautious dash to their minivan and within seconds are already giving chase.

No Hugs

Slowly and to the left, Ryson passes the still smoldering charred remains of what was once a minivan, he knows what was in it but how it has succumb to such a state of destruction is unknown. Will also passes the minivan from the left, allowing May a fleeting glimpse of the interior as they pass, her statement is one of troubled confusion, "No telling what was inside, only that what's left is no longer what it once was." They both harbor a frightening conclusion, and both refuse to speak it out loud.

Ryson decides to wait for headlights behind him before he turns right, it's so dark his own headlights barely punch through the thick moonless night and he would rather make it easier to be found than not.

Hoping it's the right set of headlights, he taps the brakes and makes the turn, immediately pulling over and coming to a stop. Headlights off, foot off the brakes, but leaves the van running.

Better judgment not being a deciding factor, Ryson moves the interior dim switch to about half way in hopes of chasing some of the darkness out of the van and maybe even some of the fear.

He turns to face the children in the back and is not sure what to say or even what language to say it in, but something tells him to simply speak from the heart, "I'm quite sure you kids have no reason to trust anybody anymore, so I will not ask you to trust me or my friends who you saw pop up from behind that create and who should also be here very soon to help us, but what I am going to say is still the truth and I will prove it to you, you just give me a chance."

"So, sit tight, keep the singing and dancing down to a minimum while my friends and I figure out how we are going to get all of you back home to your families, friends, and loved ones. And from this moment on, nobody is going to touch you or hurt you, they will have to get through me first," he winks, and fights back the tears.

Will checks the rear and side view mirrors before making the right turn, May also takes a look behind them, they see the same thing and it's just darkness. Will turns off the lights and pulls in right behind Ryson.

May and Will get out the van while expecting Ryson to do the same, he does not, instead he motions from his open window, it either means come over here or he is waving to the queen.

As May and Will walk to his window, he says out loud but does not look back, "These are my friends, but until you get a little more comfortable with that I will not let them in the car just yet."

May and Will come up to the window still unaware Ryson has passengers, their first question is, "what the hell is going on?" and the second, "Why are we stealing minivans now?" Ryson does not answer nor does he give them a chance for a third question. With a flick motion of his head towards the back seat, it draws their attention into the back of the van.

Looking over Ryson's head and left shoulder, the two fall speechless, weak kneed, and slack-jawed, both of them having to use the van for support.

Will jumps right in with a plan, "Well, for sure, we've got to get off the street, we need to burrow somewhere for a little while tell things cool down and we decide what to do next. How about May and I take the lead? We stay on this road and look for someplace to hide, you follow a couple of hundred yards behind us so we are not bunched up, this should make us a little less visible."

The look on Ryson's face not only says he agrees but also relieved he is not here alone. Before they walk away, May looks at him and says, "You okay there, cowboy?"

He lifts both hands, palm side up, and says, "Not a scratch. Now go."

May is looking across Will's chest and out his window when she says, "What is that? Stop the van, Will." When he does, she now says, "Back up and turn the wheels to the right." As the headlights begin to sweep the darkness to their left, what illuminates is at first confusing but it only takes a few seconds for Will to make the connection.

"They are harvest silos, you see how each one has a large door in the bottom and a ramp to the top, when they harvest whatever they grow in this area, it's all brought to these three silos and then probably sorted and sold right from here, and so maybe if it's off-season, this place could be empty."

Will takes the Mac 10 machine pistol and bravely walks the 30 yards on the dirt access road leading to the silos, leaving May and the van, so Ryson does not drive past them.

When Ryson gets close, May reaches over with her foot and taps the brakes, he slows, flashes the headlights, and pulls in right behind them. At this same time, Will steps back out onto the road looking at both May and Ryson through their windows, he points to May and says, "You drive, sweetheart, the road is in really bad shape I'll guide you from out here."

Now to Ryson, he says, "You follow her real close and we should all be okay."

The three silos are approximately twenty feet high and maybe one hundred fifty feet in diameter, there placed in a triangle formation with a half a football field sized space in the middle. Will leads them to this place. As they pull in, May drifts a little to the right as Ryson pulls up alongside to her left, they both have Will in their headlights when at the same time they flick out the beams. As the darkness quickly fills the space between them, they hear Will say, "Honey, we're home."

They both reach Ryson's window at the same time and they hear him say, "Get in. both of you come around to the other side and get in the passenger seat." As they pass in front of the windshield, Ryson says to the five small passengers in the back, "These are my friends, they won't hurt you, nobody's going to hurt you."

May crawls in first, using part of the passenger seat and center console to kneel on while facing the back section of the van, Will right next to her with both knees on the passenger seat, looking over the seatback also in the same direction, Ryson sort of side saddles the driver seat to his right side and now all three share the same sight and all three share the same sadness.

There's just enough light inside the van for everybody to clearly see each other. Ryson speaks up like he's forgotten to introduce friends at a party, "Silly me, where are my manners?"

"Well, this lovely lady right here, her name is May, and next to her is Will, and my name is Ryson, the three of us are not quite sure what to do next but one thing for sure, we are all in this together."

"How do you know they understand you, Ryson?"

"I don't, you try"

May basically says the same thing only in Spanish, sadly the five children's silence remains the same. Now May says, "How about you take those hats off so we can get a look at you," she now motions this action as if she herself were wearing a hat. This brings no affect.

Sensing the stalemate, Will finally chimes in, "All right, little ones, it's okay, you just let us take care of you, and don't listen to Ryson here. Of course, we know what to do, we would not have come all this way without a plan. Now, how about the grown-ups go have a talk-about and you five get comfortable and sit tight." Just as he exits, he asks, "Anybody object to me opening the sliding door so you kids can get some fresh air?"

Their little faces void of emotion or reply.

The three huddle in the dark, just out of earshot but close enough to still see the kids. It's a quiet discussion, first about what happened back there, and why was that van torched after mutilating those inside, and how are we now in possession of five small children.

Both sides are astonished by what the other has to say, then the three just stand there shaking their heads, and now quickly moving on to the second part of the discussion, and that is, what to do next?

The first decision is obvious and they might as well get comfortable with it because indeed, they will be spending the night curled up in the vans amongst the silos.

Will now becomes somewhat serious because of the training he received from the F.B.I. a couple of years ago.

"Okay, here's what I know, first of all, there should be no physical contact with the children, I think why that is, is obvious. Another thing we are not supposed to do is in any way discuss with them their recent captivity."

"This second part I know will be quite difficult, because how do you not try to hug this filthy place right out of those kids. But according to the F.B.I., any physical contact will only prolong their ability to trust us, or anybody else for that matter. And the best thing Ryson and I can do is put hands on them when it is only and absolutely, necessary."

May agrees to all this and now says, "Well, right now, let's see what we can do to make them a little more comfortable, they probably need to go to the bathroom and would maybe like something to eat or drink."

The sight that awaits them inside the van seems to be a step in the right direction, but what the large hats and boots once concealed is now exposed and three are forced to lay witness, and even in the orange glow of an aging dome light, it's all too apparent that these kids are not returning from a fun filled theme-park weekend.

There is no place to hide, the three looking at the five and the five judging the three. The battle wounds the five equally suffer range from, bite marks on the face and neck, couple of black eyes, bruising around the neck, face, and head, and one of the little girls has been shaved bald and has some sort of damage to her right ear. All five are between, perhaps, four and six years of age, all are light-skinned with hair color ranging from blonde to light brown.

Ryson smiles big like this is all about farts and giggles, then says, "Well, good day to you, young sir, and here we're thinking we got a whole basket of little girl kittens when in fact there's also a young pup." Ryson continues, "Well, I hope you all brought plenty of camping gear because it looks like we are going to spend the night, what do you mean you didn't bring any camping stuff? Who goes camping without stuff? Well, good thing for you, May, here, brought plenty to share. So why don't you five sleep in this van and Will and I can sleep in the other. I promise May will take very good care of you and we will be right in the next van if you need us."

"Good night, ladies and gentlemen."

They both now turn and walk away, they hear May as they do so already jumping in with both feet.

First, let's get rid of these things, I am quite sure we are not going to need this stuff any longer. May scoops up the rain hats and boots the children left in a small pile on the floor and shoves them under the minivan, "Now, who has to go to the bathroom? Let's get that done, then we can come back and we'll make a picnic in the van, we don't have much, but it will be plenty, now let's go find a place to go potty."

Ryson and Will pause behind the van waiting to see how those instructions pan out for May, and to their warm surprise, the children do indeed step out of the van in only their socks following May and the flashlight.

The minivans are parallel to each other with approximately five feet between them, so Will and Ryson maintain a level of whisper from the front seat well into the morning hours as they discuss, plan, and work out what happens when the sun comes up. The two of them fall asleep where they sit, not so comfortable in their physical position but definitely how they see the next twenty-four hours. They will run this new plan past May in the morning, and in the meantime, both sleep, but both on high-alert.

The sun comes up soft and peaceful, stirring May from the latter part of a dream where she had the power to grant children anything that they wanted and in return, she begs for their forgiveness, to which some give, some do not. She wonders as she wakes which of these kids have already been here too long, therefore, trust and forgiveness shall always be thin, shallow, and translucent.

May, as quietly as possible, pulls the passenger door latch, letting the door drift open as she unfolds herself from the passenger seat and gets out, doing her best to close the door just as quietly.

During stretches and yawns, May scans the area but does not see Will or Ryson, after a visit to the makeshift bathroom, she heads up the tree-lined road that leads to the main road and about halfway up this, she finds Will and Ryson walking in her direction.

They both say it, but with perfect timing so it sounds like one voice in stereo, "So how'd it go last night? We peaked in this morning and noticed you also got those damn raincoats off, so how hard was that?"

"It's the clothes underneath the coats that was the hard part, and that is something we've got to deal with, and I mean, right away."

"Their clothes our all mismatched, some tattered, nothing fits. It's obvious nothing ever gets cleaned." May's voice cracks and she begins to cry but continues, "There's all these stains and smells, oh God, the smells."

The group hugs, allowing May to use themselves as support, and they agree, cleaner clothes priority one.

The three move closer to the van but only close enough to spot movement if it should occur.

Will starts, "First thing we need from them is their tiny little thumbprints, while Ryson is doing that, you and I will head back to the train station for clothes and supplies, so he and the kids can comfortably stay here for as long as necessary After we return with what we have gathered, then you and I head back to our hotel and use the phone to call Art, hopefully, we can also fax him the thumbprints."

May shakes her head yes and says, "Art, yes. I don't know how, but I'll just bet he and Lila have already thought this through."

May is already texting Art and attempting to calculate the time to when that phone call might happen before the guys realize that's what should happen

150

next. May holds her phone out so the other two can see it and says, "how's this?"

It reads, "Need to talk private, going to use landline at the hotel but need to drive back. I think maybe noon, I will text when we get close. We are all okay. 3.4.5."

Arts reply, "On standby, be safe. 2."

"So let's wake up this sleepy bunch and fill them in. You get their fingerprints, May and I will get back with some supplies as quickly as possible. Then we take those prints and we go talk to Art."

"The children do not seem to be affected by any of this and if they are, they sure don't show it, they seem pretty content just being left alone."

Ryson watches May and Will disappear, he loses eye contact but you can hear them putter and clunk all the way to the main road and then speed away.

He has not yet turned around simply because he knows they are watching him, five tiny pairs of eyes piercing into his soul, he takes a deep breath and mumbles, "Yeah, this should be easy, fingerprints."

He turns, smiles, then gathers what he needs from the glove box.

Ryson withdraws a white piece of paper along with a black marker, stepping out, and over until in front of the five pairs of wide-eyed curiosity onlookers comfortably sitting inside of the van.

With outstretched arms, the marker in one hand and the paper in the other, he calmly first explains what he needs from them, then he demonstrates, he puts a nice black coating on his thumb from the black marker then presses this on to the paper, once he has a decent print, he shows the paper to the kids, smiles and says, "Easy peazy, whose next?"

After fingerprint fun, Ryson rearranges a couple of stacks of wooden crates and a pallet or two, making a makeshift cabana like structure to which he, too, hides from the sun.

Angel Cooks

"They are not going to know they're doll's clothes, and even if they did, they are not going to complain or care. Just the fact they're clean and the clothes fit is all that will concern them I'm quite sure."

May was far more disturbed then she let on, but the tone in her voice tells Will to leave her be.

They hold hands as they walk back to the van, they don't say much because there is not much to say. In this place, it seems Ryson was right, everything here is poison.

They put the two bags of clothes in the back, then head inside the market they parked in front of. They buy at a limit in case anybody is watching or paying attention, it's just the basics, food, and water. They make the return trip back to the harvest silos using the same route as to the market and avoiding the rain forest building and probably still a dog filled burned-out minivan.

Two hours and seventeen minutes, Ryson checks his watch when he hears a car on the main road heading his direction, he can hear it slow, then turn onto the road. He now stands at the ready with a Mac 10 trying to get a look at who it is.

He moves out of the way letting Will pull right back alongside the other van, the three unload what the two brought back, Ryson is astonished when he realizes they also brought back two bags of children's cloths, including socks and shoes.

The two are aloof when Ryson asked, "How did you find this here? What! Macy's have a sale downtown? So what gives?"

May takes the clothes and heads towards the children, Will motions to Ryson to follow as he walks a small piece up the road and stops. When Ryson is at a speaking distance, Will in a grit your teeth sort of way because he doesn't like saying it, he mumbles, "It was a doll store."

Ryson quizzically responds with, "So, it was a doll store."

152

"Yeah, well, any other place but here."

Will shakes his head in disgust, "We find this market and park right in front, but before we go in, we notice down the street is what looks like a children's store, so we wander down."

"From the outside and because of the sign in the window it appears to be a doll store, the sign reads 'In's And Out's' and under that another sign reads 'Dolls And Desires.'"

In the window are four various height square platforms and on top of each one is a doll, their different sizes ranging from infant to maybe nine or ten, so we go inside hoping to buy some clothes.

The dolls in the window are fully dressed and do seem a real to life like, if you know what I mean, but once we go inside, they have a few of the dolls in various ages undressed and on display. These are not just dolls, they are exact replicas and I mean, exact.

"Absolutely anatomically correct, boys and girls, I mean skin tones and textures, hair, eyes, they look like real children, they just don't walk and talk, well…at least, I don't think so, we did not get that far with our Q and A with the proprietor. We picked out a bunch of clothes and got the hell out of there, and evidently, May don't be wanting to talk about it. So, let's just let this one slip away."

There is a part of Ryson that wishes he found this surprising, but it's only a tiny piece because it's more disturbing than truly unexpected.

May joins the two and is glad they're not still discussing the doll store, she has a solid defiance about her and is going to do her best to forget where those clothes came from. It's in her voice and in her movement that shows she is not proud of it, but she will get over it.

The first couple of words she stumbles with, but composure gets the better hand. I just sort of laid out some of the clothing and told them it would be okay if they want to change into something cleaner and better fitting, "I made sure to place the little boy clothes, closer to the little boy." Mays voice cracks as her armor weakens. Ryson is closest and he does not hesitate to hug her, telling her, "Even once you realized where you were you stayed and you stayed for those kids. May, you're a third of why we are here, we share this as equals. May…you have our respect. You have already been tough as nails, my God, you were born for this and I'm sorry to say that. But, I already see your devotion to these children, to all children."

153

May lightly pushes him away in tears with a three-star general look on her face and says, "It was necessary, and the feeling is absolutely mutual, they kind of shake their heads in tandem then pull Will in for a group hug."

"Yeah, yeah, yeah, your both great, the three of us are super bitchin' and I'm already dusting off my mantle for the Nobel Peace Prize," they laugh and deservedly so.

May dries her eyes and asks, "Did you get fingerprints?"

"Yes, and listen, here's something else, tell Art to call Danny, Art will know what to do, Danny is my brother-in-law and can probably get satellite maps of this whole place."

Impressed but not enough time to seem so or ask questions, May and Will take the thumbprints, some water, and say goodbye for now to the kids, this time Ryson does not watch them leave, instead he turns bravely and heads back towards the silos.

Ryson slows as he passes the minivan, but does not look in or make eye contact. In his normal tone and volume, he simply states, "If anybody needs anything, all they have to do is ask, I'll be right here."

It's hard not to look at them, but on his approach he could hear them rustling around with the clothing and thought best to give them their privacy.

From Ryson's makeshift crate cabana, when he leans forward and looks right, he can see the minivan but he cannot actually see what's inside, when he does this the first time to check on the kids he sees a small light blue, stained T-shirt be thrown out and land in the dirt just outside the minivan door.

Before Ryson can get completely leaned back and comfortable with a smile on his face and hope in his heart there's a smell. It's faint, but it's closeness feels as if it seeped from his own skin, it's warm and sweet and then familiar.

It's the same warm sugar smell from just a few days ago while sitting in his own kitchen. Ryson gently sniffs the air around himself trying to capture all he can before it's lost to a gentle breeze. To his delight, instead of fleeting as before, the smell grows in thickness and strength, it's intensity warms to a point where he is almost certain a fresh batch of sugar cookies has just come out of the oven.

The moment lingers and the smell stays close. Ryson, in fear of chasing away the experience, stays perfectly still.

Only when the smell begins to fade and then disappear, altogether does Ryson realize he had closed his eyes and allowed himself to be taken someplace safe and comfortable.

Curious if the smell had reached the children, he leans forward, looking for any sort of reaction from them, and to his surprise, on the ground joining the blue T-shirt is now a whole pile of the same like clothing.

The rest of the day slow rolls in comparison, a text here and there, a text when May and Will left their hotel in King's Thone with a promise to text again when they got close. The smell does not return and all the old clothes and rain stuff Ryson gathers then is placed in doubled up trash bags, tied tight and placed some distance from them. The smell, no doubt, came from a place from where only he knows the way, because the smell from the clothing was indeed different and far more atrocious.

"Be there in twenty, everything okay? 4.5."

Ryson responds with, "All tens, everything's fine, we be just chillin' 3."

Ryson knows it's them from a long way off and finds no reason for the Mac 10 security patrol, instead, he stands at the very same spot where they are going to park. As they pull in the three trade smiles, May brings the van to a stop and the ignition to off.

Before she can do so, Ryson already has her door partly opened for her and asking, "He make you drive, May?"

Knowing her dislike for it, her response is predictable, "Yeah, just on the way back."

Ryson smiles and says, "That heartless heathen, what can you do?"

There is a slight giggle between them as Will walks over.

"I told you we'd be back before sundown, now what's so funny?"

May was just telling me how much she loves to drive.

"Ah, she did great." Will says this as he is peeking through the window of the van the kids are in, he now gently backhands May's hip and says, "You see this?"

May is extremely pleased as the large smile indicates, when did they do that.

"Shortly after you guys left, I put all the old stuff in a bag, that's it over there." Ryson points,) "Thought about burning it but did not want somebody to see the smoke, not that I think anybody would have, considering there has been nobody on this road but us since we got here, I don't know where this road goes but clearly there's nobody in a hurry to get there."

Will has this quizzical fracture in his face when he makes eye contact with Ryson and says, "Yes, odd to say the least, out of all the other roads and all leading in different directions, you choose this one and this direction. Well, we're glad you did." Will now turns and walks away, the other two follow.

When they reach an audible safe zone away from the kids, Will speaks first, "Art sends his best and yeah, we are real lucky he's on our side. The first thing he tells me after I explained to him exactly what we've done and what we have he says is that's okay because we were going home anyway, now he just has to make plans for eight, and obviously we won't be using the international terminal."

Ryson butts in with, "What do you mean we were heading home anyway?"

"Yeah, Ryson, evidently Art has been keeping tabs on the son of a bitch you put down the day they took the twins, and it seems somebody has finally claimed the body, and not only that, but the exit visa for the remains list Argentina as its destination. When the dead guy is leaving or exactly what city, Art still does not know, although, the exit visa is only good for ten days, so it's going to be soon."

"Ryson, I'm sure you don't want to leave here. And by choice, May and I would also not be leaving, but this and them, let's take these five back and yeah, I say we follow whatever lowlife piece of shit claims the other lowlife piece of shit to wherever the two pieces of shit go. Hell, we're almost in Argentina right now, so we're right on top of them and to be able to follow a Tiger Team member, dead or alive, could for sure put us very close to the machine in which we hunt."

"There's a sad calm, it's the sign of a weathered soul that leaves Ryson quiet," Will knew this would be hard and therefore, let's him choose his own destiny.

"Stay, if you must, if you can tell me in all honesty, Ryson, that your chances to succeed are better if you stay. Then May and I can only agree and she and I will take these kids back and then return, *pronto*! The way we see in we can be right back here in 18 hours and try to finish what we started."

"No, everything I feel right now says finish taking these five kids to safety and far, far away from here, and yes, I would love the chance to pay a house visit to the machine in which we hunt. How sweet would it be to kick in their front door and ask a few questions."

May nods her head and says, "Damn straight, like Wyatt Earp chasing down the cowboys."

Ryson smiles with true happy infraction and says, "Listen, May, I've been meaning to ask you this, but only because I find it all so pleasantly entertaining... But why all the western expressions?"

"It was my father. When he was not teaching me the way of the world and how to defend myself in it, one of the things he truly loved to do in his spare time was watch American westerns, he loved them with such passion it grew upon the rest of us like a boomtown in the old west."

"Well, okay then. I guess all I can say is... Please, never stop."

Ryson now returns to matters at hand, "So can I assume than there is some sort of plan to get the eight of us out of here?"

"Well, Mr. Willows, it just so happens the one in fifty roads you could have randomly chose is the very same road that leads us right the hell out of here, we know this because you also managed to park next to something your brother-in-law could see from space." Will looks up and slightly raises his right-hand palm up, "Yes, Danny and Chelsea send their love and say Pat is doing more with less medication all the time."

"I knew Danny would help, so what now, Will, where we going?" Ryson does his best to sidestep any tears but can't stop his eyes from watering up.

Will moves in one step closer to Ryson and says caringly, "Less medication. Ryson, that's always a good sign."

May now does the same and says, "I've seen people, strong people, come back from worst, you be strong for the both of you and anything is possible," now she says, "and I can't wait to meet this Danny guy."

Will agrees.

Ryson smiles and says, "Believe it or not, he's a tree doctor for the U.S. Forest Service."

They laugh, than May says, "He must be pretty damn good at taking care of trees if he can do it from space."

They laugh a little more, but it's a pretend kind of happiness and all three know it.

"Well, either way, I guess the maps he sent Art were pretty impressive, it's too bad Art could not have sent them to us, but no way we want anybody knowing where we're going. It's important us *hombres* keep a low profile."

Will jumps back in where he left off, "So, anyway, after the first phone call to Art, he tells me to call back in three hours and sit tight, keeping all communications down to a minimum. Three hours later, we call back, and Art already has the better part of a master plan in place and moving forward, it also seems he's calling in a favor from the Colombians."

Will does not stop talking and nobody interrupts.

"So, our part in this is quite simple really, tomorrow morning, we split everything up equally between both vans, May and I in one and you and the kids in the other, both vans should have enough gas to get where we're going, so if we lose one along the way, then we all pile in the other and finish the journey."

"And where exactly are we going, Will? You still have not told me that."

"Remember now, that this is Art talking, and between him and Danny, we have to trust them, because this road or where we're going is not on the couple of maps we have, the only directional help Art gave us was to go right the first time the road splits and go left the second time. And at the end of this road is a place called 'Asuncion,' there is a large diamond mining operation which is a conglomerate owned by four countries in South America and of those four, Columbia is one."

"We are supposed to remain in the dirt lot at the end of the road, we also must stay within eyesight of the runway, but proceed no farther," Will stops like that's the end of the story. He's waiting for Ryson to say the same thing he did.

"Okay, so, then what? That's exactly what I said."

That's when Art informs me he does not know yet. He says, "Sometime during the ride there, he will let us know."

The three of them discuss some of the obvious exit scenarios, and one or two somewhat more whimsical, but those just for fun. They really do not expect Art to fly in with the Nixon helicopter and rescue them, but amusing nevertheless.

Night eases gently in the space around them, it fills the world with something far less frightening tonight, they have dinner and each one attempting to be just a little more comfortable when it comes time for bed, they stick to their assigned van cabins with focus on getting some sleep.

The sun and the warmth that rides with it awake all eight at almost the same time and each of them welcome the day like an old friend. They get done with what needs to be done and say goodbye to the three harvest silos, glad for the refuge and just as glad to leave them behind.

It's one of those roads that always look worse in the distance, you always know that what you have right now is as good as it gets and for sure this road is steadily going to deteriorate, and considering the bumps and ruts already encountered, it does not look good.

"A long forty minutes into the ride," Art texts and its their first excuse to stop and take a break. When Will hits the brakes, Ryson does the same and both look for a way to pull off the road. In mere seconds, both vans empty and the occupants scatter about; May and her five in one direction, Will and Ryson in another.

All eight return to the road and share the small space between the two vans, three of them discuss the progress and Art's text, the other five remain quiet and in May's shadow.

Art's message was simple and to the point, "two have been positive I.D, Wow. Keep moving and be safe. 1.2."

May responds for the group, "That's our plan. 3.4.5."

When the road splits, they go right and of course the travel gets worse, Ryson has already been staring at a check engine light for the last 30 minutes and each time the minivan bottoms-out in one of these god-awful potholes, it seems to glow that much brighter. When the temperature gauge again starts to climb towards hot, Ryson beeps the horn, then stops, but does not turn the engine off or get out, instead, he motions for Will to come to him.

May and Will both exited their van and soon are at Ryson's window, Will stops there but May moves to the sliding door and pulls it open, "You kids okay?" Not expecting an answer she finishes, "Just sit tight," now she smiles and says, "good thing we didn't take the bumpy road, ha."

"What gives, Ryson? why we stopin'? I've got a check engine light on and the temperature is climbing fast. Also, the whole front end feels like it's coming apart on even the smaller bumps now. The wobble in the steering wheel sometimes is so bad I can barely hang on to it."

"So what would you like to do about that, Mr. Willows?"

"I say we do nothing, we let fate have its day," May says this as she turns to face Will. "We don't have enough water to keep dumping it into this wore-out bucket of bolts."

Ryson agrees, "Yeah, let's just keep moving until this thing will not."

Will steps past May so he two can check on the kids. He winks and says, "Sorry about this guy's driving, all the really good drivers had other stuff to do," he chuckles and slides the door closed. there is a smile from one of the five, it might have been the little boy, it happened fast, but it was enough to make Will feel like it was Christmas morning.

Will can see the next split in the road up about a mile and is already thinking about going left as he hears Ryson honk the horn, when he glances up to the rearview mirror, he sees him angle the minivan off the road doing his best to get as much of it off to the side as possible.

In one quick motion, Ryson is out his door and pulling the sliding door open, then releasing the handle, letting the door travel fully open on its own. The kids use Ryson as a sort of swinging stepstool, one by one, they file out and are lifted from his knee and placed towards the front of the van and immediately start walking towards May and Will.

Ryson does not wait to put the last child out of the van down, instead he carries her to where all the others are now standing.

The eight watch as the minivan spits and sputters, then erupts like a steam filled geyser, they hear one of the radiator hoses finally bursts and watch as it blows with enough force to bulge the hood of the van, this they take as their cue and decide it's time to go. May gets in the back with the kids, Ryson as the passenger and Will still at the wheel.

After going left, the road begins to narrow and now it's to the point where it's more of a path better suited for a pack mule.

Gunfire brings Will's foot to the brake pedal, it sounded far off and in the direction they're heading, the second short burst of automatic gunfire confirms the fact that, yes, it is far off but indeed coming from somewhere towards their destination.

When the three phones go off at the same time, they are all sitting in silence, anticipating the next burst of gunfire and so focused on it that the text message from Art damn near causes the three of them to wet their pants. As for the other five, it's clear they found the response more frightening than the message because it's May's yelp that causes them to go big eyed.

160

"Exit on standby, text when you have runway visual. 2."

"Roger that. 3.4.5.," May responds. The other two simply read it and silently agree.

I guess we keep moving, I am not sure how much more this old girls got in her. Will scans the engine gauges as he says this with a gallon of hope.

They go maybe another mile before the road finally wins the battle and the right front wheel snaps and folds under the van, sending it nose first to a sudden stop, gouging the bumper into the earth.

Before they walk away with what they needed versus what they could carry, Will climbs on top of the minivan attempting to get a look further down the road. Will speaks out-loud reporting what he sees when he sees it.

"You know, it looks to me like the road ends in another hundred yards, and to the right of that it looks like there might be a clearing, can't completely tell because of the trees in the way, but let's go have a look, shall we?"

In less than a hundred yards, the road does, indeed, end, and the eight of them find themselves standing in a small dirt lot and adjacent to this with maybe fifty yards between them is what looks like the back portion of a runway.

May, of course, does the honors but the three agree what to say. In lot, runway visual, all eight okay.

Several nervous minutes slowly tick by before Art reply, and it's important the procedure is fully understood.

"In this order. Exit inbound twenty minutes, take nothing on the plane, just yourselves, no guns, you will be in the crosshairs. You get ten minutes after plane has come to a complete stop, so hustle! Text when you're away, okay? 1.2."

There's some thought but no discussion, May hits send, "Okay. 3.4.5."

May now squats so at eye level with the kids, "So I guess we are all going for a plane ride, sure beats airport security." They pile all they carried here behind some trees and proceed to hatch a dash to the plane plan.

It's decided. May will carry one child and run point, leaving the guys to carry one in each arm, doing their best to keep up.

The DC-10 lumbers in a slow float approach from the west, it's four engines barely above idle, the pilot doglegs left and brings the slow moving giant in shallow and probably with his feet already on the brakes, it's the kind

161

of approach that says, he does not have enough space to safely get slowed and stopped but is going to do it anyway.

From the far end of the runway, they could hear when the DC-10 touches down and now can clearly hear it struggling to get slowed.

With most of the runway now consumed, the aircraft makes a sharp right turn and is now heading straight for them, the thought to turn and run is only that, because now the aircraft begins a large circular left turn, bringing the tip of the outer wing within ten yards of the dirt lot and almost over their heads, the eight are frozen in astonishment as the plane completes this maneuver, ending up back on the runway, heading in the other direction slowing to a complete stop.

Several precious seconds tick by and nobody moves, the spectacle is jaw dropping to say the least. "High, ho silver," she yells, and May is off and running, she does not look back, only forward with the child in her arms and a sense of bravery so pure that even to this day, she barely remembers making that dash to freedom.

The eight arrive at the plane to find stairs and an open door but nobody to greet them. When the engines begin to rev up from an idle, they quickly climb the stairs and shuffle onto the plane. A woman's voice is heard over a loudspeaker, "Pull in the stairs, close the door, find a seat, buckle up, it's going to be somewhat of a steep departure. No worries though, I got this."

The engines continue to rev, the plane's nose leans forward but the wheels remain locked to the runway, there is a point when you can actually hear the engines reach maximum power and then wham! The movement forward is so severe it seems as if you're going to be pushed right through the back of your seat.

After a couple of minutes, the plane levels out, giving May back the use of her arms, her text to Art is simple, "Eight away, thank you."

Art responds, "Nicely done, talk to your pilot."

The loud speaker squawks to life with the same woman's voice as before, "Give me a couple of more minutes and I'll be right down to say hello, go ahead and get comfortable, but you should probably stay in your seats."

Anna is already making her own introductions even before she can finish descending the ladder from the upper level and cockpit.

"Sorry I wasn't there to help you guys aboard, but when it comes to the Colombians and their hospitality, it's best to just do as you're told, they gave us ten minutes idle ground time, we only used eight. That was quite the skedaddle you manage to muster, and the whole time hanging on to these precious, little jewels."

Anna forgoes the last rung of the ladder and just short hops it to the floor. When she turns to greet her guest, it's the children she locks onto, only glancing briefly at the other three, "I've only got a couple of minutes, so I will make this quick, we have no co-pilot, it's just me and my name is Anna, Anna Bacanya. But you can call me Anna Banana."

All five children smile, but none bigger than Anna's.

"Aren't you four just as pretty as can be, and of course, good day to you as well, my fine sir." Anna moves in close and begins to check and adjust their seatbelts, her approach and contact is met with more smiles when she says, "Nothing to fear as long as Anna is here, I for sure am the very best airplane pilot in the whole world, there is none better than Anna Banana. So just sit tight, I will have you home before it gets dark." Anna takes a couple of steps back and nods her head and says, "Safe as can be."

Ryson question of, "Where we going, Anna?" sends her into a one heel spin and now facing the three, she smiles, and on her face is a look of confidence with an equal amount of pretty. At 5' 9", thin, and skin the color of dark amber, Anna checks her watch. When she flips her light brown hair back into place, she starts in.

"We are currently flying low in-between the borders of Bolivia and Argentina, we will soon be over Chile and then into international waters of the South Pacific, where we shall then make a right turn and climb to twenty seven thousand feet slipping into a jet stream, which should push us along fairly quickly, and forgoing any unseen difficulty's right across the equator. Our destination is Long Beach California, good ole US of A."

"In the back of the plane is some bottled water and such, I don't quite know what's there but help your selves, there is also a bathroom, don't forget to flush," Anna now spins towards the ladder she ascended but continues to speak as she moves that direction.

"When we level out at cruising altitude, I will come back and we can chat," before Anna reaches for the ladder, she turns back towards them and with her right hand, she makes the sign of the cross, then closes just one eye and bows her head. The prayer she now says is one of her own, "Thank you, Lord, for the gift of flight, please keep us safe, for we are not angels with wings of our own, our faith and love we give to you with one eye open to the heavens and the other we shall trust that which you show us," Anna repeats the sign of the cross, "In the name of the Father, the Son, and the Holy Spirit, Amen."

It seems almost playfully, she now spins back towards the ladder, quickly bounding up and out of sight leaving Ryson, Will, and May only to speculate, how, who, where, and why.

Anna's second appearance comes with it, of course, some candy for the kids. With that dispensed and being eaten accordingly, she now turns her attention back to Ryson and the others.

"Before you go firing a bunch of questions at me I can't answer, why don't I just tell you what I do know, starting with this magnificent beast to which you are currently riding in the belly of. My sister and I assembled, repaired and restored it ourselves."

"It's only been on the market a couple of weeks when from out of the blue, excuse the pun, an offer from a Mr. Arthur Match of our asking price plus ten percent if I deliver it to someplace called," Anna withdraws a folded piece of paper she had tucked in the sleeve of her one-piece gray jumpsuit, "War Era Planes Of Distinction with a touch and go pick up eight before that."

"I could not say no, I always do enjoy a challenge," Anna now replaces the paper to her sleeve, what she says next it's obvious she has already subjected to memory. "We are cleared for I.L.S. approach to runway one, left, our call sign will be Tango, Charlie, Delta, 11, 0, 9er. Call back at the outer marker for this museum will be whiskey, Alpha, bravo, 45, 45, so how did I do?" Anna comes to a silence and checks her watch. The smile on her face says it's only here she wants to be.

"Anna, who's flying the plane?" Will does not wait for an answer before he ask the next question, "and wow! Just what did this magnificent beast cost?"

Ryson and May acknowledge as to their questions being the same.

"I appreciate the collective thought, but I can really answer only one. When you restore vintage aircraft for the purpose of flight, the first things you have to do is retrofit modern G.P.S. and autopilot systems, meaning, this old girl can almost fly herself, she just won't land or make critical flight attitude adjustments, that just means she won't auto-correct for turbulence, it could knock us off course."

164

"In regards to the money aspects of this little Q and A, how about who ever this Arthur guy is, you ask him. And the very next time I see my sister, perhaps I will ask her as well."

They all share a little chuckle because they believe her, and she herself does not really know.

Anna now turns her attention back to the children, but does not step closer to them, "Okay, so I got some airplane flying to do, but I will be back to check on ya in just a little while, so in the meantime how about yuz bez ah chilling like Frosty on Christmas morning."

Some tiny smile, some do not.

Before she turns and retreats up the ladder, Anna points at a large, red hand button on the bulkhead, "If there's any problems you push that, Anna comes a runnin', get comfy, relax, I'll be back, yes, like Arnold."

There is no third visit from Anna. When she checks on them sometime later, all eight are sleeping soundly.

There is a series of bumps, yaws, and slight wiggles as the plane drops in altitude, but it's only enough to gently rattle awake those that were still sleeping. Everything outside the window comes into focus in one quick snap, causing Ryson to pull away from the window wide-eyed and somewhat panicked.

This very brief moment surrenders its self to sadness and anger, anger because he has seen firsthand the machine that took his children. Sadness because of those children they bring back, none of which was his own.

It's the sight of the dome they built to house the Spruce Goose that tells Ryson this is a reality, he's home.

Anna's voice is well camouflaged in the tone of her favorite superhero, but there is a certain stress component to it, lending her passengers to some concern when she announces, "This runway is going to come up just a little short of slow and easy, there is no cause for concern, it still within safe limits, the thing is I will have to get on the brakes a little harder than normal, so synch down those belts and stay in your own seats. Anna will have you standing on firm ground in just a jif."

Anna joins them at the door as the eight prepare to go down the stairs hand-in-hand. When the door is fully open and the ladder extended, there at the bottom of the stairs is a man dressed in a mechanic's uniform with both hands stretched out in front of himself as if he is trying to catch something precious falling from the sky, with a look to match. His voice cracks just a little when he says well above normal tone, "She is magnificent!"

The eighth descend the ladder, leaving Anna in the doorway, they have already said their goodbyes and traded phone numbers, they already know she wants to stay and talk to the guy at the bottom of the stairs.

The eight quietly descend and begin to move past mechanic guy, it's Will that asked, "Is there someplace passengers need to go?"

Without making eye contact, mechanic guy says, "There were no passengers on this flight, just the pilot. Have a nice day and God bless!"

When he's done with what is clearly a pre-meditated response, he smiles and flicks his head over his left shoulder.

It's not quite dark but there is enough gray to keep things from being seen in the distance, the eight scoot quickly off the tarmac and towards a small lighted hanger, the only one well-lit and with its large door halfway retracted. Inside they find Art and Lila, the two are standing alongside each-other while having a conversation with the two young females who occupy a full-size white utility van, one girl in the driver seat and the other seated in back. The driver door is ajar as is the double doors at mid van, leaving no secrets inside.

The two girls in the van stay put as the group of eight come into the hangar, Art and Lila turn from the van while moving towards the eight, they meet closer to the large door than the van. It's hugs, handshakes, and kisses all around, except the children, they stay close to each other and quiet.

It's warm and genuine but also fleeting, the reunion goes quick when Art's tone and emotional state ramp up as he answers the question, "What's with the girls and the van? I don't think we are all going to fit." Ryson says this with genuine concern and curiosity.

"The van and the two in it belong to a local organization for child protection and foster care," Art delivers this reply as if in some aspect there is room for discussion when in fact there is not. "We can trust these people, I need you three to trust me," Art takes a short step back so what he says next is heard by all, including the kids, "I have worked with these people before, and they are who they say they are, they are also these kids best chance at recovery and being reunited with their families just as fast as possible, you three did good, but let's let these kids finish their journey with the people that know how to get that done, okay?"

May steps forward and hugs Art, this triggers a group hug, and as silly as it seems or looks, this just meant all five are again on the same page.

They follow the van out of the hangar and stand quietly while it fades, then turns, it's a somber moment but quickly replaced with the promise of dinner at Art's favorite Italian restaurant.

A few steps towards Art's Land Cruiser and the parking lot it's sitting in, Art barks into the darkness as if the words simply escaped on their own, "We okay, Anna?"

And from somewhere, there's a reply, "Like a penguin through winter." They all laugh when Art says quietly, "I think that's good."

The five had agreed, all conversation regarding the last three days would be in its abridged version until they were someplace more private, the only thing that was clearly discussed during dinner was when Will remembers to again ask the question, "Art, please tell us, how much does a vintage D.C.10 completely restored and even retrofitted with modern electronics cost nowadays? Please tell us because Anna would not, or could not, we're not sure."

The table gets quiet, including Lila. Art pauses for a second or two, not so much to gather his thoughts but to build on the anticipation. He's having fun, and not the only one.

"Well, before you go looking for my hidden cachet of gold bars and precious gemstones, you should know, we did not actually purchase the plane, we only brokered the transaction, really, all I did was connect the dots, Lila's the one who crunched the numbers and made the money work. The museum where the plane landed actually purchased the aircraft, and that price was three point two million dollars. The bummer is, that's because we guaranteed an additional ten percent for the extra stop and fuel, our charity, Project Mother's Day, takes a three-thousand-dollar loss, but I think we can all agree, it was worth it."

May respectfully chimes in, "Yes, and I'll just bet there are five young children who would also agree."

Things get a little quiet, forcing one of Lila's nervous responses, "Would somebody please say something funny?"

Ryson quickly steps up to the plate like he's been waiting a while to repeat this one, "I got a joke, I heard this a couple of weeks ago on the freeway and almost took out a section of off ramp at 14th St." He already has a smile and is having to do his best to control his laughter even before he starts.

"Supposedly, just last year for B.B. King's birthday his girlfriend goes out and has the letter 'B' tattooed on both butt cheeks, I guess marking B.B. King's territory forever, anyway, after the few friends who were invited to the small birthday party get together, go home, the girlfriend now tells B.B. that this year for his birthday she got him something really, really, special, and all he has to do is stand there and close his eyes."

"When B.B. does this, the girlfriend now backs up a couple of feet and turns around putting her backside towards B.B. Now she pulls down her shorts and panties letting them hit the floor. Bending at the waist and grabbing her own ankles, she now tells B.B. to open his eyes."

"BB's quiet for a few seconds, then in real puzzlement, he says, 'Well, that's great, but who the hell is Bob.'"

The table roars, almost to an embarrassing level, all five found that very funny, and also decide perhaps it's time to go before they are thrown out for disturbing the peace.

There is less laughter and more of things turning back towards business in the ten-minute ride from the restaurant to Redline Financial, nothing to specific, it's like they're trying to decipher one another and just testing the temperature of the water.

They all five logjam at the back door from the parking lot waiting for Art to successfully pair the correct keys for two locks that look very much alike. It's exactly ten p.m., they know that because for the few seconds it took Art to find a light switch, the clock in a microwave was the only thing visible as they came through the door.

When the lights come on and before anybody gets comfortable or too far away Art steps a little closer to Ryson in a way that says he is going to ask a question, the others are also thinking this and are glad Art says it first.

"So…are you going back?"

Ryson makes eye contact with Art and says nothing. The quick glance around the room tells him they are all waiting for an answer.

"You guys are looking at me as if this decision is mine alone to make," Ryson looks at May and Will who are now leaning against the sink with their arms crossed. "I don't know about you two but I am quite sure now that we have been there done that, that is not a place where one person alone will survive for very long. I think that is extremely obvious."

"Yes, I do admit it was extremely hard to leave, and it was a decision even though you may not know it, three of us did make together. But we knew us leaving as a team with what we had was not only the right thing to do but also our best chance at survival."

"So, if you're asking me would I choose to pursue this, well, of course, I would for all of the obvious reasons, but also I think the possibility of even the tiniest bit of success going at this alone is slim at best."

Ryson now shifts his attention to Art and Lila, "Now, I don't want this to sound all worshipy but what you two did to get all of us out of that, wow, it seemed at the time nothing less than a miracle, then we get back and you two are all like, all we had to do is connect the dots and crunch the numbers. Well, I just don't think it was all that easy, probably a little more to it than that."

"So, you know what, this really is decided by you four, not me. I go back either way. Yes, I go back either way."

Lila comes in for a hug, then waiting till after to say, "Ryson, Art, and I's commitment to this is permanent, till you say otherwise."

May and Will in stereo like it was planned, say, "I'm all in, then May finishes with. like we got something better to do, I don't think so."

When its Arts turn to finally chime in he does so with the voice of a leader, "All right, my good people, so then let's talk about what happens next. It's late so I'll make this quick just to give us all something to think about."

"I have to first say, and I realize we already have, but I'd like to say it again nicely done. Five little lives get a second chance because of what you three did, our hats are off to you." Lila gives them a small standing ovation and even a couple of yahoos.

Ryson and Will give a little bow, May curtsies.

Art keeps talking, "Like I told you, the dead guy, the kidnappers left behind has been claimed and an exit visa was issued for the body two days ago, this means the feds have released the body and no longer have interest in it as evidence. This exit visa was issued to an Adam Gentos as the chaperone and Argentina as the destination. What we don't have is a picture of the chaperone, nor has there been airline tickets purchased for either one."

"The exit visa expires in seven days and some odd hours, so the two of them will for sure be leaving soon, so let's think about that because somebody should be on the flight trying to figure out who this guy is and somebody on the ground with transportation ready to follow."

"Okay? you follow me?"

"All right, so let's talk about some more wow factor," Arts tone changes and now he tells everybody to grab a juice box from the fridge and let's sit for a few minutes, Art waits in a chair at the table for the others to get settled in around him, but also for the cherry blast he asked for.

Art is already thumbing through a small tablet of paper as the others nestle in, and when he finds what he's looking for he looks up for just a couple of seconds, then says, "Those five you brought back, three of the girls we could find no match to the prints you sent, I trust the fact that child services will find out where they belong and do the right thing."

"The other two, the boy and a girl, their prints came back a match almost immediately, with photos. Turns out they're brother and sister, their parents, believe it or not, own a pro sports team right here in L.A., and will just leave it at that because they absolutely do not want to be identified."

"The kids were taken from somewhere in Brazil about three weeks ago while the family was on vacation, these guys break into the hotel room while the parents are out, the nanny puts up such a fight they end up killing her. And the kids are gone.

"So, needless to say, the parents are quite thankful for what you did. They wanted to give us a reward. Of course, I informed the good people there at child protection services; we are a non-profit organization who can and will only accept legal donations. And anything the parents would like to donate would be graciously accepted."

"Next thing I know, some guy is calling me. In all fairness, I never told anybody he couldn't. In fact it was really cool that he did, because he's offered to allow one of us at this table a one on one interview with Arlington Waters, just before his new show airs tomorrow night, remember, he's the one that exposed that whole day care pornography ring a couple of years back. Well, I guess he's become quite the voice in the fight against child abuse."

"His new show, Under Care Or Control, has already gone national and it has not even aired the first episode yet. So who's it going to be?"

All four look at Ryson and he looks shocked and genuinely startled. "Really, since when did we decide I would be the voice of Project Mother's

Day?" Ryson's question is left to dissipate for a few seconds in silence, leaving the others to simply nod their heads in agreement.

"Ryson, who better than you?" this question from Art opens the floodgates for the others.

May fires next, "Well, you really are why we're here, and I, for one, considering the last four days, think you might just have something to say regarding child abuse."

Lila jumps in, but just for fun because it's late and she wants to call it a night, "Think of it like this, Ryson, now you have a reason to finally take those acting classes you always wanted, and you know damn well your hearts just going to go fluttering when you get to meet Mr. Waters for the first time."

They laugh and chuckle.

Like I said, "Let's think about those two things, we'll call it a night and how about we say back here tomorrow at 11 a.m.?"

They all agree and say good night. Ryson, May, and Will leave first through the back door, but before Ryson reaches his car, he decides to leave it and walk home, he waves as Will pulls out of the parking lot and already feels a sense of loss as they disappear into the darkness.

Ryson checks his watch and counts the hours he must spend alone, it's 10:30 p.m. His plans, a long, slow walk home, but first, a stop at the fountain.

Angry Hero

It's a short walk even at a snail's pace from around back to the street out front, things go dark inside Redline Financial as Ryson walks past the front door, a few seconds later, he can hear a car start and motor away from somewhere out back, assuming it's Art and Lila, he mumbles out loud in a feeble attempt to chase away some of the shadows sneaking around the inside of his head, "See you in the a.m., sleep tight."

Ryson saunters past, the dental complex and is pleased to see the open gate in the fence surrounding the fountain, without hesitation, he wanders through like he's been expected. The place is quiet, there is very light traffic on the street and no foot traffic since he left May and Will in the parking lot.

There are three light poles in a triangle pattern around the fountain but only the one furthest back is on, it alone does not illuminate the fountain and surrounding area with any real penetration, so when Ryson spots movement on his approach to the fountain, he freezes.

What was a tall dark shadow, in an instant, collapses in on itself and disappears within the water catch basin of the fountain. Confused and thinking perhaps just shadows in the night he sort of bravely moves the short distance required to place himself just at the two foot sitting wall surrounding fountain.

From near the center of the fountain, which is maybe ten feet from him, the collapsing shadow he witnessed on his way in now rises silently to an erect stance of at least six feet tall, the shadow remains motionless as does Ryson. Some seconds tick buy then the shadow moves.

"What the hell is that?" this is more of a question Ryson asked himself, but does so out loud.

The question causes the shadow to spin quickly, putting the two of them only a few feet apart and now face to face.

The light is minimal but it's enough, the two let whatever words they had partially formed retreat and both stand silently, but in a familiar presence with the other.

The man standing in the fountain with a full-length trench coat with a hood knows instantly why this seems as though the two should share this feeling of "Hey! Don't I know you?"

Ryson feels this as well but to him it's a place that's very, very dark and full of pain, blood, sadness, and despair, this emotional state weakens his legs and knees. Frightened by this euphoric embrace, he attempts to be assertive when he makes the statement, "So, what, you just climb in there and start stealing people's wishes? How sad is it if you have to go through life living off other people's hopes and dreams one nickel and dime at a time."

When the man standing in the fountain speaks, his voice seems to pierce even the darkest places in Ryson's head when he says, "That's pretty big talk from a man I had to save from bleeding to death in a parking lot at the mall the day before Mother's Day."

This sends Ryson to a sitting position on the short wall surrounding the fountain.

Terrance moves to Ryson and sits next to him, leaving his legs inside the fountain and his boot's still in two inches of water that did not drain from the fountain's catch basin.

"Your first question surely will be, did I see or hear anything that would explain how you and another would come to dead and bleeding to death where and when I found you. The answer is, absolutely not. There was just you two when I got there, it was after I wrapped your face and neck to stop the bleeding that the woman who dialed 911 showed up. I left telling her I was going to get blankets when I heard sirens from a few blocks away. As I stood up, you opened your eyes for a second or two, you looked right at me."

"Yes, yes, thank you. The paramedics left it in their report that had those tourniquets not been applied I would have, without question, bled out. Now tell me how is it you end up in both places? That day at the mall, now here doing what in a fountain, I sure the hell don't know. And, what is your name?"

"Fair enough, I can see how these are some things you might like to know. Why you find me in this fountain is the same reason I was at the mall a few days ago, and this needs to be kept between just you and me. I'm looking for

173

something, it's extremely important to me and sadly enough it was tossed into a fountain as payment for a child's wish somewhere here in Orange County."

"My name is Terrance Lorden. And it's nice to meet you, Mr. Willows, all up right and not bleeding profusely. I made a point to read the papers that Sunday in hopes of getting some details on what I had stumbled into, and afterwards, as always, I wished I had never learned to read. You look as though you survived the ordeal somewhat intact, but what about the kids."

The words "Tiger Team" fall from Ryson's lips in a blurred mumble as he slightly bows his head and droops his shoulders, "Okay, but just remember, you asked."

Ryson is somewhat reluctant at first, so he takes a deep breath and is not quite sure he can continue, but to his surprise, starting with, "The emotional collapse and soul screaming horror of realizing your children have been taken seems to kick some large boulders out of the way because it opens a floodgate." He unleashes the sadness first, then this abridged version comes full circle, leaving out anything too incriminating but definitely not candy coating the horrors and atrocities.

Sadness, anger, contempt, fear, and quiet rage fueled this delivery, ending with a shadow in a fountain. Terrance is without response or interaction, he only sits quietly through the barrage as it chomps at his sole one large bite at a time.

The last few words trail away into the night, leaving both of them consumed, wet eyed, and angry.

Guilt sneaks up on Ryson as he realizes Terrance is wiping tears from his face and still has not uttered a single word, "I am sorry, Mr. Lorden, perhaps just because you knocked, didn't mean I had to open the door so far."

"You can call me Terrance, I think, given the circumstance, we can dispense with formality and go right to first name basis, and there is no reason for you to apologize, you just caught me off guard. What was once the gift of life is now a sentence to sorrow. I don't know whether to applaud you for what you did and the courage in which you did it, or do I apologize for saving your life and sending you on a journey to hell."

Ryson stands and takes a single step away from the fountain, then turns to face Terrance, "Yeah, I thought about that, and in all honesty, I love you for what you did. I have not thanked you for saving my life, but maybe, someday I can."

Terrance makes only one remark, "Fair enough." Ryson turns and takes another couple of steps away from the fountain, again, he stops and turns back towards Terrance.

"Hey, Terrance."

"Yeah, Ryson."

"You can tell me, what are you looking for? and can I help?"

Terrance swings his legs out of the fountain in a 180, but staying seated and now again the two face one another, "Just the nickels, and for everyone I take I leave a dime, what you can do to help is promise me you will never remove a nickel from a fountain in Orange County, ever."

Ryson responds with, "Fair enough."

Before Ryson can get turned around to leave, Terrance asks, "So, what are you going to say to the world tomorrow night?"

Ryson turns and walks away, but not without saying, "I wish I knew, I guess I just politely ask for donations to our charity."

They let the silence steal back the night, Ryson leaves quietly. Terrance, back in the water.

The walk home is peaceful and over too quickly, it's straight to the shower and then straight to bed.

The rising sun begins to tap gently on the back of the curtain, the warmth already sneaking through the tight weave lands peacefully on the exposed part of a leg closest to the window. Ryson feels the day role from the night and in more ways than not, wishes there was another direction for the rising sun.

There is a window over the sink in the kitchen and through the thin, yellow curtain, Ryson spots movement while rinsing out his favorite mug. Drawing aside just the left half of the curtain, he spots the neighbor girl, Francine, just as she gets down on all fours, then headfirst crawling waist deep in a large bush on their shared property line out back.

It's only nine something and with nowhere else to be, Ryson stands in the moment, willing to spend the minutes and see how this plays out.

Francine is dressed in an ankle length moo-moo, and given her bulk, the garment could probably termite tent the house, she has a light sweater over this and on her feet, a pair of sneakers, no socks.

Out the side of this bush springs a cat just as Francine makes a short quick lunge, the cat, the same cat Will gave her bounds away and disappears.

Because Francine's hurried attempt to back out of the bush and give chase, the long moo-moo gets caught up around her knees, so as she gets most of the way out all she can do to escape is role backwards onto her butt, then onto her back, unfortunately because of her well-rounded mid-section, she rolls over more to her left side, and this all happens so fast Ryson cannot close the curtain quick enough as to avoid eye contact with her.

Ryson expects to see painful embarrassment on Francine's face, instead all that's there is smiles and laughter with a look as if she would be willing to pay for that experience. Now she says something to him but with the window closed, it's just silent mouth movement.

Sliding the window open and not quite sure what to say, Ryson says, "You okay, Francine?"

There is a large, brown envelope on your porch, not quite sure who or when, but must have been early.

"Did you see which way Mister Zippers went?"

"Yes, Francine, back towards your house."

"Thanks, Ryson, I love that fuckin' cat."

"Sure thing, Francine, have fun."

Ryson leaves the window and curtain as is to go check the porch.

There is nothing written on the outside of the large, brown envelope lying on the doormat. From inside, the envelope he withdraws four sheets of paper while still standing in the open doorway, three of which are stapled together, one is not.

The single piece reads "Wrote this because of you. If you read this, then read only this. Your friend, Terrance."

It looks to be some kind of hand written poem, which is titled Heavy Is Thy Hammer.

After closing and locking the front door, Ryson heads back to the kitchen, pulling the chair in close to the table where he now sits and reads.

When only a page in, he leans back slowly in his chair, completely consumed by the emotional state in which this was written. With the pages read and now laying on the table in front of him, he's in awe and afraid to move in fear of chasing away the moment.

He reads it a second time, already knowing that next time he reads this, it will be out loud and on national T.V.

When the faint sounds of days gone by begin to ramp up in volume, Ryson knows it's time to go, because as empty as this place is, there's just too much he can remember and the phantom sounds of his family at play dig far too deep. As he locks the front door, he hesitates to retrieve the key from the lock, what he's thinking is anybody's guess.

The five blocks to Redline Financial are becoming familiar territory, keep this up and I might have to actually buy a pair of walking shoes.

Ryson slows somewhat as he passes the coffee house and fountain, the short glance he takes at the fountain when he walks by is only to ensure it's still there, that brown envelope in his hand is proof it was not a dream.

He only knocks because the door is locked, Art is on the phone when he comes through the curtain to unlock the door, he gives the deadbolt a quick flip and backs up.

Ryson comes through the door, expecting Art to scoot out of way, instead, Art finishes his sentence, something about digitizing maps, then hands the phone to him.

"It's your brother-in-law," Art smiles, turns and backtracks, but before he gets too far away, Ryson lowers the phone and gives a pssssst. When Art turns to face this, he hands him the envelope, quietly saying, "Read this, then have Lyla do the same."

Art again turns, this time, disappearing back through the curtain.

"How's things, Danny?"

"Real good, Ryson, nice to have you back."

"Hey, Danny, thanks for all your help, Art tells us those maps you produced were the only part of the puzzle he did not have, and then there you were. Real nice, Danny. Thanks, man, so how's Pat?"

"Better, Ryson. This morning, she and Chelsea have gone to the grocery store, I guess tonight they're serving up some stir-fry. As for the maps, Chelsea and I just want to help, and we will do anything we can, Ryson. We've already told Art, all he has to do is ask, and if it anyway possible, consider it done."

"You guys are the best, and I'm sure Art plans on keeping you two in the loop. Now listen, Danny, I am not quite sure what's going to happen but there is a chance I'll do the live intro for the show 'Under Care Or Control' tonight, so maybe record it if you can, I don't know what channel or time, I might later, not sure."

"I know the show, it's with that Arlington Waters guy, he's really good, and I'm sure the show will kick ass. You get on that show, you best bring you're A game. Just remember, with him it's all about the kids."

"Again, thanks, Danny, for sure duly noted, now, when the girls get back, you tell them I send my love, and I will keep all of you up to speed as often as possible."

"One more thing, Ryson. The capacity to save any at all makes you very special, be safe, my brother, we're here when you need us, you hear what I'm saying?"

"Yeah, Danny, love you, too, bro."

Ryson follows Arts path through the curtain as he hangs up. In the back section of Redline Financial, Ryson finds Art standing motionless, it's clear his lights are on but the empty stare says there's nobody home. Lila is sitting at the table facing Ryson's direction and now turning to the last page of the poem.

The moment slows, and all three are now entrenched in the pull of what Terrance has written, it draws you to a place of balance and dismemberment but mostly it's an acidic burn for the contempt of mankind.

When Lila finishes the last page, she returns the poem carefully to its brown vessel and places it in front of her. Ryson and Art, somehow, without discussing it, agree to let Lila comment first. Her head comes up slowly, gravity stealing a few tears before she can reach for a napkin, there is a sorrow in her eyes even past the tears that weakens Ryson's knees when their eyes meet.

That's some friend, her voice flutters and she smiles, "You are going to read this, right? Tell me you intend to share this with the world."

"Yes, Lila, that is my intention and I am glad you agree."

Before Art can inject his approval and two cents, the tapping on the back door means May and Will have now joined the party.

Lila stands and they all join at the back door for a group hug. There is a somber silence to the room and both Will and May feel the heaviness in the air, "What's going on, yeah, what gives, guys?"

"I assume this is for everybody to read, am I correct?" Art waits for a reply before he retrieves the envelope from the table and now hands it to May.

"Yes, of course, now how about a cup of coffee," Ryson moves towards the stove, then drops his head playfully overstated when Lila announces the damn piece of crap coffee maker broke again this morning, and right after that, I threw it in the dumpster.

"Hey! Wait, don't we still have some of those cans of iced coffee in the small fridge upfront?" Before Art can finish this sentence, he is already moving towards the curtain, "let's let those two read that and we'll go check," Lila and Ryson give chase as Art leaves the back space in search of the canned java.

May and Will pull up chairs side-by-side, May reads it first.

May says nothing when she's done, she quietly hands the poem to Will and drifts off to someplace scary in her own life, cry, she will not, this poem is about the anger, and she agrees.

The pull-tabs popping in the other room fish them both from the depths of some very deep water. Will slides the pages back to their respective vessel, as if they were priceless documents, carefully closing the envelope and leaving it on the table.

When the three return with their *café* in a can, there's only one extra, "You two can share or wrestle for it, either way this is the last one." May enters first, placing the can of iced coffee on the table, "So what did you think?"

"Where did this come from and who is Terrance?" Both these questions come from Will. May's only response was, "Wow."

Ryson sits at the table across from Will and tells those still standing to do the same and listen to this, he replays the encounter at the fountain last night, also being sure to include Francine and cat this morning, just because that was funny.

They all agree, the purpose for Heavy Is Thy Hammer is predetermined and without question.

Art addresses the table, "Okay, so moving on to more pressing matters. You three need to repack a minute bag and have it ready to go, keeping in mind, of course, we know now that whatever you take with you, you may not be bringing back. I guess we chalk that up to a lesson learned."

"Who goes where and how, Lila and I have spent some time discussing," Art now gets very matter of fact. "It really comes down to the fact that whoever claims the dead guys body could indeed I.D. Ryson, especially if they get on the same flight, so that can't be."

Lila politely nudges in, "Our best approach as Art and I see it, is you two on the plane, Ryson on a different flight heading to the same place, ahead of you two, if possible. That gives you two several hours to hopefully figure out who this guy is, and hopefully before he gets off the plane."

Art nudges back in, "Yes, and then this information is relayed through our e-box and with just an ounce of luck Ryson is ready to give chase. You two rent a car and now also through the e-box, you three regroup and decide what to do next."

Art pauses waiting for a response, when none comes, he applies his own rebuttal, "You do realize this is a democracy? We can discuss other options."

"Like that of a N.A.S.A. launch sequence," the three chirp in, one at a time.

"That plan works for me."

"You just say when, sheriff."

"I don't know, man, I really need to check my day planner."

They all laugh.

Art stands up, he looks like he is almost in tears, "I don't know how the three of you settled into such a clique so quickly but use that, trust each other, be safe. Be smart."

"Now, go, get out of here, put your life in order, pack, and stay close to your phone. And, Ryson, good luck tonight we'll be watching. They want you there by four." Art now makes eye contact with him and says, "Ryson, just be yourself and read that, seems pretty easy to me, and who knows, could be a career in showbiz your destined for."

"Yeah, right after I run for president."

"Be that as it should be, now get."

The three leave out the back, and away. Art and Lila, business as usual.

There is a private gun club and range nestled in the small hills of Orange County, and a couple of blocks from this is a place called Leonard's Firehouse Hoagies, after packing a small carry-on bag, Ryson decides hoagies and guns is how the next couple of hours shall be spent.

Ryson would be lying if he said he wasn't even a little nervous as he leaves the gun club and heads down town. Security at the front gate does indeed have him on a list, the guard hands him a small hand-drawn map and says, "Park only in the yellow spaces."

The gate goes up and with it, maybe his lunch, it's building eight.

There's a door inside a door inside a door, this makes up the front of building eight. After parking in a yellow space, Ryson heads through the smaller of the doors, the sign on the front says "Pedestrian Traffic, Building eight."

There's a small reception area just on the other side of this door, the fact that it's unmanned causes Ryson to stand quietly in search of why that might be.

"You must be Mr. Willows."

Turning to face this assumption he finds the voice moving towards him and coming from a well-dressed man, fortyish with a smile on his face that runs from ear to ear. When happy man in a suit gets close enough for a handshake, Ryson replies, "That I am."

Distance required for a handshake collapses quickly and in an instant, he is enveloped in what starts as a hug, but then, he feels the man lean into him and now it's more of an embrace.

"Thank you, thank you."

These quiet words softly fall from his lips and Ryson feels him just for a second, weep. "You know when something is real and you know when it's not," Ryson returns the embrace but says nothing.

The separation goes just as the embrace because it takes a moment for this new friend to recompose, but when he does, it's clear he is somebody of importance.

"So glad you could make it, we've got a couple of hours before the lights go on, and some time before that, they will need to check your height onset for camera position. In the meantime, help yourself to whatever is in the green rooms," he now hands Ryson a walkie-talkie and says, "when the questions Arlington wants to ask you have been worked out, I'll see to it you get a copy well before airtime. You okay? Everything all right?"

"Well actually, I was hoping to read this," Ryson hands snappy dresser the envelope, "but I am flexible."

Snappy dresser pulls the pages from the envelope and begins to read right where he stands, he consumes the poem very quickly and when he's done, it's obvious he's moved and quite surprised to be so, "Wow, that's really good, absolutely you can read this instead of the interview, by far a much better intro, you get six minutes, how you spend it is up to you. So how about now? You okay? Everything all right?"

"Yes, that's great, thank you."

"No, no, no. You don't have to thank me, Mr. Willows. What you do and what you've already done, believe me, it's thanks enough," fancy pants checks his watch on his left wrist and is honestly disappointed when he realizes it's time to go. "Ah, geez, listen, Mr. Willows this was really good, but I'm afraid I've got to go. Whatever else you might need, you just holler it into that walkie-talkie, somebody will come find you."

They shake hands. No hugs. Fancy pants turns and heads off the way he came in, he holds up the envelope as he walks away, "Somebody will bring this back shortly."

Down the corridor to his left and on the wall at the entrance is a large dry erase board, and on it list a couple of shows that are in production and the green rooms assigned to them, Ryson heads this way.

He is stirring sugar into his second cup of coffee when somebody on the other end of the walkie-talkie asks as to his whereabouts, "Hello, Mr. Willows. This is Jerry Lanes. I am the producer for Under Care Or Control. I just have a couple of questions for you. You tell me where you are."

"Hi, Mr. Lanes, I found coffee in green room four. I'll wait for you."

"I'm on my way."

Ryson is almost giddy when Jerry comes through the door and he realizes who this is, his attempt at being nonchalant is useless, Jerry knows right away he is a big fan.

"Hi, Mr. Willows. You can call me Ryson, Mr. Lanes. And believe me, it is my pleasure to meet you."

"All right, so here's what happens next. This poem you're going to read, this is a real piece of work, but what you need to do is clarify who wrote it before you read it. This way there's no question of copyright. On a more personal note, those who have read this including myself, fear for those that would harm a child but absolutely believe they only get what they deserve. So for six minutes, you may tell a very large part of our population just exactly how you feel about that."

Jerry heads for the door but before he exits he turns back to face Ryson, "Yes, this is going to go very well, relax. Somebody will come get you when it's time."

The studio is much smaller than he expected, and because of this, it all seems much less intimidating. The backdrop is of several grammar schools in and around Orange County, he knows this because a couple do look familiar.

From thin air, Jerry appears at Ryson's side with pointers like Ryson is in the biz now, "You feel good, you feel loose, there's only the one camera, so where to look is obvious, the poem is already on the prompter so just read off of that, there's two ways to go here, sit or stand? We'll let you choose."

"It's a no-brainer, stand," this single word comes quick like he was already thinking about it.

"All right, then, ready in three, people, lose the chair," Jerry vanishes, the lights reset changing the ambience to a more grayish shadowy calm.

"Take your spot on the blue tape, Mr. Willows, when you see red on the camera, the world is yours, good luck," these instructions come from a speaker from somewhere overhead.

When the small red dome light brightens to life, it catches him off guard and turned slightly sideways to it. For just a second, it seems maybe this is not going to go so well after all.

Turning to face the camera straight on, Ryson slips his hands in his front pockets, and in his posture the sense of competence makes him seem almost bulletproof.

He starts with, "It seems somebody I confide in was obviously listening, so, no, I did not write this, but this is absolutely what I said, and now I will say it again.

"True fear in the heart of a child is where all sadness is born, to harm a child is to place upon them your own fears.

"To cast upon the young, the evilness of mankind, if this is your desire, then this makes us enemies.

"And so shall heavy be thy Hammer, a cold sharpness will come quick with my blade as will darkness follow my bullets.

"I have seen too much, I have seen who you can be.

"And may your God abandon its pity upon your putrid soul.

"And if it's no God you fear or an eternity condemned to hell, then let that dying breath come slowly and as your life trickles from your body, Know this.

"In the eyes of us all, there is no one more deserving of its loss than you.

"As you can see, o, yes, the anger runs deep, the hatred even deeper and the sadness deeper still.

"But it's the pain on their tiny faces, we all need to see, it's the destruction of who they once were we all need to see, and we all need to know I alone cannot save them.

"As are the crimes obvious and with intent, so shall be the punishment and all of us it's keeper.

"Place no pity upon my visit to the gate, I shall not ask forgiveness from my God for the sins I have committed, but instead thank him for the strength and hunger to have consumed the souls of those who would inflict their filth upon a child.

"And for those children we cannot bring back, the ones we could not save, the ones consumed by this vicious sadistic system, weep not for their loss but also for the journey that took them there.

"Now hold that breath you just let whisper passed your lips, because it's here you search your own soul. Yes, to save them all, it's always a possibility.

"And so shall some come home, damaged indeed, but not beyond repair.

"I leave you with this final thought, and these words did indeed come from the man that wrote this.

"The fragile innocence all but destroyed far too soon as if it was somebody's toy. And gone for just now are the sounds of happiness and joy, but if ever there was a grace of God, then it's in the resilience of a child that all is not lost. Sadness today is thy borrowed, for it shall not be kept as a tear in my soul, but only as a flesh wound."

Ryson for a moment holds his place, he then removes his hands from his pockets as even he himself takes time to digest what he's just done. He takes a short breath and reads what's left on the teleprompter.

"I now turn you over to Mr. Arlington Waters. Thank you, and enjoy the show."

The studio lights remain dim for just a couple of seconds and then it goes dark.

"We're clear people, nicely done."

After this announcement, the lights come back on, and the dozen or so people in the studio applaud with all eyes on him.

Jerry is extremely pleased, this is obvious given the warm smile and firm handshake.

"Nicely done, Ryson, you're a natural, you sailed through that like wings on a hot air balloon."

"Thanks, I think… Now how do I get out of here?"

"My pleasure, I will walk you out myself while they are in commercial."

Ryson is only a couple of feet from the door and the goodbyes when his phone vibrates to life from a forgotten place in his back pocket. The message reads "Time to go, hurry back, and you did great. 1.2."

Tiger by the Tail

Ryson makes eye contact with the cabbie parked outside the back door of Redline Financial as he walks by. They both smile and seem to know they share a fifty-minute destiny.

Before he can knock, the door opens and Art appears, not because he timed his arrival to the second but simply to tell the cabbie to sit tight, it'll be just a couple of minutes.

"Hey, there's our man of the hour," Art holds the door so Ryson can slip by, once inside, Lila is quick to give a small round of applause and then a hug.

"So how did I do?"

Lila answers this question as she backs up a foot or two and gives him the visual ounce over, "Excellent! Not only was it completely understood and well read, but you brought to it what it meant and who you were speaking to. Now how much exactly do you weigh? And that includes the bag you packed to take with you."

Art stops Ryson's attempt to answer because he assures him it's irrelevant. Lila agrees, but with her it's always going to be about the numbers.

"I wish you had time to watch the recording and then maybe sign some autographs, but it's time to go," Art smiles big, then adds, "you really nailed that. Sweet."

"But you really do have to go," Art hands him a piece of paper and a cell phone. "The cell phone is already active, we'll use the same e-box as before, that piece of paper has May and Will's flight info, but stay out of the airport, we don't know who's going to be there to meet our bad guy. Car rental is in one of two parking lots, you will have to find it."

Ryson finally wedges in and slows Arts roll, but turns to Lila and asks, "Maybe you can tell me where I'm going and how I will be getting there?"

Lila glances at Art and says, "I guess you could have started there, but then where's the mystery in that?"

Lila now takes both of Ryson's hands in her own as they stand face to face, "Well, let's just say things are about to get a little cheesy. Art, you grab that bag out of the fridge and I'll finish the itinerary."

"There is a charter flight once a week out of L.A.X. and on this flight is a whole bunch of cheese, it's flown all the way to Argentina with a fuel stop halfway, then landing in the city of Di Loma, which is a couple of miles from the Paraguay border. This is the same place our bad guy is headed. Your flight leaves in a couple of hours, that nice man out back will take you, your one piece of luggage and this bag to gate seven of the international terminal," Art holds up the bag, this has bottled water and some snacks, it's a long flight. "You are on the manifest as third pilot, pilot in training. This should put you on the ground in Di Loma three hours before Will and May. Well, in a perfect world anyway."

Art hands Ryson the bag as he also says, "Yeah, in a perfect world. So you let us know when you get there, now get."

"Yes, sir, Mr. Match," Ryson hugs them both, "I'll text when I get there." He almost turns to walk away but hesitates, "Thanks you guys, maybe this time we bring back my own kids."

Together, they both say, "Yes, Ryson, you do that. Be safe."

Fifty minutes later, the cab driver pulls up in front of a large sliding gate and stops. It's dark and there is nobody around. On the other side of the gate stands two large airplane hangars, all Ryson can see is the small door in the back of both buildings.

"This as far as I go, already been paid, have a safe trip."

He steps out of the cab with a bag in each hand feeling a little like an exiled immigrant and with a look on his face to match. The cab backs away, U-turns, and then swallowed by the night.

"Are you Ryson?"

This question floats through the darkness and but from where he cannot tell, but he answers anyway, "Yeah, and who wants to know?"

Now a figure steps from the shadows and to the gate, "It looks like you're coming with us."

This shadowy stranger now pulls the gate open just far enough to allow Ryson clearance, and at the same time, handing him an I.D. badge telling him, "Put this on and until you step off the plane in Argentina, you are Roberto Gutierrez, understood!"

He does not wait for a response, "Follow me, be quiet, we taxi in about twenty minutes."

With the cargo inspected and I.D. badges checked, the three are allowed on board and cleared to taxi. The only place for Ryson to sit is in a jump seat tucked inside what looks like was once the bathroom.

By the grace of all that is holy, Lila, the sweet angel that she is, thought to put two books in the bag she packed for Ryson to take with him, and now those two books are in their own right, precious, and for now all that matter.

Most of the plane has been allocated for cargo, so between all the crates and cargo netting, there is not much room to move around, and the two pilots, although they have been civil, it's clear they're not looking to make new friends, so he reads.

May is still looking over the notes on the way to the airport she took during their conversation with Art this morning, scanning as if in this she left herself secret clues.

"Geez, May, how hard can this be. I think we get the gist of it. I mean really, how many single male passengers named 'Adam Gentos' do you think are going to be on this flight anyway?"

When they're within sight of L.A.X. from the 105 freeway, the driver informs them because of the current safety procedures in place he can only take them as far as the parking structure for the international terminals, from there, you have to take the shuttle. Will sounding only half as annoyed as he really was says, "Yeah, we know, did this a week ago."

With the first book read, Ryson was now passing the minutes, trying to get a look through the very small circular window in the door on the other side of the plane as they prepare to land and refuel.

Because of a large donation made recently to Project Mother's Day, Art was nice enough to purchase all three seats in row 12, thus giving Will and May a little more space in the coach section of the plane.

Will's ability to I.D. the bad guy were little to none, he was having much more fun watching May over analyze every male passenger who got on the plane. When she started taking notes on some of the passengers, Will gave up looking for the bad guy altogether because now he's just curious as to how long this will take her.

Finally the motion like it always does, gets the better of Will and reality melts, sending him fast asleep, leaving May to stand vigil on her own.

The pilot Ryson has not yet met is all of a sudden standing right in front of him, he says something in Spanish but all he got was, "Something, something, something, Banyous."

Pilot one recognizes the silence as a communication problem and shouts from the cockpit, "He has to pee."

Ryson answers with a question of his own to the man standing in front of him, "So why tell me? I gotta go to."

Again from the cockpit, "Because you're sitting on it."

All three with nature's call answered strap themselves in and prepare for takeoff. Ryson does not even wait for the plane to level off before he jumps right into book two.

Turbulence somewhere over the North Pacific is enough to rattle Will from a snow day he had as a kid, and to make it worse, the turbulence wakes him on the fastest part of the hill.

When Will glances over at May, he is pleased to see her covered in a blanket and fast asleep. This means two things. one, she no doubt ID'ed the bad guy. And now, with any luck, Will can jump back into that snow-covered thrill ride that makes being a kid as good as it gets.

On some strange level, there must have been some bonding over the whole toilet thing because there's a shout from the cockpit to buckle up and ready for landing. It's the first warning he's heard. Ryson smiles and laughs to himself, thinking, *Yeah, sure now there's probably going to be a bunch of hugging and kissing along with a tearful goodbye when the three of us have to part ways.*

No hugs no tears, all he gets from the pilot is, "Leave the badge on the plane and your quickest way off the tarmac is towards the grass and out the yellow striped gate."

By the time he finishes these instructions, both pilots are already down the stairs and heading away from the plane they just landed.

Ryson waits until he is actually in the rental car before he text his arrival, but he does before he leaves the lot.

"On the ground and in car, going to find a view, then auto-camp and wait. 3."

"Excellent! Sit tight, others on time. 1.2."

This comes back after Ryson has already left the lot.

Finding some high ground adjacent to the airport and with a good view of it and some of the surrounding area, he settles in and welcomes the next hour or so to just sit still.

The business around the two of them as the in-flight crew do a first pass at cleanup is enough to gently stir May and Will from a light slumber. They rattle around somewhat before Will finally ask, "So, my dear, for whom have we hunted?"

May is busy putting on her shoes and does not bother to look up to deliver her findings, "Row 17, seat C. Window. Over the left wing. Approximately thirty years old, five feet eight inches, one hundred and seventy pounds, blue jeans, dark gray hoodie, brown hair, clean face, tan slip-on loafer's size nine and a half."

This makes May herself laugh and she finally looks up, "Yeah, that last part, it was a guess."

Will joins the laughter.

Before they can even get off the plane, May is already poised to hit send just as soon as she gets a cellular signal on her phone. Just a few steps into the terminal, she gets three bars and hits send. She sees the message from Ryson and knows he's ready.

It's only a minute or so and he responds, "On it, eyes are open. 3."

Neither the bad guy nor May and Will go to luggage pickup, evidently all three only brought what they could carry. May sends the text "Out front door now, but knows the minute or so delay probably makes this message irrelevant. All they can do now is hope Ryson can I.D. the bad guy and give chase as the two of them head to car rental as quickly as possible."

"Tiger by the tail, heading east. 3."

Ryson waits till he is actually in pursuit to send this text. He watched bad guy come out of the airport and walk to a white utility van parked not far away. When he gets close to the van, a man who could be bad guy's twin brother hops out, then reenters on the passenger side. Bad guy gets in the driver seat and away they go, with Ryson a safe distance behind.

May finds it difficult to not cheer for joy when she reads Ryson's message, instead she calmly shows the phone to Will, who also has trouble containing his emotions.

Choice of cars was easy at the rental agency because they only had one minivan, dark blue, piece of crap. With its only redeeming qualities being it has a full tank of gas and it did start, they leave the airport heading east.

May keys in the message "Leaving now, heading East. 4.5."

But before she can hit send, this message from Ryson buzzes in.

"Already stopped, not far, hotel row. Find me left side, between the hotel Hamptons and Hamptons East."

May simply adds to her message "Roger that cowboy, on our way."

It's dark, but the five or six hotels are well lit, therefore, illuminating both sides of the street, so finding the Hamptons was fairly easy.

When Ryson sees May and Will pull into the alleyway separating both sides of the Hamptons hotel, he steps out of his car. Will pulls alongside the same piece of wall as Ryson, placing the vehicles nose to nose.

Ryson quickly climbs in the minivan through the sliding door, it's a pleasant reunion and it's hard to tell who is more pleased. And all the while Ryson keeping his attention out the small windows in the back of the minivan.

Will gets first question, "Where we at, Ryson? And what are we looking for?"

Without looking away from the back windows, Ryson's answer is one of fact and then tenderness, "Across the street, that white van there belongs to our bad guys. That van and what looked like an exact double of the guy you shared a plane with were waiting, your guy takes over the driver side and they come straight here. I assume they checked into the Rising Star Hotel because they have not come out."

There is a humble tone that now takes over along with Ryson's gentle spirit. He withdraws his attention from the back windows and says, "Again, here you guys are, making these decisions and putting yourself in real danger, it's like what we're after belongs to you, but it doesn't. And simply saying thank you seems like such a tiny piece of gratitude. I mean this guy were chasing, this fucker's bad news man, he had every intention of killing me that day and I'm sure he still would, given the chance. We are not safe. And yet, here you guys are."

"Ahh, geez, cowboy, you have got to remember, Ryson, it's your kids, it's my kids, it's their kids, it's kids. This is where my true purpose and intentions lie. The fact that were all on the same team is just fate. The fact that we now share the same space, these are decisions we all made for ourselves. Watching you read that piece on T.V. not only moved me, but also assured me I was on the right team. So, no, there's no reason for you to thank me."

It's quiet for a couple of seconds before Will adds only this to May's statement, "We share that."

All three are for a moment at a loss for words, it's May who reels them all back in, checking things up so the guys don't have to, "I don't want to be sounding all too girly and everything but I see no reason for the three of us spending the night in the van when we're parked right next to a hotel."

May stops there and waits for a response.

"I second that, and choose the girly approach as well." Will chimes in last and has already worked out a schedule for twenty-four-hour surveillance, "Ditto on the let's not sleep in the van. Let's park the car in the back, turn things around, and we can take turns in three hour shifts watching the bad guys, because for sure, sometime tomorrow morning, they will head back to the airport to pick up their dead buddy, so who's ever on watch when that happens, follow at a safe distance and text the rest of us, we will catch up. And remember to keep the texting basic."

May draws third shift, and surveillance goes as planned through the night. At 5:15 a.m., during May's shift from three to six, without warning, the interior lights come on in the white van parked across the street, May sees nobody approach or get in, but now the headlights pop on and the van starts to back up, there's no time to think about it, all she can do is grab her phone and start some serious one thumb typing before the van has backed all the way out to the street and is now driving past her.

Mays first message is simple "On the move, heading back towards airport. Stay tuned. Be ready."

Her second message some minutes later is "Airport, yes. Six minutes later… Waiting."

By the time this waiting message shows up. Ryson and Will have scrambled from a sound sleep to bug out while truly neither of them has quite woken up.

May's next message is quite specific and seems already well planned out. And even if Ryson and Will did disagree, there's no time.

"Returning, don't think they're stopping. Hey, 3. Take point. Leave. 5. Then 4-5."

Couple of minutes behind you.

Will's reply as he and Ryson scramble and move outside is "Roger that, princess."

May smiles, Will knows it.

Ryson allows the van a couple of blocks for leeway before turning out onto the street and pursuing. May and Will wait until both vehicles move out of site, then do the same.

Camp Diablo

There's enough light traffic on the road they all share to easily blend in and the white van so highly visible Ryson is able to give the bad guys plenty of space, keeping himself always at a safe distance. This rolls-on fairly close to three hours.

There are several large hills in the distance and zero signs of population, so when this large billboard appears alongside the road a short distance in front of him, Ryson has no clue what this billboard is in reference to, only that it reads Lost Angels. And in both lower corners is the mark of Vinzaya, this part he understands and the cold sweat that begins to build assures him that they indeed are back in Paraguay, and without question in the area known as Neighbors Cradle.

The small border town of Lost Angels springs suddenly from a valley floor as they drop in elevation through a wide sweeping left-hand bend, Ryson has little choice but to enter the small-town unannounced and unprepared. He lost sight of the bad guys and their van as they made a couple of switchbacks while dropping into the valley, there was only the one road so for sure they had to come through here and maybe even stopped.

The large, white van is easily spotted and for a moment he is relieved, but as he slowly passes the van, which is parked nose in on the right-hand side of the street in front of what is clearly a place to eat, he now becomes just pissed.

Speaking to himself as he passes, "Got to a agree with that, I could eat that dry hide off a sunbaked dead rhino, you fuckers." Moving up a couple of more blocks, he makes a left at the first alto, then U-turns, and parks.

May reads the text from Ryson out loud a couple of minutes before they reach the sign "In town, first alto go left, look left. 3." And so to them the sign makes a little more sense, but still just as scary.

"Roger that, cowboy." is all the text reply May sends.

194

Will U-turns and pulls in behind Ryson. The three now stand behind the minivan stretching and quietly discussing. It's decided they will take turns getting gas and a quick cruise through the open-air market they passed as they came into town. May and Will go first and hurry back, putting them in position as planned to follow the bad guys if and when the time comes.

Ryson heads to food and for sure spends what's equivalent to a week's salary here on foodstuffs and bottled water. At the pump and after the wait and with only a few gallons delivered, his cell phone text chirps from inside the car, leaving the nozzle still in the tank but no fuel being delivered he checks his phone.

"Giddy up, same direction. East out of town. 4.5."

Without panic, Ryson sends "On the way." Finishes gassing up and leaves town biting the top off a box of granola bars.

They have not traveled more than a few miles when the back-left tire blows out almost sending the minivan into a deep gully alongside the road. Will fish tales back the other way and indeed saving them from disaster.

Will does a quick inventory for the jack and checks the spare tire before May sends this message to Ryson "Flat tire, we have what we need, we will catch up. 4.5."

Not sure who or what got their first, May reads Ryson's response as he is driving by and waving "Okay, Tiger by the tail."

From this distance and through the trees all he can tell for sure is the white van fades right and then disappears. When Ryson reaches the spot, the van disappeared, he finds a dirt road that splits from the highway off to the right and up through a forest covered hill. He gets a fleeting glance as he rolls past and spots the white van about a mile up this road.

Ryson motors past, allowing a minute or so buffer before he pulls over and quickly text May "Stop.3."

Will gets pulled safely off the road and they wait.

"Sit tight, doing some recon. They have stopped. 3."

May reads this second message than answers with "Standing by. 4.5."

Ryson leaves the car and backtracks on foot using the dense vegetation alongside the road as cover while he makes his way back to the turn off. Still using the dense vegetation for cover, he casually leans out of it and left to get a look up the road where he last spotted the van. The road is empty and ascends to a crest where it disappears. Trying to get a better look, he follows a shallow drainage ditch for twenty yards or so when he finds a large open area adjacent to the road big enough for a car to completely turn around. Just a few feet past this and on the same side of the road is a sign, it's quite large and it reads "Turn Around Now!!" with two exclamation marks assuring you understand its importance.

Quite sure whoever put up the sign also created this turnaround area to do as the sign instructed. Ryson steps out onto the road still trying to get a look at the top of the hill. Just near the crest, the road drops away and its path no longer obvious but clearly at the top of the hill there is a structure, he finishes exploring the turnaround and some of the surrounding area before he sends a text to May and Will.

"On my way to you. 3."

As he sends this, he is already hustling through the bush back to his car.

"On south side, can't miss us. 4.5."

After a U-turn, Ryson pulls off the road as far as he can, alongside the minivan, putting his car the furthest away from the road, he is in a hurry and they can obviously tell this, so even before he can get his windows rolled up and exited the car Will has already started the van and has it in gear. Ryson climbs in through the sliding door already engaged in conversation as to why they need to be in a hurry. And they go.

The road our bad guys pulled onto and out of sight is just a couple of minutes up ahead, it's definitely a private road but there is a large area for turning around just a few feet up this road and before the private property sign. I looked it over pretty good and I'm sure we can hide us and this minivan in the overgrowth along the back of this open area.

When they have the turnoff insight, Ryson does his best to describe what he found and how best to pull forward up the road and almost to the sign, then backing down and into the turnaround clearing, stay to the right of the two large trees and back right through the bushes, there's a small clearing just on the other side of these bushes so be ready to stop.

He and May can both tell that Will takes a quick moment to bounce this around in his head, and then to their amusement, he says, "Yeah, that old trick, yeah, I can do that with my eyes closed."

Will has a switch, and moving this to a forward position, he learned to do at a very young age and now as he reaches the spot just before the sign, his focus clears like Austrian-Crystal and he skids to a stop, throws the minivan in reverse, and hits the gas. It gets real bumpy as they go through the bushes and all three, even though hanging on for dear life, are still smacking their heads into the roof. Will hits the brakes hard, bringing the van to a quick stop so well concealed you can barely tell where they came through the bushes. They all three exhale, May sighs with a "shoe-doggie."

"As primitive as this is going to sound, and I am almost embarrassed to say it, but we really need to acquire some kind of weapons, and yeah, even if it's just a tree branch as a club and a couple of large rocks we can throw if we have to, but we have got to find something."

"Potty in the woods comes first, then they each set to their own tasks, but as a collective, they watch and they listen."

Ryson journeys to the far edge of the clearing past the large trees Will just missed backing in here, and it's here he finds a well-worn footpath heading up the hill, same direction as the road and towards the structure at the top.

The three discuss what to do next while standing on this path as if they've not already decided. It's agreed, they take what caveman weaponry they have and go take a look.

Maybe, midway up the hill, there's a loud rumble towards the top and getting louder by the second and for sure moving towards them, the three freeze and then squat to a huddle in the thickets along the path.

The rumble is actually two military deuce and a half's painted forest cameo and a covered cargo area in back. The three from their squatted position get fleeting movement between the trees but have no trouble seeing the large trucks moving down the road and towards the highway, there is plenty of vegetation between them and the road keeping all three well hidden, they stay still and let the trucks finish their descent and exit, they hear them do so as they reach the highway and motor away.

It's a stereo effect as Ryson hears May and Will whisper, "Rain Forest Apartments, same kind of trucks."

Nobody says it but all three are thinking the same thing, *Vinzaya*.

May moves first, taking the lead as they finish their assent up the hill, the other two follow With clubs in hand like a caveman clan.

There's a thick row of tall shrubs separating them from the plateau at the top of the ridge, not less than five yards on the other side of the shrubs stands a small single-story ranch house and on the left side is a covered patio under that covered patio sits the white van they chased here. It's parked facing away from them, leaving the back of it about six yards from them and the shrubs.

They all three freeze to frozen, afraid to move, whisper or even blink. Several seconds go by before their first breath, the second breath is followed by the sound of something moving towards them from somewhere off to their right. It sounds maybe like a jeep of some kind, it moves closer to them then slows. They cannot see it, but it sounds like it runs over some loose stacked boards. It now accelerates and clearly heads down the hill.

As their attentions return back to that of the van, it suddenly starts up, the backup lights come on and it begins to move in reverse heading straight towards them, the van angles somewhat as it clears the corner of the house, only stopping within a couple of inches from the shrubs and four feet from the three standing behind them.

When the van starts to roll forward, it does so with obvious caution, it moves straight ahead and disappears but does not head down the hill.

Ryson steps through the shrubs first, quickly moving to occupy the space under the overhang the van just surrendered, then just as quickly May and Will join him.

The small ranch house they now stand behind has obviously sustained some very recent damage, it is minimal, couple of broken windows and numerous scattered bullet holes, but this says not only will they find the front door unlocked but nobody home as well. They pause only long enough to inspect the inside of the house through the broken windows, then decide to move in the same direction as the van.

Just several feet into their pursuit, they find what's left of what was once a large wooden gate that at one time stretched across the road it now lay ruined atop of, and who ever tore through it clearly did not bother to knock. This is what they heard the Jeep role over as it left, which also means this is the road that leads down the hill and to the highway. The road sweeps slightly left then falls from site.

The dirt road they're currently standing on runs along the top of the ridge, where it goes is unknown because of the surrounding foliage, one thing for certain, it's where the van went and the two guys that are in it. Without discussion, May announces, "This way," and puts her cave girl club over her shoulder and says, "Let's go find our boys," as she puts one-foot forward.

Will quickly grabs her hand and with a quiet voice he gives a, "Shhhh! You hear that?"

Then answers his own question, "Yes, something's coming, heading this way from that direction and moving fast, we need to get out of the way."

May and Ryson have already confirmed the noise before Will can finish and already the three are with quick steps to and through the same shrubbery, they stepped out of when they got here, only now thirty yards further away.

The white van hard slows sliding somewhat into the sharp left turn, it needs to make in order to access the road down, it's front bumper just a couple of feet from the three behind the shrubs, there's no time to react, all they can do is wait for the van to pass and pursue on foot down the hill and to the minivan.

The van over slows its movement as it prepares to manage the large wood pile blocking the road, it's front tires bounce hard over some of the metal support system and lifting arm for the large gate that now lay in large pieces across the road, sending the van to a sudden stop with a thud.

They can hear and watch the driver attempt to escape the wreckage in reverse and then again trying forward, after a couple of more failed attempts the van's engine goes quiet.

There's a strange buzz in both Ryson's ears, he knows when those two get out we take them down. He whispers quietly while firming the grip on his club, "I'll take the driver, you two, this guy, don't kill him. I think we're going to need them."

Ryson hears both van doors open at the same time, his movement quick and calculated as he clears the shrubs and then the back of the van, the driver sees him coming and makes a feeble attempt to withdraw the revolver tucked in his waistband.

The amount of air that escapes the driver's chest as Ryson's tree-branch-club lands solid to his midsection sends Ryson's hair waving like he's standing in the wind, and once all that air is gone, bad guy crumbles to the ground, attempting to force tiny puffs of air into his lungs to fend off suffocation.

Ryson grabs his gun and feels a rush of adrenaline surge through him like high-voltage, it leaves him speechless and quick breathed.

"You all right over there?" these words sail away with the breeze because Ryson does not hear them. The rage catches him by surprise. This piece of shit who now lies crumpled at his feet may or may not have had anything to do with the kidnapping of his two little girls, but just the fact of who they have in the back of this van and where we all are right now says to him, this piece of shit deserves nothing less than one thousand deaths and each one far more painful than the last.

Heeding his own advice the gun in his right hand does not explode five times, therefore and forever, leaving piece of shit without a head, instead, Will's second attempt to inquire as to Ryson's status does not go unheard.

"I'm good, how about you two?"

"No problems over here," May clocked this fuck pretty good but I think he'll live, and now we own a .45 auto. Ryson's response to this is, "You can add a short barrel .38 to that inventory"

Conscious and able to move on their own, Will throws a couple of quick knots around their wrist and then ties them to each other using straps they found in the van. The quick interrogation goes nowhere, it seems the bad guys don't feel much like talking and when asked, "Where is the dead guy you had in the back of this van, you know, the one you picked up at the airport."

All Will gets is shrugged shoulders and well-practiced confused looks.

May's the one that finally ask the obvious, "Where does that road go? and who lives here?"

Ryson seconds the question, "Yeah, where does that road go?"

It's decided that because of their unwillingness to cooperate, Will uses the rest of the straps, hog tying the two together after forcing them through the shrubs, leaving them lying back to back on the footpath, leading down the hill in a seriously knotted state of affairs that even Houdini himself could not have escaped.

Clubs and guns, the three step back through the shrubs, they share several emotional components but fear is not one of them, they say nothing to each other for the first several yards until they do agree that the van now blocking the only road in or out here it's probably a good thing, or maybe not, either way, where this road goes is what currently concerns us the most.

The road lends itself to obscurity and it appears to be by design, they move quickly staying close to the trees, lining the right side of the road in-case there is a need to duck and cover.

There's a large stand of fruit trees up ahead and from this distance, the road looks as if it dead ends there, but in fact the road cuts hard left, then sweeps right skirting the fruit trees. The thin sliver of gray smoke rising from behind the trees is a clear indication to press on.

Surprise is another emotion the three do not share as they come around the last row of fruit trees and find another single-story ranch house, this one somewhat larger than the last. The large driveway it sits at the end of gradually drops a few feet to a fairly large plateau to their right. The road along the ridge continues on another twenty yards or so in front of them then looks as if it just spills into a dead-end being gobbled up by the larger foliage.

They move into the fruit trees for cover and head towards the house for a better look.

This structure has far more damage than the first one. Still hidden in the trees, they move to within just a few yards from the corner of the house, and for sure, somebody opened a can of whup ass on this place, every window busted out, part of the house is so riddled with bullet holes you can clearly see some of the interior, the front door and all its framework has been torn from the house and is now laying in the driveway.

May's voice starts off a little thin when she says, "Well, I guess we won't have to knock." But then gains some strength when she finishes with, "Yeah, Will, why don't you go take a look."

She and Ryson snicker, then pretend to nudge Will out from the trees.

Will surprise them both when he steps from the trees towards the house with the .38 in his right hand and looking like unengaged hitman. Will moves to the large opening that used to be the front door placing his back against the wall, takes a short breath, then quickly over his right shoulder, he steals a look inside the house.

There is a look on Will's face and because of the short distance between them it's obvious to May and Ryson he has seen something he could not have expected. The second look is slower and much more thorough, and now again on his face and in his eyes, the world and all that's wrong with it.

Will turns to face the interior, putting his back to May and Ryson, he holds his ground for a brief moment, then bravely steps forward into the house where he is quickly consumed by the shadows and disappears. From the shadow comes a hand but only a hand and it says "Come, share the pain."

He does not have to ask twice nor was his first gesture misunderstood, they all three now share again the same space and do indeed sadly share the pain.

The entryway is that of a circular space about the size of an average bedroom, there are three large openings in front of them spaced evenly within the curvature of the wall, making the center opening the furthest away. Doors and framework that once closed off these three openings now lay scattered amongst the rest of the debris.

To their left, the wall where the door once was it so badly damaged it's possible to see most of the interior of the large room that lay beyond. The same large room Will could see from his peeks while at the front door.

Even though everything in this room has been rendered useless, debris and no longer usable, but whatever walking cyclone came through here, what it was before that is still painfully obvious. This one room occupies about one third of the house and in it, they have created a complete movie studio with lights, cameras, props, and backgrounds. The props, backgrounds, toys, and furniture all being geared towards children and the many ways to abuse and damage them.

The three move into this room only because the back wall has two large openings where there once was doors and through these the walking cyclone continued, this is obvious by the amount of debris piled just inside the openings.

Two smaller rooms that appear along the wall to their right they could not see until now, and they, too, have had their doors removed. The first room is empty except for a large four drain set into the cement floor, the mix of thick foul odors seeping from room two, and as they move closer, they can now see the large pool of blood on the floor that tells them this is going to get ugly. With the door and framework gone, there is no reason to go into the room, what's there is quite clear.

Room two also has a floor drain and to it the blood in the doorway has left a trail. The room itself has been converted into a mock public restroom like that you would find in a park or rest area off the highway. Everything in the room is damaged or completely destroyed. In the far back left corner is what looks to be a crumpled-up cloth backdrop of some kind piled purposely with the intent to conceal.

The smell is strong enough to keep the other two at bay, Will is the only one that steps closer to get a better look. He leans through the threshold and quickly scans the interior of the room, but then retreats quite rapidly, taking the couple of steps backwards to rejoin the others.

The moment idols with panic until May, big eyed, says, "What?"

Will still hoping to question his own reality shockingly answers, "Looks to me like there's a very small hand sticking out from under that pile of backdrop material in back of the room."

Both Ryson and May make a move towards the room, Will quickly snatches Ryson by the wrist and says, "Let May go." Ryson stops and makes eye contact with Will, he says nothing, then nods his head.

The training May's father provided for her was at times quite intense, but also, saw to it that what he could not teach her he found others that could, it's these lessons that now allow her to step over the blood and into the room.

The two watch May as she makes her way around the broken toilets and shattered sinks coming to rest in a squatted position over the small hand and backdrop, lifting the material and tilting her head downward they hear her gasp. May gently replaces the material, being careful to cover everything, then quietly makes her way out of the room.

Ryson and Will are standing close enough to each other, May can hug both at the same time as she steps over the blood and out of the room. Quietly, as if she does not want anybody to ease-drop, she whispers, "There are two little boys under that pile of stuff, both look to have been strangled and it gets worse from there, I'm guessing very close to the same age maybe five or six, one darker skinned than the other."

They feel May tremble, and again they share the pain.

May moves first, keeping movement brief and her still in control of her own emotions, she glances down at the pool of blood and says, "That did not come from those little boys under the tarp, the wounds they did have could not have accounted for that."

May now turns to the closer of the two openings at the back of the room and begins to clear the debris preventing them access to the back part of the house.

The amount of sophisticated equipment is only equaled to the thorough destruction of it. What they didn't push out of the way, they stepped over and into what is or at least what was a pretty serious D.V.D. replicating station, all of the equipment looks high-end and there was a lot of it.

This back part of the house is in an "L" configuration and most of it is littered with the bits and pieces of not only the equipment but out of the several thousand D.V.Ds, not a single disk has been left intact. Many hundreds of these D.V.Ds had already been packaged and provided with cover art depicting just about every possible sadistic thing you could do to a child. And now it all lays on the floor, broken and torn, no doubt, as is all the tiny souls lost in its creation. The amount leaves the three of them silent and motionless.

There is a pull cord curtain may be twelve feet long and almost ceiling to floor hung on the very back wall and it looks to be concealing what is most likely a sliding glass door, what's odd about this and they all three agree, it's the only entrance or exit left in one piece. Ryson is closest to it and does indeed hesitate exposing whatever awaits on the other side.

With a couple of slow pulls on the cord, the thick curtain moves away from him maybe about four feet, it's enough. Through the sliding glass door is a site that so sickens Ryson he can only question his own sanity as he backs away from the door.

"Please tell me that's not what it looks like, ah jeez, what the hell is that," Ryson mumbles this already in tears.

May and Will are slow to the window, "Who could blame them."

The place it took Ryson they were not in a hurry to follow.

On the other side of the glass is a high walled bricked in outdoor patio about the size of the average living room. In the far-left corner is a charred pile of small bodies, maybe half a dozen. And from it a thin whisper of a grayish smoke rising from the center.

In the far-right corner, two men lay dead. Their lives removed by the many bullet holes they share, one man wearing only pants and is missing his left arm from the elbow down, and above the elbow a crudely fashioned belt tourniquet. The other guy is fully dressed but missing most of his head. From the blood and body debris on the wall behind them, it is obvious they all were executed here, but only the children were burned.

"As specialized as they were… Ryson, there is no way what they took from you ends up here. You may or may not want to hear this but what they took from you is far more valuable than this." Will pulls the cord back the other way, then adding, "There's no reason to go out there."

The three-stay standing, seemingly comfortable with just staring at the closed curtain.

"My father, if he were here right now, I know exactly what you would say, first of all, he also would have closed that curtain and then these his words spoken as if he were '*Foo Man Chu*.'"

May's voice gets somewhat lower and she frowns her forehead, "What's done here is done, focus on the living, we shall, because life is far more precious than death." She steps away from the curtain, trying desperately to put something else in her head, but also adding, "I don't think we should stay much longer."

The other two silently agree, and they also step away curtain.

The rest of the search is uneventful, snagging a few small bottles of water along the way, they end up back at the circular entryway, but only now from the other side. The three step cautiously out of the house and back onto the steps out front, pausing only long enough to take probably the single most desperate cleansing breath of their lives and decide what to do next.

The property just past the house seems to stop at a large wooden fence, the fence stretches from the point where the road out front ends to somewhere back behind the house. On the other side of the fence, all they can see because of its close to eight-foot stature is some of the taller trees.

It's decided to double time back to the first house, do a quick search there and then as May's father would say, "I think we have some questions we would like some answers to." And as Will put it, "Let's go talk to our boys we left tied together in the dirt."

As per Will's promise, they hope to find their prisoners right where they left them. Before they search the house, Will steps part way into the bushes, just off the road near the house and confirms the captured two are still lying on the path, and says, "Both look as if they just can't wait to answer all our questions."

House number one if they turn a blind eye to the bullet holes and broken windows, they could find no connection between the two. This one has been left largely intact along with all the normal furniture you would expect to find in an everyday run of the mill three-bedroom house.

From separate paths, the three rejoin near a food pantry off the kitchen, all three frozen in place by the picture hanging above the door. It's a cheap piece of art showing Moses parting the Red Sea and the caption reads "Anything is possible when you choose to help others."

The sign has a disturbing sense of stolen normalcy, this place and the one down the road where the dead are still burning are without question; one in the same and it should all be burnt to the ground.

Ryson hears the tiniest of whistles in perfect tone coming from each ear, and as the sounds meet in the center, it resonates leaving almost a kind of itch on the back of his skull.

"You guys hear that?"

May and Will both crank up there audio alert and respond with, "No, don't hear anything. What cha got?"

Will says this as Ryson steps into the pantry.

"It sounded like one of those cheap plastic whistles you'd get out of an old box of cracker jacks, and it sounded like it came from in here."

When these words trail off and silence returns to the pantry, there's a child's whimper, the frail cries bounce quietly inside the pantry and don't seem to be coming from any one direction. Ryson stands puzzled, attempting to echo locate the source of the whimpers and finds the cries grow louder as he gets closer to the floor.

To a squat, then to his knees, now with both hands on the floor, he leans down with his right ear shaking his head and saying, "Yes, below us somebody is crying and it sounds like a child."

May and Will step in and confirms, "Somebody cries below."

Inside the pantry, the floor is just a floor, no rugs, no secret stairs, no trapdoors. They split up, they know what they're looking for. May finds a sort of mud room by the back door and under a thick oval rug in it, she uncovers the small door they knew they'd find.

"Guys, I think I have it," she waits for backup and guns drawn before using the finger pull to slowly open the door. A small amount of light creeps up and out revealing a set of stairs, leading down to what is obviously a basement.

"You and May go, I'll keep watch."

Ryson descends the stairs first. He has his gun somewhat forward but already knows the gun will not be necessary.

As they near the last couple of stairs, the small amount of light coming from somewhere unknown is enough to see what's down here. The room is equivalent to perhaps a two-car garage and for the most part, fairly empty, but there, in the center of the room, on some kind of rug, or blanket, sitting cross-legged, are four small shadowy figures. There is no movement from them, all four have their backs to the stairs and one of them is quietly whimpering.

Ryson moves off the stairs while May stays put looking for some sort of light switch. May backs up almost mid-stairs and now quietly announces, "It's going to get bright."

The light quickly gobbles up all of the shadows, allowing Ryson to safely navigate to a space in front of the four children, the children will not look up but there agitated fearful state assures him they hear his approach and know now where he stands.

The room gets very quiet, Ryson's last breath long gone and forgetting to replace it, he slowly goes to his knees, not just because for the lack of oxygen but what sits in front of him seems to squeeze his own life from the world in punishment for all the atrocities bestowed upon them.

The plastic whistle again resonates in Ryson's head, this time, causing him to scratch, and from this movement, he seems to obtain some level of clarity and knows what to say.

"I came here looking for my own children, instead I find you. I will keep looking for my two little girls, but for right now, we would really like to get you kids to safety and then as soon as possible help you get home. You do not have to trust or believe me right now, but who here would like to leave this awful place?" Ryson does not attempt to conceal the few tears that run down his face.

All four children stand and no, there is no reason to smile, in front of him and now, at eye level, he sees four horribly damaged young souls, they all four look as though they have been used like pieces of machinery, there are two little boys very similar to the ones found under the background material in the second house and although they are both bruised, battered and left in a torn and tattered state, they are the ones with the least amount of visible trauma. The next is a young boy ten or eleven he is the one Ryson heard crying and for good reasons, and on top of that, he also has his right arm in a makeshift sling. The last is a young girl, maybe thirteen, she can stand but obviously not without pain, she has some minor lacerations on her face and neck but no blood.

Ryson stands and says, "That nice lady on the stairs, her name is May, the nice man you find after that, his name is Will, my name is Ryson. We are not going to hurt you, but it's time to go."

They all six leave the basement, then all seven leave the house.

Before all seven go through the bushes with the intention of joining the two already there, Ryson stops them all and quickly takes a squatting position in front of the four children, he tries to make eye contact with them when he asks, "Can you tell me if there is any other children here?"

With surprising clarity, the ten-year-old boy looks right at him and answers, "On the bench outside blue house, they looked hurt."

"Blue house? Where is blue house?"

Before he can answer Ryson's question, the girl mumbles something that sounds like, "Blue house good, green house, bad," she does not lift her head so it's hard to tell.

The ten-year-old boy fearfully forces a look down the road towards the other location and only says, "Big fence, blue house, green house."

Ryson knows in an instant the fence the young boy is referring to, the one that was too tall to get a good look as to what was on the other side.

While standing and already backing away, Ryson glances at May and Will but before he can announce his intentions, May's the one that speaks first, "Yeah, yeah, yeah, now go. We will wait on the path with the first two, now hurry, I really do think we are running out of time."

He spins on both heels and is away at a full sprint. The other six carefully move through the bushes and onto the path.

May goes five yards down the trail and stops, this leaves them another five yards or so of cushion before the other two that are still laying across the footpath, tied close enough together they look like one big worm. She turns to face the five behind her, and whispers allowed, "Okay, let's wait right here for Ryson to get back."

May now sits and is pleased to see the children do the same and closer to her than she had expected. Will moves past the kids and takes a seat next to May making sure to face the children.

"We did not hurt those two," Will motions with his head down the path behind him and May. "Yeah, we tied them up but that's just because we don't know if there good guys or bad guys just yet, and we did not come here to make friends with the bad guys, so for the time being, we'll just leave them right there."

Will winks and smiles but gets no response, but that's okay.

Ryson starts with the fence closest to the house and begins checking it for a hidden gate as he moves towards the road out front, pushing and pulling as he goes.

Will turns his attention back to May, being sure to speak loudly enough so nobody thinks is trying to be sneaky, "Listen, May, we're going to need that big van out there, so for sure we gotta open it. Here's what I'm thinking, we can use the minivan to maybe nudge it loose, clear the broken gate out of way, and now we have plenty of space." Will hands May the .38 and kisses her on the forehead, looks her in the eyes, and asked, "You good here?"

"Just be quick. Maybe while you're gone we can makes s'mores."

"Save some for me," Will stands and gives a silly sort of salute then dashes away. He first stops to readjust the straps on the two still uncomfortably lying on the path. They're still not saying anything, so Will offers a piece of advice before he is up and away, "Be still, she will shoot you."

Ryson is perhaps ten yards from the house when a three-foot section of the fence surrenders its secret to even the slightest touch. The piece is hinged on the back side allowing it to swing in and left. Surprise one is the fact that the road out front does not stop at the fence, it actually makes a quick right turn and continues on for another fifty yards putting the end of the road almost parallel to where he now stands looking through the fence.

Surprise two, the casket, it now sits in the dirt off to the side of this newfound peace of road, left by somebody who was obviously in a hurry.

With caution and without stepping through the fence, Ryson leans.
in far enough to get a look down the fence line to his right.

This place, the horrors, there's just so many. And now this.

The words blue house, green house escape his chest on their own, he hears the words trail off and somehow, they sound as if they belong to him. The hand he used for support as he leaned through the fence he now uses to hold himself up.

Maybe fifteen yards away, there sits two side-by-side, eight by ten average looking, wooden, garden sheds, the one closest to the fence painted blue, and of course, the other with a four-foot gap between them, green. Attached to the blue shed is a bench and on this bench sits crumpled and obviously injured, three small children, two leaning on each other for support and the third in the fetal position at the other end.

The two huddled together are so close in detail to his own children, even from this distance, it wobbles and weakens his legs forcing him to hang onto the fence.

It's a single heartbeat that re-delivers the strength to his legs and he's through the fence, then quickly moving towards the bench. He is fixated on the two children huddled at one end of the bench and this hurries his approach, it's frightening to see that with just minor changes in hair and skin color these two could be his own, the age, the size, the clothing, his own.

The large pool of blood under the two at one end freezes every muscle in his body, allowing the momentum to carry his frozen state another couple inches in the form of a standing skid.

Neither of the three look up. Ryson with barely the emotional strength to look down, time stands still.

The damage to these three is different, the scene as horrific as any they have seen here thus far, but this is different.

The small child closest to him, perhaps a couple of years older than the other two, her injuries consistent with that of either a severe beating or perhaps auto accident of some sorts. Either way, it has left her balled up and unconscious.

The other two, ah, geez…the other two.

Their injuries do share some similarities but these two are handcuffed together and they were placed here on this bench leaving one of them to bleed to death, most of her clothing is stained with blood. Handcuffed to her is her twin. This child is conscious but because of the severe swelling in her face, her eyes are only that of a thin sliver. And through those tiny windows, all he sees of her soul is fear and pain.

The words ring hollow as does the promise, but the truth carries the strength so the message need not be trusted.

Time kicks forward at full speed, Ryson is already moving to recon when he tells the three on the bench, I have to do a quick check of these two sheds and then I take us all and we leave this horrible place.

Blue house, green house, what destructive purpose they're meant for is unclear, both sheds share the same dirt floor, and both scattered with dirty blankets and from the smell of things, the hole dug in the center of each shed was being used as a toilet.

Ryson re-approaches the bench at a fairly quick pace and given only the one option, he simply scoops up the two in one arm and the one in the other, doing his best at keeping all three held in close, so all four are ready to move quickly as one.

Without wasting time trying to go through the hidden gate, he heads straight for the road, passing the casket, then a quick left turn at the end of the fence. From here, it's just empty space and a dirt road, they move as one and do so quite quickly.

Will finally gets traction under the front tires of the minivan after rocking forward and reverse a few times, and when the old girl finally hooks up they rocket from the hiding spot at full speed on-to the road, fishtailing several times till Will brings her under control.

As Ryson and his cargo approach the rear of the white van still stuck in the gate debris, he can hear something on the road down below and heading their way, he does not wait for a visual before closing the distance on the row of large bushes he intends to pass through to rejoin the others.

Ryson slows only enough to get turned around so as to place his back to the bushes, allowing himself as shielding for the children as he backs quickly through the brush while doing his best to announce quietly, "Somebody's coming up the road!"

May quickly fires back and can also see that Ryson has his hands full.

That's going to be Will with the minivan, he's hoping to unstick the larger van with it, now leave them with me and you go help him. May holds up the .38, assuring him these kids are in good hands, and also that Will is unarmed.

Ryson slowly goes to his knees in front of May and places all three along-side her as she sits with the four they have already collected, he waits for May to make eye contact with him, she already has tears in her eyes when she does.

"I'm so sorry, May, Ryson stands and takes a step back, I'm so sorry May."

May can say nothing.

Ryson comes through the bushes in mid-flight and lands stumbling on both feet with a vigorous wobble, the face plant is something he could not avoid. He belly skids face down. Being unhurt, he uses momentum to help propel himself back to his feet, but not before Will gets a good look at the maneuver.

Will brings the minivan in slow and allows the bumpers to just kiss before he finally says something to Ryson, "Not bad, maybe next time, you try that with a one and a half gainer and maybe you make the podium."

211

Now Ryson pretends to stick the landing while brushing some of the dirt off his front half as they both take time to laugh about it, "So, if you're done performing, why don't you get in the van, start it up, put it in reverse, I'll nudge ya. See if you can back out of that mess."

This plan goes well, Ryson backs out of the debris, Will backs up and turns the minivan around. They both get out and together clear a path through the gate pieces. When the space cleared is equal to that of the van, they stop and, in the road, they take a breath and, in this breath, Ryson tells Will who he brought back from the bench at blue house.

Will hugs him and says, "You did the right thing, we take them all, nobody gets left behind. And as for the fucks we followed here, well, they too must come with us, at least until we know who and or what they are."

"Yes I agree, so let's load 'em all up and get the hell out of here."

Knowing what awaits, they cautiously and quietly come through the bushes, what they find they could not have expected, the sadness it brings, par for the course.

Will is already removing his shirt well before they reach May and the kids. Gently, he drapes his shirt where May now has none because hers she used to wrap the dead child in after somehow she un-cuffed the one no longer with us, leaving the cuff to dangle on the other because she had no way to unlock them.

Will goes to his knees while better placing the shirt on May and asking her, "You okay?"

May begins to button the shirt and at the same time stands, her answer is a question but it does answer Will's question, "You two get the van unstuck?"

"Yeah, May, they are both ready to go."

May turns and now faces Will and Ryson, "I think what we should do is put Ryson and the six kids in the minivan. Me, you, and are two prisoners in the larger van. We will also bring her, and just secure her as best we can. I'll drive, you keep watch on our dirt, cowboys, we take the lead, find a safe place to regroup, calm down, and work it out."

There are no replies, just movement.

They stop at Ryson's rental car only long enough for him to grab what's in it. Maybe they come back for it, maybe they don't.

Half Baked Butterflies

May chooses to head back towards the town of Lost Angels, she got a glimpse of what was here on the way up and is already attempting to recall what looked safe.

Could be a private airfield.

"It's a stretch, May, but what the hell, it looks as good a place as any, yeah, May, turn here."

Maybe thirty minutes from the small town of Lost Angels, there's the bottom of a wooden milk crate nailed to a tree alongside the road, and carefully painted in yellow lettering on it is written "Oscar's air survey."

May turns right and stops, leaving the back half of the Van still visible from the road they just turned off of. Ryson is a mile or so back and can't see them. They let him get close, May pumps the brakes a couple of times and when Ryson does the same with the headlights, they continue on.

Ryson makes the announcement to all six of his passengers when he sees it's time for a turn, "Looks like we're going to make a turn, that's good because I was tired of this old road anyway."

Ryson hopes for a response, any response, from any of them. Sadly though, this announcement sails away, but at least they're all conscious and nobody's crying. In the short time that May was alone with the children, she did manage to administer a small amount of first aid, she also determined the child unconscious on the bench had suffered a concussion and somehow, her wrapping a torn sleeve around the child's head has helped her condition and she's been awake ever since.

The first few rusted out auto carcasses do not seem to account for much but within another mile or so, they find themselves driving alongside one very large junkyard. There are several roads leading off the highway that seem to in no particular design wind through it. May chooses one after slowing, so Ryson could catch up, and now they wind through what is obviously a community dump, this is decidedly so by what others have discarded. The range of debris is mostly non-organic and quite vast.

They twist and turn until they can no longer see or be seen from the highway, May chooses a small clearing behind a rusted out mostly disassembled school bus where she asks, "This good?"

"As good as any, my dear." Will leans and kisses her on the cheek, then adds, "Nicely done."

Ryson's first comment when he gets out is, "Isn't it great that no matter where you go, there's always a dump." His second comment is, "We got perhaps an hour or two at best before the sun goes down and it gets dark." He does not have to say anything else before the discussion leans towards, "How do we get everybody through the night?" They both kind of wait for May to take the lead, "It just seems she has a knack for nesting and usually a plan to go along with it."

After securing their prisoners in the rusted-out school bus and converting the minivan to sleep seven, including May, in the reclined driver seat. They now rifle through the stuff the two bad guys had with them in the van when captured.

The center console and glove box, May tears into like a one-year cake embrace, while Ryson and Will go through the two backpacks one more time.

"Oh, here we go, finally somebody's wallet."

At first inspection all they find in the backpacks is some clothing, few snacks, a couple bottles of water, and two cell phones, but now Will withdraws a wallet and cannot open it fast enough.

"Now here's a slice of interesting info, Mr. Adam Gentos, the guy we followed from L.A.X., to here with his dead buddy, just so happens he's a pilot. And if you ask me, I think these two had someplace to go and maybe there's a plane involved."

All three check on the children and do what they can with what they have to provide them with all the comfort they can muster. With this done, it's time to ask the prisoners some overdue questions. And Will knows just where to start.

On edge is one way to describe Will's demeanor as the three of them come onto the bus and take seats near the other two, you could also say he looked as though he was a trigger pull away from even a single wrong answer. Ryson and May are more than willing to just follow along and see where this goes.

Surprisingly so, Will's approach is quite simple and extremely effective, "I can shoot you both and not look back because of these children and what we've seen today and of course where we found you. So I think I'll just be honest with you and will see where that takes us."

"The three of us came here looking for two children very similar to the two children we found handcuffed together, but instead, we find what we find and we also find you. The problem we have now is how do we get these children to safety and some very needed medical treatment, figure out what to do with you and get back to our search as quickly as possible. Also I, would like to add, and this is more directed at you, Mr. Gentos, we think you might have access to an airplane. Oh, and let's not forget, her and I have followed you since you arrived at L.A.X. and we all boarded flight 1441. And last but not least, we are in no capacity affiliated with any sort of legal bureau, not even the cops, local or otherwise." Will pauses and let's a couple seconds tick by, "So what you got?" Will says this as if he's waiting for a family member to respond.

Adam has an accent but his English is perfectly understood, and he too in all unseen truth chooses the honest approach, "Seems you already know my name so how about I start with why we're here, that airplane you think we have access to we do indeed, it's a twin engine Beechcraft and it was purchased by my family from the Gurauno family, that was their place we just left."

"The purchase of this aircraft was not usual nor was it the first time, but when it came time for money to changed hands, we are told the price has been greatly reduced and that the Gurauno family would like us to do them a favor. And when the Gurauno's ask for a favor, you really don't have the option to negotiate."

"What they wanted is what we did. Problem being, of course, when we get here, we've got a dead guy in the back of the van and nobody here to greet us or do as they promised and provide a ride to the airport. So we hide from whatever military troops were already there and as soon as they go, we leave the dead guy and then get stuck in what was the front gate."

Things are obviously going well, so Will continues, "So where is this aircraft and who is he?"

Felipa takes Wills cue and begins to speak on his own behalf, "Felipa, Felipa Marquez, Adam and I are cousins. As for the plane, believe it or not, but you are already on the right road, it's just a couple of miles past this junkyard, the small airport is known as Oscar's Field."

It seems like Felipa starts to tear up when he gets a little more serious. This man struggles with the words not because he plans deception, the reason being, he himself is a father, "Those children you rescued from the Gurauno place, you, you need to know, Adam and I know nothing of those people in any regards as to the abuse of children, we are both fathers ourselves and would not be a part of that. I myself would defend those kids as if they were my own, meaning, you do not have to ask twice for our help."

Adam jumps back in softly, "If it's honesty you want and that's what it takes for you to at least trust in some of what we're saying, we give you the plane and I as your pilot. The keys and bill of sale are in a coded exterior cargo hatch. The code is 5445. The tail number of the aircraft is TG 771 and we will have to gas her up."

Will now throws a bluff, "Yeah, well, maybe we don't need you to be our pilot. I'm quite sure I will be just fine without ya. I've flow much bigger than some twin-engine Beechcraft, I can assure you."

Adam's response seems genuine, "Godspeed, my friend, we will not even report it missing. But it's going to be a long walk back to La Paz because Felipa here forgot his I.D."

Will calls a huddle and the three get off the bus for a pow-wow. After a short discussion, Will returns to the prisoners, May to the children, and Ryson to the dead.

Ryson removes the child from the larger van while being careful at keeping her tightly wrapped, he's decided to place her in the trunk of one of the nearby cars and does so, making sure the trunk closes but does not lock. He then readies the van hoping to get some sleep before it's his turn to take watch.

May settles the kids, closes the sliding door, and quietly takes her place behind the steering wheel, her seat reclined to maybe halfway.

"Alright, you two, so here's what's going to happen. In the morning, you and my partner will go check on the plane first thing," Will makes eye contact with Adam while nodding his head, now he looks at Felipa, "You stay here, we wait for them to get back. Until then, stay on the bus and nobody has to shoot you."

216

As he says sleep tight, he is already stepping off the bus.

May is just finishing the text she intends to send Art, holding it up and out the window as Will comes over to say good night, he reads it at a whisper, trying not to bother the kids.

"We need to talk, Will call in a.m. need to find secure line, it's important. 3.4.5."

"Looks good to me, May, now hit send and get some sleep."

They share a kiss before May rolls up the window. The text from Art comes back as expected "Be safe, sleep tight. 1.2."

Daybreak's the following morning with May on watch but still in the front seat of the minivan, the light roles in from the east slowly, taking back most of the places to hide, and with each chased away shadow so goes some of the fear.

They all share half of what's left, the word breakfast was used more than once but really it was just a few granola bars and bottled water.

Before Ryson and Adam climb in the larger van to go, he checks the juice in his phone and assures May and Will he keeps them up to speed as they go, they both climb in and now he hands Adam the keys and says, "Seems you already know the way."

"La Paz, that's Bolivia, right?"

"Yes, Felipa and I, born and raised."

"So how is it you two cousins find your way into the sadistic realm of this Gurauno family?" Ryson's grip on the .45 stiffens just a wee bit.

"With us and them, it's just about the aircraft. My family has been involved in one way or another in the black-market gem trade for almost one hundred years, and in this business, it's all about fast and low, of course, with this approach, you tend to chew up a few planes and the Gurauno's are a main supplier of laundered aircraft. Nothing more, nothing less."

The last few minutes of the ride are spent in silence, Ryson on high level alert and Adam choosing to speak only when spoken to.

When most of the airfield has come into view, Ryson instructs Adam to pull over and park, with this done, he now says, "All right, Adam, so why don't you walk me through this, and at the same time, tell me what we're looking at."

"Well, that there in front of us is Oscar's field, who Oscar is, I haven't a clue. That airfield as far as I know is owned, operated and maintained by the Gurauno family. The fact that it looks somewhat dilapidated and uninhabited is perfectly normal and I am quite sure this is by design. I can't read the tail number from here but a good guess says that twin engine job sitting out there in the grass is our girl. Fifteen yards past that is a hard-packed, natural runway."

"So how do we gas that baby up?"

"Teamwork, my good sir, teamwork. There is no tow vehicle here, so we will have to push it over to that large tank on legs just past that second outbuilding over there. From there, you pump, I'll see to it that the gas gets in the right place."

The text Ryson sends May and Will is simple but keeps them engaged "Found the bird, going to juice it up. 3."

Ryson hits send and says, "So then, let's go do that."

There is a rickety wooden fence more of it down than up surrounding most of the area, except where there could be a large gate but is not. At the nearest corner past the opening sits a narrow two-story structure with windows all the way around it, most likely a curator's quarters.

Unobstructed by friend or foe, they park right behind the plane and indeed the tail number is TG 771.

Ryson opens the external cargo hatch and withdraws all of what's in there, putting both, the keys and bill of sale in his own pockets.

It moves easier than you might think and once the fueling is complete, they reverse the movement, replacing the aircraft exactly the way and where they found it.

Using the keys to unlock and lower some steps, they both now climb in, they decide to not start it, hoping to avoid any attention to themselves, so instead, Adam goes through a preflight check and determines when it comes time, she'll start. Ryson suspiciously agrees.

Back in the van, U-turn and now heading to rejoin the others the text Ryson sends reads "Done is done, see you in twenty 3."

"Be safe, all okay here. 4.5."

Leaving the prisoner bound and confined to one end of the bus, Will and May have done their best to make the rest of the bus a living space for the kids, knowing they would need the minivan to go call Art. Just finishing this task and rearranging the children in it when Ryson and Adam slowly roll in and come to a stop.

Before Ryson hands off the relay baton and Will speeds away on the next leg of this race, May jots down all the important info from the aircraft bill of sale, Art, for sure, is going to ask for it. As the two of them pull away from the junkyard, May sends this text "Heading to secure line now. Maybe one hour. 4.5."

There's been no other traffic on the road in front of the junkyard since they got here, so when the sound of May, Will and the minivan fade into the distance, the midmorning solitude now reclaims its surroundings, leaving his tired soul weathered and alone, except, of course, for the eight lives his hands now hang in the balance.

The two already have a plan and now their instincts prove correct, the internet *café* they found in town is one of the few places that has contact with the outside world and when they ask the young man who seems to be in charge for a direct phone line to an international operator, his smug response is both appreciated and in need of an ass whoopin', but now is not the time so May lets it go.

Two rooms, and of that hallway, smug boy motions with a nod, "Choose one, fifty bucks a visit, the line is private, who you call is your business."

Will pays him, May is already on her way.

May dials direct, Art picks up on the first ring. There's only a couple of breaths in-between as May brings Art up to speed and when she finally comes to a stop an empty silence fills the phone line, then Art calmly replies, "Give us a couple of minutes."

The silence returns.

When the silence breaks, it's Lila's voice that says, "You okay, May?"

"Yes, we're fine, Lila, but I can't tell you how good it feels to have you and Art on the other end of this phone. It's been hard and we've seen some horrible things, Lila, stop right there, May, there's plenty of time for that later, right now you listen to me."

"What you three have done, again, is absolutely remarkable, and you May, geez girl, some stuff you're made of, ha. But what you must do now is get those the world thought lost forever to safety, once that's done then you three by whatever grace fuels your passion shall continue. And, May?"

"Yes, Lila."

"You stay strong, your destiny awaits."

219

"Well, I don't know about that whole destiny thing, Lila, but the fact you think so means a lot."

Lila now prompts May as she calmly asks, "You've got pen and paper there with you?"

"Yes, I do. Okay sit tight, give us two more minutes, May."

As Lila comes back on the line May hears her mumble, "One three seven, in the red. Still there May?" Not waiting for an answer Lila starts in, "Your heading is simple, you tell Mr. Pilot head due south, keep it low, your direction should be towards the western coastal region of Chile, once you get airborne, let us know, will go from there. Also, your one hundred and thirty-seven pounds over maximum for that aircraft, the one cousin has to stay, but you bring everybody else. Okay, May?"

"Okay, Lila, thanks, you're my angel, hug Art. I'll text you once we are up and away."

"You three, be one, be safe," May hangs up first because Lila waited.

May is already texting Ryson before their out the door "On our way back, time to go, Felipa stays, we're too heavy. 4.5."

Ryson understands the message but keeps it on the down-low, not too sure how Felipa is going to deal with this.

"Ryson, here's the minivan," making its winding approach to him and so heads up the small road towards them for a private talk about.

Will expects some kind of a fight when he tells the two cousins one of them is not getting on the plane, so he breaks it down like this as he unties the both of them.

"We have a place to take these kids, I'm not telling you where that is till we're on the way. It's going to take every drop of fuel this planes got in her to get there, I lied, I can't fly it, so that leaves us a 140 pounds over maximum and this means Felipa has to stay. Our plan right now is to cram the ten of us in that aircraft, take these kids to safety, hand them over, refuel the plane, and head straight back here."

"We leave Felipa at the airfield with both vehicles, giving him options as to how he waits for our return. And when that happens you have our word, You two may do as you please."

There is no room allowed for discussion, they all retake the vehicle space each used on the way here, May takes the lead and to Oscar's field they all go.

It's only a twenty-minute drive and still no traffic, odd enough is that fact but stranger still, as the airfield comes into sight, May can see at the far end of the grass runway is what looks like an overturned military jeep.

May pulls off the road and stops, Ryson does the same, leaving just a foot or two between them, only, he does not know why. Still looking forward May says, "When Ryson told us what happened here this morning, he never once mentioned an overturned jeep at the end of the runway." Will now looks at Adam who is sitting tied to his cousin Indian style in the back of the van, "Was that there this morning?" May is already exiting the van before she hears his answer, Will waits but only to confirm their suspicions. It's a fearful reply of, "No."

And it makes Wills guts queasy.

There's a discussion with the three as they stand behind the minivan for cover, it's decided the large van with Will in the driver seat and the dead child still in the back with Adam and Felipa and May riding shotgun go check on the jeep, it, being the faster of the two vehicles, in case a quick getaway is necessary, if not, then everybody but Felipa get aboard the plane, letting Felipa to make his retreat in the large van.

The text comes through from Will "All looks clear come on in." Ryson slides the phone in his front pocket while telling his passengers, "Oh, this is gonna be fun, I just love to fly, I think I should have been born a bird, chirp, chirp."

Already past the dilapidated fence and narrow building but still fifty yards from the plane, Ryson spots movement at the far end of the runway near the jeep, he cuts hard right and hits the gas, following the fence line on the inside, hoping he was not spotted.

At the far corner of this fence, it goes left twenty yards and stops at the first of the two outbuildings whose back walls actually make up this part of the fence. A quick U-turn now allows him to pull up parallel and almost scraping the passenger side mirror as he brings the minivan to within a few feet of the corner along the side of the outbuilding, when he brings the minivan to a stop, looking forward, he can see just the tail section of the plane they now call their own.

Ryson is quick to exit the minivan and does so in silence, placing his back against the wall of the outbuilding in front of the van, he shuffles forward until he can get a look over his right shoulder and around the corner.

There are now two men dressed in military fatigues and carrying AK-47s and quickly heading straight for the plane as Felipa is making his retreat.

Staying tight to the corner, Ryson watches the two men hurry over and take positions in front of the folding steps leading into the plane, clearly, they have not seen Ryson because this puts their backs to him.

Raising their AKs and shouting something in Spanish Ryson could not make out, one of them now steps closer to the plane, placing his left foot on the first step of the folding stairs.

As Ryson breaks cover away from the corner, he moves to his right, allowing the building to hopefully conceal whatever happens next from the children still sitting in the minivan.

The .45 auto up and gripped tightly with both hands, Ryson shouts, "We don't want any trouble!"

The closer of the two in fatigues spins slowly in his direction, probably not sure what he heard. He's not fully turned when he and Ryson make eye contact but as this happens, soldier boy squeezes the trigger on his AK, sending it full-auto even before the barrel gets pointed in Ryson's direction.

Ryson drops to a sitting position with arms and legs stretched out in front of himself, safely allowing the last few bullets to sail high over his head. He fires twice, both rounds finding their mark and each hollow point bullet life canceling in its own right.

One down and now the other starts to spin. The attempt to re-aim is unnecessary as Will appears in the doorway of the airplane, the .38 already exploding, sending second soldier to the ground already dead when he gets there.

From very loud like the breath of a dragon to a silence that comes so quickly, it has the feel of a vacuum to it, the moment freezes for several seconds. Both, he and Will, shocked by the events.

Ryson gets to his feet as Will comes halfway down the folding steps. The quiet still lingers but now the vibrations at their feet pin them like stone and both seem unable to move.

With the vibrations now comes a rumble that rolls in from the far end of the runway, it's loud and sounds like a couple of very large diesel trucks. The sound appears to eminent from empty space because where the rumble seems to travel from there is nothing to see but an overturned jeep.

It sounds like one of the diesel trucks eats the other and from this, a thick, oily, black belch rises from somewhere near the jeep. Just as soon as all eyes are on this the rumble grows and from a hidden tear in the earth out crawls the backend of a very large tank, it continues to rise till almost vertical, there's another thick, black belch, bringing now to level ground the whole tank. Will, May, and Adam, knowing it, climbed up the embankment backwards at the end of the runway. Ryson only assuming Satan himself spit this out from the gates of hell.

As the tank comes level it jellies and settles, they all find comfort in seeing the main gun is pointing 180 degrees away from them, it's direction and maneuver clearly obvious and with intention because as soon as it settles, the main gun fires. The tank bucks back violently, sending sound and a shockwave in every direction and a fifteen foot flame out the muzzle. Where the big bullet of Satan's machine goes they don't know.

The shockwave covers quickly the hundred yards, forcing Ryson to slightly shuffle backwards while sending Will in full retreat back into the plane.

Ryson can hear what sounds like small arms fire, it's far off but definitely in the direction the tank has fired. When the tank fires a second time, the blast radius seems to double in size, keeping him in a backward shuffle and reaching to cover his ears.

The hand signals and sign language gestures are more than enough, what Will actually says while he's reaching for the cord to haul in the folding steps, Ryson could not tell. What is important and they would all agree, back in the minivan and get the kids out of here. As he turns to do this, he sees the door of the plane seal shut.

Couple of long strides puts him back at the minivan, and yeah, the kids are a little shook up but nobody's hurt. Ryson climbs in the driver seat, the key in his hand and ready to go, the minivan cranks once at normal speed but the three or four cranks that follow slow way down, making the sound like you dumped in something sticky. The engine does not catch but instead, fades to a strange clicking sound, then silence.

Now at least when the tank fires for the third time, Ryson is buffered on this side of the building along with the children. But he also knows they're, sitting ducks all stuffed inside this minivan.

223

It's clear that the skirmish is not directed at them, but how far off can some real collateral damage be.

The side of the building Ryson pulled up to ever so snugly and almost touching he did so one for cover, but also there's a single entry door here and he did not want any surprises coming out of it, but now he's forced to place the minivan in neutral and with the door open and one foot on the ground, he pushes, it's just dirt and grass, so it takes all the strength he can muster to push back far enough to unblock the door.

Mr. Ninja exits the minivan with every intention of going with the two legged, flying, kung-Fu door kick, but before Ryson puts this plan in action, he decides to perhaps check at least the integrity of the door. If it's a solid steel door, then perhaps a different approach.

A good thump with his boot at the lower part of the door not only determines its construction but in surprise it creeks open with a squeak about three or four inches then springs itself close. Placing a hand at mid-door, even a slight push sends the door halfway open. Not waiting to see what's inside, Ryson just knows that's where he and these children need to be.

All three are sitting on the floor of the plane in the thin strip separating the eight seats, Will, being the most forward and using the cockpit windows to keep his eye on the tank, all three keeping low enough to stay well-hidden and hopefully unnoticed. Adam is furthest back in the plane and able to use the last small window on the right side to try and answer May's question.

"I can't tell, but I can't believe they drove out of here and I didn't see them."

"Text him, May, see what's up,"

Will watches the tank fire for the fourth time and says, "Son of a bitch, I'm glad sure as shit we're not on the other and of whatever is coming out of that large ass piece of pipe."

May, somehow and for some reason, finds enough space between sheer terror and utter conundrum to find humor in this, and knowing Will was not trying to be funny, causes her to for just a second or two laugh out loud.

The vibration in Ryson's front pocket will just have to wait, he already knows who it is and what they're asking.

There's two wooden style picnic benches that great him as he brings the first couple of kids into the building, he chooses the table closest to the door and places two of the three children he found on the bench at Camp Diablo, the four year old still wearing a handcuff on her left wrist, and the six year old with the arm of a long sleeve shirt still wrapped around her head, both are conscious so when he sets them down, they have no trouble staying put.

The few windows scattered about allow enough light to safely navigate and also determine what this place is for, it's not an airplane hangar like he thought, but instead just a place for storage, big and small, big because of the twenty-foot garage style door in the front of the building. Small because built into this larger door is also a smaller one.

As Ryson whispers, "You two just sit right here," the door he used to bring them in begins to slowly creep open. First startled, then surprised to see all of the children who were still in the minivan now coming through the door. The thirteen year old girl comes through first and even though she is still having trouble walking and maintaining her balance, she is carrying one of the five year old little boys and then right behind her is the eleven year old boy with his arm in a makeshift sling and not without struggles of his own, he is carrying the other five year old little boy.

Ryson quickly helps in assisting all of them to the bench and seated before he finally checks his phone.

"You okay? 4.5."

"Minivan's a no start, all in building closest to you, side door was unlocked, we're okay, what now? .3"

May reads this out loud as she gets a better look at the building Ryson and the children should be in.

Her reply is simple and with exclamation as the tank fires for the fifth time just as she hits send. This is all Ryson receives before something jams the communication systems including cell phones "Stay Pink"

Not sure what to make of this, he stands in silence at the smaller door inside the larger one, trying to get a sense of what's going on through the thin aluminum siding that makes up this part of the building.

Twice, he reaches for the handle on the door and twice, in his head, the silent screams retract this motion, the door if he was to open it half way, he could then see the plane and those on board. This thought is chased out of his head when the tank fires and the whole building vibrates like the tale of a large rattler. He turns to face the children and sees all eyes big and looking back at him. His heart skips a beat and these words come from a place he knows not. He raises his volume, ensuring to capture all of their attentions.

"Can anybody here tell me what a half-baked butterfly might be?"

There is no vocal response from the bench but the eyes shifting to something less frightening.

He makes his approach to them slowly and unassuming, then adds along the way, "And I don't mean butterflies that just need more cooking."

Now there's a couple of tiny smiles.

Ryson takes a seat at the bench and continues, "It's a caterpillar. So now let me tell you a little story."

"In a wonderful land far, far, from here there once lived a caterpillar, I believe her name was Waylow. Well, one day, while Waylow lay basking in the warmth of an early summer day, she finds that she feels different and for reasons she could not explain, decides to climb a very tall, wooden fence post. Waylow's journey to the top of this post goes fairly quickly. When she gets to the top to have a look around, she spots a giant, oak tree way off into the distance and right then, she knows her journey does not stop at the top of this fence post. She just knows that large oak tree is where she should be."

"Waylow crawls down that post and begins the journey to that mighty oak."

"I wish I could tell you Waylow's journey was filled with fun and wonderful discoveries but quite sadly, it was not. Some very bad things happened to Waylow along the way, some of the other animals she encountered were very mean and did things to her that made her very sad and very scared and most of the time, it hurt. But, each time Waylow managed to somehow escape."

"Waylow awakens one morning to find herself shivering in some tall, wet grass, she crawled through the night and now has no idea where she might be. As this little caterpillar began to warm with some of the rays sneaking through the tall blades of grass, she finally looks up."

"And, yes, there, above Waylow, stands the single most beautiful oak tree ever in the whole wide world. Well needless to say, Waylow, right away, begins to climb and does not stop until she reaches one of the very top branches. It's here, high a-top this mighty oak that seems to almost touch the sky, she begins to build around her a cocoon, and in here, she hides for many days until something magical happens and she becomes a butterfly. So my question to you is this, 'Do you think that the butterfly remembers being a caterpillar?'"

He knows if pressed somebody would give him an answer but he also knows he already has one, "Well, I believe that they do, and you know why I think that?"

"The way I see it is this, I figure how can any of us know when we have found happiness if we don't understand sadness, I also believe the more sadness you encounter, the bigger the happiness you will find."

"So, when Waylow, who we shall now call Willow lets a strong breeze take her from the branch high atop that oak tree as she spreads her beautiful new wings, she, for sure, knows now what it means to be happy. And when I take all of you away from this place, you too shall understand what it means to be truly happy."

The silence that follows is neither of sadness or sorrow but only of hope for a better tomorrow.

At first, it sounds like somebody taps loudly on the thin aluminum roof, but with the second tap comes a sound Ryson has not heard since Vietnam, those are bullets, and he could tell the caliber was quite large because of the amount of light chasing the bullet through the hole. They are actually coming through the side of the building but up high almost at the roof and with the sound that of a sizzle, they go through the building and right out the other side.

Four or five of these large caliber sizzles, zip through, only stopping when there's a large explosion outside, it's different than the tank gun firing and quickly following is a series of lesser explosions but still quite intense in their own decimal level.

Death seems almost imminent for him and the lives he swore to protect, and so Ryson begins to formulate another story in his head, but before he can produce the first few syllables, the smell of warm sugar cookies again swirls around him. Ryson now lingers in this euphoric state for several seconds before asking, "Do you kids smell that?"

None reply but some do as Ryson and begin sniffing the air around them.

Will hands May the .38 revolver and quickly runs down the order in which things will happen next. First thing he does is open the door of the plane and lowers the steps, now, he says to Adam, "Get up here and start this plane, and if it moves even just an inch, May here is going to blow off one of your kneecaps. I've got to drag those two dead guys to the other side of the plane before Ryson comes through that door with those kids, we can't have them tripping over the dead to get in the plane."

Ryson hears the twin engines start and roar to life, moving quickly to the door, he tells the kids, "Don't move."

The first few inches Ryson proceeds with caution, then opening the door slowly as he tries to focus through the bright sunlight outside. When the blur sharpens, his focus lands on the tank and he's quite surprised to see it smoldering and in complete ruin.

Now he knows it's time to go, as the door comes fully open, Ryson sees Will placing the two A.K.s on the floor of the plane and then moving them to the left side of the doorway.

Ryson whistles, Will spins, their eyes meet and Will now moves to Ryson at a full sprint.

There's no time for sentimental reunions, they both rush into the building, gather the children and rush out just as fast.

Will takes the lead as he carries two, the thirteen-year-old girl and eleven-year-old boy trailing right behind him, leaving Ryson to follow, carrying the other two.

Quite quickly, Will and the two that follow are up the steps and into the plane. Ryson is within a few feet of them when he spots movement out of the right corner of his eye.

Near the smoldering tank, a soldier of some sorts stumbles in Ryson's direction and without warning, raises his right hand while firing three times with the handgun in it. Ryson turns his back to this as to provide a shield for the children and then quickly handing the kids to Will who is ready to haul them on board.

Bullet number three luckily catches Ryson empty handed because the impact to his right upper thigh sweeps him off his feet, sending him to an unconscious state when the back of his head and shoulders slam to the ground.

May moves first, she's like a shadow, and moving quick, she grabs up one of the AK-47s. She is past Will, out the plane, and down the steps in far less time than it took to write this. What's remarkable here is that both the thirteen and the eleven-year-old also move towards the door to help Ryson, only being slowed and then stopped by Will's quickness to alter their intentions. Letting them know their help will be needed, Will says, "Stay here, when we get him this far, you help pull him in."

May goes to one knee and takes a shooter's position between Ryson and the bad guy with a gun who is still stumbling this way. Squeezing the trigger, she's surprised when it goes full automatic, emptying the thirty-round magazine in just a couple of seconds. The first few rounds miss their mark because May flinches, but the fifteen or so after that scramble Mr. stumbles and it ain't pretty.

They get Ryson to his feet and then to the plane, it's more of a two-person shuffle with Ryson's legs just dangling behind, and as asked, the kids are at the door, they all push, pull, shove, and drag until everybody is now inside the plane.

The plane is already moving before Will can get the steps pulled in and the door closed.

Adam taxies to the end of the runway opposite the tank and jeep, hoping there is enough space between here and there to bring them aloft without an impact.

The twin-engine aircraft strains and shutters but does indeed clear the obstacles and they do get airborne but not before two bullets find their way into the aircraft, one comes in the right side and harmlessly leaves out the left. The second bullet strikes the only person on the plane that was already dead.

There's really not much blood. Right after May applied a tourniquet, the bleeding stopped rather quickly, Ryson is conscious but no doubt, the headache he's feeling is from a concussion. May does her best to get everybody safely seated and situated before she text Art "Adam and Will have control of the plane."

May now sits, hit's send, and takes a very needed long breath.

Lila reads the message first only because her phone is closest, she reads it out loud so Art does not have to, their calls won't go through that's why May's texting "All aboard and airborne, quite the skirmish when we left. 3. Took a bullet upper thigh. Stable but has a concussion. We are on course."

"Understood. Stay your course. We will get back to you. Hugs all around. 1.2."

May reads this to the plane so all others are up to speed.

There is a collective calm in the cabin, and for now, all seem at ease with just watching the world fly by at only a few feet above the earth.

Ninety minutes later, the quiet buzz of May's phone catches her in a daydream somewhere between her favorite pizza and a half day soak in a much-needed bath. The first part of the message seems fairly important so May quickly relays this upfront.

"Hey, you two, looks like we have a course correction, 17° south, by 70° west for about another ninety minutes. We are looking for half an old lighthouse, and somewhere just west of this there is an airstrip. Two says if we find ourselves over water, we've gone too far. He also says, 'Danny assures him there is an airstrip,' he says we'll see it. I guess we are going to have to trust him." The last part of the message says "Read Privately, was going to arrange fuel for the plane, no need for that now. Everyone comes home, minus the pilot."

The next sentence is followed by several exclamation marks "Do not get off the plane. Park it, shut it all down, stay put. Let us know when this happens! Be safe, Godspeed. 1.2."

May responds "Understood. Thank you, you are the angels. 4."

She then forwards this to Will.

When they finally do spot half a lighthouse, there is approximately eighteen minutes of fuel left, they turn and head west, following the Chilean coast into the desert region, but only for a couple of minutes, the landing strip was clearly marked by scattered debris along either side. How ironic that the aircraft to which has failed in the attempts now defines its boundaries. There are four or five small aircraft that look like they crashed on landing and now the bits and pieces outline the edges of the sand and grass runway.

There's not much wind, so the approach and landing is fairly straightforward. They are within a couple of hundred yards of the beach so it's not hard to see how this landing on a more windy day could go badly very quickly. They do as instructed, May sends "On the runway, all in one piece. 4." And now they just sit quietly.

Lila is just finishing a conversation with somebody on the other end of a satellite phone when May's text's beeps in, she quickly replies with a "Very good, sit tight. 1."

Art walks into the room as Lila finishes her conversation. When he hears her say, "Roger that, I say again, they are on the ground," he gestures with, "Touchdown!"

Raising both hands high over his head.

The silence and paranoia become too much, even with a concussion so Ryson breaks the quiet with a question, "so, hey, what the hell happened to that tank?"

230

Things go quiet again but now in a weird way. May is closest to Ryson and now she look's him straight in the eyes and says, "Yes, that's a very good question."

Will turns a one eighty in the co-pilot seat and now he two makes eye contact with Ryson, "So, yeah, here's the thing about that, first of all, when we drove to the end of the runway, there was no tank, but there was a dry riverbed, and they were obviously using that as a sort of hidden highway. What made the tank explode I haven't a clue, but I think we're all pretty lucky it did. We, for sure, were its next targets."

"Just as our cell phones go down, there is a round hatch cover that suddenly opens at the back of the tank and up pops some guy with a pair of binoculars, he still in the tank, so I could only see him from the waist up. He starts scanning our area and of course, spots the two guys on the ground and when he does, now he shifts his view to the building you and the kids are in, and now the turret starts to move and that big ass barrel along with it."

"I actually had my hand on the airplane door and ready to make a run for that side door you said you guys went in, and try to get you all out."

May jumps in here and finishes Wills story, "I was looking right at it and it simply exploded. I did not see it being attacked, no rockets, no R.P.Gs, no bombs, just one real big boom."

This quiets them all and leaving them to be collectively startled when May's phone again beeps to life.

May looks up wide-eyed after reading this and simply states, "It looks like it's time to go."

Will asks, "Where we going, May?"

"Well, here's what it says. Exit the plane, head towards the beach, now follow the horn. Leave the pilot at the plane, destroy the weapons. 1.2."

Adam finally looks concerned as he asks, "How am I supposed to refuel the plane?"

Will has no intention of sugarcoating this and besides, now they are in a hurry, "Listen, Adam, here's how I see it. And no, this is not a discussion."

"If you get caught with your hands in a cookie jar, chances are you've eaten some of those cookies. You and your cousin, Felipa, did not show up at that place on accident. But still, the evidence is circumstantial. Therefore, you are not dead, only stranded."

Adam nods once or twice and chooses to just sit quietly.

The group are only a few yards from the plane and doing their best to move towards the beach when in fact they do hear a horn.

It's somewhat slow going, especially when they hit sand, Ryson can only take small hops on the good leg and even that, each time he lands, the pain makes him wince and light headed, so he's letting Will support most of his weight, he and Will both carry a child, May is carrying the other two. The older ones are doing their best in helping May carry hers.

About every twenty or thirty seconds, there is a blast on this horn, it sounds like a car alarm only a little higher in octave. This place and the landing strip are absolutely deserted and it feels almost like being in a quarantine zone so they press on heading down the beach, looking for whoever belongs to that horn.

They are less than one hundred yards from the plane when further down the beach, they spot a small pier, they can no longer see the plane because of the embankment that separated the landing strip from the beach, but they know where it is.

There's only one boat parked at the pier and it seems safely to assume it's whom they're looking for.

Of the two groups, when they do make eye contact, the three on the pier move quickly to help the group on the beach. When they are all face-to-face, it's the woman of the three that speaks first, the two males that hurried with her stand quietly. All three in their twenties and maybe thirties and all three definitely American.

"Good afternoon, my name is Sophie, Art sends his best, and also I might add without the help of somebody named Danny, we would have never found this place. These two fellows here are Mark and Tony, that little boat there is going to take us to a bigger boat and then that boat takes us all home, well, as far as San Diego anyway."

May jumps in with a question because she seems to be struggling with this the least, she does so humbly and with a couple of tears rolling down her face, "Where did you people come from?" she then adds, "and sadly, there is still a child on the airplane and yes, we would all like to go home."

Sophie steps forward hugging May and the two children May still has glued to her hips. As she backs away from this embrace, she says, "Let's just say we were down here helping out some whale friends of ours and you sort of took priority. So let us help you. And we already know about the little girl still on the plane."

Sophie glances at one of the men standing next to her and says, "Tony, go, and you better hurry because we're leaving."

Tony outruns the last part of the sentence, probably did not even hear it, "I guess we could also do something about that bullet in your leg," she smiles at Ryson and says, "that's got to hurt."

Ryson smiles back, "Yeah, just a little."

Before they all get on the small boat, they pause and wait for Tony who is now only thirty yards from them and in his arms still tightly wrapped is the small child he went after.

Sophie announces the fact that they can call her Sophie, she's a doctor and will be in charge of all their medical needs, starting right now. It's slightly choppy and only a twenty-minute ride but Sophie begins to assess the damages to Ryson and the six young children now under her care.

The bigger boat Sophie mentioned is actually a very large cargo ship, there's still a quarter mile away but even from here, it seems enormous, with easily two hundred shipping crates stacked on the flat deck two and three high covering two thirds of the ship. The back of the ship consist entirely of what looks like a three-story apartment building. There is a large space between these two monolithic structures and in it a crane that rises from the deck like a large yellow sunflower.

As if she possesses a clairvoyant nature, Sophie glances up and out of the front windows and says, "Oh, it's much easier than you might think." All eyes are forward and out the same windows, so now Sophie elaborates.

"You see that big, yellow crane on the deck of that ship? Well, because this is a very special little boat, we are going to pull up alongside and that crane is going to pluck us right from the water, all we have to do is sit still and enjoy the ride."

Sophie's simple mechanical breakdown of as to how the little boat gets on the big boat was correct in its end justifying the means but the actual procedure was at times heart stopping. Or as some would put it, "Wow, now that was an e-ticket ride!"

The platform they are lowered onto aboard ship must be cushioned because instead of a spine compression landing they were expecting, it felt almost like being lowered onto a large bed of springs, if anything, it was uneasy because it seemed the small boat never does come to a rest.

They're greeted by several people as they all get off the small boat, one of which is the captain who is also the only one who speaks at this time, "Welcome aboard, I am Capt. Martin Ricks, sorry we could not come to a complete stop, but the minute we do that, it then raises a question on radar. These fine people here will assist you to your quarters and the little one there will be taken downstairs where there's a cold storage, I'm sorry to say, she will not be alone."

"Dinner is at seven, we can talk then. Right now, we I must get this old girl back up to full speed or she'll never make the head currents out of the South Pacific." As Capt. Ricks walks away, he slows long enough to say, "Tonight's pizza and a movie, if it and I believe it is, Thursday."

The float home consist of showers, food, and sleep, they manage to communicate with Art, all the children are ID'ed and of course, from Ryson, one bullet extracted.

From the deck, Ryson is helped downstairs to medical, they park him on a table face down and promise somebody will be along shortly with some food and water. About thirty minutes later, Sophie shows up with a bottle of water and oatmeal cookies.

Sophie's not saying much as she begins to gather what she needs, she drops some items into a stainless-steel bowl, the sound echoes far too long in the small room and when it does fade, Sophie comes to a standing rest. Ryson hears her exhale but it's more than that. He knows that sound and he also knows no matter how hard she tries, she will never push out all the ugly. Ryson turns his head and lifts it from the table, so he can see her and her him.

Sophie stands five foot ten inches one hundred and sixty-two pounds, thirty-one years of age, chestnut hair, medium toned skin, quite pretty, and a demeanor to match her looks. But today the ugly of mankind has shit all over her and all she can say is, "Those kids are such a mess, and that poor little thing down in the freezer, my God, and as if what killed her was not bad enough, the bullet in her tiny little body came post mortem. Now what sort of sick sadistic beast shoots a dead four-year-old child?"

"I wish I could tell you it's not as bad as you think but clearly and considering where we found these children, I cannot. But what I can give you is this… Just as we took off, two bullets were fired into the plane at us, one went straight through, the other, well, you already know."

Three days drift by before they arrive to a full stop and an anchored position two miles off the coast of San Diego. Reversing the procedure in calmer seas and at a full stop still not without a fright but at least it did not seem death defying, and in no time, they were back on land. The only conversation on the way in was when Ryson asked Sophie, "Just how is it she comes to know Art?"

Her response as his would be, vague and without a real answer, "Oh gosh, Art, Lila and I go back quite some time, maybe someday we all get together and talk about it. Or not."

Sophie is sort of weird and gets a wee bit serious, it's quite obvious she is fighting back some real emotion when she says, "I admire what you three did and who you came out of there with, and in the eyes of us, all there is no more greater sacrifice. I myself stand and salute."

The three really don't know what to say, it's finally May that states the obvious, "Don't sell yourself short, cowgirl, you would have done the same."

The boat slows as they come into a series of private docks and boat houses, above one of these private docks rest a parking lot and staring down from this and behind a locked gate, is Art and Lila. In the parking lot above them is Art's suburban and a large white utility Van.

Sophie has a key and therefore, exits the boat first, she is to the gate quite quickly, letting Art and Lila through. They share a three-way hug and some quiet words are exchanged before the three head back to the boat and help the others.

They all go up to the parking lot together, leaving Sophie and the driver at the gate and also surrendering the crutches as promised.

This group was no more easier to say goodbye to then the last, but they do, and yes, there were some shared tears when this had to happen.

There is a serene moment amongst the five as they watch the van and all the tiny little faces disappear. It's warm to know that some thought lost forever are now heading home, but there is no mistake as to how truly successful this trip was.

These words are shared by all, but not spoken, "What next?"

Art slices in, saying, "All right, people, it's a three-hour ride, we've got plenty of time for all the proper Q and A we care to discuss, now let's go."

No Rest for a Desperate Father

It's 1:27 a.m. when they pull up in front of Ryson's house, well-fed, and Ryson ready to try out the new crutches. The ride back from San Diego with a stop for dinner and a drugstore did absolutely assure them all, that this is not over, the only real concerns were how long before Ryson is up and running, and where to next. The collective decision for the evening was to not make any decisions, other than all in tomorrow night, six-ish, Redline Financial.

The day lingers like that of a hangover you did not see coming, it's a slow and wobbly morning with a couple of phone calls, and several pieces of furniture forever scarred with impact marks from newly acquired crutches.

Ryson first called Danny and then a brother. This took the better part of the morning, frustration staggered into lunch with Ryson finally collapsing on the couch and ordering some Chinese food for delivery. At 2:08 p.m., Ryson declares the recovery period now over and slides the crutches under the couch. As he mumbles, "What recovery," and stands. The pain reminds him to at least for now he should refrain from any and all marathons, "Ha, ha, not really a problem."

Will's phone call at 4:50 interrupts a pretty serious session of pluck it, trim it, shower, and shave, but Ryson welcomes the interruption, "What's up, Will?"

"How you doing their hop along?"

"I'm good, although I can't say the same for the furniture. It's amazing what real damage a thirty-dollar pair of crutches can do. My leg is now the least damaged appendage in the house."

Will laughs and says, "I'm sure there's a way to write that off on your homeowner's insurance."

"Na, they are still mad from when I filed a claim for the garage being too small."

"Yeah, having somebody else take responsibility for your small unit can be a bit tricky."

Now they both laugh.

"Listen, Ryson, why I'm callin' is this. May and I are still at her place but heading your way soon, do you need us to stop and pick you up?"

"Well, now, let me think this over for just a sec or two… You first call here making fun of the handicap, then you insult the size of my unit, and now you want to take me for a ride. Should I be bringing my own blindfold and shovel or will these items be supplied when we reach the middle of nowhere?"

Now just Will laughs, and this time, it's genuine.

"No, but really, thanks, guys. I already made arrangements. How are you two doing? You two get some rest?"

"Yeah, we did all right. I think it's more you we were concerned with and how long before we go back at this."

Will can sense the wrinkle in Ryson's emotional state and in his hesitation to answer there also lays of course a large sense of gratitude.

"If you two are still in this, I am without question. And as for recovery, I am first a father and what's left will just have to wait."

Things for a second or two get quiet, then Will in his best brotherly voice says, "Ryson."

Ryson answers, "What?"

Will's reply, "I love you, man."

Again, they both laugh and it's a good laugh.

The phone call ends simply with a, "See you at six."

The horn chatter out front means the arrangements Ryson made have arrived. It's only a few minutes after five but he's been ready since about four, the house is too lonely and at the same time so full of loud memories, he finds it almost impossible to be here alone.

A Rio-Grande with something overloaded in caffeine, with extra whip cream, and a chill at the fountain is all the destiny required.

Ryson over tips the cab driver, first because the man said very little and second, because he did not have to repeat where it was he wanted to go. As blue car company car forty four pulls away, Ryson glances towards Redline Financial, he's looking that direction but moving forward towards the outdoor order window, and still his attention is even beyond this, so much so when the pretty little thing at the window ask him, "What's it gonna be?", it takes him by surprise.

He orders the Rio-Grande, coconut, ridge-runner, extra snow, then scoots left, not just to wait for his order but for a better look at the fountain.

This time of year the nights tend to stay in the eighties and tonight is no exception, what seems different is that it all feels so comfortable, even the hot cup in his hand is not without a simple sense of pleasure.

There's others around but nobody seated at the fountain. When Ryson takes a seat the piece of cement, he chooses feels like he's slipping into a Barca-lounger in his own living room. It all feels so right, just as it did the times before. And of course, the ever-present smell of warm sugar cookies.

At sip two, some of life's harsh realities fade, at sip three, it all seems less entrenched in misery. Before sip five, there is a sound some ways off, and with a gentle tug, at first, it draws Ryson back to the cement he now sits on, the noise gets louder and becomes rhythmic like a very large footed duck in a sprint for its life.

Ryson only has to lean a wee bit left to get a clear look through the open gate space and then the sidewalk, after that the street. From the sounds of things it's moving along the sidewalk out front and from right to left. The sound slows and instead of a flash past his field of view, the noise produces a man, maybe thirty years old, dressed in tan sweats and flip-flops. He's been running hard and by the looks of things, this might be his first time.

As this six-foot-tall man with light sort of complexion and dark hair, turns into the fountain area from the sidewalk, their eyes lock, flip-flops more so than Ryson's.

It's more of a quick shuffle as flip-flops moves to where Ryson is sitting, he stops and bends at the waist, left hand on his knee and the right hand stretched out with open palm, when he's five or six feet away, it's clear he has something to say but at the moment, he looks more like a large mouth bass on the floor of the boat.

With no clue as to where this is going, Ryson sits patiently as if this man was expected. Several seconds go by before Mr. flip-flops has gasped long enough to finally form some words, still not standing but keeping eye contact he says, "My name is Afrin Shivers, and you are Ryson Willows. I was looking for Art, but you will do."

Afrin now stands while saying, "I have some very important information and you, my friend, are going to want to hear all of it." Afrin takes a deep breath, then adds to it a tiny smile, "But first, let me get a cup of coffee."

His confidence and self-sacrifice tells Ryson he should probably listen to what Mr. flip-flops has to say.

Afrin returns with a Rio-Grande of his own and a half dozen little bags, and each holding a different pastry. The space he chooses to sit is to Ryson's right, putting the pastries in the space between them, he then says, "Help yourself, I have no particular favorite."

Afrin again has his wind about him, he has no agenda other than the truth, and woven tightly to a calm spirit, he lends himself believable, "Just so I have your attention, why don't I start with what I know about Vinzaya?"

Ryson turns his head but not really enough to make eye contact and says, "Ya, why don't you do that."

To his surprise, his voice does not crack but what defenses he had are now down.

"You have to jump a little further back then Vinzaya to understand what's there and who chooses it not to be."

"The sick warlord fuck before Vinzaya viewed the entire population under the age of sixteen only that of a commodity, in which he fueled his army in hopes of one day to control all of Paraguay."

"Well, as usual, the next crazy fuck with enough money to buy an even bigger army takes over, and that was Vinzaya."

"Mr. Vinzaya, you see, fancies himself as a family man and even has several children of his own, so the fact that most of the money coming in was from all the many ways to profit from child destruction did not sit well with him. His plan, and I know this to be true, is to remove all of the adolescent element from the country, leaving in place the infrastructure used to support and disperse this filth to know to be reused for global distribution and production of cocaine. And I am sure you already know some of his methods for removal."

Ryson flashes backwards to the dead they encountered, and the dogs. His voice is cold with a chill that just seized his system, "How do you know this and how did you find me?"

Afrin snags up a couple of pastries, thus explaining some of his two hundred fifty plus puffy nature, eating both quickly so he can answer.

"Let's start with how I found you, it was actually Redline Financial I found first. But only because they're listed as your employer."

"I first put two and two together after seeing you on T.V. Your name looked familiar so I looked it up and found the incident at the mall."

Afrin pauses here and wants to say something personal but does not, "Now… Sometime later, my contacts aboard the morning star, that's the cargo ship you floated home on, tell me about a beach grab and identify you in one of the photos I sent them."

"So now I understand why you would go into the Neighbors Cradle and that's why I ran here in flip-flops. My apartment is three blocks from here, third floor, I can actually see this area from my kitchen window."

"About an hour ago, I finally came up with the new address for Redline Financial, then I realized where it's at and I grab a pair of binoculars, hell, they weren't even focused before I see you standing there ordering coffee, and now, here we sit. Believe it or not."

Ryson finally grabs up one of the small bags of pastry, keeping quiet as he does and even after discovering it's a slice of pumpkin bread. Oh yes…his favorite.

Afrin does the same, but it's a large scone and he eats it in two bites.

There's a lot of questions Ryson could ask but there's only two that truly concerns him, "How do you know all this about Vinzaya and the Neighbors Cradle?"

Afrin's voice sombers to a sad place, but also a place of anger.

"I, too, am looking for somebody, though it is not a child, it is a man that has hurt many children, and our last deadly encounter was in Paraguay. He'd been arrested at the airport and they called me first. The rest is not important, what's important here is to know that whatever children are left in that part of the country are most likely marked for death, and are being eradicated as we speak."

"I wish I had more in regards to your own, but I do not and for that I am truly sorry. I do know this cleansing Vinzaya has taken on started in the lower northern region and given the direction and of course what I have already seen it stands to reason things will get bottled up through the thin mountain corridors leading into Argentina because this will be the only way out on foot."

"Those that survive the onslaught most likely will be heading that direction." Afrin pauses and takes a breath, "He wants real bad the last two little bags of pastry but in the wake of new friendship he snags up only one. Well, that's what I got, Mr. Willows. I hope this aids in your quest and rest assured if our paths do cross, we are, indeed, allies."

"Mr. Shivers…" Ryson says this kind of short and quick but means no disrespect. Afrin stops and turns around.

"Yes, Mr. Willows."

"You ever hear of a Tiger Team in that area, or anywhere else for that matter?"

"No, sir, but if you're looking for some help, I'll just bet the Colombians would like to know Vinzaya's intentions."

Silence fills the growing space between them until the sound of Afrin's flip-flops can no longer be heard.

Ryson sits, but only long enough to finish the last scone, washing it down with the last of his Rio-Grande. Coconut. ridge-runner, extra whipped cream.

One thing for certain, the short walk to Redline Financial was one without pain in his leg, only panic in his heart.

With it being a few minutes after six when Ryson knocks out-front, it's no surprise the rest are already here. He knows this because they all come to greet him at the door.

All feel the quickness through the meet and greet, so not surprised when Ryson announces soon after, "You all better sit down for this," then breaking the trail with only a slight hitch in his get-along to the kitchen, first with the intention being a show of strength, second, a place to sit down.

They're all juiced and coffee before Ryson unloads the encounter at the fountain. There's some questions along the way but no real answers, when the aquatic tale comes to an end, only silence follows in its wake and for several seconds no one has much to say.

Breaking the silence first, of course, is Lila. The rest then follow with a piece of their own, "Well, I guess now we know for sure in which direction you three head next… And I got a pretty good idea how you're going to get there."

"For sure, we know what we're looking for… And God knows we know now some of what to expect. And let's not forget, we make a pretty damn good team…"

Art looks at Will after this last comment and as serious as the moment will allow says, "Ah, yah, Will, we been meaning to talk to you about that."

241

The table in an over stressed rebound erupts in laughter.

When the laughter settles some, Will comes back with, "Yeah, sure, we have guy with a bad leg and can't stay out of the way of bullets and I'm the one that's outed."

More laughter.

Without slowing for the turns Art jumps right into hatching a plan, he starts with transportation, and then abruptly he screeches to a halt, "O, wait, I, also, have some new business."

I would like to entertain the request for a new member. All eyes now on Art, quietly.

"You guys remember Sophie, right? Well, when she got off that boat to say hello she whispers to Lila and I, she tells us what you three did is where she has always wanted to be."

"I said call me only because Sophie and us go back a long way. This afternoon she comes by. I explained to her for some of the forty or fifty minutes she was here that we are right in the middle of things and at least for the time being not looking to change or add personnel. She understood, from then on, the three of us just hung out and got caught up."

Art takes a breath, letting it soak for a couple of seconds, on the exhale, he remarks, "But now I am not so sure."

Lila's concerns are torn and shared equally between the safety of the team versus mission success. So it's obvious she wants Ryson, May, and Will to judge Sophie on her own merits, and when she says all this, they all do agree. Lila also adds that her and Art know Sophie to be exactly who she says she is.

"One thing for certain, what I know of Sophie, it's always been about the kids, was the same for her father, but I'll let her tell you about that," Art stands then finishes, "let's do this, I'll call Sophie see if she wants to come visit and Ryson, why don't you call your brother-in-law, ask Danny real nice maybe he can find us some satellite maps of these mountain corridors I hear speak of."

May's question as to what other maps Art might already have of the area in and around Paraguay, comes well received, he points Will and May at a drawer in a file cabinet saying, "Yes, yes, start there."

Only Lila hears the quiet tapping on the back door, she knows right away Sophie's tapping to listen first then to be recognized. The tapping gets a little louder before Lila calls out through the closed door, "I hear you, sweetheart, don't get your sea panties all in a bunch."

Sophie's arrival catches the three by surprise when Art said she was not far from here who knew he meant fifteen minutes.

Sophie's arrival also brings with it a sense of comfort and friendship like they have all been doing this for years, the meet and greet goes quickly as they get right into things.

Ryson is sitting closest to Sophie so when he turns to say this their faces are only inches apart, "Sophie, we have already done some things I don't think are going to go over real well when and if the day comes for judgment at the pearly gates. I don't question your motives or ability I think my question here is one of moral aptitude."

Sophie understands exactly what Ryson is asking and loves the way he did it, "Hey, I'm sure we've all done things were not proud of, and I'm no exception. It's not judgment I fear, it's knowing I did not do enough before I get there."

Sophie does not stop here but she does humble some in her delivery, "My father was a doctor, he later went on to specialize in pediatrics, he then went to work for the United Nations. So now here's a man who witnessed firsthand and up close child neglect and abuse on a global scale. Four years later, he comes home and decides to spend every day for the rest of his life helping children, which is exactly what you did."

"My father, Franklin Naples, built pediatrics facilities across the country and some of those even specializing in advancements in modern medicine along with psychological and behavioral studies. So I grow up in this environment and all I can dream of is one day to work right alongside my father. And yeah, he did encourage me to become a doctor, although I myself, for obvious reasons, chose to go into pediatrics."

"After he died, I just sort of went freelance, I just spent the last two years with Greenpeace and hands across the world delivering aid to some of the thousands of abandoned children in Nubia and Botswana."

Lila jumps in because she's quite sure they have all heard enough, "Her father built the dental complex three buildings down from here, the one with the coffee house is attached to."

Sophie taps back in, "Well, it used to be a pediatrics facility, my father's the one who commissioned the fountain next to it, and it's because of that fountain I still own the building."

What Sophie just said is now bouncing around inside of Ryson's head like a bullet in multiple ricochet, he turns towards her, again, only inches apart and says, "So, you own the fountain?"

The question he asked next even surprises himself, "Have you ever noticed that no matter the time of day or night, the constant smell of fresh baked cookies?"

Confused and curious, Sophie replies, "No, I have not, but what's also strange is the fact that once a year, I have the fountain cleaned from top to bottom, all the money in it is donated to charity, and this year of the 147.00 dollars in change recovered from it, there were no nickels. Only dimes, pennies and quarters, no nickels." Sophie shrugs her shoulders and finishes with, "Life's a mystery, it's what makes it livable."

Ryson says nothing else, the conversations drifts back to the matters at hand, minus a vote, it was just not necessary, Sophie was one of them well before she walked through the door.

Art scoots from the table like he's trying to escape when the printer in the front office chatters to life, saying, "Danny, maps," as he does so. Then chasing the chatter to its source.

At 9:50 p.m., both phones share the same time and along with it the same message...in tandem and from across the table Art and Ryson check their phones and as if they were twins and using the same brain repeat the message in stereo, "At the front door, F.B.I. can we talk?"

And the room staggers to a halt where quiet is king. The eyes dart from one another in silence until they have all shared an inquisitive look when Lila finally says, "You two should probably go check the front door."

Art sweeps the door inward and engages the two like new friends, "You two look like somebody's come knocking on friendships door, and yet. the suits say this ain't social, well, that's okay to, come on in."

Margo speaks first and clearly it's been prearranged because Tom looks content to just idle in the conversation, "Nice to see you up and about Mr. Willows, and good evening, Mr. Match."

"You can call me Art, so how can we help you two this evening?"

"Interesting enough, help is exactly what we've come to ask for. I'm sorry, Mr. Match, I did not introduce ourselves, I'm Margo Hops and this well-dressed fellow here is Tom Marks, we are F.B.I., child safe care services branch."

The two pairs of eyes stealing a strained peek through a small opening in the curtain belong to May and Lila. Will and Sophie chose to remain seated, they really did not need the visuals. The girls are far enough away from the four at the front door, thus allowing them to whisper quietly to each other.

"You put those two in street clothes and there quite the handsome couple, yeah, she's kind of pretty but he looks like he could be hard to train."

They both giggle and continue to get their spy on.

At 3:30 yesterday afternoon, the wife and child of Senator Neil Thompson and a friend of hers were both at a breast-feeding clinic given by the hospital, both had newborns approximately 14 days old, both women attractive and first-time mothers.

"Geez, Margo, lighten up, I thought we were here unofficially, remember, hear no evil, see no evil, there be no evil?" Tom intervenes while letting Margo cool her F.B.I. jets a little.

"Listen, you two, what Margo is trying to say is this. The senator's wife and a friend were kidnapped with their infants while leaving the hospital yesterday and have not been heard from since. Why we bring this to you? Because of how it was done and by who."

"Most likely this was what's known as a 'wet nap' and chances are, done by a Tiger team. What we believe happens is the newborn being the primary target, the mother is taken simply to care for the infant until sold, after this happens, the mother is either sold as well, or kept for profit or pleasure, or just killed."

"We assume there were three, two assailants and a driver. They moved fast and it was well planned. Hell, they even brought titanium B.Bs and an-air gun which is just about the only thing that will shatter the tempered glass lense in the security cameras and not make any noise. The fact that one of the women was a senator's wife was coincidental and this we're pretty sure of."

Margo rejoins the explanation then takes over, "So, that brings us back to why we've come. Twice you've gone into Paraguay and twice you've come home with a handful of children, and we are sorry none of which were your own. We also know you're probably going back. Don't ask. We are the F.B.I., and so far you've done nothing to, shall we say, offend us."

"Where's that picture, Tom?"

From an inside breast pocket, Tom withdraws what looks like a single playing card and on it two women's photos from the chest up. Both photos sharing equal space on one side of the card, and on the back of the card, a phone number hand written in red ink.

Tom makes a notable effort in handing the card to Ryson, and only Ryson.

Margo now seems content to let Tom finish their visit, so much so that her hand is already on the door.

"That number on the back is a direct line to a systems opp center for an elite three-man strike team, if you obtain visual on either of these women, dial that number, answer the questions, and stay away from the target if possible, I hear these three can come in pretty fuckin' hot so stay out of their way, they will already be in country and probably closer than you think."

"Any help in locating these two will not go unnoticed, and you could make some pretty important friends here."

Before Tom follows Margot out an already open door, he turns just enough to give Ryson a quick side glance and says, "We really do hope you find what you're looking for."

Even after the door comes fully closed, Art and Ryson just sort of stand there, kicking this around in their own heads for several seconds before Art retreats and Ryson follows towards the back. On the way Ryson asked, "Should we have told them anything we have already learned?"

Art's response was, "If the FBI ain't askin', then we ain't tellin'."

The conversation out front was heard by all and excepted as just another twisted piece of an already decaying situation.

The rest of the evening unfolds as Sophie is brought up to speed and somewhere through the hours guided by Western Henry's B.B.Q several pots of coffee and a half dozen maps Danny sent over, the six of them collectively agree on where they need to go and why they need to be there.

Before Art sends everybody home, he asked several personal questions, one, of which, clearly he was disappointed in the answer, knowing none of the four had any experience in parachuting seem to trouble him and yet, at the same time, clearly he was amused.

As they bunch up for good nights at the back door, Sophie, who has already begun processing tonight's information on a level to help the team, stops and says, "You know, that guy Afrin is right, the Columbians are not going to like this, and I'll just bet if played right, they could become an ally."

Art smiles and nods his head, "I'm already dialing the number, now go, keep your phones close and get some sleep."

Cargo Drop and the Hunt Continues

At 8:40 a.m., all four our rattled from a deep sleep with the same text message from Art "Good morning all and to all a morning filled with everlasting adventure, you four need to be at Chino Hills Jump Academy, Chino Hills airport."

10:30 a.m. "Your instructor will be waiting, you get two hours, you best learn all you can because there will be no time for a practice jump. The instructor will explain the rest."

The message no doubt carries with it a caffeine injection seeming to buzz all four wide-awake without a cup of coffee, all four respond bravely "Got it."

Art let's this settle for a couple of minutes before sending message number two "My place after. Lunch will be waiting. P.S., Lila says to focus, it's easier then it seems."

Again, all four bravely reply "Got it."

There was no time to work out a car pool so now the three vehicles sit side-by-side in the parking lot of Chino Hills Jump Academy and the four that brought them here, just now going through the front door.

The small lobby is quiet and without a receptionist but the large chalkboard on the far wall and in large, green lettering solves the what to do now question. Art's four. Room two please.

"Cecil, hears the four come into the room, he has his back to them as he is drawing simple stick like depictions of some sorts on a large chalkboard." Without turning around, Cecil barks out, "Good morning boys and girls, take a seat be right witcha," then somewhat softer he says, "we have a lot to cover, because today my four brave Jedis you must learn to become a piece of Air Dropped Cargo and I'm told we only have two hours in which to do this."

Cecil continues to speak as he turns to greet his four pieces of cargo, "My name is Cecil Childs, but most people call me, Cease. Excuse the obvious misalignment when I use the term crash course in skydiving but today that's just what we got, so let's get right to it."

Will knows instantly when Cecil turns around that he has met him before and if he wasn't so concerned with how to become cargo he might have brought it up. The other three also hold their tongues, not because of who he is, but what he has to say.

"It can take many years to learn some of what there is to know about skydiving, that's why early on, these drop methods were perfected for both, troops and cargo, thousands of troops have been dropped into battlefields the same way, and with minimal impact casualties, so pay attention, take some notes and you may indeed survive the drop."

The two hours paddle by in a river of quick moving information, Cecil enjoys what he does that's obvious, but all four found it unnecessary to over address the need for notes, "Basically, it comes down to jump, float, hope to fuck you don't die, and only a minimal amount of parachute control to prevent the latter from happening. You simply jump and surrender to gravity with no back-up plan available. Yeah, like cargo."

Cecil finishes with a couple of personal notes in regards to his own theories and beliefs, "I make sure I tell everyone that comes through here this piece of life-changing insight, I, too, was terrified on my first jump but somewhere on the way down I realized it was hard to accept death as a consequence when living feels this good, I've been jumping ever since and each time it feels better than the last. Now, get, I promised Art you four would be driving away by 12:40."

Time being the dictator, Will forgoes the four one with Cecil, how he knows him will just have to wait, or never come about at all.

The short walk back to the parking lot seems like it's done in two stages, the first stage being denial, the conversation lends itself to hopes that this new be like cargo knowledge is only to be used when all else has failed. The second stage is not reached until they are in the parking lot. And this conversation is nothing more than and they all four do agree, "We would not be here if this was not part of Art's plan in getting us where we need to be."

On the way back to Redline Financial, things are fairly quiet, and in their heads all seem separated not only by distance but also in a wee bit of childlike apprehension.

The back door to Redline is propped open about halfway as the four arrive in three separate cars. Single file and some space between them they enter the back room, Sophie being the new kid was chosen to go first and now, she just above normal voice calls, "Art? Lila?"

Ryson pulls the door closed behind him leaving all four in a straight line now looking at a table completely set for six, minus the lunch they were promised.

Ryson, because he is closest to it, hears Art's voice on the other side of the door, "Well, now, that's a fine how do you do, locked-out and we brought the food."

Now he hears Lila, "I guess we eat what we can and slide the rest under the door."

Ryson's smile indicates it's his turn to be playful as he says loudly enough to be heard through the door, "Well then, I hope you brought plenty of thin-meat because I am starved before he opens then pushes the door slowly outboards."

Lila comes through the doorway first and she's carrying a large pizza box, Art is right behind her with the other two.

"Sorry, it's just pizza," Art says this but not without insult to Lila, "just pizza! Yeah, well, then I guess Elvis was just some country singer, I'll have you know there is not a better pizza to be had in all of Orange County, now sit and eat, you four are on a tight schedule."

For the first slice or so the conversation rotates around light laughter regarding this morning's learning experience and of course, how really damn good the pizza is, then to things more pressing.

"I'm sure you all noticed that there was and still is six place settings at this table," Art says this in such a manner it causes the others to stop and listen. "Those of you who did not return from this morning's assignment would not have even received a phone call, we would have simply removed the place setting with no questions asked, that's a policy we all must know exist, yesterday, today, tomorrow. Nobody here is being held accountable, your presence is by choice only. Everybody up to speed on this?"

From the other five this question goes unanswered, they just collectively and quietly nod their heads and smile.

"Okay, so now that we've satisfied the legal department, let's talk about the scary stuff. Art stops here and pauses as if he's attempting to gather the last few thoughts on what he wants to say. You know what, why don't I just lay out the facts and the fiction and we will see how well it all sticks?"

"Fact one, there is a chartered flight booked and waiting at John Wayne international to take the four of you to Central America in less than three hours. Exactly where in Central America I am still not quite sure, we are waiting for Anna to call and tell us that. You three remember Anna, right?"

"So those are the facts, I do wish there were more of them. This thought from Art he says out loud and it's quite genuine. Now here's what is supposed to happen next. Or better known as the fiction part of this little story. Anna, right now, is in a military aircraft salvage yard and evidently she has recently purchased a vintage B-17 flying Fortress. She tells me she only purchased the aircraft for parts, but it will fly. The connection we had was poor at best but she got the gist of what I was asking and is going to find a landline and call back."

"But how I see it is this. There's no way to land something that large anywhere near where you four need to be. So you will have to jump, and not only that, it also has to happen in the dark."

Art waits suspended for a couple of seconds for some sort of outburst but when none comes he simply takes a breath and lets Lila take over.

"This jump, easy peasy," Lila does not say how or why she feels this way, leaving only that her confidence speaks for itself.

"That B-17 is going to lumber in at low power and seemingly to defy gravity, hell, you could probably out walk it, it's a static line jump, Anna will talk you through it, she's not going to let you jump if it ain't all kosher. You float down, you do per Cecil's instructions, you then sit tight, and wait for the sun to come up."

"I hate to be the one to stare this scarier than hell gift horse in the mouth, but why does Anna help us?"

"Well, Ryson, now that's a good question, I wish I had the right answer. I do know, for sure, Anna's heart is in the right place and for the most part I think we can trust her, I believe she is on our side and with her as it is with you four, I'm quite sure it's about the children. So just do what she says, she wants you on the ground in one piece as much as anybody."

"Exactly where is she dropping us?" May and Sophie say this almost in tandem, then smile at one another.

Art grabs and unfolds a map from a stack sitting on the table, he spins and slides it so the four who are going, each share a view.

"You already know the place. The plane is to put you as close to Oscar's field as possible, in the city of "Lost Angels," that way once the sun comes up you find one another, make your way to the airfield, and maybe you find the minivan still there. Either way, you will need transportation, It's maybe a two-hour drive from where you are, to where you need to be. The rest is waiting to be written, that's you."

Art lets the quiet settle at the table as he anticipates more questions.

Wills voice breaks the moment and it's in his question all six realize and agree, it's go time, "So, how do we find this charter flight at John Wayne International? And who gets that last piece of pizza?"

Tension leaves the room like a speeding bullet, there is some laughter, and they do indeed eat all the pizza.

Clearly the driver has been here before. He seemed to follow a path hard chiseled and etched in his memory because as he pulls up out-front of the international charter services at the airport he reacted as though he was just waking up from a thirty-minute nap. In between yawns, he manages, "Art, already took care of the tip, have a safe flight."

Chosen by vote, Will goes in alone to check on the flight, he's voted most diplomatic and clearly capable of obtaining information. The other three laugh as he walked away pretending to be important.

When he comes back, he brings four boarding passes and starts reading from a small piece of paper in his hand, "Looks like after security, we're heading to Guatemala, the pilot tells me we have a call sign and permission to touch and go, leaving four, that's us. And yeah it's just like Art said, we end up on a private military aircraft salvage lot, and I can only assume Anna and a B-17 should be fairly easy to find."

Low altitude turbulence on a slow dogleg flyby rolls the twin-engine aircraft to Portside so quickly it was hard to stay in the seat, but it did indeed provide a very good view of the ground and runway.

There are several hundred aircraft all shapes and sizes lined in long rows several hundred yards from the runway and one of those is definitely a B-17.

The pilot mumbles something about the I.L.S. being disabled and he is not cleared to roll off the runway. Now he turns to his passengers and informs them we will be breaking hard to a stop and as soon as that happens, you must exit the aircraft, "I will use what's left of the runway and go home. Everybody okay with this?"

All four have barely stepped away from the prop wash before the pilot is at full throttle and already rolling down the runway.

There is another two hundred yards between them and the B-17. They watch the plane that brought them here take flight and leave in the same direction as their delivery.

The four stand still all staring at the same location, no one more focused than the rest. Who speaks first shows first fear but the rest share their one quarter portion.

"Fuck me."

"That's supposed to fly."

"I guess we go find out."

"Maybe there's another B-17 we just ain't seen yet."

"Airborne? It looks like it's having trouble just sitting there."

When they reach the shaded area under one of the large wings, they can now hear Anna shouting from somewhere inside the aircraft, it's badly muffled but what they do get, is she's on the way.

Anna crawls out a small hole in the belly of the plane, she appears feet first, then drops the five feet or so to the ground, leaving her in a standing position directly in front of the four that have just arrived.

Anna cannot hide her jubilance in the fact she has company and does not try to do so, "I've met you three, who's the new girl?"

Anna already reaching to shake Sophie's hand.

"I'm Sophie, and you must be Anna."

"Hi, Sophie."

"Yes, Anna Banana."

"Yeah, I know, this old bird she don't look like much, and I can only imagine what you're thinking, I guess if it was me my first thought would be."

"Now here's a plane that when it comes time to jump it will probably be a relief. But I can assure you, she will fly."

Anna now walks over and takes a seat on one of the large landing wheels and finishes what she was saying, "Something I'm sure you do not know about the B-17 is the fact that the aircraft had to be completely disassembled in order for it to be considered decommissioned, because as long as the wings were still attached and at least two of the four engines start, this girl will fly. Luckily for us, this old girl was never decommissioned and as you can see, the wings are indeed attached and yes, all four engines do start and run."

Anna waits for rebuttal but there is none, even though the four do not look quite convinced.

"Well, let's go aboard, have a seat, and talk about what happens next, first text Art. Tell him you made it in one piece and we should be airborne in under an hour."

Anna's perkiness settles as she gets quit serious, she points to a yellow sort of dome light over her left shoulder that's attached near the door they used to get in and says, "That light will be our only way to communicate, when it comes on you have three minutes to attach your static lines, get the door open and prepare to jump. When the light goes out, you jump. I am going to shut down both inboard engines when we get close, it will slow and quiet our approach and that light will come on soon after that."

"I have my hands full with this old girl so there will be no time for socializing once we get underway, stay buckled in and maybe get some sleep, E.T.A., approximately six hours. Godspeed and my prayers go with you," Anna starts to choke up and finds it difficult not to, but catches hold of her emotions and shifts gears.

Anna's perkiness trickles back as she tells the group that after they jump she plans on staying in the area, there's a place to land and refuel about 70 miles away, I will camp there for at least a couple of days, "You have my number, call if I can help."

Chasing one, running from the other. Darkness seems to fill the front part of the aircraft first, leaving the night to chase the day from where they've come. And like that of life itself, half is spent in the light the other half in the dark.

It's like the expected death of a loved one, no matter how hard you try to prepare, when the time comes, it always seems so unexpected.

Shutting down both inboard motors certainly suggested the moment was close, but when the light did finally burst to a blinding luminescent call to bravery, all four were taken by surprise.

It takes Ryson and Sophie both to get the door open, the four-stand ready hand-in-hand. The light goes out and it's a blind jump, the darkness so completely concealing the planet, leaving only thoughts that it's a drop that could last forever.

No moon, but enough starlight to illuminate the earth just before impact. The four dot the countryside about every hundred yards or so but this information will have to wait for the sun to come up. They text and know all are safe but where, they know not. Art and Lila go to bed also knowing the four are safe, for now.

They all hear the same roster at sunup and for each of them it seems to gently guide the night into the today, the proud bird is far off but it's enough to remind all four they survived being cargo.

May is the first to untangle from what Cecil referred to as the "Para shelter, Cecil style."

"Basically this is a procedure, where upon landing, you follow a set of predetermined rolls and folds of the parachute with you in the middle, ending with all the loose material gathered at one, end then secured with para cord, sealing yourself inside as if snuggled in a cloth cocoon."

I think all four realize as they follow the same para-shelter exit strategy they owe Cecil a thank you for their success up to this point. Everything was just how he said it was going to be.

May jumped third so now when she stands in the fairly flat field, they've landed in she can see Ryson and Sophie in one direction and when she turns 180 degree, she finds Will. All four are now standing and looking at one another, each separated by no more than one hundred yards of ankle high grass. So perhaps, they owe Anna a thank you as well.

It takes only a few seconds before each is acclimated to the surroundings, and each just as relieved as the other in realizing how close they got to Oscar's field, and hopefully the minivan.

They huddle now on their knees in a group, all eyes forward on the direction at hand but only three truly stressed about revisiting their dead. As the four stare out from the field they're in, from what they can see it's just how they left it, but from this distance, they cannot see all of it.

They first cross a small creek, this puts them in the field adjacent to the grass runway, and at the far end still sits the exploded tank and overturned jeep, they cannot see the minivan as of yet, but relief does come as they realize the two dead guys have been removed.

Spaced out and in single file, they move to the outbuilding in hopes of finding a ride out here, Ryson already has the keys in his hand for good luck.

The small van looks as though it has sustained some minor collateral damage but nothing too severe, and at least it's in one piece.

Ryson jumps in as the others stand silent, the van cranks right to life then idles as if it's all it's ever done, then just as quick he turns it off, and gets out telling the others, "Hey, before we drive out of here, let's look around maybe we find something for defense."

The pickings are poor, both outbuildings locked up tight so each gathers what they can find quickly. Will assures them he's driving out of here in three minutes.

As they drive away from the airfield May sends Art this text "Van for now good to go. On the move. All intact. 3.4.5.6."

Art responds "Please be safe, Lila says, ditto. 1.2."

Navigating is quite simple, the maps which Danny provided are up to date and quite detailed, Will's at the wheel, the others providing guidance and support.

They are in a semi-mountainous region with some steady climbs and just as many down-hill runs. On one of these climbs, Will announces, "The temperature is going up steady, piece of crap is going to overheat."

Saying this seems to draw the smell of rusty steam into the van, the temperature needle now slams to the right triggering a red panic light on the dash.

Because there is traffic on this road, Will pulls off as far as clear space will allow, coming to rest alongside a tree line some ten yards from the two-lane road they were just on. The spits and spiders and rising steam from the front of the van; for sure means this vehicle has given all she had and the four standing in witness as the life fluids now begin to pool under the van can only watch as their rubber wheeled chariot goes slowly into the light.

Before they can read the van, its last rights, Sophie suddenly spins on one heel, then coming to a one hundred and eighty degree stop, face on to the tree line, she says, "That's water, somewhere not far into these trees is some kind of stream or maybe even a river, either way, a couple of gallons of water might just get us out of here."

"What is she, some kind of bat and somehow echo located this stream that supposed to be back here?" Will says this jokingly because they both believed her when he and May volunteered to go look.

Ryson gets the hood open a second time and begins to vent out some of the heat hoping to cool things down before May and Will get back with water.

Sophie stands and leans on one leg against a tree near the front of the van, the map she holds in her hand she's hoping shows them the nearest place to find new wheels.

There's been no traffic on the road for the last couple of minutes so as the pair of motorcycles makes their approach, they do not go unnoticed. Because the vans hood is up and blocking his view, Ryson has to lean his head out to get a clear look at who's coming.

The two on cycles have already begun to slow as all three make eye contact, he does his best to not invite their attention so he makes no gesture for help or needing assistance. To help sell this, he puts his hands and attention in the engine compartment, hoping to look as though he has the repair under control.

Ryson does not discourage the two on cycles and they pull off the road as they pass the minivan, coming to a stop twenty feet or so from him, they both lower their kick stands but only one gets off and makes a rather suspicious approach.

Ryson now moves to the side of the van closer to Sophie, still pretending to fix something but now he can see this guy's movement in his peripheral and also doing his best to not show it.

Locked and loaded, Ryson has already committed to a violent act of hand-to-hand combat, but only as a matter of survival, and yeah, this has the stink of blood ugly written all over it and he knows it. As does Sophie.

"What's the problem?" These words in Spanish ring monotone. The voice is just angry and destructive, it carries flat and without compassion.

Ryson does not look up, he only answers, "Just a squeaky belt."

Motorcycle boy is now only a couple of feet away and already lifting his shirt and with the left hand reaching for a 45 automatic handgun tucked into his waistband.

Any thought here is pointless, one must simply react in order to survive.

There's no chance in preventing bad guy from reaching for or withdrawing the gun. All Ryson can do is make a desperate surprise lunge reaching for and then grabbing just behind the .45, with his right hand.

The momentum and equal force is enough to prevent the gun from moving in Ryson's direction but it does not stop bad guy from pulling the trigger. The gun explodes in their hands, both sharing the recoil all three times before he can deliver a thumb forward hand chop to bad guy's throat. This ends the attack, sending bad guy to his knees at Ryson's feet.

Bad guy number two, of course, sees this go wrong. Still twenty feet away Sophie gives him the chance to cut and run, the gesture sales free and bad guy number two gets off his cycle gun already in hand.

Sophie's movement is quick, it's not calculated but what it lacks in planning she makes up in tenacity. Definitely all in, Sophie moves away from the tree she was using for cover and steps directly into the line of fire.

Sophie at best is hoping to at least distract bad guy number two long enough for Ryson to recover first guy's gun. The throw is all she had. With everything she could muster, she heaves the broken pipe wrench she gathered at the airfield.

Bad guy number two does indeed attempt to avoid the impact but stumbles over his own feet in doing so. The pipe wrench landing with a soft thud just over his left eye, putting out the lights instantly and he drops wrinkled like crumpled debris.

For a few seconds, the air around them seems to discharge, giving the two of them a chance to take a breath and produce a clear thought. They both here traffic approaching but cannot tell from which direction, realizing it doesn't matter and that they only have a few seconds before somebody cruises by paying too much attention.

Sophie takes off first, the words, "We got to get that guy over here and out of the way trailing behind her."

Ryson, as if being pulled along one word after another, gives chase.

They dash the twenty.

 feet at full speed, Ryson with a wobble catches Sophie just as they reach the guy crumpled near the motorcycle. Each reach down and grab an ankle and in perfect harmony pull hard leading to a semi-sprint back to the minivan, and bad guy number two flopping, along behind like a full-size ragdoll.

Out of breath and in between puffs when they get back, Sophie says, "Let's put them both in the Van and send all three down the hill."

Ryson sees no reason to argue or disagree considering two of the three bullets fired from the bad guys 45 tore through the radiator, the third disappearing into the engine compartment and now oil is mixing with the water already on the ground.

Both bad guys are piled in the minivan and left in their unconscious state on the floor in the back, Ryson slides the door closed as Sophie is quickly getting in the driver seat. Ryson moves past the van on foot towards the two motorcycles as Sophie gets the key turned on, the transmission put in neutral then pops the emergency brake.

The road they were on continues to travel up the mountain, but what now lies in front of Sophie is a short space with a moderate decline, and just past the motorcycles, the ravine drops away, leaving a fairly good-sized ditch following the tree-line down the mountain.

Sophie lets the slow pull of gravity move her safely past Ryson who is already moving one of cycles, he stops to watch as Sophie exits the van landing on both feet in a slow walk, then calmly closing the door as if she expects it to be here when she gets back. Ryson watches the van as it quickly picks up speed then disappears along with the tree line and down the mountain. Sophie does not.

Together, they push the second cycle into the trees, placing it alongside the first making sure them and the cycles are far enough back to be well concealed from the road but also not too hard to find when May and Will get back with water they no longer need.

Of Course, there first question is, "Where's the van?"

Followed up with, "What's with the motorcycles?"

These questions come amongst some huffing and puffing, then in stereo, they ask, "Were those gunshots?"

Ryson starts with, "Well, the good news is, we are now armed with a couple of .45s and some spare ammo, the bad news is, these two motorcycles are now what we have for transportation."

Sophie takes over about halfway at Ryson's request, she ends the story of how we got here with, "Well, if the two guys are the only ones that can drive these damn things then, hell, May, that makes us biker bitches. They do their best to laugh quietly although they're not sure why."

Will moves onto the road first and as planned motors away, Ryson hesitates so they stagger their travel, for now. Sophie takes the moment at idle and asks, "What do you think they wanted?"

Ryson purposely does not hurry his response, he wants to be honest and so gathers his truth, "I think it's just like Will said, they wanted everything they thought we had. And I think they would have killed all four of us to get it. I told you before we left, everything here is poison. You did fine, and you're going to be okay. Now hang on, it's been a while since I kicked around a steel horse."

Sophie replies, "I'm good."

The first five or six miles seem almost bearable but the lack of any privacy or protection proves to be much more difficult than expected. On a couple of longer straighter stretches of road, Ryson could catch a glimpse of Will a mile or two up ahead and if there lack of blend is anything similar, and he's sure it is, then they best find better transportation soon.

A long sweeping curve seems to cast a sleepy lullaby over Will, his vision narrows obvious by the squinting in his eyes, it's not sleep that calls him, what it is only he knows. Why he follows, even to him, sometimes, that's a mystery. May's voice in his ear as she leans forward and says, "You going to be stopping for that?" startles him, as if he's at home cat napping on the couch.

I was thinking about it, Will pulls slowly to a stop taking his place last in line of a long-line of stopped traffic. It's only a minute or so before Ryson rolls in along-side. Before there can be a discussion as to what now, Will leans left, telling Ryson, "Let's go have a look."

There's just enough space between the road and the drop-away shoulder to slowly pass the thirty or so vehicles now using this quarter-mile stretch of asphalt as a narrow parking lot. The last car they come to looks as though it has spun around a couple of times and now facing the wrong way, it also blocks the small space the motorcycles were using, so all must stop.

Will stops about even with the front of a large panel truck whose driver has also joined the group now trying to clear the car off the road, it's tough going for the five involved because not only do they have to get the car turned around but the only place to push the car out of the way is further up the hill another twenty yards.

May becomes fixated to the point where she almost slips forward towards transcendence, completely captivated by the woman in the large panel truck Will stopped next to.

From May's position on the back of the cycle and directly to her left, sits a woman in the front seat of the truck whose driver is one of the five trying to move the car.

The woman is dressed in perhaps a sarong, where it covers her head, part of her face, and most of her body. Clenched in a swaddle, she has what looks like an infant held against her chest.

This all seems normal enough right up until the woman holds the child out at arm's reach as if playfully interacting, but when part of the child's blanket falls away, it becomes painfully obvious that it's just a doll. Even more painfully obvious is the fact that the woman clearly believes that doll to be a real child. May slips further into a trance like state as she watches this woman fuss, rub, kiss, and cuddle that doll as if it being her own flesh and blood.

The words, "Hang on, we're moving," come slowly to May, the sudden jerk of the motorcycle snaps her from a hypnotic state, allowing her to glance back and finally getting a good look at the woman's face. It is partially covered but the noise of the motorcycle as they take off causes her to look up and directly at May.

There is a rush of ice cold adrenaline quickly flicking every nerve in May's body, she knows the face and it's the face of a senator's wife.

Calm, cool, and collected, May simply leans forward and whispers in Will's ear, "I need you to put a couple of miles between us and that truck we were just stopped next to, and I would suggest you do it at wide open throttle, I'll signal to Ryson and make sure he keeps up."

Will shifts down and throttles up no questions asked. Not even a "yes, dear."

All four are moving at one hundred plus and only May knows why. Life and its nearest components blur by as one trail of color leads to the next. Now again, May leans forward, "That's good, first place you see, get off the road."

Will nods and throttles back.

They continue to pass around the photo the F.B.I. gave Ryson, they are well off the road as they wait for the truck to drive by and hopefully share in May's discovery, And then, of course, give chase.

Far too many minutes go by, there is some passing traffic from that direction but what did not go by was the large panel truck.

They all four decide to double back, May assured them there were only two possible exits from the road between here and there, both were dirt and neither looked all that inviting.

The first exit off the road they come to it's obvious there's no need to even slow, there is enough dense vegetation blocking the entrance that had something just driven through their they would know. The second exit maybe a half mile further down the road does indeed have the same amount of growth blocking the entrance, only this one looks like somebody just drove a Mack truck through it.

They all attempt a quick glance to see something at a thirty-m.p.h. drive by but because the vegetation is so thick along this part of the road all they know for sure is something big went that way.

It's another quarter mile before they find enough shoulder to safely get off the road and talk about it.

There's not much of a discussion, they trust the fact May knows what she knows and now they all four need to know the same.

The decision is to push the cycles through the dense brush right where they're at, there's a slight embankment and thick brush but after this the going looks doable allowing them to backtrack, hopefully putting them directly across the road from where they hope a large panel truck was last seen.

The going is fairly easy, they've got to get everything over a couple of down trees along the way but they find pushing a couple of street bikes through the forest not all that difficult. The road is several yards to their right, the sound of occasional traffic zipping by assures them there staying on track.

At first and from a distance, it looks like somebody's house, but in fact, as they slowly creep a little closer what they find is what they assume is a firewood cutting station, complete with a makeshift wooden structure lean-to and a fire pit. The cut wood that has been left on the ground is quite rotten, meaning probably nobody's been here in a while and the heavily overgrown path leading to the road says chances are this place has long been forgotten about.

Guessing they are close, they park the cycles and go check the road.

Across the road and slightly left, they can see the spot where something large punched a hole through the foliage.

Because the F.B.I. entrusted Ryson with the photo he's chosen as the volunteer to go take a look.

Ryson's plan is overly simple, signified by how fast he draws it in the dirt.

"I will head back the way we came-in maybe go one hundred yards or so and cross the road there, I'll do the same thing we did to find this place, then see if I can't sneak peek."

After crossing the road and burrowing through the tall thickets, he moves steadily for only a couple of minutes before the sounds of others from somewhere up ahead slow his pace and caution his approach. Using the trees and taller bushes for cover, he continues to the point where he spots the large panel truck through a small circular row of trees and this of course further cautions is quiet approach.

Keeping to the outside edge, he moves to the panel truck keeping the three or four-foot-thick bushes and tall trees between them for cover. Inside the back of this truck, which is not covered, looks like just cheap housewares and some dilapidated furniture. The cab of the truck is empty, this, he checks thoroughly as he continues to sneak by.

The outbuilding he comes to next because of the thicker bushes here he can't get a clear view, it looks like just that of an oversized wood shed, not in too good of shape and from here there is no sign of a door.

The thought of stepping through the bushes here to check the contents of the shed through some of the worn boards is halted almost with fright because of how close the voices are.

Using his quietest heel to toe step, he only moves a couple of feet further when the truck and camper shell come into view. The pickup truck is of average size but the camper shell in and over the back of it by comparison is not. The slightly oversized structure has also been retrofitted with certain key components giving it an almost house-y look.

The truck and its house-y shell are parked pointed away from Ryson, giving him a pretty good look through the door that's being held open by way of a bungee-cord. By making slight adjustments to his view through the thick wall of bushes, he is able to piece together some of the layout and contents inside the camper house.

Closest to the door, still draped in a sarong and clutching something to her chest is indeed the senator's wife, her face is exposed enough so that first he can tell who it is, but also there's a strange droop to it as if all the muscles in her face have slightly surrendered. The small, stuffed chair, she is sitting in, appears to be level, yet, her posture remains at a slight lean.

Sitting next to her is a man maybe in his forties, dark, slightly overweight, and engaged in a conversation with somebody sitting directly across from him. Definitely male, judging by the tone of his responses, but because of his position the sound of his voice is the only clue as to who the other guy might be.

Laughter and then some loud conversation erupt from somewhere further past the pickup truck, halting Ryson's decision to head back.

Almost to the front of the truck when the conversations stop, Ryson freezes, the distance consumed is just enough to follow the last few words back to their maker. The sight through the bushes slows his breath not so much for the two well-armed men sitting in folding chairs under a lean-to similar to the one they found across the road, but for the two empty chairs next to them and the guns that have been left leaning against these two chairs.

Without wasting time to turn around, Ryson puts one foot behind the other, and as if he could control time, moves the dial backwards and slowly reverses the last couple of minutes.

When he again can use the small outbuilding for added cover, he stops and slowly starts to turn around.

Just on instinct alone, the muffled dog bark quickly sends Ryson to a squatted position just a couple of compressed feet off the ground, the second bark is just as muffled, but now more curious than startled, he realizes the barking is coming from inside the small outbuilding.

The sound that follows trickles through the outer shell slowed only by Ryson's denial, the sad whimper of a frightened child is something he did not expect to hear. Then again comes the whimpers of a child. Ryson stands and is now face onto the back of the small outbuilding. What separates them is three feet of bushes about six feet tall and one million miles of apprehension.

It's not a matter of can; he force his way through the thick bushes but how quietly can it be done. He backtracked far enough to avoid visual with those in the camper house, but still this only separates them by thirty feet or so once he comes through the other side.

Like a thin ninja, Ryson makes one last quiet sideways push and although a little scratched up comes through the bushes undetected and no worse for wear.

In the small space behind the wooden structure, he now stands next to and the bushes, he just stepped out of, he waits frozen and listens.

Outside the oversize woodshed, all is quiet inside, however, Ryson can hear a faint sound of paper rustling and the occasional low throated dog growl.

The shed is in fairly decent shape, forcing him to quietly scoot towards the far corner where a large split in one of the corner boards he's hoping gives him a look inside.

His eyes adjust fairly quickly through the slit because of the light flooding in from the open door on the front side. What he sees first is the two large dogs tied to a broken part of the doorway and resting just inside the shed staying in the shade.

It takes another couple of seconds for his eyes to adjust to the darker part of the shed and slowly that image begins to paint it's disturbing picture.

In the dirt, at the back wall, opposite corner from him, sits four small figures in a semi-circle, all four have their hands bound at the wrist in front of them, forcing each to reach into one of two brown paper bags with both hands and then eat whatever was retrieved.

The shadows are tricky, but as each, at some point, find just the right beam of light Ryson one by one sees most of who they are, there is not a whole lot of time to stand and visually draw a picture in his head of each one, clearly and increasingly the two Dobermans are catching wind of his presence, one has already stood and sniffing the air, like it's located something to eat in Ryson's direction.

The four young girls in age ranging from perhaps eleven to fourteen are no doubt frightened, abused, damaged, and even in a woodshed full of shadows through a split in a rotted out plank the road they've traveled is clearly one of pain and despair.

No movement now is more important than to just back up and disappear through the bushes from which he arrived, the scar left in his arrival makes the exit, through the bushes, less painful and far more simple, but that act itself is one of shame and self-contempt.

Ryson knows to back away now gives all those concerned a better chance at success, there's more here to recover then just four innocent angels, he only wishes they could know that they've already been saved and he has no intentions of leaving this country without them.

He moves quick but not like in a retreat, he moves quick because there's children in danger.

The all four gather in close as Ryson dials the number on the back of the photo, as he keys in the last number, there's a short breath before he hits send, he now lowers the phone and calmly says, "For sure, both sides will put their targets at higher priority than the others, what stops these guys from coming in, taking what they want, and destroying what they don't need, including us?"

It's finally agreed to hit send is in all reality to trust the F.B.I. and as Sophie simplistically stated, "They trusted us."

Ryson hits send, and waits.

Broken Blade

The woman that answers is pleasant and perky, she sounds like he's just reached the front desk of a theme park, "Good afternoon, how can I help you today?"

Like instructed, Ryson's answer is, "I have positive visual on target one one four"

Still pleasant but not as perky, the woman now addresses Ryson like an old friend, "Well now, aren't you a sweet dear, I am so pleased you called, and now if you just sit tight for a few, our friends will buzz you when they are close. Before you hear the dial tone, know that I've hugged you."

The line goes quiet and it's almost as if he could feel the electronic embrace, then, dial tone.

"Okay then, that wasn't too strange."

Ryson explains and now the four of them half expecting something evil to just fall from the sky.

May's curiosity finally gets the best of her and more than anything, she really is just pondering out loud, "What the hell do you think she meant by the whole, hug thing." Will jumps right in, he's already thought about this, "I think it's some sort of lingo, probably means once you hear a dial tone, they have your position locked and now you can hang up."

There's no argument, just a strange level of anticipation.

Twenty-seven slow minutes later, to what almost sound like alarm chirps beep somewhere north of their position and almost instantly Ryson's phone barks to life with this incoming message. They all group to read it.

"That's us," four clicks out, "we're coming in. All weapons on safety. We are friendly."

"Should I reply? Just tell them okay."

Ryson decides to play the game a little and sends this message "Roger that. All weapons on safety."

The vehicle that rolls into camp is impressive to say the least, and the three in it seem no less threatening than old friends on a fairly extreme hunting trip.

The four-wheel drive open, topped buggy looks modified but not too overstated, although it definitely has the appearance that it goes where it wants. The three who climbed out once it gets stopped are all maybe thirtyish, and definitely American. The jeans and shirts are of local attire, the boots and side-arms are not. All three are well armed but out of respect, leave the assault weapons in the buggy.

No hugs, no kisses, no introductions of any kind. The one who was sitting shotgun as soon as he gets cleared of the buggy asks, "Target one one four, who of you has had visual?"

The first question stings like that of a military chain of command, luckily before anybody can answer or react the mistake is realized and the approach softened up.

The driver now steps more forward than the rest and he takes a more civil approach, "You will have to excuse Mr. Warm and Wonderful there, he's not much for the civilian population. As he puts it, they all lack discipline and the ability to conform."

Mr. Warm does mumble a sort of sorry but it does not seem all that genuine.

"So, now, let's try this again, the driver remains at the helm as he takes over the questioning."

"First, let me just say, no matter how the outcome, you four did what we could not and for that we are grateful, now please, one of you tell us why we've come."

Ryson, of course, speaks up and in just a couple of minutes brings the trio up to speed starting with the stopped truck, and of course in detail what he discovered across the road.

The driver now nods and flicks his head towards the man who was sitting in the back of the buggy, and with no words being spoken, backseat boy moves like the wind and he is quietly out and away from camp in an instant, his movement precise and silent.

The air around camp is not much on the social side, both parties seem willing to wait for Wind Walker's return before committing to any sort of problem-solving engagement.

When W.W. returns, he does so from a different direction from which he left, all four expect the other three to huddle and discuss the fate of all the rest, surprisingly enough, they do not, instead Mr. Wind Walker calls a huddle to all parties currently concerned.

"You four can call me Ed, as for these other two, Hell, they're so covert they don't even know each other's names."

They all three laugh, must be an inside thing.

The very first words he speaks, instantly makes them all friends, "Yes indeed, they have located our target, and he's right, we've got to get those kids out of there."

The driver again takes the com and it's quite impressive how quickly he begins to formulate, "How quickly can we move the kids out of there once the fun starts?"

"Hell, this is no different than central America, and you know damn well they been using them dogs as vicious canine nannies, and we also know their intentions are to lock them all up together through the night."

"And what of the sentries?"

"There's five, but I only had visual on two, the other three, maybe cutting wood? It sounded something like that."

"And our target?"

"Just like he said."

Driver man ponders this for a second or two, just long enough for things to go quiet. His voice indeed showing some concern when he says, "I hate to say it but one of you is going to have to help, if we expect to get everybody out of their unhurt."

"You would have to sedate Ryson to the point of an unconscious drool-bath if you expected to keep him out of this fight." This seems to be common knowledge, so no surprise to hear him speak first, "Hey, you boys get what you came for, I'll go for the kids."

"Yes, that works. But your gunna have to haul ass because every second after first shot fired, those kids will be in danger of being mauled. What makes this even worse is we need to go right through the front door, it'll be their only weakness. So you will have to hang back and wait for that first shot and only then do you make your move to the kids. If you jump early, good chance not of us come out of there alive."

268

Wind Walker Ed intervenes here with an addition of his own, he now makes eye contact with Mr. Warm, the man that was passenger and says, "Let me see your Bowie." With only a slight hesitation, he does so. Ed now withdraws his own knife he had strapped to his waist and left leg, both Bowie's a force to be reckoned with, and announces, "These two ladies should give those little ones a fighting chance, hell, at minimum at least some defense."

"There was I'm sure enough room between those boards along the bottom end of that shed, I'll slide these two right alongside a couple of those kids, I think they'll know what to do if need be. But yeah, you better fuckin hurry with that .45 of yours. Excuse the language, ladies."

"It'll have to be dark, we risk loss otherwise. Leader man says this and it's obvious his many years of military training is forcing him to keep to the advantage."

The three hours or so before dark, there was some light conversation but all in all in general terms; all seven understood this is only a place where paths cross and neither has understanding as to where the others path may be leading.

At dusk, when the gray shadows begin falling towards dark, the mood in camp changes, it's not like in the movies, nobody's banging heads or bashing forearms, except for some greasepaint, communication headsets, and some pretty serious assault rifles, the three of them seem fairly calm.

After they rattle off some strange lingo testing their communication systems, Wind Walker bolts with the knife in one hand, a side arm in the other, he's the only one without an assault rifle. He, without warning, has already moved into the darkness leaving the words, "Give me ten, come in hot," to fall from where he once stood.

"All right, 45 on our six We will cross the road right here and like I said were using the direct approach so stay low and keep up, I'll let you know when to break for the kids."

"You can call me Ryson, and you tell me when, I'll move just as fast as I can. It's a real shame though, I am fond of most dogs."

They move into the overgrowth just off the road, same place the vehicles went through. Ryson is close enough to the two in front of him he hears muffled chatter on their headsets.

The two men freeze, listen, and they wait. The noise from somewhere behind the bad guys camp sounds a little like one of those rings you had as a kid, the one where the harder you blow into it, the more it sounds like something taking off, and sends all three to one knee.

Ryson was unaware the two in front of him were no longer there, he was quite surprised by gunfire and then the words, "Make your move 45," as they come from the darkness several feet in front of him.

The first couple of strides are quite painful, the leg has had no time to heal and although he's done his best to ignore the fact that just three days ago Sophie pulled a bullet out of there, the pain and discomfort has been difficult.

About third stride, Ryson pops through the overgrowth in midair, feet already moving, waiting for the ground to catch up, when he does finally land, he's already at a full sprint.

The inner compound is lit but only with a short flicker from a small campfire, but it's enough to keep him heading in the right direction. As he reaches the back of the large panel truck, his focus so intent the sporadic gunfire is nothing more than simple background noise.

Past the truck and several feet from the shed, Ryson slightly slows hoping to time the flying kick to the door just right. Both feet land at the same time, one on the ground in front of the door, the other flat, right over the latch, holding the door closed. The impact on the door splinters the doorway, where the latch was inserted, allowing the door to swing inward a couple of feet.

When the door rebounds, the return force because his foot is still in the air in front of him, it damn near sends him tumbling backwards, this only avoided due to the fact the other foot remained firmly planted.

Using the side body approach, Ryson leans into the door as he brings the .45 in his right hand and the flashlight in his left more towards the center of his chest and attempts to enter the shed.

At first, there is some resistance, the door feels almost spongy, Ryson leans back and this time with more force towards the door it surrenders, but only a few more spongy inches.

There's now a vibration in the door and from inside the shed, there comes a sound, the vibrations seem almost sonic in nature due to the speed with which they are being generated, the sound is simply that of perhaps something being deflated.

Before Ryson can reset for another attempt, the door and he, along with it, are now poled into the shed by way of what feels like a massive vacuum, the force pulls him in rather slowly but the torque is unescapable.

As Ryson readies for impact against the back wall of the shed, the vacuum suddenly let's go, his body frozen, skids to a stop, and the shed door slamming shut behind him. In front of him, three or four boards of the back wall for just a split second seem to go translucent, there's a slight silver burst maybe the size of a dime, and then silence, and then once again... The smell of warm sugar cookies.

The small beam of an under powered flash light now frantically dances in the dark, the .45 giving chase as if the two are connected, Ryson is first looking for movement from the dogs, and then, of course, the safety of the children.

It's very dark, and only the thin beam to illuminate who's who and who's where, the children, all four our semi-huddled against the wall of the shack to his left, the dogs are at his feet against the back wall, the toes of his boots almost making contact.

Both dogs are of medium to large size, short haired, and now lay motionless on the ground in front of him. The several large stab wounds through each, rendering them no longer a threat. Assuming this was done in defense, Ryson now shifts his attention to the kids.

All four girls are still bound at the wrist with their hands in front of them. The oldest girl whose maybe fourteen has one of the large Bowie in her hands and with the business end pointed right at Ryson. Bowie number two, he does not see.

The polite knocking on the door is done softly and without urgency followed by Ed's question of concern, "You okay in their, 45?"

Ed is able to pull the door outward due to the damage done when the door was closed last, he steps in taking a place next to Ryson and says, "Okay, boys and girls, cover your eyes it's about to get sunny."

Then there was light.

Ed, the Wind Walker's, first words are, "Where's the other one?"

"The one she's holding is mine, the other I don't see, do you?"

Ed glances down at the dogs and his remark is one of confusion and mystery, "Well, somebody in here used it on those two because there's no blood on the other."

"What's that?" Ryson question leads them both to a shared squat because at their feet is the handle of the knife partially buried in the soft dirt of the floor.

When all Ed retrieves is the handle from the dirt, minus the blade, they are both speechless for a couple seconds. Ed stands first and then slowly backs out of the shack, knife handle in both hands mumbling, "That's just not possible."

Ryson stands and faces the children, all four still in a frightened defensive posture and one still clinging to the hopes she can defend the rest, "I know, sheesh, what a day."

Ryson takes a couple of steps closer to the girls, then slowly he goes down to both knees, his hands resting on his legs just above the knee cap, he then calmly continues, "Yes, I'm sure you've had a lot of bad days lately. Well, I think you've had enough and I'm here to see to it that every day after this, they get a little better every time the sun comes up. So for now on, you may perhaps look forward and face each day with a smile."

"Now, about that knife. I'm not going to take that away from you, if you can't decide to trust me even a little, then you keep it, but I'll just bet the four of you would rather go home, this part of your life is over, all you have to do is walk away, now let's go, and leave the knife behind."

Ryson stands, smiles slightly, softly nods his head, and exits the shed. He hears the girls get up even before he's clear of the doorway.

Ed and the owner of the broken blade are patiently waiting outside the shed, one holding half a deadly weapon and both anxious to retrieve what's missing.

Finding the strength to look back is in itself an act of bravery for several reasons, but only one is sure to bring all five closer together.

The campfire that once provided a minimal amount of light is now quickly approaching bonfire status and with each thump of another log being added the shadows are driven further away.

Ryson knows when he turns to face the children, he, again, will be confronted with all of the sadistic atrocities of mankind and in that moment and forever he to shall feel their pain.

Ragtag tattered and torn, par for the course, this place consumes these children one vicious act after another and those that survive will forever be left to struggle with what they once were.

No tears this time, Ryson stares the four down, never shifting from their eyes and already thinking the large panel truck he now stands next to is how all drive away from here together.

"Safety is number one for you, girls, so how about just for now you climb in the front seat of this here big ol' truck where you can stay nice and safe."

Breaking eye contact, Ryson opens and rolls down the door and window, leaving the door ajar, he backs out of the way, giving the girls unobstructed access. They do indeed climb in, the oldest of the four climbs in last and closes the door.

Ryson takes a breath and reaches for his phone, the text reads "All clear, come on over." Bring all backpacks, we got new wheels. After hitting send, Ryson looks up and magically, there stands Ed, the Wind Walker, and Mr. Warm and Wonderful as if they sprouted from the earth at his feet, a little startled he takes a half step back and comments on just how quietly they move around.

Mr. Warm speaks first but it's more of an embarrassing question than an inquiry as he holds up half of his Bowie knife and says, "I don't suppose you know what happened to the rest of this?"

"No, I'm sorry I do not, it was really dark and we did not even see the handle until Ed turned on his light."

Mr. Warm begins to drift away even before Ryson can finish but stops as he's turned halfway and leaves Ryson with this piece of knowledge, "In general, we do not leave any sort of hardware lying around that perhaps the bad guys could use to hurt us or others, so there's no chance we left that canvas duffel by the fire."

"It's Ollie, but you can call me Lee." Lee now glances towards the girls in the truck and asked Ryson, "Is that why you're here?"

"Yes, those and others like them, including my own two children."

"Yeah, we figured something like that, well, listen, this road out front continues on for a few clicks further before it splits, the road left is an easy mountain pass leading straight on through to Argentina. Going right a click or two, you'll find the small village of 'Casa de Norte,' it is friendly and they had a medical office, no doctor but they did have some medical supplies."

Ryson, hears Will, May, and Sophie come through the overgrowth from off the road and turns briefly to guide them in his direction, when he turns back to, Lee he is now looking at empty space.

It is not only unsettling but also frightening to see firsthand just how one of these ghost teams operate, as strange as it was, the respect lingers as does the feeling he's somehow made a new friend.

273

All eyes are on Ryson when he turns to prepare the girls for visitors, "I know this is all moving really fast but the next person you're going to meet is a doctor, she is my friend and she is not going to hurt you in anyway."

Ryson steps a foot or two towards the back of the truck and the four reunite, but only long enough for Sophie to find out where the children are, she then steps casually to the open window of the truck.

The other three stay put as Ryson explains what's up, he intentionally speaks above a whisper so all can hear, including those in the truck.

Ryson's delivery stops and they all fall silent with it and listen. The buggy fires up with a growl and even from this distance is loud and sounds angry. They can't see it, they only know because of the way the sound thins to nothing it left in the same direction from which it came.

Sophie is prepared for what she finds but the extent of the abuse, even without peeling away some of the layers takes a vicious bite out of her soul leaving her weak in the knees.

As the three step away from the truck, they listen as Sophie runs through a simple list of questions that require no response only that she read their body language.

The canvas duffel-bag, buggy team did not forget, in it, they find a couple of AK-47's and maybe two hundred rounds of ammo for them, a nine mm semi-automatic pistol, kind of beat up but with a full box of shells for it.

Giddy up Cowboy is May's call to the man at the wheel as Will pulls through the brush and onto the road. Sophie and the children in the back seat, Will at the wheel, May in the middle, Ryson riding shotgun.

"Somebody should probably text Art, let them at least know where were heading."

May reads Arts reply out loud so as to keep everybody in the know. Art says "Casa De Norte, good choice. Inform when arrive. Be real safe. 1.2."

It was nine something when they got the show back on the road and that road was extremely dark, but now after an hour or so into the drive, the region has become more forested and the darkness thicker with each passing mile.

They first feel the sonic percussion inside the truck even before they hear the familiar rapid thump of a helicopter close by, it's dark and the headlights barely penetrating the road in front of them, so all they can do is roll the windows down and listen.

The helicopter passes right over them but all they see is a dark silhouette twinkle some of the stars as it fades and disappears. Who it is, seems easy, what's weird, is neither of the parties ever said thank you when it was over. I guess just all in a day's work.

The fork in the road comes and goes, it's not quite eleven as they role slowly into the small village of "Casa de Norte" and half expecting something, but pleased to find the village assumedly already tucked in for the night.

The brakes damp from the night air squeal to a screechy stop in front of the first structure they find in the dark. The small building has been whitewashed making it quite easy to find and as further luck would have it the sign on the door reads "Med Office." Smaller sign beneath this reads "No Doctor."

The door is not locked, allowing Sophie to be the first to enter, she has the nine mm pistol in her pocket, she knows how to use it but would rather keep things much quieter than that. Ryson is right behind her and for sure will not consider the noise factor if need be.

No switches, no lamps, no overhead lights. Candles placed about room suggest there is no electricity in this building. They light the first few, Sophie goes back for the kids, Ryson finishes with checking all the nooks and crannies.

It takes less than an hour to settle everybody in for the night, Ryson, Sophie, and the kids take what sleeping spaces there are inside, May and Will each take a bench seat in the truck, May in front, Will in the back. As they roll the windows up and share a kiss goodnight, May sends Art this message "In village, all okay, good night." And then is barely able to get laid down before sleep takes her so quickly she does not hear Arts reply "Sleep tight, be safe."

The message they all four awake to is puzzling in nature but it's content is understood as something wicked is headed their way "Good morning all and to all a wonderful day that follows."

"Julian more." And so shall the cavalry charge. "General, Abrams Wes". Or as Shakespeare once put it "Cry havoc and let slip the dogs of war. 1. 2."

Art lets this message brew a wee bit before sending the second half "Stay put, the Colombians are inbound to your location and would like to talk. As we expected they are not pleased, but do indeed remain our allies. Be nice, they can help. 1.2."

275

They don't see them but the soft inquisitive voices are coming from a handful of the local villagers who are now whispering somewhere near the back of the truck.

Their questions are more with concern as to the items in the back of the truck and not so much for who brought them here, one thing for certain, they believe some of the items in the truck have been brought as gifts.

Villagers are neither startled nor surprised as May and Will unfold from the two doors on the same side of the truck, both wrinkled and looking as if they just spent the night in a truck.

Only one of the villager's approaches and with some caution. Her Spanish is quick but May's onboard just as quickly and engages her like someone she's met before.

Will has had no problem keeping up so when May turns to him and says, "They think we brought some of this stuff for trade."

He's already answering back, "I think you tell them they may have all of it in trade for just something to eat." This either goes over real well or it scares them to death because in just a single heartbeat, they disperse and scatter like bits of a shooting star.

Unfamiliar voices slow, then halt their approach to the already open door of the medical office, Will stops just short of the entrance, trying to get a look inside, May over his shoulder trying to do the same.

The two older ladies that emerge from the medical office, smile politely, and quickly step through the doorway, both whisper good morning and both disappearing in different directions.

Will steps through the doorway first but does so with announcement, "Good morning, boys and girls, if you're not already up, it's time to rise and shine because here, at camp, somewhere, it seems that were already waiting for someone."

Ryson is standing only a few feet from the door as Will steps in, this puts them face to face and ten feet apart.

Will's hair nest like, clothes bent like he slept in them in a cement mixer, face wrinkled on one side like somebody tried to make waffles, and yet the tone of his voice still carries with it the weight of the world, but when Ryson says, "Yeah, maybe we should bake them a cake."

This Will was not prepared for and cannot subdue his funny-bone.

May pushes past, she too in laughter as she disappears looking for Sophie and the girls.

"Well, I don't know about a cake, but I think we traded all the furniture in the truck for something to eat, but I'm guessing cake is probably not on the menu."

"So who were the two hotties leaving your place this morning?" Now it's Ryson's turn to chuckle.

Locals come to investigate the intruders. At first, they seemed a little antsy but after Sophie told them she was a doctor, they lightened up. It seems this place only gets used every couple of years or so when they round up all the free range livestock in this whole region.

Wills nods his head, saying, "Well, that explains the oversized barn and large holding pens."

"Yeah, the rest of the time it's just a dozen or so locals that maintain the place."

In a way, not unlike those days spent in Vietnam, two helicopters scream in from the west, coming in low and in formation. It first shakes, then seems to ripple the ground beneath their feet.

Curiosity draws them to the doorway but only Will steps out, the sudden flashback slows Ryson's exit and for a moment, he feels the horrors of war.

When Ryson does step out and stands next to Will, the two helicopters pass directly overhead, one staying the course and disappearing over the mountains behind them, the second banks hard left and re-approaches.

The helicopter settles into a nose-in hover, but the two hundred yards distance between them does not allow to see who's in it. They can only watch it settle gently to earth and hope, in fact, they really are allies.

Two men exit the helicopter with the blades still in motion but slowing down, both men slightly ducked and heading towards the medical office, both men well-dressed, the one a couple of steps behind the first, also well-armed.

Both men approach with smiles and an eagerness to meet them as if they have been waiting for weeks to do so.

"Sorry about the guns, but this Vinzaya fuck is already putting up quite a fight."

They all four shake hands while forgoing formal introductions because man one never stops talking. Man two, the one with the assault rifle, takes a couple of steps back where he remains quietly on guard.

277

"Our common ground here is the kids, I've spoken to Art a couple of times in the last twenty four hours, and I do understand why you're here, he would not tell me who you were looking for, only that they were children."

"The fact that Art did call puts me in your debt. If this plan of Vinzaya's had continued to move forward unchecked, he could have caused a lot of serious fuckin' problems."

"And as for the children in this godforsaken hellhole, we will gather them along the way. We are all family men and most of us parents many times, so you needn't question our attempt at being extremely thorough. Believe me, we will check under every flower and all the places the sun won't reach. And all them, we find we will move to this location." He stops here unexpectedly and with the warmth of perhaps that of a brother he places his right hand on Ryson's shoulder and asked him, "So who are you looking for, maybe I can help."

It's an act of true compassion and Ryson knows it and therefore, does not hesitate to tell him.

This rattles around for a few seconds and it's obvious there is a connection but it seems fairly deep.

He nods, "I think I have somebody you might want to talk to. As soon as I can locate him, I'll send him this way."

"So here's what you should not do." Man one drops his hand from Ryson's shoulder and now goes back to business, "Make no mistakes about it, we have arrived and in large numbers, our purpose here is simple, we've come to raise hell, havoc, and high water and do not plan on leaving much behind. This place will no longer function as is or as it was. Who comes here and shits next is their problem. But, for sure, Vinzaya will be taking a beating."

"Down the road a couple of miles is a fork, the one side comes here the other is a mountain passage leading into Argentina, your safety ends at that fork, anybody carrying a weapon past that split in the road will be shot on sight. But our aggression ends there. Understood?"

He waits.

"Yes. Believe me, we do not want to get in your way. It's only the children were after. All the children, if possible," Will says this simply to be heard.

Ryson agrees then adds, "Thanks."

As the two men walk away, somebody says, "You tell Art we're even when you leave here with more children than you know what to do with."

Ryson says this but he's not quite sure they hear him, "Our pleasure."

But then comes a thumbs up from the man not carrying an assault rifle.

Check Point Vinzaya

Only after the rotor thump begins to fade do May and Sophie step out from their place of eavesdropping. The four now stand in the early morning sun and all four the same question. What now? Then the obvious.

"Text Art, perhaps he and Lila have some words of wisdom."

May does her best at bringing Art and Lila up to speed without supplying too much information to others who might be monitoring the cell systems. The last line of her message reads "Already some havoc, the roads aren't safe. 3.4.5.6."

Squeaky wheels and nervous chatter from a couple of goats sneak around the corner of the medical office, the sound is heading their way and quite close. The four have just enough time to glance left, catching the appearance of two of the older ladies they've already met; one is holding the end of a rope that seems to lead to the source of the squeak and chatter.

The other end of the rope and the two goats it's tied to now come into view and harnessed to them is a flat-bed cart with four small rubber wheels. The cart itself is maybe four by nine and no side rails and approximately ten inches off the ground.

The two ladies do turn and smile but their progress remains the same, only coming to a stop once they reach the back of the large panel truck.

Movement again from the same corner, the goat pair appeared from re-draws their attention. This time the two ladies who step into view are carrying open-topped wicker baskets and a couple of goat skin pouches.

Their approach is quite friendly, all smiles and already chattering well before they even get close. When they're finally close enough to hear what the woman speaking is saying, all four our quite surprised to hear her speaking perfect English.

The two ladies, who are similar but definitely do not seem related, scooch past and into the medical office with what they've brought, but as they do, the woman speaking, politely says, "We should go inside, it seems you're making some of the locals nervous. Some think you've come to put the sign back up."

Sophie, right behind them, already engaged in damage control, the rest follow quietly, giving Sophie the chance to speak for all four.

"No, ma'am, we know nothing of the sign nor do we intend to erect one. So tell us please why they would think that. We're only here to save some children, and I think we can all agree there is plenty of that to do," Sophie's a little hostile and it shows.

The chatty one now slightly leans more towards humble and with a much softer voice, says, "You're right, and we have no reason to suspect otherwise."

After placing the baskets and goat pouches on a table, both ladies now head back to the doorway but only one steps out and away, the other continues to speak. About four months ago, she now turns and re-faces the four standing at the table, this was right after a large round up, so there were still a few of the local boys finishing with cleanup and repair when this group comes rolling in here calling themselves Vinzaya and saying this is now part of their territory.

They were heavily armed, military trained, and it was obvious they were looking for resistance. When they found none, they put up a large sign claiming this territory as their own and take three of the older boys when they leave.

It seems at this point she has something else to say because of the way she pauses and takes a breath, she does not, instead, she smiles and kindly thanks them for the furniture, assuring them it will all be put to good use. She is already halfway out the doorway when she, without looking back, says, "Enjoy your breakfast, don't be afraid to ask for more if need be."

"Would you like some help?" Ryson says this as he is already heading towards the doorway.

"No, no, no, eat, enjoy your breakfast, we've got all the people we need, Thank you."

The meal consisted of cheese, flatbread, goat's milk, and two different kinds of dried meat, not sure what it was but it all was delicious. Except the warm goats milk, must be an acquired thing. But even still, between the eight of them, only empty air was left in the basket and goat skin pouches.

Halfway through breakfast, Arts message certainly supercharges the moment but it's Lila's reply that sends them all to the think tank, including Art.

"You know who says from space he can see several roads that crisscross through the mountain region behind your village. One in particular, quite large, east to west, and connects you to the mountain pass into Argentina. Where you wanted to be. Maybe 3 miles away. P.S. Lila says, 'Be Vinzaya?' 1.2."

They all receive the same text and while reading it, it was the only quiet time of the day.

"Be Vinzaya?"

The all four know this is important, or Lila would never have said it, they just don't know how.

"Will, you know what?" Ryson glances sideways because of Will's location, "What?"

"I think it's time we woo these ladies into giving up some real info. So let's go out there and be just as damn charming as we can be."

The girl's kind of play along each adding a couple of their own innuendos, as to who can be more charming.

Several times during breakfast, they heard the goat cart squeak away than squeak back, so there was no surprise when Ryson and Will reach the back of the truck and find it almost empty.

The last three items in the truck are a fairly worn and torn leather loveseat and a couple of cheap, pine, heavily stained tables. Could not sell that crap at a swap meet in Bangladesh, but these women seemed quite pleased with the day's haul as they load these last three items onto the cart.

Ryson figures to try the direct approach first, given the happy mood these three ladies are obviously in, "Our sources tell us there's a road behind this village and they say that road connects to the mountain pass leading into Argentina. Our two questions being, is that true and will this truck fit?"

The woman whom they've already spoken, she now as politely as possible sends the other two women on their way, followed by two goats and a squeaky cart.

"Did the children get enough to eat?"

"Yes, ma'am, but I wish they'd had eaten more than they did, I guess the fact they can eat at all is a testament to their own strength and endurance, their ability to survive is as of yet still unknown, but at least now they're safe," Ryson moves her and it's obvious. Although that was not his intention. She does soften and answer his questions.

282

"Yes, it's a main collection road. Come round up time, they park trucks that size and bigger on it, then load the animals as they are brought in from free range. And yes, it crosses the road leading into Argentina. These dirt roads are not maintained and it could be a little rough."

There's a few seconds of odd silence before she continues and when she does, the subject matter has changed and she begins to soften even further, so much so she now moves to a humble approach and slightly teary-eyed.

"Please, could you take that sign away from here, we have all been afraid to even touch it, considering the fact the two man who dug it out of the ground were found dead the next day, both men attacked and partially eaten, by what we don't know."

Two large tears now tumble down her cheeks, the moment seems to weaken her and she leans against the truck then continues. They put the sign in the barn over there, next to it, on the ground, you will find a box and in it, are two military uniforms.

Two more tears give chase to the others. The three boys that were kidnapped, two of them escaped and returned a week later, they were wearing those clothes. The third boy has not returned. That one is my son. She quietly turns and walks away, never attempting to wipe the tears from her face.

Wills answers, he makes sure she hears it, "Yes, of course."

The two decide to share this new bucket of info with May and Sophie before making any decisions, but they know it's time to go for a ride.

The three put the sign in face down, it's a rather large sign, probably four by eight but just small enough to fit without any hassle. The box they do not open and probably will not, Ryson gently placing it also in the back.

It's agreed to leave Sophie in the village, thus keeping her with the kids and waiting for more to arrive.

"Well, shall we go have a look?" Will turns the key letting the truck grumble to life, all three in the front seat, all three no place they'd rather be.

Other than a few swimming pool sized potholes, the road itself is fairly easy to navigate, and was just as easy to find.

The three miles goes rather quickly, the road more or sometimes less, skirts a ravine that is probably a raging river during rainy season, there are several smaller roads jetting out in different directions along the way, so as they approach a clearing and a road the same size as the one they are on, they can only assume a right turn takes them through the mountains to Argentina, and a left, to a fork in the road, they've already seen.

Careful not to expose any of the truck to whatever traffic may be on the road in front of them, Will stops several feet short of the crossing as the engine dies down so go the windows and it's time to listen.

Ryson is the first one out of the truck after several seconds of observed silence, then just as quickly May and Will follow. The three approach the road with caution than stopping to lean in, all three checking the road in both directions.

With their backs to Argentina, the three now stand side-by-side on the road with a sweeping view down into the valley and the area known as Neighbors Cradle. They are able to follow the road as it begins to unroll at their feet, first to the fork in the road, and then bits and pieces of it as it slowly winds and disappears somewhere in the valley floor.

Way out there and more like dancing vapors, they can see a couple of helicopters zipping around, a handful of fires dotting here and there and their black, puffy smoke all caught up in the same winds now lead away like a distant ships smoke on the horizon. They cannot hear the havoc, they can only see the destruction. And yes, it looks as if somebody has opened the quiet gates of hell.

Caught up and mesmerized by the reality of life itself and the passing of it, the movement on the road a fairways past the fork idles into view and it's May who finally says, "You see that?"

"Yes, and definitely heading this way."

Ryson is the last to comment, "Maybe twenty minutes to the fork and another thirty minutes until they're right here. I'd say we have less than an hour before company arrives."

The last remark brings to the moment a level of collective thoughts that at first wanders from the obvious but soon leads all three to a thought that can only be referred to as a life defining moment. Then Will says it out loud, "How could she have known, be Vinzaya, hell, we already are. We have a sign and uniforms. How could Lila have known?"

There is now a moment of silence, it seemed only fitting to pay tribute where tribute is due.

Ryson is the one who gets to say it first, leaving the other two disappointed, "Welcome to checkpoint, Vinzaya."

Now it's May's turn, "Surrender the children, unconditional."

"Well, if you two are done playing checkpoint Charlie, whatever we do, we best be doing it now," there becomes a sense of urgency because clearly the first two vehicles heading their way, one being a large four-door sedan and some kind of small S.U.V. right behind that are moving at a very high rate of speed. The white, pickup truck is a few miles behind the first two, moving much slower, one reason being the small open trailer in tow. Past this, the road is empty and being quickly consumed by the havoc and carnage dished out by the Colombians.

Moving quickly back to the truck with details and construction for checkpoint, Vinzaya beginning to zing around in three-part harmony, shared equally as the plan hatched and immediately put into action starting with where to put the large sign they took from the village.

The sign itself is of basic construction, simply a piece of quarter inch plywood, four by eight with two by fours as legs, by removing the legs, they are left with just a four by eight piece of plywood they attached to the outside of the truck, providing them with not only a rolling barricade and checkpoint but also by leaving it concealed on the crossroad, they maintain the element of surprise.

The dress rehearsal goes disturbingly well, two guys stand down the road a few feet as May roles the truck from hiding, the large trees and bushes concealing it do a fantastic job at making their rolling checkpoint seem as if it appears from thin air. Rolling to a quick stop and places the truck mid-road, leaving only a few inches at each end. There is no way because of all the forest growth to squeeze past.

What's disturbing is just how intimidating it looks. The sign covers most of the back of the truck. It's like all the others they have seen. The background is a simple whitewash, the large letters spelling Vinzaya in blue at the top, under this, is a falling S pattern and in the spaces it creates, the words "The Dark And The Light." And In each corner, a large circle and in it a large letter "V."

As for the uniforms in the box, two shirts, two pairs of pants, both shirts O.D. green and on each shoulder, a patch bearing the same logo as in each corner of the sign now attached to the side of the truck.

"Looks good, May, scary as hell," they both agree.

May smiles and still looks deadly. She is wearing one of the shirts and sits with the window halfway down, her hair pulled back loose. On the half open window is a folded piece of burlap and resting on this is one of the AK 47s.

"It looks very real because it is."

May removes the gun from the window as Will and Ryson cover the few feet to her door. When they get there, May is just reading a text from Sophie, Sophie says "Three more to the nest." May quickly reads her own response out loud as she types it "That's great, we should be back soon. 3.4.5."

"Okay, boys and girls, are we ready to set this trap and see just what kind of horrors we can catch? Does not matter who says this, only that it's true."

Time is quickly dancing forward, they are down to just a few minutes before the first two vehicles arrive.

May pulls the truck straight back, retaking her place of hiding on the road that brought them here.

Because of Ryson's part in all this, he is closest to May, which makes him responsible for having her move into position. He is tucked in just off the road in some bushes but has clear line of sight for at least two hundred yards in the direction of oncoming visitors.

Directly across the road from Ryson, in the same kind of bushes, squats Will. All three at buzz with anticipation and ready to spring, and all three, locked and loaded.

Still moving at a high rate of speed the larger of the two vehicles comes into view. Ryson cannot actually see May but knows exactly where she's at and knows she will have no trouble hearing him, "Okay, May, start it up, be ready."

Ryson looks across the road at Will and can't help but smile, this because, when the truck rumbles to life, his eyes get big like donuts, "You ready, Will?"

Will quietly nods *yes*.

"On 3, May. 1... 2... 3."

May pops the clutch and the truck lurches forward, the movement comes quick and the truck is already half way across the road before May can two-foot the brake pedal. The stop comes just as quick with a short skid and perfect position. No way to get around. May's focus is now on the AK-47 and her target.

The large four door Sedan in front brakes hard with a couple of minor fish-tales, the smaller S.U.V. behind barely escapes impact while making the same sort of wobbly stop. When both vehicles come to a halt, thirty feet is all that separates them from May, the truck, and the barrel of an AK-47. All falls quiet.

Will waits for both vehicles to get stopped and some of the dust to settle before stepping into view. When he does, this puts him about even with the driver side door of the small S.U.V. and maybe fifteen feet away from the large Sedan in front.

Will stands angry, the A.K. in both hands held close and across his chest. Because of his part in this his role required him to wear both parts of the uniform, so along with the O.D. green shirt with shoulder patches the pants he's wearing our military khakis in green forest cameo. No doubt, he looks the part.

Will waits for Ryson's movement to be noticed by those in both vehicles before he's going to shout his commands, Will can see heads darting about inside both vehicles as Ryson steps from his place of hiding. This puts him almost even with the space between the two vehicles, but still ten feet away. He's wearing the same pants as Will, only his shirt is a tucked in white polo with a horsey on the pocket. His .45 held low at mid body, like he's ready for up close hand-to-hand engagement.

Wills voice now booms with authority, and in his best mad Spanish he announces, "Surrender the children. All children. Unconditional!"

The second time the boom of Will's voice is even louder and almost seems unnatural, "Surrender the children. Leave Paraguay. Unconditional."

The plan failed to evolve past this point and how could it. All three are· waiting to see what happens next.

The two backdoors of the large Sedan in front open and out of just the right side, the side closest to Ryson, emerge four small children. From the second vehicle, same thing, but only two children exit.

The six children seem to instinctively know and scramble quickly from the road and onto the shoulder. Where they stop and come to a huddle is only a few feet from Ryson.

"Stay down!" and a hand gesture is all that's needed from Ryson and all six drop and sit, same huddle, just shorter. All six children are white and of Asian looking descent, all are little boys, ages ranging from maybe five to eight years old, dressed somewhat similar and all six wearing what looks like those thin cheap white hospital slippers. No way they all understood *get down* but the hand gesture was universal.

"Inspection!" this time Will's command is less threatening but still quite loud.

The two front doors of each vehicle now swing open, stopping only when full travel has been reached. Both vehicles sit in silence four times ajar.

Knowing the white pickup and the trailer it tows, will soon be rolling into checkpoint Vinzaya, Ryson and Will do a quick look see into both vehicles, assuring themselves all the children have been removed.

Will now shift's his attention left where he and May make eye contact. He nods his head and kind-of flicks the A.K. in his hands, meaning he wants May to back up and off the road.

He wants to laugh as he hears May grinding away on the gears looking for reverse. The gears finally clatter, then thud, and the truck begins to drift backwards. Not until it's completely clear of the road do all four doors close.

There's nothing in Will's soul or engraved in his beliefs that says it's okay to now empty his A.K. into the wretched souls he himself has judged. But the real strength is in watching them now drive away.

Ryson stood ready and let Will make the call. The anger and contempt will not be leaving as easily.

Returning the truck to hiding May, then turns the key towards quiet, and waits the few seconds it takes for things to hush back to normal. "How much time we got Ryson?" May's question has only one purpose and that is, does she have enough time to check on the children still sitting on the side of the road.

"Everybody sit tight, they are close, May, be ready to start that thing back up."

"I'm ready, Ryson, just tell me when."

"You ready, Will?" Ryson glances across the road and finds Will with his game face on.

There is no time to move the children to a safer place, where they are at looks to be the safest option, they're far enough off the road to not be in any real danger and Ryson close enough to make sure of that.

"Okay, May, start her up. Like before, on 3."

Loud enough for sure Ryson starts his count, "1... 2 ...3," like instant replay, only this time, it's a full-size, white, pickup truck and a small, open, top trailer that comes fishtailing to a stop at checkpoint Vinzaya.

Clearly the command to surrender all children is not needed. The truck is occupied only one time and that is the driver, once he gets stopped, he is all too happy to exit his truck and offer any and all contents of the truck and trailer for safe passage into Argentina.

After a quick inspection, Will assures the man he can keep what little firewood and scrap metal he's collected, adding that indeed leaving Paraguay is the smartest thing to do.

Will takes the few steps required that puts him close enough to May who was still married to the A.K. and pointing it out the half down window, so as they can speak, "No kids, May, it all looks just as it does, and just as it seems. I guess we let him go."

May finds no reason to disagree and turns the key back to rumble where quickly she returns to grinding away the gears as if she's begun to enjoy the vibrations. Now Will allows himself a chuckle.

Ryson has just more or less been playing the overseer, making sure nothing goes wrong, while providing safety for the six he would surely defend with his life.

When May finds reverse and those gears rattle and drop into place, something pushes like hard air against Ryson's chest. As May slowly let's out the clutch, the pushing stops, but it's being replaced by at first a thin whisper of something so pleasant the smell is like vaporized happy.

As the truck finds first movement the thin whisper of something pleasant thickens, it quickly solidifies, then drapes like wet silk, the air so dense with the thick smell of warm sugar cookies. Ryson is completely unable to take a breath of fresh air.

The moment for a second or two panics Ryson, then like it's arrival the thin whisper of vaporized happy sneaks away but does so, so quickly its absence is startling and Ryson comes very close to discharging the .45 in his right hand.

Although still dizzied from the lack of oxygen, he is not without the ability to bellow the command, "Stop or I will shoot you! Don't let him through, we need to talk."

May hits the brakes, leaving only a couple of feet for escape, to which there is no attempt to do so. Reluctantly, the pickup small skids to a stop, leaving only several inches between it and May's A.K. 47.

Will is quick to the window, then just as quick with the butt of his A.K. when he sees the driver of the pickup attempting to withdraw a handgun from his waistband.

From the other side of the road, Ryson steps to the back of the pickup still not sure what is happening.

"What's going on, Ryson?"

"I'm not sure, just don't let this guy go anywhere."

"This fuck was going for a gun, now he's going to need a bucket of titanium to put that jaw back together, he's out but not dead, probably wishin' he was, 'cuz yeah, that's gotta hurt."

There is a strange tickle to the tiny hairs in Ryson's ears as he stands looking into the back of the pickup, it's almost as if there should be sound but there is none, focused on the lack of sound tickling his ears, the odor takes a few seconds to register, he need only to alert his sense of smell and on the next breath, the odor unmistakable. Vomit.

Before he can even ask for help emptying the back of the pickup, May is already there and reaching in.

"You smell that, May?"

"Yeah, somebody barfed."

"Let's get this crap out of here."

There's only a few pieces of firewood and some of what looks like pieces of an aluminum fence to remove before the bed of the truck is empty. What this reveals is what is obvious a false bottom. The thin corrugated aluminum is slid into place, locking it in tight when the tailgate is closed.

Ryson drops the tailgate, so he and May from both sides of the pickup can slide the corrugated aluminum out at least halfway before it hits the small trailer and stops.

No words, May cries. Ryson reaches in and removes the only child that is clearly still alive. All May can do is reach in and confirm the death of the other two.

There are two separate chambers in the bed of the pickup, both chambers the same size and run the full length of the truck bed. The chamber on May's side of the truck is still thick with the smell of vomit and exhaust fumes.

All three girls looked to be about the same age, maybe six or so. All three girls were gagged with a thin piece of cloth tied at the back of their heads.

Their hands and feet bound together, leaving them on their sides and bent at the knees.

The differences of course are the two that lay motionless, not quite sure whether they drowned in their own vomit because of the gags in their mouth or were first asphyxiated by the obvious exhaust leak on their side the truck.

Will is standing over May's shoulder, the two of them forced to share the moment because neither of them want the other to walk it alone.

Ryson moves quickly in removing the piece of cloth around the little girl's head and mouth, he almost has her untied as he reaches their truck. May left the driver side door open, so for now, after Ryson finishes untying her, he plops her on the driver seat, smiles, then says, "You are safe now." Then winks.

Ryson turns away with the intention of gathering the other six kids and placing them in the truck as well. This puts him face to face with bad guy in the pickup, well, that is if he wasn't slumped against the steering wheel.

Through the front windshield, Ryson can see this guy's twitching funny like he's thinking about waking up. Two strides and he is at and opening the driver side door and just as quick grabs the back collar of Mr. Slumpy, pulling him from the pickup and letting his filthy existence fall to the dirt, face up at his feet.

Ryson's boot, it seems, without asking, comes to a resting position on the throat of this demon and it's here he is faced with the task at hand beneath his feet, so he looks to the heavens because hell is just a little too close for comfort.

Not sure how long he stands heavy here, but it's only a soft nudge and May's voice that makes him step away.

May now stands were Ryson was, she lowers the barrel of her A.K. 47 to the demons mid-chest and quite calmly says, "A bullet for every child I know you've killed today."

Thunder times two means it's time to go. The noise is like a slap to the cortex, stunning the senses. This awakening brings May, Will, and Ryson to a place once again in the middle of the road. (Not A Metaphor)

The sight that spills before them is certainly one of calculated destruction, it's quite clear from their vantage point where the Colombians started, where there at now, and which way there heading. The smoke the fires the gunfire and chaos quickly consuming Neighbors Cradle.

All roads as far as they can see have already been cleared and most now remain guarded.

We need to go, no one else is coming through here, and I get the feeling we are about to have our hands full. Both guys offer just a simple, "Yes."

Like machines, each sets to their own tasks, each knowing their place, and each okay with it.

May takes the little girl from the front seat of their truck, allowing Will to climb in and start the multipoint maneuver to get the large truck turned around.

With the one she already has, May joins the other six kids. She kneels with caution, then sits, allowing the child to stay safely in her lap.

There's a cycle of life here, it's movement obvious as is the destruction it causes, but up until now, all they have seen is already the damage done. For lack of a better word, the six little boys look almost new, yes, there are already signs of abuse but at this point it's cosmetic. Obviously, these six children have been slapped around, fat lips, couple of black eyes, and they all have several small cuts on the tops of their hands. But in comparison to the one she's holding and the two still in the bed of that pickup, night and day.

Six will leave here with true hopes for Mother Tomorrow and one who can only leave here broken. All will leave Checkpoint Vinzaya, permanently scarred.

With everybody in the truck and ready to go, Ryson now gently places the two children he has wrapped tightly with seat material from the pickup in the back of their truck, he wipes the few tears that still sting his cheek, then cuts the large sign from the side of their truck letting it fall facedown, only to return to the earth from which it came.

Hell, Havoc, and High water

The short ride back to Casa De Norte is one spent in reflection and forward thought, not so much in conversation. There is a text to Sophie along the way, saying "We are on our way back."

Their return to Casa De Norte is overshadowed by a beehive of already ongoing activity, they parked alongside the medical office in an attempt to avoid colliding with the two open top jeeps that comes racing in like something's on fire, but what's really making all the noise is the helicopter now hovering directly overhead. Both jeeps are occupied with the driver and then half a dozen or so kids. The helicopter drifts and then lowers some hundred yards away, it's hard to tell where or if it landed because of the amount of dirt thrown up by the rotor wash.

The two jeeps U-turn, stopping only long enough to unload their passengers through the open doorway of the medical office with a synchronized delivery system, making it look as if they've done this before.

With their vessels empty the jeeps, single file, flick away like fleas from a poisoned collar.

Next through the doorway is May with a child in her arms and the other six close behind. Before Will and Ryson can follow, they hear a voice erupting from the rotor wash dust cloud.

The voice sounds panicked and the man that emerges through the cloud even at fifty yards away can be heard quite clearly, "I have two more in the heli, I can't carry both, they need help."

Fly boy does not wait for a response, instead, he about faces and charges back into the now thinning dust cloud.

They both take off at the same time, but in all fairness, Ryson's injuries have taken some of the giddy out of his giddy-up. When they almost reach the helicopter at the same time they, find the pilot in the back seat unstrapping two lifeless bodies, "They were both breathing when I took off, but not conscious."

293

The one he unstraps first is a male, definitely in mid-teen years, dark hair dark skin, "Somebody get ready to grab this kid."

When the strap let's go, the pilot just sort of nudges the boy towards the door, only hanging on long enough to watch him fall chest first into Will's open arms. The momentum carries Will and the boy backwards five or six feet, Will on one-foot spins, maintaining balance, and speed with a beeline for the medical office.

Ryson steps up just in time to catch passenger number two who is now semi-conscious. She is the same as the first but only female, could be his sister. Both are wearing grey overalls and are soaking wet.

She at first struggles with the fall, then surrenders completely into Ryson's arms.

Before the pilot crawls from the helicopter, Ryson and Will both hear him holler, "I was told those two were from the river, but they look like first they were thrown down a mountain."

As Will nears the medical office, his passenger now becomes semi-conscious and even somewhat coherent.

Together, he and Ryson step into the medical office and into adolescent abundance. There seems to already be a sense of chaotic control, so they deposit with announcement the two they bring to the party, and then slowly back through the doorway from which they entered.

Before they can get turned around, the voice sneaks up from behind, "Thanks for the help, now which one of you is Ryson?"

They both turn before there is an answer.

Confirming it's the pilot, Ryson quietly announces, "That would be me."

"I'm told you would like some information regarding some twins, is that right?"

Ryson's heart dances out of rhythm and his skin gets cold. Slow tongued, he replies, "Yes, I would, what can you tell me?"

"It's not much but you're welcome to it. A few nights ago, I'm here on a regular run I do twice a month and sometimes the cargo is undetermined, meaning they don't always tell me. But I don't cargo children for anybody. So when this fat fucker shows up in a minivan with these kids, I threatened to kill him and would have if it not for me realizing, I do that and no way those kids get off that mountain by themselves. He's pissed, so what. He then loads them back in the van and disappears into the night."

"They did not all get out of the minivan, the three that did get, out I saw fairly well, the two that did not, not so much. They were twins, and maybe four or five, the third girl, maybe six or seven, I remember her because she had a funny sort of haircut like she did it herself. Can't say for sure but the two that did not get out looked very similar to the twins that did."

Ryson finally finds his tongue and would like to get specific, "The two I'm looking for are my own. And yes, they're twins, girls, brown hair, green eyes, four years old, and very much the same."

As Ryson describes their clothing, something catches in the pilot's memory.

"Yes, I remember a penguin shirt, but neither of the kids was wearing it. When fat fuck pulls the first two from the van, one of them is holding a doll, and drops it. Both kids pick it up and what they had it wrapped in was a small penguin shirt, big penguin on the front, some smaller ones on the sleeves."

The pilots radio he has strapped to a harness across his chest starts chirping like parrot chatter, but before he steps away to answer it, he adds this last freezing piece of info, "If it helps, I also remember the older girl with the odd haircut, she was wearing an oversized sweatshirt and on the front of it was a large sunflower."

This leaves Ryson and Will speechless, the pilots radio squawks again, sending him in the direction of his helicopter, "Gotta go, hope that helps."

There's a moment needed to thaw before Will states the obvious, "Those three you found on the bench at Camp Diablo, the older girl, funny haircut and sunflower shirt, same girl, you think?"

There just is no time to process this, only that Will adds, "We get home, maybe you find a way to ask her what she knows."

The rumble at their feet meant something heavy was heading up the small road. The military jeep they see first, even though it does contain five passengers and a driver, does not explain the rumble that seems to ripple itchy under their feet.

The jeep moves quickly to the spot right in front of them, then carefully comes to a stop just as the rumble comes into view, "Where would you like that parked because it stays?"

The driver gives Ryson and Will only a second or two before he first gestures to the man driving the large truck, then answers his own question,

"How about we just put it over there for now and you help me get these kids inside?"

Sophie greets the three men just a foot or two inside the doorway, her arms open and already taking from Ryson, the small child he cradles with what is an unknown bandaged leg wound. The other four children are some years older and able to walk in on their own.

May catches the driver of the jeep before he leaves the two he brought in and retreats, "Excuse me, sir, I'm sorry to sound all like queen bee and stuff but we are already out of the few medical supplies that were here, and it seems the only thing we do have plenty of is freshwater and kids."

Pleasantly, the driver responds with smiles and a wink, "Yeah, we thought so. I think you'll find everything you need in that truck we parked out front." Spinning quickly on his heel, he adds, "There is already more children on the way."

The two children Will walks in with now brings the adolescent total to thirty three, not counting the two left purposely in their truck parked in the shade of an overhang alongside the medical office.

Like damp sand in an hour glass, time feels like it clogs to a halt for all four at the same time. Where is forward from here is a glance they share not in panic or fear but only as a question as to how we all leave here together.

Odd as it may sound, when Anna's name is first bounced around, it, for some reason, seemed like a long shot so the text May sends is simple and direct "To our friend, Anna. Sort of seems like soon for us and the dozens we've collected it's going to be time to go. Can you help? May."

"Indeed, my four flightless angels. Have already spoken to Art and know where you are. Trying to bridge the gap as we speak. By road is not an option. Some very unsafe sixty miles between us. Anna."

No sooner do these words fade away after May reads Anna's text out loud does the obvious sound of something pulling up out front stall any discussion or reply. Two short chirps on a horn sends Will towards the doorway first, another chirp pulls him through the doorway.

Out front will find's a full-size passenger van, it's the kind with too many windows like maybe for sightseeing. The driver is already out and on the other side, where he can open a set of double doors, as he does this, he informs the three children inside, "See, just like I said, 'Safe, sassy, and in one piece.'"

Will scoots right and allows the three children to step from the van and directly into the medical office. To Will, the driver simply states as he walks past, "I believe those three would like to go home, he then follows the children inside."

There is a respectful dominance in the driver's voice when he says out loud to anybody who will listen, "To whom must I bow, for it is a promise I shall not break." He now looks around the room, then adds, "There will be no child left behind."

Ryson steps closer not only to get the driver's attention but also to shake hands if need be, this man carries with him leadership, and he seems like somebody who gets things done, so Ryson does not hold back, "I think bowing is a bit much, but what we could use is a way to move all of these children sixty miles from here, and obviously none of it can be by road."

Quickly, this man seems to calculate sixty miles in every direction, the words he mumbles one at a time string together the facts to which Ryson has but one answer.

"Sixty miles, that's the B-17 we flew over on the way in, she your bird? no wait, that had to be Anna, is that how you leave this place? Sweet."

Ryson's answer, "Yes."

"Done and did, my good man."

Now he shakes Ryson's hand, who, for some reason, saw it coming and reaches humbly for the embrace.

"We will shuttle the first few at daybreak, by that time anything living that should be here will have already shown up. Couple of helis and a couple of hours after that we should all be heading home." He again looks around the room and seems quite pleased, then says, "Everybody okay with that?"

There are more than four voices in the room that collectively answer *yes* to that question.

Art and Anna receive the same message from May "Found a lift, the first batch heading your way at sun up. Where the wind takes us after that?"

Anna's reply "Can't wait. The more, the merrier."

Art and Lila's reply, "Destination already plotted. Be safe and Godspeed."

The last jeep rolled in some time close to midnight, the driver of assuring Ryson and Will these are indeed the last two. Something about his conviction and slowed attitude gave merit to his statement and as he drove away, neither of the guys could find a way to not believe him.

Most in the crowded medical office seem to find a place they can call safe, no matter how narrow the window and stay still through the night. Some even sleep. Ryson does neither. He knows somewhere near his own center, he's not coming back.

At first light, the incoming thump though still far off had a call to it, the tiny tap in your chest was just enough to calmly wake those still sleeping. The explosion that soon followed was not as calming and rippled the very earth beneath their feet like Christmas ribbon candy. This brings everybody who can to their feet and Ryson just as quickly to the door.

Like a graceful four-dimensional air ballet, two helicopters stay in tight formation through most of their approach, their movement quick and precise, as if one was flying the other.

With only a few inches of space between their blades, they hover, then gently lower to a space on the ground no more than thirty yards from where Ryson is standing. Both helicopters idle down but not off. The pilot closest to him swings his glass door outward and follows the momentum to extract himself, making it look more like he was pulled, then climbed from his own helicopter.

When the pilot is close enough that he knows he can be heard, it's clear his design and the details are non-negotiable, "Here's what we can do. 1 pilot, one adult five kids. Or one pilot, six kids. Those numbers we leave up to you but let's go now. That explosion you heard was only one of three and there will not be a whole lot of dry real estate after the third. We got maybe, couple of hours."

The second time he says, "Let's go now," he is already turned and heading back to the helicopter from which he was seemingly pulled.

As rehearsed and planned out the best they could, Ryson and Sophie each gather five children, four of whom can move on their own and one they will have to carry. Ryson and who he cradles are through the doorway first, as is four right behind him. Sophie's next as she follows Ryson and his bunch towards the helicopters, her four tucked in behind her and doing their best to move quickly.

Ryson and his group pile in and buckle down inside the first heli, Sophie does the same in the second one. Both helicopters now spin up but only leave the ground one at a time.

The sight, even from a distance, is nothing short of a masterpiece, if you could paint this just how it looks, only those who have seen it would trust even the most vivid rendering.

Clearly, a cash crop and definitely planted but not cultivated, are what once was most likely to separate fields of sunflowers, but over the years, they have crept up and now inhabit not only a couple hundred acres on either side of the runway, but all of the runway as well.

As though nested at one end of the flower covered runway sits a vintage B-17, its nose pushed right up against a rockslide, blocking the last fifty yards of the runway. The damage to the flowers is so minimal the plane looks like it was lowered from above and now nests in a spot with five and six foot tall sunflowers and fifty acres of them in every direction.

Anna darts from a shaded area under the wing when she hears the helicopters approach, and then to a full sprint through the sunflowers as she sees where the pilots have chosen to land.

Anna is at the skids of the helicopter even before they are firmly planted on the ground, she seems to know time is of the essence and manages to help empty both helicopters in just a couple of minutes.

With Anna at point, they reuse the trail she broke getting to them while trying to put some space between and what is now a full-blown sunflower cyclone and themselves as both helicopters lift off at the same time.

As they reach the plane and quiet once again remains dominant, Anna's first question is, "How many more children should I be prepared for?"

"We have sixty-three children Anna. In ages ranging from four to fourteen. Two of those, I am very sorry to say were D.O.A. The rest and including these ones here have clearly weathered some pretty serious storms but all are conscious and have been well cared for by yours truly there. Sophie has tended, bandaged, and over-all in general, repaired every single one of them."

Ryson finishes his answer with a question of his own, "Anna, why is there a runway here?"

The three set to work at getting the first ten kids in the plane and strapped to one of four, long, metal, bench seats that line both sides of the aircraft while Anna explains where they're at.

"This runway was built as a cargo drop for the larger supplies and equipment needed to build the small airport that's not far from here, that's why it was never paved, it's the same airport I had fuel delivered from yesterday.

Yeah, I've been here before, and believe it or not, the rockslide blocking the rest of the runway was expected, the sunflowers were not. I refer to this place as Runway Manual 180 because we will have to turn this plane around using nothing more than brute strength and determination."

When the thump gets close, Ryson and Sophie prepare for the sunflower cyclone with scarves pulled tight around their heads, covering their mouths, and providing only a narrow slit for vision.

Leaving Anna to safeguard the children and finish preparing the aircraft for those that will follow, Ryson jumps first and through the sunflower field he charges and of course, Sophie giving chase hot on his heels and again feeling alive for the sake of a child.

The favor Anna needs to ask for she will have to do face to face so on the last round of helicopter deliveries, it is Anna who leads from the airplane fully scarfed and into the sunflower cyclone.

The first helicopter Anna greets with a smile and after helping May and the four children out of it, climbs in to powwow with the pilot.

Leaving the decision to pilot number two, Anna now gets on the radio and ask him for the same favor. He does not reply. Instead simply slips from the heli and now he and Will share the burden of carrying the dead.

All that is said as he and Will hustle past heli one and Anna is, "Good afternoon, Anna, now let's make this quick. Were already late."

With all the kids safely seated and strapped down, the six adults converge on the tail of the airplane where Anna is already barking commands and instructions, "All right, everybody's hands right here, squat at the knees, back straight, and on three stand and lock your knees. One, two, three."

To six of them, the fact that they got the tail off the ground came as an absolute surprise, "Okay, we're stepping left on three and do not chase the momentum, keep it nice and steady with no stopping tell I say so. On three." One. Two. Three. One hundred and eighty degrees later, Anna very softly says, "Right there, stop, now let's put it down."

The two helicopter pilots, before they turn and hurry off do take the moment and hug each of the five and from the heart, they whisper to each one, one at a time, "God bless you."

Even at a distance of sixty miles, the back to back explosions could not only be heard but also felt. And nobody could agree more when Anna states, "I think that's our cue, time to let the wind do the talking."

The four large engines come to life one at a time and each engine alone shakes the world around you, but as all four begin to breathe as one the shaking stops. From zero to fall throttle, the plane dances through the flowers and without effort lifts and they are gracefully away.

Anna points the aircraft towards the South Pacific and nobody looks back. The hardest part for all of them, including the children, is knowing they all had to leave a piece of themselves. And it's a piece they chose not to surrender.

Leaving Hope Far Behind

The word melancholy…drenched heavy with despair, covered in a thick layer of sorrow, then splashed with idle surrender, and layered upon all this a sense of leaving hope far behind, and yet, most on board share the grace of God, or at least someone who is God-like. The plane drifts on a cushion of unstable dreams for a better tomorrow, all aboard say very little and the conversations are without joyous salvation or celebration but do indeed share a common tone of pleasure for those that have been rescued. Their first stop is Costa Rica, where they must refuel before the last leg can safely place them on the ground at Chino Hills Air Museum, Orange County, California.

The yellow school bus can be seen as they make their final approach, it stands out like a large banana on a sea of black asphalt and of course not far from this stands Art and Lila. As Ryson, May, Will, and Sophie begin to prep the children for landing, Anna's voice rings calmly over the speaker system and even though she's using her best "everything is going to be just fine voice," it's what she does not say that brings the four to apprehensive attention.

"Things have been getting a little warm up here and also, I am not cleared to land with passengers, so just as soon as we come to a complete stop, I need everybody to exit this aircraft lickidy split, and don't worry, my young travelers, Anna banana will be down to help you all get off without so much as stubbing even a single precious toe."

The plane drifts in and lands with the soft touch of an angel, then rolls slowly towards the school bus, where it now comes to a stop just a few yards from it. Will is at the door and lowering the exit ramp as if he's done this a hundred times on a hundred different B-17s and per Anna's request, they all began to disembark with the speed and efficiency of a well-oiled machine. Art, Lila, and the two young women in charge of the school bus lead the children on to the bus and see to it all are properly situated.

Will and Ryson carry as Anna and May lead the last few kids off the plane and all finish helping the children to and safely in a seat. It's now everybody, except for Anna and the kids, notice the smoke coming from both outboard engines as they watch the school bus drift away as if it was nothing more than a group of school children heading home after a fun filled air museum field trip. Ryson is first to ask the obvious, "Hey, Anna, is that something you were already aware of?"

Anna's reply is without panic but indeed her answer is of some concern, "Yeah those two started smoking some time ago, we were flying on just the two inboards for the last hour or so but no biggie, we could have coasted in on just one engine if necessary." Art and Lila both hug Anna at the same time and say, "Nicely done, Anna, you're the best," now all join in for a group hug and a well-deserved "thank you."

Anna now comes clean with her reply, "Yeah, it was touch and go at times and this old girl, no doubt, a handful, especially without a co-pilot."

"Anna, I assume you're staying?"

"Yes, for what these people paid for this thing, I figure it's the least I can do."

Art now turns his attention to the other five, "Well, shall we have some lunch before we head back?"

Lila now speaks for the whole group and says, "No point in answering that question, lunch it is, let's talk."

Shanghai Gardens, Art chooses this place for three reasons, first, no doubt the best Chinese food in Orange County, second, his love for Chinese cuisine, but most of all, he knew that at one thirty in the afternoon, the place would be fairly quiet. They take a large table and gather around in no particular order, the girls ordered first, then the guys, and now the table softens to just above a whisper as Art opens the door for quiet conversation.

"I have not nor has Lila begun to plan a new direction which would bring an end to our means, we both are not quite sure how to proceed, one thing for certain and I think we can all agree on this, and that is there seems to be no reason to head back into Paraguay or the Neighbors Cradle."

Art now makes eye contact with Ryson and continues, "This in no way derails our intentions, we simply must refocus our objective with any and all information we have gathered up till this point, so tell me what you learned from the Colombians and again from that place you refer to as Camp Diablo and what that place and the Colombians have in common."

Quite obvious the words Camp Diablo sting with a high dose of the devil's venom because the four that were there all now share the same look of saddened despair.

"That place…" Ryson stumbles and struggles as he now brings back to the surface what horrific cruelties they uncovered there, "that place…was nothing more than a sadistic machine in which to devour the young and bring their pain and suffering to those sick mother fuckers who, by choice, choose to create the demand… Please…I'm so sorry, please, excuse my French." Ryson finishes the rundown and refrains from further outburst of his own emotions.

As the last few words stumble from Ryson's mouth, Art and Lila move closer to each other as they share the same broken heart. The table and those around it seem to now hover quietly in a place of shattered spirits and shame.

Before everybody can fall to a place of a reachable sorrow, Art pulls themselves back using the sheer strength of his own willpower, "Okay, so now tell me about the Colombians." The other six now follow Art's strength and rejoin the party of broken hearts.

"Well, the connection between Camp Diablo and the Colombians is this, I asked one of them who showed up and who seemed to have a level of hierarchy if, in fact, he could share any information in regards to my own children, and after providing him with their descriptions," he pauses for a moment, then tells Will and I he might know somebody who could do just that, and will send him to us the first chance he gets. "Sometime later, this helicopter shows up with two of the kids we brought back," but before he leaves, he informs Will and I about a situation he was confronted with just a few days ago while what he thought was a scheduled pickup of an undisclosed cargo, he tells Will and I that when he arrived at the location within the Neighbors Cradle, he was approached by a man several children and that he and the children were his cargo, he states that this man had with him a young girl who was wearing a sweatshirt with sunflowers on it and also he had with him a set of young twins, and in a minivan parked nearby were another set of twins that matched my description of my own children. He goes on to say the twins this man was dragging with him had a doll that was wrapped in a small penguin shirt just like the one I described. His story ends with him saying, "I do not cargo

304

children and would have killed this man but thought better of it for the simple reason he did not want those kids left to fend for themselves."

Art and Lila have by now already connected the dots but it's Art who speaks first, "The redhead on the bench with the two you found handcuffed together," he stops there and clearly finds it difficult to continue, so now Lila takes over. "The redhead and the two you found on the bench in all likelihood shared the same minivan and for reasons unknown were left at that bench where as your two were not."

Art regains some of his composure and now brings to those at the table a glimmer of hope.

"So, seems easy enough, we learn from the young girl in the sunflower shirt and red hair where your kids are, of course this will have to be done through her therapist, but I will see to it that we know what she knows, that young girl and her family owe us all at least that much, and I happen to know she lives in a state not far from this one, with that information, we will plan what must be done next and how we proceed. The way I see it, those who were left on that bench wore done so because of how badly they were injured, but your two were not," Art says this to Ryson with such conviction and believe it is hard not to believe in it and therefore, he brings hope to a place where there once was none.

They all eagerly crack open the after-lunch fortune cookie and all do so for the same reason because without hopes for a better tomorrow, today is nothing more than a pathetic step backwards.

It only takes a few minutes to reach the back-parking lot of Redline Financial after exiting the freeway and it's here, Ryson, Sophie, Will, and May say goodbye to Art and Lila but with a promise that all will return when once again called upon.

The path in which Ryson now travels is one of borrowed hope and translucent dreams, but what he can do this perhaps convince Pat to come home, now more than ever he needs her by his side, he no longer sees any reason why he should carry this beast of burden alone and upon his own shoulders without her, she needs to rejoin the real world whether it be for hope or despair, he needs her, loves her, and misses her.

The following sunrise finds Ryson already awake and cleaning the house, it's a simple stall tactic but for sure if Pat decides to come home, at least it will be clean when she returns, the stall tactic comes about because in the name of all that's decent he should and will not call the house looking for Pat at least tell after nine, so clean, he shall. 9:17 a.m., the butterflies that dance in his stomach do so for two reasons. The first, of course, is indeed expected, the second, and this even he does not expect, but as he begins to dial the number, he knows in his heart the feeling he has left hope far behind still squeezes the soul, this he must keep to himself and not let the fear spread.

Surprised and almost speechless when Pat answers the phone in a voice that takes him back to a time when things were different, "Hello and good morning."

"Well, good morning, Mrs. Willows, and also the love of my life, how are you?"

"I am not quite sure I have an answer to that question, even I myself wonder that very same thing each and every morning the sun comes up."

"Well, how about I come out and see you today? That is, of course, if you have not already made plans?" Pat's reply again takes Ryson to a place of unexpected normalcy.

"Don't be silly, after all, I can't live here forever, so how about I pack some stuff and that way you will not have to drive back alone."

"That sounds fantastic, Pat, love you, see you about noon."

"Okay, babe, drive safe, love you, too."

The phone goes quiet on both ends and each of them idle for just a moment in a place of anxious uncertainty.

The first part of the drive out to Hemet brings to Ryson a strange sense of troubled understanding, he can't help but wonder why Pat seemed so much her normal self, yeah, sure, he could still hear some residual narcotics slurs in the few words they exchanged, but for the most part, she seemed in a strange way almost too coherent, surely she must know if he had fantastic news regarding the twins, the joyous announcement would have been the first part of their conversation. This thought stumbles around inside of Ryson's head but only long enough for him to blindly scatter some happy dust on a suppressed reality.

The world rolls by and somehow, Ryson finds a sliver of hope within it as there is by surprise, happiness in his heart, and a pleasant whistle at his lips, the tune for which he whistles is of no particular melody only that it seems to brighten his day and lighten the load upon his shoulders.

Without warning, the small market suddenly appears up the road a few yards and to Ryson's complete astonishment, as if he's being guided by some unseen force, he hits the blinker, taps the brakes, and prepares to make a right turn into the dirt lot surrounding what he still refers to as Little Joe's stickup market, although he now knows the actual owner's name is Josephine and she is quite the disturbing little creature with a voice that of a diving pterodactyl, her hair and body thin straggly and the color of dried figs. Ryson also knows she has fake tits, and this, even still, troubles him because there's just some things in life, no matter how hard you try it, just can't fixed. Yes indeed, the woman quite unpleasant to look at, even if her tits were made of solid gold.

Ryson pulls in and stops within just a few feet from the front door and now finds it somewhat difficult to get out of the car and face this unpleasant creature, but indeed, he shall, he has a debt to pay and acknowledge an act of kindness that must not go an answered.

Cautiously, he steps through the doorway and heads straight back to the ice-cream counter with the pterodactyl screeching as she leaves her stool behind the front counter and gives chase, "How can I help you today? Is there anything in particular you're looking for?"

Ryson's reply comes on the fly as he is not quite ready to stop and make small talk, "Just some ice-cream please." He takes a deep breath as he reaches the ice-cream counter and Josephine finally catches up, she drifts in behind the counter before she says, "Only got chocolate, vanilla, or strawberry."

Their eyes finally meet as Ryson does his best to put on the face of somebody who is not overly concerned with the looks of others, he now withdraws a one hundred dollar bill from his pocket and places it on the counter between them, "Actually, I am here to ask a favor of you, if you could please see to it that half of this money is spent until it runs out on every kid who walks in here and wishes to buy ice-cream, and the other half, you may keep."

Josephine is quite pleasant and more than willing to fulfill Ryson's request, but not without asking the obvious, "And so why is that?"

"I am just returning a favor and have no idea who this kid was."

Without further inquiries, Josephine simply replies, "Consider it done."

Ryson smiles politely, turns, and walks away as he says, "Thank you and have a wonderful day."

There is no amount of momentum that can carry Ryson away from this place fast enough, not even if he could climb atop a speeding bullet. Uncertain as to exactly why this is and why he finds Josephine so horribly offensive, he chooses not to over examine this complexity as he quickly motors away without looking back.

It all seems far too quiet as Ryson pulls into the driveway, he truly expected to see Danny already on the patio and working his culinary skills on the barbecue with a spatula in one hand and a beer in the other, but instead, there is nothing but quiet, it's not until he exits the car when finally he can hear sounds of life coming from inside the house, the swift rhythms of C.C.R ooze through the woodwork filling Ryson's heart and soul with a song, he begins to sing out loud as he taps on the side door of the house just off the driveway.

Chelsea is quick to the handle as if she was standing at the ready for Ryson's arrival and gently pulls the door inward, "Well, looky here, before us, stands Mr. Willows, the children's Angel of rescue."

"Well, it's not all good news I'm afraid," is Ryson's reply before he chooses to step through the threshold.

"We already know. Art has taken the liberty to enlighten us as to the current situation," he called last night and as he put it, "just a heads up in hopes of making things somewhat predigested before your arrival, that man's heart is bigger than all of Texas, and indeed you are an angel of rescue, I mean my God, Ryson, sixty five children, that in every way provides you with hero status." Chelsea now steps forward with tears in her eyes and damn near hugs the air from his lungs.

"So, where's Pat?"

"Upstairs, changing, she got spaghetti sauce all over her shirt, give her a few minutes, she will come down when she's ready. In the meantime, how about you go in the other room and convince Danny to put on something else, please!"

"Why? What's wrong with some good old Creedence Clearwater?" Ryson now begins to sing along to what's being played, "Do, do, do looking out," but before he can continue, Chelsea interrupts, "Oh god, not you too, you do realize that song is really just about some guy who can see out his own ass, right?"

It takes Ryson just a couple of seconds to put the joke in order, and now he smiles real big, shakes his head, turns, and walks away, "I'll see what I can do."

Ryson finds Danny on the couch glued to the T.V. and some sort of visual coma as he, in small movements, bops his head in tune to what's being played, Ryson knows from experience how badly Danny hates sports commentary, so there is no surprise in finding him watching the third round of the World Cup with just background music and no sound coming from the T.V., he has no intentions of bringing Chelsea's request to the surface, instead. he quietly slips in beside Danny and takes a seat.

"Hey! What's up, brother? Did not hear you come in." Danny now disengages from the T.V. and puts one hand on Ryson's shoulder and asks, "How you holding up, buddy?"

"Well, all things considered, I suppose it could be worse but I don't dare question how, so how's things around here?"

"Oddly enough, not too bad, yes, not too fucking bad."

"So, how's Pat? You think she really will come home with me today?"

"I do indeed, her and Chelsea been making spaghetti and meatballs all morning and both seem in pretty good spirits, although Pat is still taking some fairly serious tranquilizers but at least now she is taking much less, therefore, I believe much less is needed, and that's a good sign."

Like a breath of fresh air, Pat appears on the stairs with a smile on her face and a warm hello at her lips. Ryson stands with the same smile on his face as he moves toward her rather quickly, they both now share a lasting embrace, one of which neither of them seem willing to let go.

Caught up in the moment, Danny is close to tears when Chelsea comes into the room and playfully remarks, "Geez you two, get a room."

This statement brings something a little less dramatic to the room and now Chelsea announces, "Okay, everybody to the kitchen, let's have some lunch."

During lunch, Ryson confirms the fact that, "Yes, indeed, there is a young girl who was rescued and brought home and it is her who will most likely bring to light where they must go next in search of the twins," he also re-cements and especially to Pat that hope in finding the twins is as strong as it ever was and he has every intention of pursuing this, even if it takes him through the gates of hell. Ryson's tone and convictions are quite sincere, even though he himself has doubt.

Lunch drifts mostly around the past and not so much about the future, the only real piece of tomorrow is when Ryson bravely asks Pat if she will be joining him on the ride home, to this her reply is a genuine, "Of course, I am, already packed and ready to go." Although she still no doubt lingers somewhat in a place of foggy apprehension, her voice carries with it a genuine slice of enthusiasm and this for sure brings smiles to all those concerned.

After lunch, they all share in the cleanup. Pat and Ryson making sure all is clean, dry, and put away before they attempt their exit, this is a strange and somber moment, as is the long embrace they each share with one another. And as a very wise man once said, "Never say goodbye, only whisper the sweet sounds of love and a promise that stays close to the heart."

For most of the ride home, things are fairly quiet inside Ryson's truck, Pat is clearly trying to take it all in and doing her best at coming to terms with the way things are, they are within a few miles from home when finally Pat begins to loosen up and the chatter between the two seems more like old times. Just as the house comes into view, Pat's question rattles Ryson like that of a bite from a cobra, "Do you really think everything is going to be okay?"

Ryson's reply staggers from his lips as if the words themselves escape on their own, "I think we have to."

Cold Heart

The next couple of days painfully idle by as Pat and Ryson spend the time doing some light housework and in general, just staying close to each other. Before Ryson went to Hemit and brought Pat home he closed the kids' room and so far it remains the same, neither have had the stomach or the heart to push through the sadness and venture inside, both only slow in passing but never come to a complete stop.

On day three, Art calls the house, it's 9:30 a.m. when Ryson's phone vibrates to life on the kitchen counter as he is just finishing his second cup of coffee and doing his best at forcing down some over toasted frozen waffles, he already knows who it is well before he stands and checks from whom the vibration comes.

"Good morning, Art, and, so what brings you buzzing on such a fine morning as this?"

Art knows without asking how are things, So the choice to not do so is simple, instead he just jumps right to the point, "Hey, buddy, can you be down here by11:00??"

"Sure thing, Art, no problem, what's going on?"

"I have some place you need to go, and hey, how about you leave Pat out of this for now."

Arts voice now takes on a tone of genuine concern, "So, how's she doing, Ryson?"

"I guess as to be expected, she sleeps a lot, but I think that's probably for the better. So 11 o'clock then, should I bring something?"

"No, Ryson, just you and your truck."

Neither say goodbye because both know now is not the time for pleasantries.

Lila is closest to the door when Ryson taps with the gentleness of somebody who knows they already hide from the truth, she opens the door and cannot embrace him quick enough. Ryson's response is of course to first return the affection but as the reality sets in now comes, the second response, "Geez, nobody gets this kind of welcome," and less sadness soon follows.

Art now walks into the room and replies, "I wish I could say you were wrong about your assumption but sadly I cannot, let's just sit down and get on with it." Art's tone becomes quite condoling as he relates what he knows, "In about one hour, a Miss Colleen Redin will be at her office in Santa Ana and would like to speak to you in regards concerning your twins."

"Now before you go asking me what she has to say, I can only tell you she refused to say anything to me, except that the news was not good, and I think she only did that because her and I have some history together."

Art now slides a piece of paper in front of Ryson and says, "That's the address and directions."

Ryson's head droops as he stares at the piece of paper and the room takes on a frigid sense of despair, Art and Lila remain, silent giving Ryson a moment to gather his composure and are willing to wait as long as necessary. When Ryson does finally lift his head, there are no tears, he simply and calmly says, "Well, let's just hear what she has to say before the world dissolves beneath our feet."

"Promise me one thing,"

"What's that, Art?"

"After you hear what Colleen has to say, you come back here first, unless you don't feel like driving, in which case, I will come get you. I guess what I'm trying to say is, no matter what happens, we are still in this together."

From the mouth of what sounds like a condemned soul, comes the words, "Well, I suppose, but I cannot guarantee where my head will be."

Lila, who has remained silent, now says, "That's okay, we're family now and like Art says, 'No matter what happens, we are all in this together.'"

The three share a group hug at the back door as Ryson quietly slips away, and all three knowing he and he alone must first face this demon from which there is no place to hide.

There is not much conversation between Art and Lila after Ryson departs as both find it almost impossible to consider the most obvious outcome, so they wait for Ryson's return in their own private house of pain, they, of course, realize, no amount of speculation or false expectation, will deliver either of them from a place so dark that if there were to be light at the end of the tunnel from where they now stand, it would be impossible to see.

Two hours and twelve minutes pass but seems more like one hundred lifetimes before once again, they hear a soft tapping on the back door, this time, however, Lila is not so quick to the door but not because she fears the cold slap of a harsh reality, instead it's her legs and feet that now fail her, the body has gone numb and is unwilling to do as the mind commands, as if she's been heavily sedated.

Art moves towards the door but is not sure how he does it, he already knows that this day and the ones that follow will forever change life and the way he sees it. There, before him, as the door swings inward, stands a man shattered and fragmented, Ryson's eyes, cheeks and the front of his shirt now wet with what can only be the million tears from a man now broken, Ryson staggers through the doorway arms crossed at his chest and barely makes it to the table where Lila already sits when his knees finally give out and he's forced to take a seat in the chair closest to him.

Art joins the table and takes a seat as the three now sit in silence, life around them seems to move forward but at their table, all things linger in a world where sorrow is king. Ryson must be the one who speaks first and he knows this, although, for a very long moment, he cannot find the strength to piece together the words that will, no doubt, bring back the tears, "They are gone, both have been killed and buried."

As expected, the tears return.

Art and Lila move in closer, each placing an arm around Ryson's shoulders and now all three bring tears to the table. It is silently decided to let linger the minutes before asking any questions, and when this time fades away, Art finally ask what neither really want to know, "So, please Ryson, tell us what Colleen had to say."

Ryson lifts his head, wipes the sadness from his face, and now brings to light what nobody wants to hear, "Well, I'm sure you already know that Colleen is the therapist that is working with the young girl we rescued from the place we refer to as Camp Diablo and yes, she did indeed learn how those three kids came to be on that bench outside of the blue shed."

It's quite obvious Ryson wants to get through this and one clean sweep because it all flows as if just one dreadful continuous sentence, "First of all, I believe the facts here speak for themselves and that's for the simple reason while my children were locked inside the blue shed with several other kids, they spoke of me by name, and also how I was in the military and how sure they were that I was going to come save them." Ryson's voice cracks and he is not the only one at the table who feels perhaps he's not going to finish, but to their surprise, he continues.

"Five children were removed from the blue shed and loaded into a minivan, two of which were my own and the young girl with the sunflower shirt, the same girl who is now receiving therapy from Colleen, they were then driven through the mountains in the dark until they reached a clearing of some sorts, it's here they find a helicopter, the man driving the minivan now removes three of the children, the same three I found on the bench and leaves my two tied together in the front seat and now, he approaches the helicopter with the three he has already removed. The young girl in the sunflower shirt, who I found on the bench, tells Pauline that in the short conversation between the helicopter pilot and the minivan driver, things become very angry because the pilot refuses to transport the children and even threatening to kill the driver, this helicopter pilot is most likely the very same pilot Will and I spoke with during the last rescue when the Colombians laid waste to the neighbors cradle, so now the driver of the minivan is extremely upset as he drags the children back to the van and quite physically, he shoves them back in and speeds away as he mumbles to himself in anger." Ryson pauses here and takes of breath then falls silent as a few large tears form in the corner of his eyes. Art and Lila attempt to brace themselves as if waiting for a bomb two explode.

Only a few seconds ticked by before Ryson now finishes what he started, "On their way back to Camp Diablo, the guy driving is moving way too fast and loses control of the van and plows first through a ditch, then cannot stop fast enough to avoid a head on collision with a large tree and because the twins were in front seat, they were both thrown through the windshield."

Art and Lila at this point would like to interject, thus saving Ryson from having to state the obvious but he does not come up for air and sadly continues to, "The driver, of course, now gets out to check on the condition of my children and soon returns to the minivan and retrieves a shovel."

The tears now fall from Ryson's eyes and trail down his cheeks, then fall to the table like oversized rain drops before he can stem the flow.

"Oh, God," is Lila's response, she thinking this slow journey through hell is perhaps over, but, sadly it is not. Ryson continues.

"Colleen tells me at this point the driver now picks up both kids and heads into the mountains with the shovel top up under his arm, when he returns a short time later, he does so with only the shovel."

There's times in all our lives when the world comes at us with such chaos and disorder it feels as though you have just been kicked by a mule right to the stomach, and indeed, this is one of those times as the three sit at that table with only hatred for all of man-kind and yet again, Ryson finds the strength to continue.

"I guess, somehow, the minivan survived the impact with the tree and is able to back out of the ditch, although, as for the other passengers, they most certainly did not fare as well. The driver now returns to Camp Diablo and leaves the other three children on the bench where I found them, and of course, leaves one to bleed to death while still handcuffed to her sister."

"Now before you to start asking me how Colleen can be so sure the children thrown through the windshield were mine, she assures me the description she got from the young girl who brought back was absolutely and without question correct in every detail, including the socks they were wearing."

There are no amount of tears that can relieve the pain and sorrow of what has just been dealt, so all three now sit at the table in dry eyed silence.

Before standing and after Ryson clears his throat of what feels like a gallon of white glue, he mumbles in a soft tone, "I have to go home and somehow tell Pat I failed to save our children and now they are dead because of it."

Lila's brain goes numb from the impact so Art must now speak for the both of them, "I know you will find no comfort in these words of reason, but listen Ryson, this was not your fault, you did, we all did, all we could do." These words, of course, fall upon a darkened spirit and Ryson leads through the door the same way he came in; a shattered man in a field of dismembered debris.

It's the lack of any sort of emotional response that Ryson not only finds deeply concerning but also it's as if Pat's soul has left her body when the only words she can bring to her lips are, "I'm sure you did all you could do." Ryson, of course, gave her the abridged version in hopes of sparing her any further anguish, but clearly because of her reply and complete lack of visible distress, he realizes she has come to a place of absolute denial and quietly slips inside her own sense of false reality.

Ryson looks into Pat's eyes, places both his hands on hers and whispers, "Sweetheart, we will together get through this, we just have to be strong, and most important, we have to be there for each other." Ryson so much wants to share his tears and a lasting embrace with her but Pat pulls away, as if she has not heard a single word of what's real since they sat down.

For the time being, Ryson is content to give Pat some space in hopes she will soon process this horrific slice of life they have been given and perhaps begin to come to terms, so the healing can begin.

The rest of the day and into the night, there are no further words exchanged. Ryson orders a pizza for dinner and is forced to not only eat half himself but sadly enough, Pat has not even come downstairs.

At 9:40 p.m., Ryson quietly crawls in bed and listens contently to the slow rhythms of slumber as Pat lays next to him and he can only wonder if she will ever be able to get past this.

Sleep for Ryson is slow in coming, the visions of not only his own children but all those who have suffered the tragic loss of childhood innocence he finds dreadfully menacing and cannot seem to shake the feeling, as though this slow walk through hell is not quite over.

Sunrise catches Ryson by surprise as does the fact he somehow managed to stop the screams in his head long enough to get some sleep, there is no hope for the cleansing dawn of a new day, nor does he falsely believe things will get better anytime soon, Ryson lays quietly for some time before he finally decides to roll over and wakes Pat in hopes she's ready to at least talk about how she might be feeling, the first touch of her shoulder seams cold and the reality eludes him, the second touch as he slides his hand down the length of her arm seems colder still, and yet the denial remains.

"Pat, you okay over there? How can anybody with so many blankets piled on top of them still feel frigid as if we are in the midst of winter?"

There comes of course no reply or movement from her, just cold and motionless. The terror begins to creep in, like a slow moving landslide as Ryson touches her one last time, and now comes the sting from the panic laced venom of a thousand rattlesnakes, he has no words, his body gripped and wrenched with disbelief, he lay there, trying to put this all in perspective and cannot, his blood turning cold is something they both now share, and each now possess that of a cold heart.

Heavy Is Thy Hammer

Death from accidental overdose is what they're calling it, but in all, reality how can you truly know for sure? I guess you believe because it hurts just a little less.

And now the painful task of informing the others, the loved ones, the friends, and even those who were considered just close, and each time, the words are spoken the pain is renewed. It's now in the days that follow, the house becomes so silent and empty, Ryson can feel the heavy weight of true sadness upon his shoulders as he barely has the strength to stand. The first few that come to the house in the days following the funeral bring with them their own demons and of course, offer up their own brand of comfort and support, this, of course, is well received, but in all honesty, serves in no way any kind of true relief.

The painful sadness and the deep dark fathoms of despair fill every living moment of Ryson's life, there is no escape, there is no belief things get better. There are those who truly reach out to Ryson and who are more than willing to go the extra miles in hopes they can help him recover, but even their attempts fall short and drift by like desert sands being swept into the breeze as all hope seems fading away.

The minutes slowly tick by, the days painfully inch forward, the weeks pass unchecked and the months idle at the edge of life unlived. Ryson spirals and slips into a self-exiled land of shattered hopes and dreams as he now finds himself far underground and, in a darkness, so vast there is no way out, the only obvious exit is one he considers on several occasions and that is, of course, a suicidal solution. He finds any and all kind words and attempts for compassion from others nothing more than painful reminders of who he once was and therefore, avoids the world at large, he parked the truck in the garage so nobody knows where he might be, and only answers the phone occasionally just so it appears as though he still has some life left in them. This dance with

317

the devil is nothing more than just that, he even lies to his own brothers regarding his health and well-being, when, in fact, he's hoping, at some point, he can find the strength to pull the trigger.

For the first time in weeks, Ryson turns on a light inside the house, up until now when the sun went down and things got dark, he could find no reason to change the way things are, if the dark comes, so let it, day or night, either way, really makes no difference in how he sees things, but tonight was different. The rain seemed to be falling in such heavy sheets curiosity got the best of him and something about watching the rainfall has always in some degree lift his spirits.

Ryson now stands in the open doorway at the front of the house and becomes transfixed on the heavy downpour of rain that seems to be falling at such a rate he expects to see a small boat motor past at any moment, he willingly allows his mind to drift away and is happy to do so. The car that pulls up out front goes completely unnoticed until the passenger side door opens and it triggers the interior lights to flicker on and illuminates the two who begin to exit the vehicle, first to the curb is a woman who quickly deploys the umbrella in her right and, she is then joined by the man who exited from the driver's seat and he, too, now stands quietly under his own umbrella, both stand motionless on the sidewalk, gazing up at Ryson, as if the sadness in their hearts is responsible for all the rain.

As the two from the sidewalk begin to make their way to where Ryson now stands, he's not quite sure how to interpret their approach, *Are they heading in the right direction? Are they lost? Or have they just come in an attempt to sell him something he does not want?*

When the gap between Ryson the two strangers close to just a few feet, the woman speaks, and it's in these few words is heart dances oddly in his chest and all three seem to know destiny has made a connection, "If you are who we hope you are, we would like to speak to you in regards to our missing children."

Ryson's mouth opens without his permission and the words, "My name is Ryson Willows," fall from his lips in a self-startled sort of way.

"We are sorry to have just shown up here unannounced and without your permission, but we have no other place to turn" These words pull tears from their eyes as the man under the umbrella continues to speak, "Mr. Willows, may we please have just a few moments of your time?"

Oddly on autopilot, Ryson steps aside and allows the strangers to come through the doorway and into the house and as they do so he says, "Of course I will listen, I'm just not sure why you would come talk to me," he then adds and for reasons, he did not understand, "please, excuse the mess, me, and the house."

"You do not have to ask for our approval, Mr. Willows, we are well aware of what you have been through, if anything, it is us that should be asking for your forgiveness, like I said, we just had no other place to go and nowhere else to turn."

Ryson leads them into the kitchen where he offers them something to drink, they both decline and now all three sit at the kitchen table, and oddly enough, they all seem to share the same expression.

"So, why me?"

"It was all about connecting the pieces, but first let me introduce ourselves. My name is Randolph Baylor but most call me Randy and I'm okay with that, this is my wife Miranda, and we also live here in Orange County, not far from here actually."

In the brighter lights of the kitchen, Ryson now takes a more comprehensive look at the two strangers he has allowed in the house. Mr. Randolph/Randy looks to be in his early forties, brown hair, green eyes, perhaps six feet, one hundred and ninety pounds. Miranda, about the same age, brown hair, brown eyes, thin, seems somewhat underweight for her size, but still quite pretty.

"The first time we saw you it was on T.V. and this was before our children were taken. After they went missing from the pool area at a resort in Acapulco, we, of course, began a twenty four/seven frantic search in that country using all available resources and after several days of complete dead ends and absolute no clues as to where they might be, we were told to come home and contact the F.B.I., under extreme duress, as you could well imagine, we leave Acapulco in hopes of finding some help here in the U.S."

Now Miranda steps into the conversation, even though quite clearly it's tearing her heart, "Yes, at first, it seemed like they would indeed help, but after a week or so, everything got very cold between us and all they would say is. We are doing all we can." Miranda stutters to a stop and can no longer find the strength to continue so Randy again takes the lead.

"They would not tell us why, all of the sudden, our case no longer had priority except that things were getting very complicated on an international level, but the last time we saw them as we were leaving, one of the F.B.I. men slipped me a folded piece of paper and on that piece paper was your name, so after some digging, we find an address and some newspaper headlines regarding the day your twins were taken from you at the mall, and also, we are aware of what happened to your wife just a few months ago and for these tragedies in your life, we are truly sorry and do indeed understand your pain. That's all we know and what this means to us is at this time unclear."

Ryson finds this whole situation in a strange way somewhat healing and finds himself surprised at how quickly he warms to these people and now begins to tell his own story, it is again the abridged version but by the time he is finished, all three again share the same teary-eyed facial expression, and indeed like I said, "Destiny has made a connection."

Randy and Miranda have already decided they would like very much for Ryson to go and find their children but neither seem to have the courage to just come out and ask, so Randy continues with a softened approach, "We were on vacation in Acapulco with the kids a couple of weeks ago when out of the blue, this man calmly strolls up to us while we are lounging poolside and watching the kids play in the shallow end of a large kiddie pool, and for what we know now was simply just a distraction, sucker punches me and claims I have been fooling around with his wife, maybe a minute or so pass as I convinced this man he has the wrong person were at which time he simply turns and quickly walks away. Now as we regroup and return our attention towards the kids, they are nowhere to be seen, the lifeguard on duty at the time tells us and the management during some kind of commotion in the water, he did see a man and woman enter the pool and carry out two small children and yes, they did put up somewhat of a struggle but says he just figured it was because they simply did not want to get out of the water."

"All we really remember about the man that hit me was he had a tattoo on his neck that spelled the word 'death' and next to it was a couple of 'dollar signs.' He was for sure of Spanish or Mexican descent, dark skin, dark hair, and spoke with a Spanish accent."

Clearly the words "death and dollar signs") strike a nerve with Ryson because his head and shoulders droop as he exhales, and when Randy finishes his description of the man that hit him, Ryson quickly asked the question, "How old are your children?"

Randy just as quickly fires back, "Alisha, she is six years old, brown hair, brown eyes, light skin, wavy hair well past her shoulders, and missing her two front teeth, she also speaks at times with a slight stutter."

"Kyle, he is four years old, brown hair, blue eyes, light skin, and has a birth mark on his left shoulder that which resembles in size and shape a three-leaf clover."

These descriptions flow from Randy as if they had been rehearsed, but in fact it's because in the last two weeks he has repeated them what seems like close to one thousand times, before he can pause long enough to take a breath, Miranda now slides a photo of the children with their description on the back across the table, leaving it to rest in front of Ryson, and now all three sit in silence for several seconds.

"Please help us, Mr. Willows, we can pay you whatever you want, or, whatever it takes."

There is a rush of new life that enters Ryson's lungs as he takes a breath, and in the first time in months, he does not exhale the putrid stench of his own pathetic existence, "I cannot promise you anything, but what I will do is first thing in the morning I can look into this with somebody who might have some insight on how we might proceed."

"Does this mean you're going to help us, Mr. Willows? And like I said, we can pay whatever it takes."

"Please, call me Ryson, and yes, I will do whatever I can, and no, I do not need your money. You two go home, try to get some sleep, and I will call tomorrow, is your number on this photo somewhere?"

"Yes, on the back, thank you so very much, Mr. Willows, you give us hope."

The mental strength and capacity to sleep upstairs still eludes him, but at least, as he slips away tonight on the fold out bed in the den, Ryson finds a small amount of comfort, he drifts into a peaceful slumber where things feel more in his own control, tomorrow, as the sun rises, he, too, shall rise and in this new day, he begins to take something back.

As hoped and just as he expected, Ryson awakens with a renewed purpose in life, why this seems so definitive he does not quite understand as he lays there trying to grip the reality of this new spirit. The loss he has had to endure still squeezes the soul and stabs deep at the heart, but what now flows through his veins is a cold mixture of anger, contempt, rage, and revenge. He did not choose this path, it was thrust upon him by cycle of life so cruel and unjust if given a chance he would certainly, without hesitation, search and destroy.

These thoughts of balance and revenge pull him from that couch with clear intent to clean himself up, shave the beard, cut file, and clean, trim what need be trimmed, and once this process complete, he shall then walk to Redline Financial in the shoes of a different man.

As Ryson pulls the door closed behind him he stares down the thin walkway toward the sidewalk out front, he knows that one thing for certain, and no matter how sadly painful it will be, he must sell this house and leave this place to the wind.

It's mid-October and finally the temperatures have begun to proceed towards the cooler end of the spectrum, giving Ryson the need to zip up the thin jacket he so gladly now remembered to bring with him, the air feels clean and crisp as he shuffles along in oddly high spirits towards a high octane, double shot mocha and perhaps some kind of pastry. As Ryson approaches the coffee shops outside order window, he does indeed glance towards the fountain and wonders, will *it still be a place of warmth and pleasure or has it now been forever tainted by sadness and loss*, well, perhaps on his way home he can test it's virility, or maybe not.

As Ryson gently taps on the front door of Redline Financial, he checks his watch after noticing there were no lights on inside, he is about ready to back away from the door and already thinking, *Maybe a second pastry*, when he sees Art pop through a curtain with a smile on his face like he already knew who was knocking.

Art is quick to the door and with a smile so big it seems to cover most of his face, he says, "Good morning to you, Mr. Willows, isn't this an unexpected pleasure."

"Morning, Art, it's nice to see you as well, hell, it's just nice to get out of the house and breathe some fresh air. I am sorry for the fact I've been so un-social, but to be honest, I was not sure the sun would ever rise again."

"And yet, here you are." Art seems unable to abandon the smile on his face and now, almost in giddy-like fashion, tells Ryson, "Come on back, I have some muffins to go with that coffee."

322

As they come through the curtain, Ryson surveys the room and finds it empty, so somewhat disappointed he asks, "Where's Lila this morning?"

"Her and Trina are off to see grandma and then to the movies, so it looks as though it's just you and me, but make no mistake about it, Lila will be very disappointed she was not here this morning. So tell me, to what do I owe the honor? And don't go all girly on me with 'I miss you, you are just so damn fun to be around I could not stay away.'"

They both chuckle and indeed this lightens their spirits.

"Well. sure, no doubt part of the reason is in fact your charming nature and party personality, but there is something else."

"Well, take a seat and enlighten me."

"Last night I had a visit from the Baylor's," Art says nothing but just a simple shrug of the shoulders. "No, you do not know them, but what they came to tell me we are all far too familiar."

Ryson brings Art completely up to speed and now waits patiently for his response, even though he could already tell by Arts reactions what his first question would be.

"And they're sure about the tattoo? Death and dollar signs?"

"Absolutely, Art, no mistake."

"Well, one thing we know for sure, and that is if this guy was branded with that tattoo, most likely he is part of a Tiger Team."

Art is quick in his deduction and reasoning and to Ryson surprise offers up some of his own insight, "From the intel I have gathered since your last visit to South America, these guys were chased away from that continent and have now set up shop somewhere in Central America, now, exactly where that might be is anybody's guess. Before we continue in this conversation, tell me straight, Ryson, is this something you're interested in pursuing?"

"Yes, Art, I would like to help these people, I was unable to rescue my own children but perhaps I can somehow be of help to others, and yes, before you ask, I would for sure like to get my hands on a Tiger Team and exact some well-deserved pay back, seems somebody needs to slow their roll." Ryson now humbles and looks Art straight in the eyes and says, "We have rescued so many, why stop now?"

"Well, all right then, how about you give me some time and I will see what I can come up with."

"Cannot ask for more than that Art, thanks. Now if you will excuse me, I have to gather some boxes because the sooner I move out of the house, the better."

"Now that sounds like somebody who still wants to make a difference. How about some of us come over tonight and help you do just that? I do not want to brag, but they do not call me Sir Packs Aplenty for nothing."

They both laugh and quite obviously, they are once again on the same page.

For a fleeting moment, Ryson does consider abandoning his desire to visit the fountain as he approaches the coffee shop but finds the pull of its wonderment just too great and cannot ignore the connection between him and it, so there he stands as he did the first time they met, in awe and quite moved by not only its construction but also the meaning for which it was created, the children, and how it is up to all of us to ensure their futures. Ryson drifts away from that fountain on this day, and on this day, he pledges to himself, "Live life for the children and keep safe the world in which they live in."

With the intel gathered by Art and the maps provided by Danny, it's quite clear this rescue will focus in Central America and no doubt will require some serious aggression in order to achieve the primary goal, recover the Baylor's children, and also it seems there are others being held in the same encampment. It is also quite clear what is needed will be a far more cohesive and better trained rescue team.

Ryson and Will remain, they are accompanied by some friends who they met along the way, one of which is Ollie, he is the one they met during the rescue of target 114, the other is Cecil, the jump master from Chino Hills jump Academy, who turns out has three years of sniper experience, along with several years of military and special ops. Sophie will be joining the team but will stay with the plane along with the pilot in the staging area, her contribution to all of this is of course to provide any and all medical needs required by not only the children they rescue but also the rescue team if needed.

By the grace of unseen forces, they are indeed successful in rescuing the Baylor's children along with six others, and in Ryson's heart, the accomplishment finds a place far beyond just bravery, to him, the call from the tortured young shall remain answered as long as he can draw breath.

And on through the following years, members come and go, but what remains constant is Ryson at the helm and those that choose to rescue bring freedom to the young and continue to chase the demons and no doubt, slow the role of those who choose to damage the life of a child.

Heavy Is Thy Hammer.